Code Zero

Also by Jonathan Maberry

Novels
Extinction Machine
Assassin's Code
King of Plagues
The Dragon Factory
Patient Zero
Dead of Night
The Wolfman
Fire & Ash
Flesh & Bone
Dust & Decay
Rot & Ruin
Bad Moon Rising
Dead Man's Song
Ghost Road Blues
V-Wars (editor)
Redneck Zombies from Outer Space (editor)
Out of Tune (editor)

Nonfiction
Wanted Undead or Alive
They Bite
Zombie CSU
The Cryptopedia
Vampire Universe
Vampire Slayer's Field Guide to the Undead (as Shane MacDougall)
Ultimate Jujutsu
Ultimate Sparring
The Martial Arts Student Logbook
Judo and You

Graphic Novels
Marvel Universe vs. Wolverine
Marvel Universe vs. The Punisher
Marvel Universe vs. The Avengers
Captain America: Hail Hydra
Klaws of the Panther
Doomwar
Black Panther: Power
Marvel Zombies Return
Bad Blood
Punisher: Naked Kills
Wolverine: Flies to a Spider

Jonathan Maberry

Code Zero

St. Martin's Griffin
New York

CODE ZERO. Copyright © 2014 by Jonathan Maberry. All rights reserved. Printed in the United States of America. For information, address St. Martin's Press, 175 Fifth Avenue, New York, N.Y. 10010.

www.stmartins.com

The Library of Congress Cataloging-in-Publication Data is available upon request.

ISBN 978-1-250-03343-7 (trade paperback)
ISBN 978-1-250-03342-0 (e-book)

St. Martin's Griffin books may be purchased for educational, business, or promotional use. For information on bulk purchases, please contact Macmillan Corporate and Premium Sales Department at 1-800-221-7945, extension 5442, or write specialmarkets@macmillan.com.

D 10 9 8 7 6

This is for all of the organizations and individuals who do what they can to help our returning veterans by providing jobs, helping them get the benefits they've earned or working with them to find new ways to serve their country even out of uniform. To help a hero is to be a hero. Bravo and brava.

And, as always, for Sara Jo

Acknowledgments

As always I owe a debt to a number of wonderful people. Thanks to Dr. John Cmar of the Infectious Disease department of Johns Hopkins University Hospital; Dr. Steve A. Yetiv, Professor of Political Science, Old Dominion University; Dr. Pawel Liberski of Laboratory of Electron Microscopy and Neuropathology, Department of Molecular Pathology and Neuropathology, Medical University of Lodz, Poland; Philadelphia police officer Bob Clark; Michael Sicilia of California Homeland Security; the staff, presenters, and conferees of DragonCon in Atlanta, Georgia; Nancy Keim-Comley; Melinda Leigh, Katharine Ashe, and Chris Redding; the International Thriller Writers; the crew who helped me with video game research: J. P. Behrens, RJ Sevin, Stephen Goodman, Alex Adams, Stephen Reider, Stephen Harvey, P. J. Stanton, Garrett Cook, William J. Bivens, Herb Dorr, Mike Therrion, Charlie Miller, Tony Baker, Gabrielle Henderson, Henry Rysz, John Leasure, Tony Baker, James Frazier, Ken Varvel, Paul Merritt, Phillip Bolin, Mike Chrusciel, and Bill Versteegan; my literary agents, Sara Crowe and Harvey Klinger; all the good folks at St. Martin's Griffin: Michael Homler, Joe Goldschein, Aleksandra Mencel, Rob Grom; and my film agent, Jon Cassir of Creative Artists Agency.

Thanks for being Joe's "friends in the industry."

Thanks and congrats to the winners of the various Joe Ledger contests: Michael Barbera, Jamie Sheffield, Christopher Duffner, and David Mickloas.

Part One
VaultBreaker

Pain and foolishness lead to great bliss and complete knowledge, for
Eternal Wisdom created nothing under the sun in vain.

—KHALIL GIBRAN

Chapter One

The philosopher Nietzsche didn't get it right. He said, "Battle not with monsters, lest ye become a monster."

That's not exactly true.

Or, at least, not all the time.

If you battle monsters you don't always become a monster.

But you aren't entirely human anymore, either.

Chapter Two

1100 Block of North Stuart Street

Arlington, Virginia

Thursday, April 14, 1:22 p.m.

Some cases start big. Something blows up or someone unleashes a nasty bug and Echo Team hits the ground running. Most of the time, even if we don't know what the endgame is going to look like, we have some idea of what kind of fight we're in. And we can usually hear that big clock ticking down to boom time. Other cases are running fights and they end when one side runs out of bullets and the other doesn't.

I've had a lot of both.

This one started weird and stayed weird, and for most of it felt like we were swinging punches at shadows. We didn't even know what we were fighting until we were right there at the edge of the abyss.

And even then, it wasn't what we thought it was.

Not until we *knew* what it was.

Yeah, it was like that.

It started four months ago on one of those sunny days T. S. Eliot wrote about when he said that April was the cruelest month. When spring rains wake the dead bulbs buried in the cold dirt and coax flowers into first blooms. When we look at the flowers we suddenly forget so many important things. We forget that all flowers die. We forget that winter will come again. We forget that nothing really endures and that, like the flowers that die at the end of the growing season, we'll join them in the cold ground.

I spent years mourning the dead. Helen. Grace. My friends and colleagues at the Warehouse. Members of my team who fell in battle. All of them in the cold, cold ground.

Now it was April and there were flowers.

In my life there was Junie Flynn. She was the flower of my spring.

As far as we knew, her cancer was in remission, though we were waiting for her last panels. But for right now, the sun shone through yellow curtains and birds sang in the trees.

I sat at a kitchen table with a cup of coffee and the remains of a big slice of apple-pecan pie. The rest of the pie was gone. There was evidence of it in crumbs and beige glob smeared on the floor, on the aluminum pie plate, and on the muzzle of my dog. Ghost. Big white shepherd.

He loves pie.

The mess was considerable. However, I had no intention of cleaning it up. It wasn't my pie.

It wasn't my house.

When the actual owner of the house—a Mr. Reginald Boyd—came home and then came storming into the kitchen, he told me, very loudly and with lots of cursing, that it wasn't my house, my kitchen, or my goddamn pie.

I agreed with those observations. Less so about his accusations that I fornicate with livestock.

Reginald Boyd was a big man gone soft in the middle, like an athlete who has gone to seed. Played some ball in college, hit the gym a bit after that. Started going soft probably around the same time that he started getting paid for stealing some real important shit from work.

"Work" was the Defense Advanced Research Projects Agency, known as DARPA. Basically a collection of the most dangerous geeks on earth. Except for idiots like Reggie, those geeks try to keep America safe.

"Get the fuck out of my house," yelled Reginald Boyd.

Ghost, his face covered in apple pie and pecan bits, stood up and showed Boyd how big he was. And how many teeth he had.

I smiled at Boyd and said, "Lower your voice."

Boyd backed a step away. "You broke into my house."

"Only technically. I loided the lock with my library card. *Loided*," I repeated. "It's a word, look it up. It means to bypass a lock. You have a two-hundred-dollar dead bolt on your front door and a Mickey Mouse spring lock on the back door. A moron could get in here. So . . . whereas I got *in*, I did no actual *breaking*."

He didn't know how to respond to that, so he glared at what was on the table. "You made coffee? And you ate my pie?"

I felt like I was in a Goldilocks and the Three Bears reboot.

"First off, the coffee is Sanka. How the hell can you call yourself an American and all you have in your pantry is powdered decaf? I ought to sic Ghost on you just for that."

"What—?"

"The pie's good though," I continued. "Could use more pecans. Store-bought, am I right? Take a tip and switch to Whole Foods, they have a killer deep-dish apple that'll make you cry."

"You're fucking crazy."

"Very likely," I admitted.

His hand touched the cell phone clipped to his belt. "Get the hell out before I call—"

I reached under my jacket, slid the Beretta 92F from its clamshell holster, and laid it on the table. "Seriously, Mr. Boyd—actually, may I call you Reggie?"

"Fuck you."

"Seriously, Reggie, do you really want to reach for that cell phone? I mean—who are you gonna call?"

"I'll call the fucking cops is who I'll call."

"No you won't."

"Why the fuck not?"

"'Cause *I'm* a cop, Einstein," I said. Which was kind of true. I used to be a cop in Baltimore before I was shanghaied into the Department of Military Sciences. The DMS gig gives me access to credentials from every law enforcement agency from the FBI to local law to the housing police. I need to flash a badge; they give me the right badge. The DMS, though, doesn't have its own badges.

Boyd eyed me. "You're no cop."

"I could be."

"Bullshit. I'm going to call the cops."

"No you're not."

"You can't stop me, this is my house."

I drummed my fingers on the table next to my gun. "Honestly, Reggie, they said you weren't the sharpest knife in the drawer, but come on . . . Big guy? Big dog? Big gun? You're armed with a cell phone and a beer gut. How do you think this is going to play out?"

"I'm not afraid of any stupid dog."

I held up a finger. "Whoa now, Reggie. There are all kinds of lines we can step over. Insulting my dog, however, is a line you do not want to cross. I get weird about that, and you do not want me to get weird on you."

He stared blankly at me, trying hard to make sense of our encounter. His eyes flicked from me to Ghost—who noisily licked his muzzle—and back to me.

He narrowed his eyes to prove that he was shrewd. "What do you want?"

"What do you *think* I want?"

"I don't know."

"Of course you do."

"No, I *don't* know."

I sighed. "Okay, I'll give you a hint because you may actually be *that* stupid."

He started to open his mouth.

I said, "VaultBreaker."

His mouth snapped shut.

"Proprietary military software? Am I ringing any bells here?" I asked. "Anything? Anything? Bueller?"

That's when Reggie Boyd tried to run. He spun around and bolted down the hallway toward the front door.

I took a sip of the coffee. Sighed. Said, "Go ahead."

Ghost shot after him like a bullet, nails scratching the hallway floorboards, one long, continuous growl trailing behind him.

Reggie didn't even make it to the front door.

Later, after we were past the screams and first-aid phases, Reggie lay on the couch and I sat on the edge of a La-Z-Boy recliner, my pistol back in its shoulder rig, another cup of the pisswater Sanka cradled between my palms. Ghost was sprawled on the rug pretending to be asleep. The living room was a wreck. Tables overturned, a lamp broken. Bloodstains on the floors and the walls, and one drop on the ceiling—for the life of me I couldn't figure out how that got there.

My chest ached, though not because of anything Reggie had done. It was scar tissue from bullet wounds I'd received last year during the Majestic Black Book affair. Couple of bullets went in through the armhole opening of my Kevlar and busted up a whole lot of important stuff. I was theoretically back to perfect health, but bullet wounds are not paper cuts. I had to keep working the area or scar tissue would build up in the wrong places. Wrestling Reggie onto the couch helped neither my chest nor my mood.

"We could have done all this in the kitchen," I said irritably. "We could have had a pizza delivered and talked this through like adults."

Reggie said nothing.

"Instead you had to do something stupid."

Nothing.

"That alone should tell you something, man," I said. "Didn't your spider sense start to tingle when you found me sitting at your kitchen table? No? Maybe you're good at your job, Reggie, but beyond that you are as dumb as a box of rubber hammers. You assumed you were being slick and careful, but since I'm here, we can agree that assumptions about your overall slickness are for shit. Ass out of you and me, you know what I'm talking about?"

Nothing.

"The question is, Reggie, what do we do now?"

He turned his face away and buried it in the couch cushions.

Back in Baltimore, Junie was shopping for a dress to go with the killer shoes she bought last week. We were going to see Joe Bonamassa play stinging blues at the Hippodrome. Thinking about that, and about how I was pretty sure I was falling in love with Junie—real love, not the unstructured lust into which I usually fall with the women who pass through my life. I don't want to get all sappy here, but I was beginning to get the feeling that Junie was the one. The actual *one*. The one they write cards and movies and love songs about. The kind of "one" I used to make jokes about, as all male outsiders make jokes when they don't think they'll ever meet, or perhaps don't deserve to meet, their one.

All of that was waiting for me once I cleared up a few details with Reggie Boyd.

I leaned over and jabbed him with my finger.

"Reggie? Listen to me now," I said quietly. "You know I wouldn't be here if you weren't in trouble. You know that you're going to be arrested. We both know that. What we *don't* know, what you and I have to decide, is where you go once you're charged. There are people who want me to take you to a private airstrip so we can send you to Gitmo, where you will never be seen again and from where—I guarantee you—you'll never return. Personally, I don't dig that option. I'm not a huge fan of enhanced interrogation. Not unless I'm up against a wall. There's a wall pretty close, though, and I don't think it's in either of our best interests if you push me against it. You dig?"

He didn't answer, but he lay so still that I could tell he was listening.

"Second option is I bust you through main channels with the NSA. That means you get charged with treason and you'll spend the next forty years in a supermax prison learning what it means to be a 'fish.' It's not a lesson you want to learn, trust me. If we go that way, I lose control of the situation and less friendly people run your life henceforth."

Reggie shook his head, still silent.

"Third option is the one I like. Yes, it still ends with you in prison— that's going to stay on the table, no way around it—but in that option it's a federal country club prison and you don't spend every Friday night giving blow jobs to tattooed members of the Aryan Brotherhood. I think you'll admit that it's a better option."

"You're lying to me," he mumbled. "You're going to kill me."

"If I'd wanted to kill you, Reggie, I wouldn't have pulled Ghost off of you."

Ghost opened one eye, looked around, closed it. Made a soft *whuff* sound.

"We don't want you dead, Reggie. What we want is for you to become a cooperative person. Totally open, totally willing to share everything you know. That kind of thing opens hearts, Reggie. It earns you Brownie points."

Reggie said nothing.

"Now, I need to make a phone call, Reggie," I said. "I need to make that call in the next five minutes. I need to tell my boss that you're going to cooperate with us. I need to tell him that you're going to help us plug the leak in the Department of Defense. I need to tell him that you're going to name names and make connections so that we can make a whole bunch of arrests. And, yes, some of them will go to Gitmo and those that don't will be doing the shower-room boogie-woogie in supermax. You, however, won't. You'll be watching *American Idol* on cable, eating food nobody's spit in, and sleeping soundly at night with all of your various orifices unviolated. Not sure if that's a word, but you get my gist."

He turned and looked at me, uncertainty and conflict blooming like crabgrass in his eyes. "How do I know I can trust you?" he said in a near-whisper.

I smiled, then reached behind the chair and dragged out a heavy leather valise, opened it, and spilled the contents onto the rug. Reggie stared at what spilled out and his color, already bad, went from pale to green. The light from the one unbroken lamp glinted from the curves and edges of pliers, bone saws, wood rasps, electrical clamps, scalpels, and rolls of duct tape. "Because I didn't use these."

"Jesus Christ."

"I know, right?"

"But you fucking *brought* them! You were going to use those . . . *things* on me."

"Actually," I said, "I didn't bring this shit." Before he could reply I got up and walked over to the small coat closet beside the door. I opened it. Two bodies tumbled out. A third lay twisted inside. "*They* did."

Ghost made his *whuffing* sound again. It sounded like laughter of a very bad kind.

Reggie gagged. Even from where he lay he could see bullet holes and bite marks.

"Two of those guys are North Korean," I said. "Other guy's Iranian. They're working together, which I find interesting as all hell. They came here and began unpacking their party favors. Can you imagine what fun you would have had with them? They'd have had to bury you in separate boxes. Ghost and I dissuaded them."

I sat down again and gave him my very best smile. The one that crinkles the corners of my eyes and shows a lot of teeth. The one I never show to Junie.

"Now," I said, "how about we have that talk?"

He licked his lips. "What . . . what do you want to know?"

Chapter Three

1100 Block of North Stuart Street

Arlington, Virginia

Thursday, April 14, 2:09 p.m.

Once he got started I couldn't shut Reggie Boyd up.

Seriously.

At one point I considered clubbing him unconscious long enough to make a Starbucks run, but I think that would have been hard to justify in my after-action report. He talked and talked and talked. He was Mr. Helpful for the rest of the afternoon.

Part of it was that tool bag. There was some nasty shit there, and Reggie had enough imagination to guess how his afternoon might have gone if I hadn't showed up. Part of it was the presence of a big man and his nasty dog. And part of it was the fact that he believed me when I said I could cut him a deal that he could, in real point of fact, live with. That much was true because the DMS had been given a lot of latitude to strike such a deal courtesy of Vice President William Collins, who was the nominal head of the CTF, the federal Cybercrimes Task Force. Collins was also a major dickhead in many important ways, but he had powerful friends all through the government. Collins had provided me with papers detailing what I was allowed to offer Reggie in return for actionable information.

Also, I think that part of the reason Reggie cracked was that once he was talking, I think on some level he felt relieved. He was out of it now. Maybe he was of that type who wasn't suited to be a criminal. Maybe by the time he was fully invested in taking money to sell secrets from DARPA, he realized that this wasn't a criminal thing, it was a terrorist thing.

It happens. Greed or idealism kicks you in the direction of bad choices because at first it's all about the money or the politics. None of it's quite real. At first it's just data on a flash drive. No fuss, no muss. But then something makes you step back and look at the bigger picture, at the actual intended use of the information you're selling, and the abstract becomes so crystal clear that its edges can draw blood. That's when you realize that you, as a part of a larger conspiracy, will be complicit in acts that could kill people. That almost certainly *would* kill people. Acts that could lead to war.

What was it he sold?

The latest generation of a software package called VaultBreaker.

It's the absolute bleeding edge of cybersecurity technology. On the surface it was an advanced counterespionage program to keep China, Iran, and North Korea from hacking into our energy grids and shutting them down. That's been a real threat for the last few years thanks to superhacker groups like Comment Crew, which sounds like a rap band but isn't. They're a group of Chinese operators also known as Advanced Personal Threat 1, or APT1, headquartered in a nondescript twelve-story building inside a military compound in a crowded suburb of China's financial hub, Shanghai. They've intruded into banking, credit card companies, power companies, Internet providers, and other places, and our cyberwarfare people have no doubts that these pricks could do us serious harm. It's a little scary that they're not even trying to hide, though the Chinese government officially denies their existence. VaultBreaker is designed to both predict attacks and respond to them, and it has some intrusion capabilities that allow it to fight back in creative ways, either by planting viruses or sneaking into attacking systems to rewrite their operating software.

The other thing VaultBreaker was designed to do was attack our own security systems. Sounds nuts, I know, but there's a logic. Once a new ultrasecure facility was designed, VaultBreaker would be used to try to crack its defenses. Each time it found a hole, the designers of the facility would then be able to address that vulnerability. Reset and replay until there were no holes left to find. Smart stuff.

And from what Bug told me, VaultBreaker was designer to play like a video game. They even hired some top game nerds to play versions of it—in very controlled situations, of course—to see how good it was. What alarmed everyone was that these gamers, most of whom were teenage kids, were better at using VaultBreaker against our best security than most of our security people were. In fact, only two of our geeks were better than the geeks-for-hire. Bug—which surprised no one—and Dr. Artemisia Bliss, a stunningly brilliant computer engineer who'd helped design the system. Bliss was gone now, of course, and VaultBreaker had been revised and upgraded many times since.

That was what Reggie Boyd wanted to sell.

He'd managed to bypass the protections in the system and burn a complete copy. He didn't have the codes to enable it, but once it was in the hands of hackers like the Comment Crew, VaultBreaker would be broken. Then it could be used for all sorts of fun and games. And by fun and games I mean it could be used to orchestrate a coordinated shut down of more than forty percent of the power grids in the United States, and—and here's the kicker—neutralize more than half of our missile defense systems. Viruses would be introduced to screw up the rest of the systems, including our satellite early warning systems and all military and civilian air traffic control.

We would be blind, naked, and bent over a barrel.

Nice.

It would also give anyone with enough computer savvy a real chance at cracking the defense systems of ultra-high-security facilities such as the Locker—the world's most dangerous bioweapons lab—as well as all of our military bases, and every bank in the world.

Vice President Collins gave us a lot of authority to get that program back, even going as far as calling off his long-standing holy war against Mr. Church and the DMS. Suddenly he was our friend and ally. Couldn't help us enough. Kind of like having Satan ride shotgun with you while you're driving a Meals on Wheels truck.

Reggie told me that he was scouted by an Asian woman who called herself Mother Night. She was his liaison to a nine-man team of cyberhackers from China along with day players from North Korea and Iran. Axis of Evil, nerd division. Reggie wasn't sure if Mother Night was a foreign national or not. Nor did he know if she worked for China or was merely acting as a go-between. He was scared of her, though. He told me that five times, though he couldn't say exactly why, beyond the fact that she "creeped him out." Very helpful.

He liked her money, though, and apparently five mil is the going price for a man's soul. Deposited, of course, into a numbered account in the Caymans. That doesn't seem like a lot, but better men than Reggie have sold their souls for less.

So, once Reggie got going he tried to buy back his soul by telling me everything he knew. He knew a lot. More than he was supposed to know. He may have been stupid in some areas, but not when it came to computers because Reggie hacked his way into the systems of Mother Night's crew of cybergeeks. He was, however, too stupid to realize that they'd figure that out.

Hence the closet full of dead guys.

Now here's the clincher. We found out about all this because our computer geeks at the DMS—Bug and his brain trust—had been using Mind-Reader to silently hack the Iranians. This popped up because it's the kind of nastiness MindReader is programmed to look for.

Oh, what a tangled web we weave.

Once Reggie provided me with a probable address for the team of cyber-hackers, I juiced him with enough horse tranquilizer to send him off to la-la land and called for a pickup. After that I made calls to assemble a team to kick their door down.

Then I opened my cell, took a breath, and called Junie to tell her that I wouldn't be able to go to the theater with her tonight.

"Are you all right?" she asked immediately.

"Right as rain," I said. "But, I, um . . . have to work tonight."

Her response was what she always said, and it said it all. "Come home to me when you can."

Not just come home.

Come home to her.

"Always," I promised, and that was no lie.

Chapter Four

Mother Night's cyberteam was in Arlington, and we hit them hard the following day. Thirty men and women in Kevlar, black battle dress uniforms and ballistics helmets. Echo Team was on point, and we had a hodgepodge of shooters from FBI Hostage Rescue, ATF, local SWAT, and some warm bodies from every alphabet group who could get a man to us by the time we kicked in the door. The Veep made sure some of his CTF gunslingers were there, too. Everybody wanted skin in this game because it looked like an easy win but a damn big one.

The prize was so juicy. A joint Iranian-Chinese—North Korean team of cyberterrorists operating inside the United States. That was like crack to political strategists. The guy from the State Department nearly fell on my shoulder and wept. This gave us all kinds of political leverage. If we could prove official sanction on the part of the Chinese or their allies, then it was an act of war, and nobody wanted to go to war with America *and* all of its allies. I know North Korea makes a lot of noise about wanting to nuke us, but saber-rattling isn't the same thing as wanting to duke it out with a country whose military budget exceeds those of the next twelve largest countries combined.

The ideal outcome would be a bloodless sweep of the splinter cell. It would be okay if they fired some shots, and I know that there are some cynical pricks on our own side who would love to spend the currency of martyred Americans, but that wasn't the plan. We wanted everyone inside to drop their weapons, raise their hands, and come along like contrite schoolboys.

That was Plan A.

Plan B would be determined by how the hostiles reacted, and in a geeks vs. shooters scenario I liked our odds.

The splinter cell was in a suite of offices on the seventh floor of a nine-story office building that was still mostly under construction. There were occupied offices on the first two floors and sporadic occupancy above that.

The eighth floor was only half finished and the landlord—who was as slimy an example of his profession as I'd ever seen but not actually an enemy of the state—rented it cheap to a group he described as "pencil-dick geeks from some dot-com thing." The joint team had people in the basement and in the fire towers. Echo Team was on the roof. Bug was poised to cut power, telephone landlines, and cell service to the area. Helos with even more backup were sitting in parking lots or building rooftops a few blocks away, and local police were on standby for traffic control and backup.

Morning dawned with red sunlight burning the underbelly of low-hanging clouds. We had observers and cameras everywhere, and an eye in the sky. As the bad guys arrived we took high-res pictures and ran them through MindReader's facial recognition program. FBI guys at street level checked tags on their cars, or on cars that dropped them off. Info was shared with local law, which remained poised to hit their residences after we took this nest.

They came in according to no pattern. I guess terrorists don't fight traffic to clock in on time. So it was midmorning before we decided that no one else was coming. Nine of them were in the building. A nice school of nasty fish.

All nine were men, though. Mother Night never showed.

Top, Bunny, and I drifted down to the eighth floor. Bunny had a breeching tool and Top had a combat shotgun. I drew my Beretta and clicked my tongue to bring Ghost to attack readiness.

I counted down.

On zero we came out of the fire tower and Bunny swung the breeching iron at the door, which exploded inward, half torn from its hinges. Top and I tossed in a couple of flash-bangs. Before the thunder of the explosions faded we were moving inside. Ghost lunged forward ahead of me and cut right. I faded left with Top beside me. Bunny dropped the iron, swung his M4 on its strap, and came in hard and fast.

The rest of Echo Team and two dozen other shooters boiled in through the door.

Everyone was yelling.

Everyone was pointing guns.

Each of us ready to kill if we saw even a glint of gun metal.

And then we all ground to a halt.

The main room was big, an open-plan office with desks and laptops. There were heavy curtains over the windows. And, true to what the landlord had said, the place was still under construction. Exposed brick, unpainted drywall, and no ceiling tiles to hide the pipes.

Maybe it would have been better if the pipes had been hidden.

Or maybe things would have gone a different way. A worse version of Plan B.

As it was, we found that there was a Plan C we hadn't anticipated.

We all looked up. Bunny stood with his mouth hanging open.

Top said, "Well, fuck me."

Ghost whined.

Nine bodies hung from the pipes.

Chapter Five

Conrad Building
North Nineteenth Street
Arlington, Virginia
Friday, April 15, 2:09 p.m.

Someone had taken a can of red spray paint and used it to write a message on the wall.

The only action is direct action.
U+24B6

"What's that supposed to mean?" wondered Top.

"I know that phrase," said Lydia. "I read it somewhere—"

It was Bug who answered. He could see the image via our helmet cams. "The top line, that's a catchphrase from the anarcho-punk movement."

"Punk?" I asked, but Bug had more.

"That's computer language," he told us. "Unicode. It's the codepoint for circle-A."

We all knew what that was. A capital A surrounded by a letter O. The international symbol for anarchy.

"The hell we into here?" asked Bunny.

I didn't have an answer for him.

We never found Mother Night.

We sat Reggie down with a police sketch artist and someone who knew how to work an Identikit. The problem was that Reggie never saw Mother Night when she wasn't wearing big, dark sunglasses and a kind of Betty Page haircut that he thought might have been a wig. She had lots of piercings in her ears, nose, and lower lip, and a couple of scars on her face. Her skin was darker than normal for an Asian, so he speculated that she might be part black. Her accent was European, but Reggie couldn't pin it down even after many audio samples were played for him.

The sketch and the Identikit picture did not resemble each other all that much, which is pretty common with descriptions by people who are not trained observers. Even so, the pictures of Mother Night were sent to every law enforcement and investigative agency in the country, and to a fair number of our friends overseas, including Interpol and Barrier.

All of the laptops at the suicide site were trashed, of course. No surprise there. But when the forensics teams searched the residences of the dead men they struck gold. Reggie's copy of VaultBreaker was hidden behind a false section of wall in one man's apartment. And that's where we caught our first break. The encryption on the software could not be hacked without the attacking hardware being hijacked to leave a signature on the disk. That signature included notations on the number of times the disk was read as well as critical information about the computer being used. It also uploaded a destructive virus to any attacking computer unless a separate piece of decryption software was preinstalled. When Bug analyzed the disk, he announced that the encryption had not been hacked.

Mother Night's team had not yet accessed the VaultBreaker software.

As lucky breaks go, that one was massive. That's when my nuts crawled back down from inside my chest cavity.

The second break we caught was that the drives had stuff on them that the bad guys really did not want us to have. Names were named. In North Korea, in Iran. And, we discovered, in China.

And in a few other places whose political stability took a serious kick in the nutsack once Mr. Church turned over the data to the State Department. And, with reluctance, to the Veep and his Cybercrimes team.

The effect of all this was pretty dramatic.

Heads rolled. Literally in North Korea, I believe.

People went to prisons and gulags. Some were disappeared. Governments denied official involvement. All players were disavowed and labeled as rebels, dissidents, enemies of various states. Blah, blah, blah.

What mattered to me was that the power grid stayed on, the missiles remained in their silos, and all of the microscopic monsters slumbered in their test tubes at places like the Locker.

The farther we got from that day in Arlington the less the DMS was involved. It became part of yesterday's box score. We moved on to other fights, other wars, other horrors.

And in doing so we believed that we had won an easy victory, kicked all kickable asses and put one in the win column for the good guys.

There's being wrong, and then there's being wrong.

This was the other kind.

Interlude One

Donleavy Building
Forty-third Street and Fifth Avenue, 58th Floor
New York City
Six Years Ago

The young woman sat on the edge of her seat, knees together, hands in her lap, briefcase open on the other guest chair. She was twenty-three years old but already had a Ph.D. in computer science and masters in cybernetic engineering and software engineering. She'd graduated from high school at thirteen and was courted by scouts from every big-ticket science school from Cal Tech to Harvard.

The interviewer read her name off the top of her resume.

"Artemisia Bliss," he said, pronouncing it slowly, savoring it. "Real name?"

"Real name," she agreed. "My father is a professor of genetics, specializing in the hybridization of ultrarare plant species. My mother is an assistant curator of the Metropolitan Museum of Art, and she is one of the world's foremost authorities on Baroque art. She discovered two lost paintings by Artemisia Gentileschi, the seventeenth-century Italian who was—"

"—the eldest child of the Tuscan painter Orazio Gentileschi," finished the interviewer.

Miss Bliss blinked, confused. "Did you look that up after I scheduled this interview?"

"No, I happen to know something about art."

The interviewer left it there. Left it for her to ponder whether that statement was true or not.

He sat back in his expensive leather chair and pretended to study the psychological evaluation on this woman that had just been hand-delivered to him. In point of fact he was looking past the pages at Miss Bliss. She was, he was quite sure, the most beautiful woman with whom he had ever had a conversation. Possibly with the exception of Dr. Circe O'Tree, who was a young but brilliant counterterrorism analyst he occasionally consulted. Dr. O'Tree was a mix of European ethnicities, with some emphasis on Irish, Scottish, and Greek. Artemisia Bliss, unlike the scholarly couple that had adopted her, was pure Asian. Vietnamese and Chinese. She was slender, but not skinny. Not like many of the Asian women the interviewer had known. Miss Bliss was in no way a stick figure. Excellent nutrition had given her height and curves. Exercise toned her and gave her the posture of a dancer. And a lottery-winning set of genes gave her an IQ of 192 and the ambition to use it.

The IQ test was not a fluke or an error. Miss Bliss had first been tested at age nine and scored 187. Everyone concluded that she was a prodigy; but the growing body of evidence on intelligence testing indicated that a childhood IQ of 180 might only translate to an adult score of about 115. However, new developments have come up with much more accurate and flexible tests based on multiple dimensions of intelligence, including analytical, interpersonal, logical, memory, musical, spatial, linguistic, philosophical, moral, spiritual, intrapersonal, bodily, and naturalist. The information in Miss Bliss's assessment had been drawn from that kind of exhaustive testing, and it deeply pleased the interviewer. He made a note to have his computer people try to hack the records of the adoption bureau in Beijing. There were people he worked with who would probably want to put eyes on any siblings or close cousins. Intelligence levels of that kind were distressingly rare.

The interviewer riffled the pages, pursed his lips, and pretended he wasn't looking at Artemisia Bliss. He had an IQ of 198, and halfway through this session he was wondering how many Nobel prizes their kids would earn. As he saw it, supergeniuses should be allowed to mate only with each other. The fact that the supergenius gene pool produced someone like Artemisia Bliss was, to him, proof that the universe as a collective whole was working to make it happen. It was an evolutionary imperative.

He placed the evaluation facedown on his desk and laid his palms flat on top of it.

"What do you know about us?" he asked.

She gave him a brief smile. There and gone.

"I know only what I was allowed to know," she said. She leaned ever so slightly on the first "know."

The interviewer decided to play along. "Which is?"

Miss Bliss raised a few fingers of her hand in a way that was meant to indicate the interviewer, the office, and everything associated with it. "That this is an interview for a possible position in a government think tank."

"But . . . ?" he prompted.

"But . . . this is window dressing for something else."

"Oh?" He wanted to smile, but didn't. "Please explain."

Another flicker of a smile. It was a trademark with her, he noted. Less than a second in duration, meant to convey a bit of warmth but also to show that she was aware that these hoops were all necessary. She didn't like them, but she'd jump through them with grace because there was a nice reward at the end.

"This is not a government office."

"You're sure about that?"

"Yes."

The interviewer pursed his lips. Miss Bliss was very composed, in a tailored linen suit in a pale charcoal, with a salmon blouse. Three earrings in each ear, which told the interviewer that she took some time for leisure and fun—a single pair of functional studs would have indicated a loner—but her mind tended toward order. She wore silver rings on two fingers of her left hand and gold rings on three fingers of her right. Perhaps an indication of qualities of her right and left mind. Her glossy black hair was pulled back at the temples with scarab-shaped clips; the wings prevented her hair from falling into her face. A sign of purpose and confidence. The interviewer filed it all away in his mind.

"Then walk me through it," he suggested.

A more pedantic person would have ticked it off on her fingers as she explained. Miss Bliss did not. She said, "There is a soldier sitting outside the building."

"Soldier?"

"He's dressed like a FedEx guy, truck and all. I got here early and stood outside to finish my coffee before I came in. Maybe three minutes. The whole time the man looked at maps on a GPS." Before he could ask her to elucidate, she held up a single finger. "A FedEx man working in Manhattan wouldn't need a GPS even if he could get a clear signal. There are so many businesses compacted into each few square blocks that deliverymen would work a tight region. He'd know it backward after a day."

The interviewer almost flipped her file open to check her birth date to make sure she was really only twenty-three. Instead he merely said, "Continue."

"Sure. The big tip-off is the fact that he has a wire behind his ear, like the Secret Service wear. It was on the passenger side at least, so it wasn't too obvious, but he has a tan and the wire is white. At the very least he should have been wearing a flesh-colored one. It spoiled the whole effect."

"You're very observant."

Her mouth twisted into momentary irritation. Like the smile, it was there and gone. The interviewer appreciated it. His compliment had been deliberately weak and obvious, and her irritation showed that she wasn't the kind of person to seek compliments like a puppy wagging for treats. She was giving information and did not appreciate a pointless interruption. He gave a small gesture with his hand to indicate that she continue.

"Inside the lobby, the menu of offices was wrong," she said. "There are a lot of insurance companies and similar firms here, and they comprise nearly seven eighths of the office space. When the government rents office space it tends to do so in larger chunks. This was the only such office. However, if an organization—federal or private—wanted to have an office for interviews in the right zip code in Manhattan, they might rent something like this. It's expensive without being a clear misuse of taxpayer dollars. The waiting room is a bit careworn, which is a nice touch, but there's some old cigarette smoke lingering, and government offices have been smoke-free for years."

He nodded, considered making a Sherlock Holmes joke, decided against it because it might weaken him in her eyes, and instead asked, "Anything else?"

She smiled now, a full smile that was beautiful but not warm. "You never bought that suit with a government paycheck. No government pencil pusher is going to wear an H. Huntsman just to sit behind a desk. Same goes with that watch. A Rolex Daytona? Seriously? That costs about the same as a semester at Harvard. So, no . . . this isn't a government office." Her smile changed, became a bit shy. "Besides, I know who you are, and this," she said, reaching over and nudging the brass nameplate holder, "isn't you."

The nameplate read Michael Chang, Ph.D.

The interviewer had to clear his throat before he asked, "Are you certain about that?"

"Yes, because I know who you are. I have six of your books, including the latest one, *Filamentous Bacteriophage: Biology, Phage Display and Nanotechnology Applications*. You're wearing that same suit in the author photo."

He said nothing. It took a great deal of effort to control the expressions that wanted to twist his face into a mask of great delight.

"You're the man *Scientific American* called 'DARPA's real-world mad scientist,'" Miss Bliss said. "You are Dr. William Hu."

Part Two
Mother Night

The opinions that are held with passion are always those for which no good ground exists; indeed the passion is the measure of the holder's lack of rational conviction. Opinions in politics and religion are almost always held passionately.

—BERTRAND RUSSELL, *Sceptical Essays*

Chapter Six

Gülhane Park

Eminönü District

Istanbul, Turkey

Monday, May 2, 3:37 p.m.

I skated the edge of the Mother Night thing again on a rainy afternoon in a lovely park in Istanbul. They don't get a lot of rain in that part of the world, and if the skies above hadn't been dark, the conversation I was having might have taken place indoors.

My friend, you see, doesn't appreciate bright sunlight. She can deal with it if she has to, but she doesn't like it. Call it an allergy to the sun if that works for you.

Even in the gentle drizzle, Violin wore a hat with a floppy brim, and sunglasses, and she kept her hands in her pockets. Ghost sat on the ground with his head in her lap, letting her pet him and play with his soggy ears. Few people ever get that close to Ghost without losing important parts. But he has a thing for Violin. For her, and for Junie.

It's all pretty complicated.

For him. Not for me.

Violin had once been my lover, and a pretty intense one at that, but things had changed. I'd changed. Maybe the world had changed. Now I had Junie in my life and Junie was my life.

What did that make Violin?

Certainly not a sister. That was too inbred a concept for me.

Comrade in arms, I suppose, though that definition was far from accurate.

We drank bitter coffee out of cardboard cups, pretending that we couldn't still smell gun smoke and spilled blood. Three hours ago we'd cleaned out a nest of Red Knights, and our nerves were totally shot. Well, mine were. I still get a case of the shakes every time I see one of those saw-toothed freaks. They are human, of course, but they're from a different genetic line called the *Upierczy*. An evolutionary spur that dead-ended, resulting in them being just enough different from normal humans to appear inhuman. Or nonhuman. However that's supposed to be conjugated. *Freaks* works for me. They are the reason we have legends of vampires. Pale, immensely powerful, and they have a real taste for O positive; but they don't sleep in coffins, they don't turn into bats, and you don't need a stake to kill them. A nine-millimeter bullet in the brainpan works nicely, thank you.

Today we'd killed five of them.

I took two out, one with bullets and one with a knife in the eye socket. Yeah, that works pretty well, too. Ghost crippled one of them, and Violin finished the job. Then she tore the remaining two to shreds. Violin was not an enemy you'd want to have. And in a lot of ways she, and the other women of the covert ops team Arklight, were much scarier than the Red Knights.

That was a handful of hours ago and now we were pretending to be ordinary folks out for the day in a light rain, enjoying the soggy park with their waterlogged dog, drinking coffee. It was all I could do to keep my teeth from chattering.

Funny thing was that I hadn't come over here to hunt vampires. I was tracking a shipment of fissile materials that had been covertly purchased by a splinter cell of the Seven Kings. We'd torn the Kings down a few years ago, but it wasn't dead. Even though at least half of the Kings were dead—Hugo Vox, Sebastian Gault, and Bin Laden for sure, and maybe one or two others—the rest had eluded us. Rumors were afloat in the seas of international terrorism that the Kings were regrouping. If they do, I think I'll quit and get a job kicking Siberian tigers in the nutsack—I'd be safer and have a better chance for retirement.

"When are you going back?" asked Violin, trying to make it sound casual.

"Tonight."

"She's expecting you so soon?"

I looked at her. The question was clumsy, and she colored as she realized how it sounded.

"Violin . . . ," I began, but she shook her head.

"I'm sorry, Joseph. That was wrong."

We had some coffee. A young father walked by, holding the hands of two little kids, a boy and girl in raincoats. He smiled at us and we at him. I listened to the sound of little feet in galoshes, pleased that each footfall made a true "galosh" sound.

Violin tried it again. "This is serious, then? With you and that woman?"

"Her name is Junie."

"I know her name."

"You never use it."

She sighed. "This is serious with *Junie?*"

"It's serious."

Violin looked into my eyes, into *me*. She was very good at reading people. Not as empathic as Junie, but no slouch. She sighed again and looked away.

"Okay," I said, "what gives? What's with the heavy sighs and leading questions? Since when were you a love-struck schoolgirl? This isn't like you, Violin."

After a long time she said, "You know that's not even my real name."

"Yeah, but you won't tell me your real name."

She shook her head.

We sipped. She petted. Light rain fell.

"It gets lonely after a while," she said.

Jesus. And what do you say to that?

"I know," I said, aware that it was both lame and more than a little disingenuous. Okay, sure, I did know about loneliness and loss. And heartbreak. All that. But at the same time I was five degrees past insanely in love. Happier than I'd ever been in my whole life. So . . . lip service felt like talking shit.

Violin said nothing, and I kept my dumb mouth shut.

The rain gradually stopped and the day began to brighten as the clouds thinned. Violin adjusted her hat and sunglasses.

"Joseph," she said, "I'm sorry I said anything. It was weak of me. And impolite."

"No."

"Yes. Please . . . let's forget I said it, okay? Let's go on being us. Allies in the war. Can we do that?"

"Absolutely."

She glanced at me, read me, nodded. And measured out a thin slice of a smile. "I worry about you," she said. "I suppose I always will."

"Believe me when I tell you that I worry about you, too."

She shrugged. "I'm used to this life. I know what's in the shadows."

"So do I."

"No," she said, "I don't know if you do."

"What's that supposed to mean?"

She said, "Have you ever heard of someone called Mother Night?"

I stiffened.

"Ah," she said, smiling, "apparently so."

"How do *you* know Mother Night?"

"A woman who goes by that name has become a player in some dangerous games."

"What games?"

"Theft of science. Two weeks ago an Arklight team hit a lab in Warsaw sponsored by the Red Knights. It was a group of scientists working on computer viruses. There was some Iranian money involved, but their principal clients were the *Upierczy*. They have been trying to obtain as much information as possible about gene therapy and transgenics. They want to force their own evolution. They want to become indestructible, invincible. They want to be like the vampires of movies and books and they're convinced genetics will accomplish this."

"It might," I said sourly.

She nodded. "Yes, and if it happens we'll lose the fight against them. But my point was that when we hit their lab it was already in turmoil. Someone had hacked into their systems and stolen everything. Research, testing data, backup files, the works. We used Oracle to hack their system but we couldn't find anything, not even a hint as to who'd stolen the data. It was so clean and thorough a job that we thought it was the Deacon using MindReader, but he said that it wasn't the DMS."

I said nothing. Church had mentioned something about the Red Knights' computers being hacked, but it was a comment in passing. And *I'd* assumed it was Arklight using Oracle. Assumptions, assumptions.

"How's any of that connect with Mother Night?"

"Ah," she said, smiling faintly. "One of the technicians at the lab said that it was Mother Night. It was all he said, though. Just that."

"You couldn't get any more out of him?"

Her smile never flickered. "Alas, he was unable to say more. However, a few days later we hit a second site in Vilnius. A testing facility for genetic enhancement. When we broke in, though, everyone was already dead. Four Red Knights and sixteen technical staff. All dead."

"How? It would have taken a hefty strike team to—"

"No," she said. "They had not been shot. Someone had released a toxin into the system. Specifically, a radically weaponized strain of enterohemorrhagic *E. coli*. It was like nothing we'd ever seen before. Our scientists tell us that it triggered a quick-onset form of hemorrhagic colitis. The victims bled out through their rectums."

"Christ, that's disgusting."

Violin's eyes were ice cold. "They were Red Knights and their servants."

I said nothing to that. The women of Arklight had suffered indescribable indignities, torture, rape, and worse at the hands of the Knights, and this went back centuries. Whatever mercy they might have had for their former oppressors was long since beaten out of them. They were now the most vicious and efficient kill team anywhere in the world. Second to none, and I do not exaggerate. I was very, very glad they were on our side.

She said, "All of the computers had been stripped of their data and there were no viable materials left. It was all gone, except for empty cabinets, ransacked computers, and the bodies of the dead. Those, by the way, had been piled up and set on fire. There was a message painted with blood on the wall that read: *Mother Night Says that you have to Burn to Shine.*"

"Oh, man . . ." I shook my head. "But even so, how does that connect Mother Night to me and the DMS?"

"Since we found that site, Arklight has been asking around. We've managed to conduct a few interrogations of Knights we captured, and with people connected to them. No one knows much, but several of them told a story about a senior scientist for the Knights who'd been found at the point of death. He'd been severely tortured and left for dead."

"Tortured by whom?"

"By a woman who called herself Mother Night," said Violin. "She asked him a lot of questions and most of it was about the Knights, their former connection with the Red Order, their more recent connections with the surviving members of the Seven Kings, and a mutual enemy of all of then—the DMS. Your name came up in the interrogation. The scientist said that he was aware of you, and of your role in killing Grigor, king of the Red Knights. Unfortunately, that was the extent of the questioning. The scientist died shortly after that. So . . . all we have is a small, fragile connection between you and someone who has been doing significant harm in order to steal computer files and research. A group who has either developed an *E. coli*–based bioweapon or who has stolen it for use."

"I'll have to share this with Church, and he'll probably want to talk to you or to your mother."

Lilith, Violin's mother, was the leader of Arklight. I have never met a more formidable woman. She and Church had some history, but I didn't know what it was or how deep it went.

"Of course," she said.

Violin stood up. When I began to rise too, she touched my shoulder to keep me seated.

"If I hear anything else I'll let you know," she said. "Goodbye, Joseph."

"Goodbye, Violin," I said.

She began to move away, but she stopped and looked over her shoulder at me. "Joseph . . . ?"

"Yes?"

"This woman . . . Junie Flynn?"

"Yes."

"Be good to her."

There was so much meaning in what she said, so many layers to it that I could not respond. It felt like there was a lump in my throat the size of a fist. However, Violin nodded to herself as if I had replied.

As she walked away I felt a weird ache inside. Almost a premonition, like maybe I'd never see her again. But that was stupid.

I sat there and took over the job of petting Ghost, who stared at Violin's retreating back. "Mother Night," I said aloud.

Ghost whined softly.

Chapter Seven

Mother Night surfaced again later that month.

It went like this.

The interrogation team finished with Reggie. They'd squeezed him like a Florida orange, and when they were sure he had no juice left, they gave him back to me to transport him to the witness protection program. Or, rather, our version of it. The one run by the U.S. Marshals is good, but in an age where computer hacking has become the most feared WMD, the protected witnesses aren't all that secure. The Marshal Service is a government agency, which means it needs to keep records, transfer information, and receive reports from the field. All of that goes through computers. Last year, nine protected witnesses who were set to testify against a coalition of Mexican cartels were targeted and killed. Five of them had families, and each witness had on-site marshals as watchdogs. There were no survivors. Forensic computer analysis proved that the system had been hacked.

We didn't want to turn Reggie Boyd over to the marshals. We trusted the agents but not their computers. The world of law enforcement is changing. A couple of keystrokes are more powerful than a bullet.

The DMS has gone old-school with its version of witness protection. Nothing goes onto any computer except MindReader. Even then, information is protected by 28-bit encryption and self-erase counterintrusion programs. There are missile codes with less security.

So, Reggie had been a guest at the new Warehouse, the DMS field office in Baltimore. My office.

Everyone I worked with still called it "new" even though we'd been in residence here for months. However, whenever someone spoke of the Warehouse, without the "new" prefix, everyone knew they weren't talking about here. Once upon a time we'd been in a different building four blocks away. That building was now a hole in the world and everything that had been in it had been vaporized by a terrorist bomb. A hundred and sixty-nine people had gone up with it. Friends, colleagues, brothers-in-arms.

Gone. On some level those of us who'd escaped that catastrophe felt it was disrespectful to simply call this the Warehouse.

The new building was bigger and it was crammed with every kind of interior and exterior surveillance and detection equipment. A sparrow couldn't take a crap on a rain gutter without an alarm ringing somewhere. Paranoid? Sure, but as the saying goes, sometimes they really are out to get you.

Ghost and I came to get Reggie a few minutes before eight on a rainy Friday. Reggie's "cell" was actually an office that had been converted into an apartment about as big as a good-sized dorm room. He had a flat-screen TV, cable with lots of premium channels, a Netflix account, and a tall stack of Blu-Ray DVDs. When I came in, he was in sweats and sneakers, and was sprawled on his couch watching an old episode of *Game of Thrones*.

"It's almost over," he said. "Can you give me a sec?"

"Sure."

I perched on the end of the couch for a few minutes, watching it with him. It was from the second season, the siege of Kings Landing. Good stuff.

Ghost climbed up between us, and while the armies clashed on the screen, Reggie stroked Ghost's fur. Their relationship had changed a bit. Not that Ghost wouldn't kill him if I ordered it, but over the last month we'd all developed an odd fondness for Reggie. He was a traitor and a jackass, but Reggie didn't seem evil. Not even a little bit. More like a cousin who can't keep out of trouble but who's fun at parties.

And, let's face it, no one in the history of international espionage had ever been more cooperative. He could wear out a crack team of CIA interrogators in nothing flat. They dreaded interviewing him because he not only gave useful information; he was the kind of guy who had to tell you every single blessed detail of every single blessed moment of every single blessed day. Once, when a weary interrogator asked him to summarize some of the less important things—like Reggie's account of driving to work or going to the gym—Reggie shook his head and said that he was afraid of missing something.

He didn't miss a thing. Not one single, mind-crushing moment of his life. I was tempted to bribe him into shutting up and never speaking again.

When the episode ended, he turned off the TV and tossed the remote onto the coffee table. "Any chance you're going to tell me where we're going?"

"Come on, Reg, you know better."

We got up. His suitcase had been packed by my people, but I allowed Reggie a few seconds to stuff some of his favorite DVDs into a bag. He looked around and sighed again.

"What?" I asked.

"You'll laugh."

"No, I won't."

He shrugged. "It's just that I think I'm going to miss this place."

"Oh, come on . . ."

"See, what did I say?"

"I'm not laughing," I said, hiding a smile. "But why on earth would you miss this place?"

Another shrug. "I like it here. The food's good. Nobody cheats at cards and you let me keep what I win. I seem to be getting somewhere with Rudy."

Rudy Sanchez was the DMS house shrink as well as my best friend. He'd spent a lot of time with Reggie, not as part of the interrogation team, but trying to map the route from law-abiding citizen to criminal and back again. He planned to publish his findings in one of those incomprehensible psychiatric trade journals that I don't think anyone really reads.

And, apart from that, Rudy was the kind of therapist who could help you find a way to like yourself again. He did that for me, and I was a real mess.

Reggie bent and scratched Ghost between the ears. "I'm going to miss the fur monster here."

Ghost nudged his hand with a wet nose.

"Despite the fact that he bit you?" I asked.

Reggie straightened and gave me a philosophic shake of his head. "Puppy-boy there was doing his job. I can't fault him for that."

Puppy-boy liked being talked about and he thumped his tail.

Dog's very strange. He won't let my brother, Sean, pet him, but he goes all goofy around a bonehead enemy of the state like Reggie. Go figure. Maybe Ghost needs to log some couch time with Rudy.

"I'll make sure the fur monster sends you Christmas cards," I told Reggie. "Let's go."

I checked us through security and we walked together out to my Ford Explorer. When Reggie saw it he whistled.

"You got the new one? Niiiiice," he said, stringing it out. "What did you get on the trade-in?"

"Less than I'd hoped," I said. What I didn't tell him was that my last Explorer had been hit by a rocket-propelled grenade. The one before that had been parked at the old Warehouse and was destroyed when that blew. This new Explorer was my fifth in four years. My insurance company freaking hates me.

The new car was next year's model. Black, with smoked windows and a bunch of extras, including bullet-resistant glass and extra suspension to compensate for the body armor. No ejector seats, though. I keep requesting them but they won't give me one. I think they're afraid I'll use it for fun. They're not entirely wrong.

"Buckle up for safety," I said as Reggie climbed in.

Ghost went into the backseat, flopped down, and began enthusiastically licking his balls. Everyone needs a hobby.

I got in, started the engine, locked the doors, and drove past the security guards, both of whom waved to Reggie.

Reggie Boyd, the cybercriminal who's everybody's pal.

Even with heavy rain, the ride should have taken only two hours, and this was something I could have turned over to any of my staff. There are more than two hundred people working for me at the new Warehouse, including four teams of top-of-the-line shooters. I should have sent some of them, but I wanted to do this myself. It was low-risk, and besides, despite everything, I kind of liked Reggie, too.

Reggie turned on the Sirius, found the Raw Dog Comedy station, and we were laughing our asses off when the team of killers came out of the rain and rammed their Humvee into the side of my Explorer.

Chapter Eight

East McComas Street

Baltimore, Maryland

Friday, May 20, 8:41 p.m.

I never saw it coming.

We'd veered off Cromwell heading to McComas, which ran parallel to I-95, when a dark green Hummer slammed us on the driver's side. The impact tilted the Explorer onto the two passenger-side wheels and drove it sideways toward a row of cement cattle guards that had been placed to guide traffic. It felt like being punched by a giant. The front and side air bags blew, hitting us hard in the face and the side of the head, slamming us back against our seats. The rain-slick streets offered no resistance as the bigger vehicle smashed us into the cattle guards with bone-jarring force. Reggie screamed. Ghost began yelping in fear and pain. I had a mouthful of air bag and couldn't breathe; my side of the car was canted inward toward me. Cracks appeared in the reinforced glass. If it hadn't been for the body armor, the car would have collapsed like a beer can.

"Joe!" howled Reggie in a high and terror-filled voice. "God, Joe!"

With one hand I fought to release the seat belt while my other hand clawed at the handle of my rapid-release folding knife, which was clipped inside my front trouser pocket. The air bags were designed to deflate almost immediately after deployment, with nitrogen leaking out of small vents; but we were so crammed in that the vents were blocked. There was almost no room to move.

Ghost's whines changed to barks and I craned my head to see the Humvee's headlights receding. I wasn't fool enough to think they were going away. They were backing up to hit us again.

I stamped blindly on the gas and the Explorer lurched forward as the Hummer roared and slammed forward again. My car was too badly damaged to drive away—even if I could see to steer, which I couldn't—but it jerked forward a few feet. Enough so the Humvee crunched into the side of the rear bay with a huge *whump*. Metal screeched and I heard one of the tires explode. The car settled awkwardly into a cleft formed by the Humvee and the cattle guards. There was no damn where to go.

Then the knife was in my hand. I flicked it open and jabbed the airbag. White powder filled the cabin, and I spat and sputtered as I twisted to cut the seat-belt straps with the knife. Ghost kept barking but I could hear other sounds. Reggie's groans of fear and pain. Car doors opening. Feet crunching on broken glass. Shouts.

Reggie was bleeding and dazed, but alive. Ghost was going nuts in the backseat and I silenced him with a stern command. Through the cracked glass I could see several figures. All wearing black hoodies and black jeans.

They all had guns.

Jesus Christ.

Panic flashed through me. The driver's door was crushed in. Reggie's door was locked and the glass was reinforced, but five armed people could definitely break in. The impact with the Hummer had twisted the Explorer's frame and the steering wheel sat askew, blocking me from climbing backward over the seat.

Shit.

I saw gun metal glimmer in the downspill of streetlights.

Then a barrage of thunder as they opened up on the car with automatic weapons. I could hear the bullets punch into the side of the car, tearing through the metal skin, flattening themselves on the steel lining. A couple of rounds ricocheted away and I heard a sudden scream of pain and surprise as one of the figures staggered and fell.

Dumb ass, I thought. *The fuck do you expect when you fire at an armored vehicle?*

They closed on the car and began trying to kick the windows in.

That, unfortunately, they might accomplish. The impact of the two heavy vehicles had damaged the glass and it was bound to give.

I clawed the torn fabric of the air bags away from me, tore open the flaps of my Hawaiian shirt, and grabbed for my gun just as the bad guys tried to open the door.

The doors were locked.

One of them must have gone back to their Hummer because suddenly they began swinging a tire iron at the glass. Little chunks of glass popped out from pressure cracks and pinged off the dashboard, the rearview mirror, and my head.

I slashed at Reggie's seat belt and shoved him roughly into the foot well. "Stay down!"

The window glass abruptly turned to white as a solid blow send a thousand microcracks all through it.

Then I jammed my back against the door, banged the door lock control with my elbow, took my Beretta in both hands, and fired at the glass, blowing it outward.

I fired, fired, fired.

There was thunder. Theirs, mine, and real booms coming from above. It all blended together into a deafening symphony of intolerable noise. The figures reeled back. Some falling, some staggering. I swapped out my magazine as I lunged across the seat. With a savage grunt I jerked open the door.

"Ghost—*hit!*"

A flash of snarling white barged past me, knocking me into the steering wheel. Outside I heard a terrible scream of pain.

Then I was crawling over the seat, over Reggie, shoving my gun hand out the door, firing at anything standing. I saw two of my bullets hit a figure, once in the chest and once in the jaw. The impact tore half his face away and he spun around and fell into the glare of headlights. My third shot blew out the Hummer's left headlight.

As I emerged from the car, I saw that chaos ruled the street. One man was down, hands clamped to his stomach as he rolled back and forth. Probably the idiot who'd been hit with a ricochet. A second man leaned against the grill of the Humvee, bleeding from a bullet wound to the thigh, fingers slick with rainwater and blood as he tried to swap magazines on an AK-47. I shot him three times in the chest and once in the head. Ghost had a third man down and all I could see was teeth and torn flesh and a hell of a lot of blood.

The first man I'd shot in the face was down, too.

That left one of the attackers uninjured. He was the one with the tire iron, and he lunged forward and swung it at my head.

If he'd backed up, dropped the tire iron, and pulled his gun, he might have had me.

Might have.

I was moving pretty fast by that point, though, going past the obstruction of the open Explorer door, swinging my gun up.

The tire iron came whistling down through the rain and hit the top of my gun so hard that the weapon was torn from my hands. Pain shot through my fingers and wrists and ran like an electric charge all the way to my elbows.

The guy stared at my empty hands as if he was stunned that his desperate blow had worked. I was surprised, too, but I didn't think a gaper delay in the middle of a fight was a good tactical move. So I rushed him, launched myself into a flying tackle, wrapped my arms around him and his tire iron, and smashed down into a huge puddle. It geysered up around us. I never heard the tire iron fall, but the guy's hands were empty and he started punching me in the face. He had small hands and he didn't really know what he was doing. I could feel his hand bones break on my cheeks and forehead and jaw. While he did that, I wrapped my aching hands around his throat and shoved him down under the water. He beat at my face, my shoulders, my chest. His body writhed and bucked. He tried everything he could to fight back, but I strangled him and drowned him in eight inches of muddy rainwater. Something inside the circle of my hands, inside the structure of his throat, broke, and then the hands fell away.

And then it was over.

I reeled back, a savage growl tearing its way from my throat as I twisted around to see if there was anyone else who needed to die.

There was no one.

The man Ghost had attacked was dead, his throat gone.

The fool who'd been hit by a ricochet lay near him, no longer bleeding. The dead don't bleed. Ghost had gotten to him while I was fighting in the puddle.

My dog raised his head and looked at me with eyes that were ancient and strange. Wolf eyes in a dog face. I knew that what he saw in return were not the eyes of a civilized man. Nor the eyes of a cop or a special operative. In that moment, I—like he—was a more primal thing. A killer. A savage.

The rain fell and fell, each drop as hard as a needle.

I looked down at the man I'd strangled.

It wasn't a man.

It was a woman.

Barely.

Her face floated in dirty water. Thin, frail. Features that might once have been lovely were distorted by the pain of her death. Eyes bulging, tongue protruding between full lips.

She couldn't have been older than twenty.

Maybe not that old.

A girl.

Dead in a ditch, with her throat crushed into an improbable shape by the brutality of my hands.

A girl who'd tried very hard to kill me.

A girl who matched the Identikit sketch of the missing Asian woman from the Arlington team of hackers.

The others around me were young, too. Three men, one other woman. The first one I'd shot in the face was a woman, too. No way to tell how old she'd been. There wasn't enough of her face for that. Only the damaged landscape of her body told me that she was female.

Young.

All of them so damn young.

I rose very slowly. The shakes started then, shuddering their way through my muscles on relentless waves of adrenaline, fear, and revulsion.

Ghost was shivering, too.

He whined in the rainy darkness.

Somewhere, a million miles away, I heard a voice. Reggie.

"Joe . . . ? God . . . are we okay?"

It was a stupid question.

No, I nearly said. No, we're not okay.

But I couldn't say that to him.

So I said nothing.

Around me there was so damn much death.

And no answers at all.

Chapter Nine

East McComas Street
Baltimore, Maryland
Friday, May 20, 8:41 p.m.

That was a long damn night, followed by a longer day.

So many questions.

From my people, from the cops, from Homeland and everyone else. From Vice President Collins's Cybercrimes Task Force. Everyone wanted to know what happened. I told the same story forty times. It didn't make any more sense the fortieth time than it did while it was happening.

None of the five dead people had ID. The Humvee was stolen. The serial numbers had been removed from the weapons, and ballistics didn't match anything on record. No fingerprints on file.

We had to wait for dental records and DNA. The woman I'd strangled was named Luisa Kan. Korean by birth, raised in foster care, and a runaway at fourteen. She was nineteen when I'd killed her.

Reggie said that she looked like Mother Night. He was sure it was her.

So who were the others? Two were Asian: a twenty-two-year-old Japanese boy named Hiro Tanaka who'd come to America as an exchange student three years ago and dropped completely off the radar; and Sally Lu, fifth-generation Chinese American, twenty years old and a junior at the University of Southern California. Last seen at the end of the spring term. We were unable to verify that she was the same woman Reggie met in Arlington. There was simply not enough evidence.

The others were Neil Cox, nineteen, a former employee of a store that sold role-playing and video games; and Arnie Olensky, a high school dropout with no work record. Both of them from Baltimore.

All of them dead.

Jerry Spencer and his forensics team worked their apartments. They found money, expensive video game consoles, including one handheld that was like a souped-up Gameboy, but which no one could identify. Bug later said that it was the most sophisticated handheld game he'd ever seen. He did a patent search on it and found nothing. It was loaded with a bunch of games, but most of them were standard first-person shooter stuff. Except for one, a *Mission: Impossible*—style intrusion game called Burn to Shine. However, when Bug tried to hack the game software it triggered a series of microcharges. The game was destroyed and Bug spent a week in the hospital. They found nothing else of value.

The phrase "burn to shine" stuck in my mind. Violin had told me that those words were painted in blood on a wall in an illegal genetics lab in Vilnius, Lithuania. So far no one understood the exact meaning, at least as far as Mother Night's organization viewed it.

Various agencies worked the case. Nobody made headway, and it eventually reached that point in an investigation where the various agencies covertly dropped out so they wouldn't be seen as the agency still fruitlessly searching.

Bug kept his people on it, though, and MindReader dug up every known fact on the five dead kids. We had a ton of information and we knew absolutely nothing.

If they had political ties to Iran, China, or North Korea, MindReader couldn't find them. No one could.

After a month, the investigation ground to a halt. There was simply nowhere to go with it. The press had bailed, frustrated by the lack of anything juicy to follow up the initial news of five good-looking kids dead by violence.

My name stayed out of it. Press releases from Homeland declined to name the "agents involved." Reasons of national security, yada-yada.

I spent some time with Rudy Sanchez, drinking beers with him in my dad's backyard, and sitting on the couch in his office. Rudy listened. We talked. He gave great advice on dealing with the shock and feelings of self-loathing that any moral person would feel after such an encounter.

Again, yada-yada.

Nothing he said, nothing Church said, nothing Junie said, could change the fact that I'd strangled a teenage girl and participated in the slaughter of four other young people. Kids.

I knew I'd take the memories of that night with me to the grave. Just as I knew that on my bad nights, on those nights when the hinges of the Pandora's Box in my damaged head come loose and the monsters sneak out, then five ghosts would be standing beside my bead. Watching me with accusation in their dead eyes.

Maybe if we knew what all of this meant, then there would be some closure for me.

Maybe.

But I doubted it.

Chapter Ten

Camden Court Apartments
Camden and Lombard Streets
Baltimore, Maryland
Tuesday, May 31, 6:54 a.m.

On the last day of May, Junie found me on the balcony of our apartment. I was in my boxers and undershirt with the macramé lap blanket from the couch wrapped around my shoulders.

"Joe——?" she asked, her voice soft and tentative.

Without waiting for my reply she came out onto the balcony and sat down next to me. It was a strange morning, with shreds of clouds scattered haphazardly against a dark blue sky that refused to grow brighter as the sun rose. In the distance a few big birds rode the thermals, but from that distance I couldn't tell if they were gulls or vultures.

Carrion birds either way.

Junie lifted the edge of the blanket and snuggled up against me.

"Aren't you freezing?" she asked.

I shrugged. Truth was that I hadn't noticed the temperature.

I kept looking at the birds, but I could feel Junie's eyes on me as she studied the side of my face.

"Tell me," she said. It was gently said, an offer instead of a demand. And it was part of our rhythm. We each had a lot of complications in our personal history; we'd each been battered by the circumstances of lives lived in the storm lands. She had every right to be more emotionally screwed up than me, God knows, but Junie was far more balanced. More at peace with who and what she was. The same cannot be said of me.

"Bad night," I said.

"Couldn't sleep?"

"Couldn't shut my head down."

She kissed my shoulder.

The winds of morning kept tearing the clouds into gray and white tatters.

"Those kids?" she asked.

"Yeah."

"Joe . . . I remember you once telling me that if the bad guy deals the play then he owns whatever happens. Those are your exact words."

"Clever words, too. I should put them on my business cards."

"Come on, Joe, what else could you have done? And don't tell me that it's not the point. We both know it is."

"You're quoting Rudy."

"No, I'm not," she said, and there was an edge of irritation in her voice. She was a smart and empathic woman, and it was unfair of me to say that she was cribbing lines from anyone else.

"Sorry. It's just that Rudy's been harping on me with that for a couple of weeks."

"Maybe you should listen to one of us. I think it's fair to say that he and I know you best. Okay, Rudy knows you better and longer than I do, but I know you, Joe. I do. And I know that sometimes you look for ways to beat yourself up over things that are beyond your control and aren't your fault."

"It's more complicated than—"

She cut me off. "I *know* it's more complicated than that. Of *course* it is. The life you live is extremely . . ." she fished for the right word, ". . . *difficult.* The things Mr. Church asks of you, the things you ask of yourself, not only push your body to dangerous limits, they constantly put you in situations where there is no good option, only options less terrible than others. I've seen that, Joe. I saw what you had to do to protect me the day we met, and what you had to do in order to save everyone from disaster. I saw it. Just as I saw the hurt in your eyes afterward."

I said nothing. Her body was a warm anchor to a better world and I closed my eyes and concentrated on the feel of her arm and breast where they pressed against my side.

"The question, my sweet love," she said softly, "isn't whether you did something wrong. You didn't. You couldn't do anything other than what you did. No, the question is whether you need to go back to the fight. We both know that this kind of war won't really end. Terrorism is a fact of our lives. It'll be here forever because there will always be hatred in the world and technology has gotten so user-friendly that anyone can reach out through the Net to do harm or cook up something in a cheap lab. I spent years talking about this sort of thing on my podcast, and it's not all conspiracy theories. This is our world."

"I know, but . . ."

"But do you have to be the one to fight everyone's battles, Joe?"

I said nothing. I didn't dare, because I knew what my answer would be.

"Joe . . . listen to me. If you're fighting because you're afraid to stop fighting, then you're fighting the wrong war. Maybe it's time to stop."

I watched the carrion bird circle high in the sky.

"Not yet," I said.

Interlude Two

Miss Artemisia Bliss looked out the window. "Am I allowed to ask where we're going?"

Midway through the interview Dr. Hu left the room to make a call, and when he returned he told her that they were going to take a drive. Without telling her anything else, he escorted her down to the lobby, where they were met by two very tall, very imposing men in dark suits. Hu knew that she was sharp enough to peg them as Secret Service or the equivalent. Outside, they got into a black Escalade that had a third man behind the wheel. The big car headed straight to the Brooklyn-Battery Tunnel.

Now they were in Brooklyn, heading west on I-278.

"Am I allowed to know where we're going?" asked Miss Bliss.

"You'll see," said Hu.

She nodded, accepting the conditions.

"You're fond of games," said Hu, coming at her out of left field.

She gave him a full second's appraisal, then nodded. "Sure. Video games, mostly. Some RPG stuff and simulations."

"I'm going to shock and possibly offend you," said Hu.

She said nothing.

"According to your debit card purchase history, you're a frequent flyer at GameStop and other stores. Are you angry that I know this?"

"I'm not pleased," she said, "but not surprised. I'll bet you know all sorts of things about me."

She smiled when she said that, and Hu's pulse jumped a gear. Was that a flirty smile? There was definitely some kind of challenge there. He kept his composure intact, however.

"Thorough background checks are necessary for reasons you'll discover shortly."

"Oh, I have no doubt." She paused, then prompted, "Games—?"

"Right. Games."

"What about them?"

"That's what I want you to tell me," said Hu. "What's your interest?"

"Amusement?"

"Please."

She shrugged. "The real answer is kind of boring."

"Try me."

"I like to solve problems," she said. "The tougher the challenge, the more fun it is."

"You bought the Legend of Zelda: Ocarina of Time. How'd you do on the Water Temple level?"

"Is that a serious question?"

"Yes. Did you beat it?"

"When I was like . . . ten?"

"You survived the jet ski level of Battletoads?"

"Sure."

"What was your best time?"

"It's not about best time. It's about remembering where you died in previous tries. I only played it six times, and beat it on the seventh try. I didn't have a stopwatch running."

"Have you done a speedrun?" he asked, referring to one his own favorite aspects of gaming, which was a play-through of a whole video game or a selected part of it, with the intent of completing it as fast as possible. Although Hu didn't compete with other gamers except a kid named Jerome Williams—known familiarly as Bug—recently hired by Mr. Church. They were neck-and-neck at speedruns of most games.

"Sure. Everyone does a speedrun once in a while."

"Did you do one of Battletoads?"

"No," she said. "Haven't played it since I beat it."

"Why?"

"I beat it, and then beat it again," said Bliss. "What would be the point?"

"To beat your best time . . . ?"

Hu smiled. "What about Halo: Combat Evolved, the Library level? To beat your best time . . ."

Bliss snorted. "Overrated. I beat that on my second try. I expected more."

"Super Mario Sunshine, the—"

"Corona Mountain level," she finished for him.

"How fast did you beat that level?"

She considered. "It's not about how fast, okay? Only gamer newbies or people who don't game care about time. It's about how. For Super Mario Sunshine, you can only get to Corona Mountain by clearing the seventh episode of all other areas. But the real challenge is the boat controls. You have to propel a boat by facing backwards and turning on the spray nozzle, then navigate through a section of platforms with either retracting spikes or fire. But you have to figure out how to use the Hover Nozzle."

Hu tried another. "What about level forty of Dead Island?"

"Not really a fan of zombie games."

"But you play them."

She gave him another of those coquettish smiles. "I play everything."

"Did you beat level forty?"

"Yes. On my third try."

"The Teenage Mutant Ninja Turtles game for NES? The underwater bomb disarm section?"

"Set the Way-Back Machine, but sure. When I was eight, I think."

"You're making me feel old."

Another smile. "You're not too ancient."

"What's the hardest game you've ever played?"

She had to think about that. "None of them are what I'd call skull-crackers. If I had to put one up at the top, maybe Super Ghosts and Goblins. I underestimated it because it was harder than I'd heard."

"But you beat it?"

"Yes, and it taught me a lot about making assumptions." She paused. "Excuse me, but are we really going to dissect every single game I ever played? I mean, is there a point to this?"

Instead of answering directly, he said, "Do you have any practical experience with game design?"

"Some."

"It's not in your résumé."

"It was just for fun."

"'Fun'?"

"Well, for the challenge. I, um, hacked into the game programs for Halo, Battletoads, and Gears of War and wrote new levels."

"Why?"

"Like I said—"

Hu shook his head. "I want the real answer."

Miss Bliss took a moment, stalling by adjusting her clothes and shifting to find a more comfortable position on the bench seat. "I . . . have a few friends who are gamers."

"Gamers of your caliber?"

"Pretty much."

"And—?"

"I wanted to see if I could create game levels that they couldn't beat."

"Could they beat them?"

"The first few, sure. But the more recent ones? No."

"Can those levels, in fact, *be* beaten?"

"Sure. Otherwise it wouldn't be a game."

Hu smiled.

"What?" she asked.

"I think you'll enjoy where I'm taking you."

"Meaning—what?"

Hu threw a different line into the water. "What do you hope to accomplish?"

She didn't turn. "Specifically—?"

"In life," he said. "With your career."

Her response was casual, with no trace of defensiveness. "I don't know. I'm keeping my options open."

"And yet you applied for a job with us."

"Sure, I applied for a job because the job description, though necessarily vague, was designed to hook someone like me. You dangled the bait of this being either under the DARPA umbrella or connected to it in some way. That's where I want to be."

Hu nodded. "And you think you'd flourish in a DARPA setting?"

She cut him a quick look as if she'd caught something in the way he'd inflected that question. Her eyes searched his for a long moment before she answered.

"DARPA . . . or something like it," she said carefully.

Dr. Hu smiled as the Escalade drove through an opening in a rusted chain link fence. Frowning, Miss Bliss looked out at the building embowered by that old fence. It was a massive airplane hangar of the kind built seventy or eighty years ago. Many of the glass panes were busted out and the gray skin was peeling and long in need of fresh paint.

Miss Bliss began to ask, but Hu held up a finger.

"Wait," he said.

The Escalade curved around and entered through a small side entrance just big enough for the SUV. Once inside, a door slid shut behind them and for a moment the vehicle was in total darkness. Then there was a shudder beneath the vehicle. The kind of tremble elevators gave. Even through the closed windows there was the sound of heavy hydraulics.

Lights blossomed around the vehicle and Miss Bliss stared in shock as the Escalade descended into what seemed like another world. Bright lights filled a vast chamber that was easily three times the size of the gigantic hangar. Where the structure above looked decrepit and abandoned, down here everything was new. Metal gleamed, computer screens glittered like jewels, hundreds of people moved here and there, many of them in white lab coats but others in blue or orange jumpsuits, green coveralls, the crisp gray of security uniforms, and even ordinary street clothes. Rank upon rank of the latest generation of Titan supercomputers ran the length of the room, their precious drives encased in reinforced glass.

The Escalade reached the bottom and the hydraulic hiss faded into silence.

Miss Bliss gaped at the room around her. Even from a distance any scientist could tell that everything here was cutting edge. Bleeding edge. Billions of dollars' worth.

After several breathless moments, Miss Bliss turned to stare at Dr. Hu.

"I don't . . . I don't . . ." She stopped and gulped in a breath to steady herself. "What is all this?"

Dr. Hu adjusted his glasses. "You could choose to work for DARPA," he said with a hyena grin, "or . . . you could come work for us."

"But . . . but who are you? What is all this?"

"It's something so new that it doesn't even have a name," he said. "We've been calling it the Department of Military Sciences as a kind of placeholder name. Something to put on congressional memos." Dr. Hu stepped out and then turned and offered her his hand. "How would you like to help us save the world?"

Part Three
Burn to Shine

They played at hearts as other children might play at ball;
only, as it was really their two hearts that they flung to and fro,
they had to be very, very handy to catch them, each time, without
   hurting them.

—GASTON LEROUX, *The Phantom of the Opera*

Chapter Eleven

On the day that she died, Dr. Noor Jehan had a premonition.

It was not an unusual thing with her, though she'd had them less often as an adult than when she was a little girl in Punjab. Since coming to America with her parents at age thirteen, her premonitions, once an almost daily occurrence, faded to a scattered few. They were rarely anything of note. She would look up a few seconds before a doorbell rang, or she'd take her cell phone out of her purse and hold it, knowing that a call was coming. A few times she bought scratch-off lottery tickets on a whim. Once she won fifty dollars and another time she won five hundred.

Like that.

Nothing that rocked her world. No insights into matters of any consequence heavier than the early arrival of a traveling aunt or the tie color of a blind date.

There were three exceptions.

The first was when she was eight years old. Noor woke from a sound sleep and cried out for her brother. His name, Amrit, burst from her and the sound of it pulled her from a dream of drowning. In the dream it was Noor who was sinking beneath black waves as the sodden weight of her sari pulled her down to coldness and invisibility and death. But as she woke, she knew—with perfect clarity and absolute certainty—that it was Amrit who had drowned.

Amrit was a petty officer about the INS *Viraat*, India's only aircraft carrier—a Centaur-class ship bought from the British and serving as flagship for India's fleet. It was vast, strong, and as safe as an island. That was what Amrit said in his letters.

But at that moment, the young Noor sat bathed in sweat, as drenched as if she had been sinking in salt water, and knew that Amrit was lost. It was almost two days before the men from the Ministry of Defence came to their house to break her mother's heart. There had been an accident, they said. A crane had come loose from its moorings, the big iron sweep had knocked a dozen men into the ocean. Six were pulled out alive, and six had died. They were sorry, they said; so sorry.

The second time was a month before the Jehan family packed and moved to America. Noor had been at school, copying math problems from the blackboard, when a bus suddenly crashed through the wall and killed her. Only it wasn't like that. She woke up in the school nurse's office, screaming about a bus, but nothing at all had happened at the school. However, that evening on the news it was reported that a tourist bus had been in a terrible accident with a tractor-trailer filled with microwave ovens. The driver of the truck apparently had had a heart attack and fallen forward, his dead foot pressing on the accelerator, his slumping body turning the wheel. The truck hit the bus side-on. Nineteen people were killed, thirty-six were injured. The following afternoon her father received a call from his mother saying that his brother, Noor's uncle, had been a passenger on that bus and had been crushed to death.

That second terrible premonition had been nearly thirty years ago.

Noor Jehan was no longer a little girl, and she was no longer in India. Now she was deputy director of the Sigler-Czajkowski Biological and Chemical Weapons Facility, a highly specialized and highly secret government base. She headed a team that stored and studied some of the most virulent diseases and destructive bioweapons on earth. A place so secret that it was only occasionally mentioned in eyes-only reports, and even those were appended to black-budget R and D filings. In those reports the facility was known only as "The Locker."

Noor was now Dr. Jehan, with a Ph.D. and an M.D. and a list of credits and titles that, even abbreviated, wouldn't fit on a standard business card. And although she clearly remembered her intuitions and premonitions, she now kept that kind of belief on a small shelf in a mostly disused corner of her mind. The rest of her life was dedicated to hard research, to things that could be measured, weighed, metered, and replicated according to the plodding but beautiful process of empirical science.

And yet . . .

This morning—early, somewhere in that blackest part of the night when the body is chained by sleep, unable to move or even glance at the clock—Noor Jehan had received her third exceptional premonition. This one was stronger than the fantasy of drowning when Amrit had died. It was more real than the deadly bulk of a bus splintering its way through the walls of her schoolroom. No, this was so thoroughly real that when Noor finally woke in the golden light of a steamy Virginia morning, she was not sure whether she was now awake or still dreaming. Because the dream felt more real than reality.

In the dream, Noor had been right here in her office on level six of the Locker. The alarms were all going off, the lights were flashing red and white, slapping her eyes with painful brightness. People were running and screaming. The wrong doors were open. Doors that could not be simultaneously open were nonetheless ajar. The air had become a witch's brew of toxins and weaponized versions of poliomyelitis, Ebola, *E. coli*, superstrain typhus, half a dozen designer strains of viral hemorrhagic fever, aerosol *Mycobacterium leprae*, and other microscopic monsters. All free, all released from containment systems that had been designed with what many had thought were an absurd number of safeguards and redundancies. Foolproof and failproof.

In that dream, Noor heard shrieks coming from shadowy corridors and through the open doors to side rooms. She was screaming, too. She dreamed of fumbling with the catches and seals and dials of her hazmat suit, but none of the seams would join. Then she heard the sounds of footsteps. Staggering steps, shuffling steps. The disjointed and artless footfalls of dying people; her friends and staff wandering in their diseased madness, wasting the last minutes of their lives in a shocked attempt to find a way out. But there was no way out. Soon the biological disaster protocols would reach a critical failsafe and then the main and rear doors would thunder down—each of them two feet thick and composed of steel alloys that could withstand anything but a direct hit from a cruise missile. The failsafe systems would ignite massive thermite charges that would flash-weld the doors in place. After that, cluster bombs built into the very walls would be triggered, detonating fuel-air bombs. Everything, from the strongest man to the tiniest microbe, would be incinerated.

And it would all be abandoned. No one would ever dig through the mountain or try to cut through that weight of steel to try and breech this place. The Locker would officially cease to exist because, in point of fact, everything of which it was composed—human staff, lab animals, equipment, computers, furniture, and the stores of biological agents—would be carbon dust.

The dream persisted. It kept Noor down in the darkness where she had to feel and hear and smell it all. It was like being forced to watch a hyper-real 3D movie that had become reality.

The scuffling of the dying staff grew louder as they came toward her office. She knew that she should stop wrestling with the hazmat suit and close her door—and her dreaming mind screamed at her dream-self to do just that—but she did not. She fumbled and scrabbled at the ill-fitting protective garment even as the first of the infected staff members shuffled through the door.

The dreaming Noor watched her dream-self look up, watched her turn toward the people, looking to see which of her friends and colleagues came through first. Dreading to see which symptoms were presenting on familiar flesh.

But then both Noors—the dreamer and the dreamed self—froze in shock.

The person in the doorway was dressed like Dr. Kim, and wore that name tag, and even had the same tie, but this figure was wrong. So . . . wrong.

It had no face.

It wasn't that the hazy air masked it, but the thing in the doorway simply had no face. It had a head, hair, cheeks and a jaw, but otherwise the face was gone, erased, just a featureless mask of white.

And the skin . . . it was the color of a mushroom. Pale and blotchy. Sickly in appearance and sickening to look at, as if it were in itself a creature composed entirely of disease. No longer human, but rather defined by the pestilential bacteria and viruses that permeated the air.

The faceless, diseased thing stood for a moment in the doorway, its head raised and cocked as if trying to find her through some sense other than smell or sight. It swayed a little as if it might fall down at any moment.

Noor wanted to scream, but instead she balled her fist and crammed it into her mouth, dreading what would happen if this faceless thing heard her.

Then . . .

The thing took a single awkward step forward.

Into the room.

Toward her.

It raised pale hands and pawed at the air, trying to find something to touch.

To grab.

Other figures crowded behind it, their mass and weight pushing the first creature farther into the room so they could enter, too. Each of them—scientist, research assistant, technician, security guard, maintenance man—was faceless.

Noor backed away as they filled the room, squeezing into it the way a liquid expands to fill a vacuum. First three of them, then eight. A dozen. Twenty.

Noor scuttled backward into the corner, her legs banged against the chair and sent it rolling toward them. As it bumped up against the first one, the whole mass of them stopped, just for a moment, as if one of them feeling something allowed them all to feel it. A sympathetic reaction. A hive reaction.

Then they began moving again. Faster, with greater purpose.

Toward her.

Noor screamed.

That was when the dream had ended.

That had been a dream.

Now she was awake. Totally awake.

Now Noor stood in her office, crammed into the corner, sweat and tears running down her face.

And her office was crowded by pale, shuffling figures. Dozens of them. As many as could squeeze through the door. They closed on her.

They closed around her.

Exactly like in her dream.

Except for one thing.

In the dream these creatures were all faceless and featureless.

In the dream they had no mouths.

No teeth.

This, however, was not a dream.

Noor Jehan screamed and screamed for as long as she could.

Until there was not enough of her left for screaming.

Chapter Twelve

Residence of the Vice President of the United States

One Observatory Circle

Washington, D.C.

Sunday, August 31, 5:37 a.m.

Vice President William Collins woke with a smile on his face.

The big windows were open to the dawn breeze and the scent of roses and honeysuckle. The trees outside were filled with birdsong.

Collins got out of bed and padded barefoot across to the chair where he'd left his bathrobe, shrugged it on, and stood by the window to watch the rim of the sun peer over the line of trees. He took a deep breath and let it out as a long and contented sigh.

Behind him he heard her stir.

A soft sound, warm and vulnerable. A rustle of sheets as she turned over, then the deep, slow sound of a sleeper far below the surface.

He didn't look at her, preferring instead to remember the way she looked last night. She'd flown into town on a private jet from Atlanta and showed up in a black dress that clung to her curves like a second skin. The delight in peeling that faux skin from her, revealing an electric blue push-up bra and matching thong. Those were probably downstairs with the rest of their clothes. They'd been naked when they made love on the stairs, and in the hallway, and here in the bedroom.

God, he'd been a lion last night. A tiger.

A beast.

He made her scream when she came, and when he came inside her the first time he roared like the beast he was.

That's how it always was with her.

It was never that way with his wife.

She was a cold fish who had be stoned or smashed before she spread her legs. And the world would have to be burning down to its last hour before she'd open those thin and prissy lips to give him a blow job.

He wondered if he she knew he was cheating on her.

Probably. Probably felt relieved, too. The more ass he got elsewhere, the less often she had to act like a sexual being.

Anger began to creep into his mood and he forced it down, letting memories of last night wash it out of him. He turned and leaned on the window frame to watch the woman sleep. Silky black hair spilled around her like fine lace. The curve of one shoulder and one breast, a nipple that was surprisingly dark against the soft golden tone of her skin. He was glad she didn't dye her nipples like many Asian women did in the belief that it would be more appealing to white men. Collins thought she was perfect the way God made her. Appealing to each one of his five senses.

Not bad for the ego, either.

Though he had to wonder if he was a bigger ego hit for her than she was for him. Vice president of the United States. Even if she couldn't tell anyone, she knew she was banging the guy who was one heartbeat away from being the most powerful man in the world. A man who had, in fact, *been* the president twice. Once when the president had bypass surgery, and then last year, during the abduction thing.

Collins had tasted that power. He had become addicted to it, and he did not apologize to himself for that addiction. It would have been a greater lie to tell himself that he didn't need or want that power again.

Goddamn right he did.

Wanted it, and would have it.

The anger crept back into his veins, and this time it took hold. It changed the color of the sunshine to an ugly brightness, and transformed the birdsong to irritating noise.

Collins felt his mouth curl into a snarl.

He pushed himself away from the windowsill and crossed to the bed, caught the edge of the sheet and whipped it away. The noise and the sudden air shift snapped the woman out of her sleep, and for a moment she recoiled, cringing, her hands instinctively moving to cover her cupcake breasts and smudge of ink-black pubic hair. Then she saw him and her sleepy confusion changed into something different. A smile that was as sly and old as all the corruption in the world ignited fires in those eyes.

"Well," she said slyly, moving her hands and rolling onto her back, "good morning to you, too. You look like you're ready to take a bite out of the day."

He grinned down at her, leered at her. Wanted her. "So do you. And it's a big damn day for you, sweetie."

"I know. I have to get back to Atlanta," she said. A shadow passed through her eyes when she said that.

"You okay?" asked Collins. "Having second thoughts?"

The woman took a half beat before answering. "No. It's just that once this match is lit, this is it. There's no turning back."

"I know."

"And we might not see each other again."

He gave her his best smile. "Sure we will."

"When?"

"When the game is reset."

She shook her head. "It's not a reset. You never get the terminology right."

"Yeah, yeah, I know. Whatever you gamers call this stuff."

"It's a new game. Brand new."

"Yes, it is," he said. "And everything will be different afterward. A new America . . . a new world."

"But *we* won't share it," she said.

"We will."

"No—"

"We *will*," he insisted. "It'll just take some time. You're going to be busy getting the hell out of Dodge and I'll be busy remaking this country into what it should have been if we'd stayed the course. So, call it a new game, call it what you like, honey. When all the fires are out, we'll find a way to get together. Maybe even out in public."

"You're a very charming liar."

"I mean it."

"What, you'll dump your wife and trot me out on your arm? The world's most hunted terrorist, and you think that'll make for good arm candy?"

"You're not the world's most hunted terrorist yet."

"Day's young."

He laughed. "You're an evil bitch, you know that?"

The woman reached up and caught the end of his bathrobe belt, gave it a sharp pull, and licked her lips as the robe parted.

She reached between the flaps of the robe and wrapped her fingers around his hardness, and with that as a handle, drew him toward her. She was not gentle about it. It hurt. But that was okay. Pain was another kind of drug. Her breasts and thighs and buttocks were still red and bruised from last night's slaps and bites. Collins shoved her back against the mattress, used his knee to roughly part her legs, and with a low feral growl thrust into her with only a little guidance from her strong hands.

He did not take her. They took each other, both of them thrusting against the other with brutality and need and a shared viciousness that was an incredible aphrodisiac for each of them.

Outside, the sun set fire to the morning and the sound of the birds in the trees changed in Collins's ears to the shrill screams of fear.

And that, too, was a turn-on.

Chapter Thirteen

Surf Shop 24-Hour Cyber Café
Corner of Fifth Avenue and Garfield Street
Park Slope, Brooklyn
Sunday, August 31, 6:03 a.m.

The girl who came into the Surf Shop was one of those twenty-somethings who could actually have been anywhere from seventeen to thirty. She had a porcelain complexion and gleaming black hair in a Betty Page cut. She wore red sneakers, black leggings, and a baggy black T-shirt that had a picture of an androgynous Asian with a shock of white hair and hugely oversized sword. The words DEVIL MAY CRY were hand-painted below the image. A loose leather belt was clasped around the shirt, hanging low on one hip. The girl wore oversized sunglasses and never took them off the entire time she was in the café.

She stood in line with the other early birds, earphones in, texting on an Android, talking to no one and acknowledging no one.

The sleepy counter man, Caleb Sykes, had seen her or a thousand girls like her every day. Most of them were underpaid secretaries who still couldn't afford a smartphone or their own laptop and who wanted to check their e-mail before heading into the city to start their day. It wasn't as common to see them this early on a Sunday, but really Caleb didn't give much of a shit.

When it was her turn to pay, Caleb took money for a Red Bull and handed over a log-in card for one of the computers bolted to tables scattered around the room. The girl paid cash, didn't tip, didn't say anything else except when she'd ordered the drink. Caleb's only thought when he saw her was that her hair looked like a wig. Just that. When she left the counter, Caleb forgot her completely. Fifteen minutes later, when the counter rush slowed and Caleb looked around the room, the girl was gone. He was not consciously aware of her not being there. She would have slipped entirely from his mind had it been an ordinary day.

However, the day was not ordinary and, as it turned out, Caleb would come to remember that young woman for the rest of his life. She would visit him in his dreams, though when that happened there were no eyes behind the dark lenses of the shades, but actual fire. The heat of that fire became so intense that it would chase him from sleep into a trembling wakefulness, and he would sit up in bed, drenched with sweat, listening to the desperate pounding of his heart.

At the moment, as he looked around the cyber café, he did not see her and did not think about her.

Until he had no choice.

At precisely 6:30 that morning her face appeared on every screen in the café. Even on the personal laptops of customers who came in for the wi-fi access. Caleb was bent over the counter running a debit card, heard the chorus of grunts and questions.

He looked up and saw the face on the monitors.

A girl with dark glasses and an anime T-shirt. Caleb thought he recognized the Betty Page haircut, but her presence on the screen did not immediately connect with a customer who had been in the store.

The girl smiled placidly but said nothing. It wasn't a static image, because at one point she sipped from a can of Red Bull.

"Yo!" growled one customer as he pounded at his keyboard in a vain attempt to break the connection. "What the hell?"

"Hold on, guys," said Caleb loud enough for everyone to hear. "Must be a server error. I apologize for the delay, let me see what I can do."

Caleb pulled his laptop closer and tapped some keys, checking the router status, running a diagnostic, doing the routine things that should have fixed this in seconds. The image remained in place. The Korean girl took another sip of Red Bull.

"Okay," Caleb announced, "I'm going to have to reboot the router. Everybody should be back online in a couple of seconds."

"I'm not paying to sit here and stare at some Japanese chick," groused the man who'd yelled earlier.

She's Korean, jackass, thought Caleb, but he didn't see any value in saying that out loud. "Gimme a sec."

He unplugged the router from cable and power sources.

Every screen in the café flickered to black for one second, and then the Korean girl was back.

Caleb stared at the dozen-plus copies of her face scattered throughout the room. He looked at his own laptop. With the plugs pulled all that he should be seeing was a no-connection screen.

The Korean girl smiled.

Caleb said, "What?"

He tried several other things. The image of the girl blipped and for a moment Caleb thought he'd solved it, but when the girl sipped the Red Bull in exactly the same way as before he realized that this was a video loop. That was weird. If the computers weren't connected to the Net and yet were showing the girl, then that meant there was some kind of video file planted on each machine. Even computers belonging to customers who came in after that girl left the store. Was that possible?

Yeah. And if it was true it could be real trouble for the café.

That girl could have uploaded a Trojan horse to all of the rental computers here at the Surf Shop, and anyone logging on through the router was probably receiving it when they agreed to the terms on the café's homepage.

Shit.

The customers were mad now. Several were badgering him about getting things fixed. The loudmouth was saying that they should all get their money back.

Caleb quickly restarted his MacBook Pro. He entered his password and for a moment he saw his usual desktop display.

And then the image of the Korean girl reappeared.

"What the hell are you doing over there?" demanded the loud customer.

Caleb shook his head. "I—I'm having a little trouble with . . . Um. Hold on, let me try something else."

He plugged the router in and waited as it ran through its opening diagnostic.

"Hey," said a woman seated by the window. She held up her iPhone. "It's not just us. It's on the news."

Everyone scrambled for their cells. Caleb subscribed to several RSS news feeds, and as soon as he unlocked the screen he saw a string of news alerts from *USAToday*, *New York Times*, *Yahoo News*, and even the BBC news. Caleb fished under the counter for a TV remote and aimed it at the flatscreen on the wall, which had been flashing advertisements from a CD-ROM. He channeled over to CNN.

And there she was. The patrons got up from their laptops and began drifting toward the TV. Below the Korean girl's face was a title credit:

CYBERHACKER MYSTERY WOMAN

"Turn up the volume," said a woman, one of the café's regulars.

". . . will auto-delete in a few seconds," the Korean girl was saying. "Good luck trying to figure out how we did this. And even if you do, so what? Big deal. Give yourself a cookie."

This wasn't the video loop still playing out on their laptops. This was a live feed on national news. And . . . the girl looked different. The hair and sunglasses were identical, but she no longer looked Korean. Caleb thought that she looked older. A young woman instead of an older teenage girl. And maybe—Chinese? He wasn't sure, but he knew that something was different.

"What the hell *is* this?" demanded the loudmouth.

All Caleb could do was shake his head.

"Okay, monkeys," continued the woman on the screen, "pay attention, 'cause there are three things you need to know and Mother Night is here to tell you."

Caleb mouthed the words, *Mother Night*.

"First, if we do not all rise up against globalization then we do not deserve to be free of the shackles welded around our necks by groups like the World Trade Organization, the Group of Eight, the World Economic Forum, and others like them. We are slaves only if we allow ourselves to be slaves. We are free if we take to the streets and take the streets back. Occupy Wall Street failed because there were too many do-nothing pussies. That wasn't anarchy. The pigs in the system haven't seen anarchy. Not yet." She licked her lips in a mock-sexy way, as if tasting something forbidden but delicious. "But it's coming. The only action is direct action."

"Jeee-zus," said the loudmouth. "What kind of Communist bullshit is this?"

"It's not communism," said a college kid seated near him. "It's anarchy."

"I don't give a flying fuck what it—"

"Shhh," hissed several people. Caleb raised the volume.

"Second," said the woman who called herself Mother Night, "because complacency is not only a symptom of a corrupt society, it's also a cry for help, I am going to shake things up. Will it take the sacrifice of one in three hundred to force the pigs in power to let true freedom ring?"

Mother Night paused to smile. She had perfect white teeth, but smiling transformed her from a pretty girl to something else, something unlovely. The effect was transformative in a chilling way. It was a sardonic, skeletal, mocking grin, a leer that was hungry and ugly.

The screen display below the image changed to read: WHO IS MOTHER NIGHT?

"Third, Mother Night wants to tell all of her children, everyone within the sound of my voice, all of the sleeping dragons waiting to rise—now is the time. Step out of the shadows. Be seen, be heard. Let your glow cast enough light even for the blind to see. 'Cause remember, kids, sometimes you have to burn to shine."

She gave another of those terrible, leering grins, then every screen went dark. TV, laptops, smartphones.

For five seconds.

And then, one by one, the screens returned to Yahoo, Safari, Gmail, and websites. They returned to normal. The TV suddenly showed the confused faces of the unnerved reporters.

Everything looked normal.

But Caleb—and everyone else at the café or who'd watched the broadcast—knew that normal was no longer a part of this day.

Chapter Fourteen

Across America
Sunday, August 31, 6:32 a.m.

Teaneck, New Jersey

Digger Hohlman sat in the rear corner of a Dunkin Donuts, head bent low, earphones screwed in, his Styrofoam cup of coffee nearly forgotten as he watched the screen. He was entranced.

Mother Night's face had suddenly filled his laptop screen. It was like magic. One minute he was watching "Awakening," a video from the deathcore band Molotov Solution, and then she was there. It made Digger's hands clench into fists and he could hear his heartbeat pounding in his ears.

After all these months, after encoded e-mails, after packages left for him in coin lockers, after the slow and insanely careful process to bring him into the Family, now here was Mother Night. On his laptop. Speaking to him.

On some level he knew that this was a general message going out to the whole world, something she said would kick open the doors and light the fires. However, Digger also knew that it was a clarion call to the many members of the Family.

Like him.

Born in the dust and promised so much more. Mother Night had told him that she would set a beacon ablaze in his skin. For Digger, who had never shone for a single moment in his life, he would shine because of the grace of Mother Night.

He bent closer to the laptop, so close his breath steamed on the screen, and he turned the volume all the way up so that her murmured words shouted in his ears.

"Okay, monkeys," began Mother Night, "pay attention, 'cause there are three things you need to know and Mother Night is here to tell you."

Digger smiled. A rare thing for him. As he listened he thought about the things he had in his backpack. The chemicals. The detonators. The blades.

All the time she spoke, he mouthed the sacred words.

Burn to shine.

Burn to shine.

Pasco, Washington

Julia Smith and her girlfriend, Rage, sat huddled together in a booth at Jerry's Java on North Twentieth Street. They were sharing an omelet with extra onions and peppers. They were dropping down, mile by mile, from their first pipe of the day.

Normally the descent to earth would be painful and sad, and the ground would be covered in broken glass. They didn't have enough cash to buy more rock, so that high was the only one they were going to have that day unless they could do some blow jobs for truckers passing through. Rage still had her teeth, and in the right light, with a push-up bra and short shorts, she could usually score three or four ten-dollar tricks. Julia knew that her own looks were too far gone. Hand jobs in the dark for five a rub was about her best.

Luckily, Jerry's had a three-dollar omelet with a bottomless cup of coffee.

They were watching the news on the tablet Mother Night had sent them. The wi-fi was free at the coffeehouse, and the tablet had a good battery as well as a splitter, so they could both plug in their earphones at the same time.

When the news feed vanished to be replaced by Mother Night, Julia sought Rage's hand under the table. They sat, fingers tightly entwined, watching the world change. This was what they had been promised was coming. This was the way out of the shadows for both of them.

Los Angeles, California

Tayshon watched the broadcast on his laptop, which he'd snuck into the bathroom. His mother's boyfriend, Isaiah, didn't know he had the computer and would have taken it away from him if he'd found out. Isaiah would then beat the living shit out of Tayshon, demanding to know where he got the laptop, why he had it, why he didn't say anything about it, and on and on. It wasn't like Isaiah could use a computer. He was an illiterate fool who thought he was a thug, but he was really just a wife beater, a child beater, and a drunk. That bastard loved using a belt, and he didn't mind if the buckle was what made contact. He made Tayshon kneel on grains of rice. Made him stand barefoot on screws and nuts. Sometimes he'd use his fists, rings and all. Trying to beat his own life's defeats and disappointments out of his girlfriend and her sixteen-year-old son. Tayshon had scars on his face and body that he'd carry to the grave because of Isaiah.

The only good part of that, as Tayshon saw it, was that the grave was right there. Close enough to touch. Offering a perfect escape hatch from the bullshit and the humiliation and the nothingness.

On the screen, whispering to him through his earbuds, Mother Night said, ". . . remember, kids, sometimes you have to burn to shine."

When it was over, Tayshon bent and put his face in his hands and wept, his thin shoulders trembling as each sob rocked him. They were the happiest tears he'd ever shed. He prayed then. Not to God, but to Mother Night. Prayers of gratitude.

Then he washed his face, opened the bathroom door, went back to his bedroom, and fished in the very back of his closet for the things Mother Night had sent him. The knives. The kilos of semtex. The detonators.

The gun.

He heard a sound downstairs. Isaiah's chair scraping as he pulled into the table for his breakfast.

Tayshon tucked the pistol into the waistband of his pants, the steel cold against belly flesh. Then he picked up the skinning knife.

When he turned the blade this way and that he imagined he could see Isaiah's face. Bloody and screaming.

"Burn to shine," said Tayshon in a voice thick with tears and strong with purpose.

Orlando, Florida

His name was Parker Kang.

He was twenty years old and he was certain that he was as old as he was ever going to get.

He was good with that.

It was perfect.

It was soothing to think about it.

No more pain.

No more humiliation.

No more loneliness.

No more anything.

He sat at a desk he'd found in an office building that had been closed during the economic crash a few years ago. He and some other squatters had broken in the night after the place had been shut, moving fast because they knew that someone would be coming to remove everything of value. Parker and his friends came in quick and quiet, using skills honed from years of living hard and surviving from day to day. Each of them knew how to disable a basic security system and open a lock. There were always a lot of chicken hawks learning from older, more experienced squatters. Back when Parker was a snack rat, living off the crumbs dropped by the real players on the street, he learned everything he could. Now he was on his own and didn't need anyone else.

Except Mother Night.

He needed her more than anything he ever smoked, huffed, swallowed, or spiked. He needed her voice. Her face.

He needed her permission to step off the ledge and fall into forever.

The laptop on his stolen desk was from her. It was nice, too. The shell was that of a MacBook Pro, but the guts were something else. Something weird that she'd designed herself. Stronger than any computer Parker had ever touched, with built-in programs that allowed him to sneak into almost anywhere. He could order food delivered from Domino's and pay for it with fake credit card numbers. Never a kick out, never a canceled order, because the card numbers were hijacked. The pizza always showed up. Other stuff, too. FedEx and UPS deliveries with clothes and equipment. Even parts for the devices Mother Night had asked him to build. *Asked.* As if he would ever say no to her.

She was the only person he believed in. The only *thing* he believed in.

Parker had no god, no angels. Like most of the kids who move like ghosts through the cities, he belonged to nothing. He wasn't like the homeless who clung to the coats of groups like Homes Not Jails and Take Back the Land. He didn't have that kind of optimism. He didn't give a cold rat's dick about squatters' rights or the plight of the homeless or any of that shit, because nothing was ever going to change.

Not unless Mother Night made it change.

Even then, though, even if Mother Night ignited a fire that burned down everything that was and cleared the way for something new to grow, Parker knew that he wasn't going to live in that world. He didn't want to. He didn't care if the changes she wanted to make would really build a better world for the disenfranchised, the dispossessed, the forgotten, and the lonely. Parker had even less politics than he had religion.

All he wanted was to help Mother Night light those fires.

There was a big table lining the wall opposite where he sat. Something else he'd boosted from the bankrupt office. One half of the table was filled with boxes of parts. The parts always came in individual shipments. Screws one day, housing another, specific chemicals another. Like that. Sometimes shipments from every professional delivery service, including the Post Office. And occasionally things were left in coin lockers for him, or in post office boxes. In those cases he'd get a key in the mail.

On the other half of the table six devices were in various stages of assembly. A FedEx carton filled with brightly colored vinyl backpacks stood open at the end of the table. Each pack waiting to be filled.

When Parker thought about those boxes, he smiled.

Maybe it was a revenge thing after all. Just a little. A baseball bat upside the head of the kind of people he fled from when he was nine. Foster parents who think orphan kids are cash cows, dogs to whip, or something to stick their dicks into. People like the losers at child welfare who can't think their way around regulations in any way that does real good for the kids in the meat grinder. Politicians who fuck up the system with regulations because they're in the pockets of landlords, big business, credit card and health care companies.

So, yeah. Revenge, not politics. He didn't want to see the system changed. He wanted to see it burn. Then he wanted to dive into those flames, let them consume him, and vanish into ash and smoke.

That's what Mother Night promised him.

It's what she whispered in his ear that first day.

The whole thing started weirdly. He came home from a day of panhandling at a long traffic light on Sand Hill Lake Road in Orlando and found his door ajar. At the time, he was squatting in a foreclosed house miles away from the tourist areas. The house was in a pretty good neighborhood, but there must have been some kind of legal thing going on about the title, because it remained empty for over a year. Parker moved in, sealed some windows with black plastic sheeting to keep light from escaping, had a friend help him move his furniture in, and took possession. He figured he had a month before he would have to move. That timing seemed to work for him. If the place was shittier, then he might have stayed three months.

But when he came in that day he saw an envelope on the floor. His name was written on it.

Parker wasn't sure how to react to that. Run, or be relieved because this was probably from someone he knew. He slit it open with his knife. Inside was a short letter and a key. And two twenty-dollar bills. Crisp and new. The letter read:

Parker . . .

You are not in danger. I will never hurt you. This key will open a box at the Your Mailroom office on International Drive. Inside are gifts. If you want to use them to help me, then I welcome you. If you don't want to help me, keep the gifts and use them to find your happiness. You are under no obligation.

I have been where you are. Every night when I close my eyes I can see the monsters and I can hear the echo of my own screams. This

*country has betrayed its own people. It has a cancer of the soul. The
only action is direct action. I am going to cut the heart out of this
country. I will light a fire that no one can ignore.*

I will do this for you and for me and for all of us.

I cannot do this alone.

It was printed on a computer, but it was hand-signed.

Mother Night

That night Parker got some friends and moved his stuff out of there.
Over the next few days he began casually passing the Your Mailroom
place, checking it out. It was one of those stores where you could rent a
mailbox. It gave you a mailing address, and it was used by a lot of squatters. Parker never used it, but he knew people who did. He also knew that
cops were aware of this, too.

It took almost three weeks of burning curiosity and nearly crippling
paranoia before he walked into the mail service store and used the key. He
waited for a time when it was busy, when there were a lot of people in
there. He slipped in, opened the mailbox, and peered inside. There was a
computer case. Old and battered. Parker bit his lip as doubt chewed him.
Then he snatched out the bag, slung it over his shoulder, relocked the box,
and got out of there.

An hour later, when he was in a quiet, secure place, he opened the bag.

Inside was the MacBook along with all the necessary cables and char-
gers. Cards for Starbucks, Panera, and other places that had free wi-fi. He
later discovered that each card had one hundred dollars on it, and when
they got low they were recharged by someone else. There was an envelope in one pocket of the bag that contained thirty twenty-dollar bills.
The last parcel included in the bag was a thick stack of CD-ROMs loaded
with games. Edgy stuff. Games that challenged him. Parker had played
enough stolen games to be very good.

And there was another note.

When you trust me, when you are ready to help me light the fires, send me an e-mail to the address below.

It was signed by Mother Night, and below her name was a Yahoo e-mail address.

All of that was months ago.

Parker had learned to trust Mother Night.

He had learned to love her.

Every night he played the games. The package had included multiple versions of Grand Theft Auto, as well as select versions of God of War III, Manhunt, Dead Rising, MadWorld, Saints Row 2, Gears of War, Postal 2, Call of Duty, Splatterhouse, and Solder of Fortune. Plus there were other games in there, stored on disks with titles handwritten on them. Anarchy I through IV, and one highly technical though very difficult strategy game called Burn to Shine, which had one side adventure in which you had to break into a high-security government facility. That one was a real bitch.

Parker later learned that when he played those games his scores were sent to Mother Night. Every time he beat a difficult level on a speedrun, she sent him money and food along with notes of praise.

Those notes were the only praise Parker ever remembered receiving from an adult. If there had been others in his life, the meat grinder had torn them from him.

Mother Night sent him links to videos in which he could see her and hear her. She was beautiful. Asian, like him, but maybe black, too. Or something. Her skin was darker than an Asian's, and she had a lot of piercings, dark glasses, and a wig. A disguise, but that was okay. That was smart.

Some of those videos had been recorded for him alone, and in those she said his name and spoke as if he were in the same room with her.

At other times the video was clearly intended for multiple viewers. A family. *Her* family. A family to which he belonged, and wanted to belong. But a family he knew nothing about. Not its faces, not its names, and not its numbers. From the way she spoke, though, Parker had the impression that there were a lot of people out there.

Like him.

At first he was ambivalent about that. Jealous that there were others she cared about. But he knew that was sentimental and stupid. Later he came to appreciate the fact that he had *siblings* for the first time in his life. Sure, in a way this was another foster family, but before Mother Night he had never felt like he belonged. And he'd never felt like he was understood.

Month after month the videos came, and he quickly discovered that when he went back and tried to view them again, they were gone.

Smart.

So smart.

Then today, a video had just popped up on his computer. On his laptop and, he later learned, on millions of computers, and all over TV and the Net.

Mother Night spoke to the whole world.

However, buried within that global message was one directed only to the members of her family. And to him.

She'd said, "Mother Night wants to tell all of her children, everyone within the sound of my voice, all of the sleeping dragons waiting to rise— now is the time."

Those were her words.

He smiled with such deep contentment that it was nearly orgasmic.

He could almost smell the sulfur on the match as she struck it.

You have to burn to shine.

Parker got up from his computer, crossed the room to the table, and completed the last few small steps necessary with the waiting devices. Then, still smiling, he began carefully placing each device into a separate backpack.

Chapter Fifteen

The Hangar
Floyd Bennett Field
Brooklyn, New York
Sunday, August 31, 6:36 a.m.

Nikki Bloomberg was the third most senior member of the DMS computer division. Only Yoda had more seniority, and then of course there was Bug.

Nikki had been part of Bug's team for nearly five years and she loved her job. Even though she worked in a glass-walled office buried a hundred feet below Floyd Bennett Field, she felt like she was an international woman of mystery. A superspy with superpowers. Working with Mind-Reader had that effect.

Each senior member of the computer team—variously known as Bug's Thugs, the Igors, or the Nerd Herd, depending on who was sending the e-mail—ran a different aspect of the MindReader network. Yoda was head of cyberintrusion, and it was his job to make sure that no opposing system could lock its doors to MindReader. That meant that he had to write code or edit code all day. It wasn't a job Nikki wanted.

Her job was to manage the pattern search team. MindReader had more than seven hundred pattern recognition subroutines, each of which could be used separately and all of which could be combined into a massive assault on raw data. All day long her team received notices in the form of small pop-up windows with keywords and case numbers. Each pop-up contained a hot link to a data cascade where everything related to the keyword was collated. It took a certain kind of mind to be able to interpret that data and make sense of it. Nikki had that kind of mind. A super anal-retentive skill set that was unattractive in, say, relationships, but invaluable within the DMS. She also had a photographic memory, without which she could never even attempt that job.

She was at her desk rerouting data threads from the pop-ups when a new one blipped onto her screen. This one came with a red flag in one corner, indicating it might belong to one of the major active cases. Nikki opened the link in the pop-up and suddenly her screen was filled with a fragment of a video clip. An Asian woman speaking directly to the camera. The phrase MindReader had plucked out and flagged for attention was this: "*'Cause remember, kids, sometimes you have to burn to shine.*"

The software pulled the words *burn to shine* out of the sentence and floated them as text on the screen. The file to which this was attached was one of Joe Ledger's.

The Mother Night case.

One of the few DMS cases that was unsolved.

"Oh my god," breathed Nikki. "She's back."

She hunched over her computer and began hitting the keys that would ring alarms all through the halls of power.

Interlude Three

Artemisia Bliss sat at one end of a massive oak conference table. Three people sat at the far end. Dr. William Hu and two strangers, a big white man and a short black woman. The woman looked oddly like Whoopi Goldberg. She could have been her twin, except that she had eyes that were as flat and cold as a Nile crocodile and a mouth that was permanently set in a frown of disapproval.

Hu said, "You understand that anything we discuss here is strictly confidential."

"Okay," said Artemisia. "Do I need to sign some kind of nondisclosure form?"

The black woman's disapproving mouth hardened.

The big white man opened a briefcase but instead of producing government forms, he removed a package of Nilla wafers, opened it, selected a cookie, bit off a corner, and munched quietly. He placed the package on the table but did not offer a cookie to anyone else. No one asked him for one.

Artemisia waited. She didn't know who he or the woman was, but it was clear from Hu's demeanor that they were his superiors. Hu's manner had become immediately deferential when they'd entered this conference room, particularly to the white man. The big man looked sixtyish, but it was the kind of middle age that came with no diminution of personal power. He wore a very expensive Italian suit, an understated hand-painted silk tie, and tinted sunglasses that effectively hid any expression in his eyes. The lenses looked flat and did not appear to have any corrective curves, so she guessed that their sole purpose was to keep people from reading his eyes. That was interesting. Either he was the most closed-in person in the world, or he was aware that his eyes were the only weak link in otherwise impervious armor. Whoever he was, Artemisia was certain that he was in charge of this place. He had a natural authority and sense of power that was palpable, and yet he did not appear to be deliberately projecting an alpha dog vibe. He simply was the alpha. Here and, she thought, probably in most situations in which he found himself. She was certain she'd never met anyone quite like him.

His vibe was extremely scary. And sexy.

She doubted he would have showed off by making a comment about her name and the connection to the artist, as Hu had done. While with Hu that was mildly flattering, the doctor's energy was more earthy and real. This man was far more aloof, and probably didn't need the ego stroke of wanting to appear hyperintelligent and well-informed.

Artemisia realized that she feared him for reasons she could not adequately understand. She was in the presence of power on a level she'd never previously encountered.

And the woman, the Whoopi Goldberg with 'tude, had a lot of power, too. But it wasn't quite on the same level.

After the cookie was gone, the big man took a handkerchief—a real one, not a tissue—and dabbed at the corners of his mouth. He folded the handkerchief neatly and placed it on the table beside the box of cookies.

"My name is Church," he said, then nodded to the black woman. "This is Aunt Sallie."

"'Aunt Sallie'?" echoed Artemisia.

"You can call me Auntie. Call me 'ma'am' and I'll kneecap you." She wasn't smiling when she said it.

"Noted," said Artemisia.

"Dr. Hu speaks very highly of you," said Church.

Artemisia nodded. She was letting her instincts guide her, and the remark did not seem to warrant a verbal reply. The man was stating a fact, not asking for agreement.

"Your profile suggests that you would be a good fit for us."

"May I ask who 'us' is, exactly?"

"We'll get to that." Church studied her for a long time. A longer time than was comfortable, and she began to fidget. She hated that, because she never fidgeted. It was a point of pride for her. The big man ate another cookie. Slow bites, a lot of measured chewing. A dab of the handkerchief. Without consulting any paperwork or computer, he said, "You were first in science and math in every school you've attended. You graduated from high school at age fourteen, you received special consideration that allowed you to earn a doctorate at twenty. You don't appear to have much in the way of personal politics."

She resisted the urge to give a dismissive shrug. Instinct told her that a reaction like that would cast her in a poor light. Probably in the black woman's eyes and definitely in the big man's eyes.

"I care more about people than political parties," she said.

"Oh, jeez," sighed Aunt Sallie.

Mr. Church gave a faint smile. "Would you mind elaborating on that?"

Artemisia felt her face growing hot. Despite her best effort she'd put her foot wrong. Still, she kept her voice controlled, her manner calm. Much calmer than she felt inside.

"I don't know enough about politics to have an opinion that would matter. Not when it comes to Republican and Democratic pissing contests. If we're talking the politics of science, then I land on the humanist side."

"Meaning—?"

"Meaning that science should benefit humanity. I have a private loathing for any science that exists for its own sake. Science should be used. It should be applied. The end result of research is practical and beneficial application."

"What about military applications?" asked Mr. Church.

"Is that a trick question?"

"No."

"I won't build nukes, I won't create bioweapons. Beyond that . . . if you're talking about drone technology that can fight an enemy in a modern combat scenario while keeping U.S. troops out of the line of fire, then . . . sure. I'd do that. Would I build a space-based laser system so the CIA can assassinate whoever's on their shit list, then no. That's bullshit and it's too much of a gray area."

"You distrust the Agency?"

"Of course."

"Why?"

"Because they're untrustworthy."

"How so?"

She took a moment to find the word that she thought would work best. "They're inept."

The Whoopi Goldberg lookalike turned away to hide a smile. Dr. Hu studied his nails.

"What makes you say that?"

Now she did shrug. "Because they get too much press, and none of it's good."

"It could be a front," he said. "A misdirection."

"Sure. But I don't think it is. I think they've had to do too much and never had enough legal funding. They let their need to accomplish an impossible agenda trick them into making bad choices. The whole drug thing in the sixties. That may even have begun as a well-intentioned reaction to the threat of Soviet expansion, but it was badly played. They broke so many laws while trying to save capitalism that it became their knee-jerk reaction. It became the easiest path to a series of short-term goals that probably looked good on reports to Congress but were chump change in terms of real global control. The space race did more to scare the Soviets, as did the Reagan-era military buildup. That's what tore the wall down and collapsed communism."

"So you *do* have politics," observed the woman.

"No," said Artemisia, shaking her head. "I'm aware of politics . . . but really what I'm aware of is the evolution of military sciences since the Manhattan Project."

Mr. Church selected a cookie, tapped crumbs off, took a bite. "Why?"

"Because that's the sandbox I want to play in, and I can't do it from the outside. All of the university research projects are in permanent stall mode, presenting only enough results to renew their grants. And don't get me started on the private sector. If I were a male Asian scientist I'd already have a job in the high six figures, but there is a bizarrely counterproductive bigotry against placing women, particularly ethnic women, in the trenches of the top military contract teams. That leaves DARPA or something like DARPA. Some kind of think tank way out on the cutting edge where results matter more than gender, race, age, or any other bias."

Aunt Sallie opened a file folder, read for a moment, her lips moving, then raised her head and gave Bliss a direct stare. "What would you say if I told you that we have transcripts of your therapy sessions going back to junior high?"

"Hmm. Two things occur to me."

"And they are?"

"First, fuck you."

Auntie measured out a slice of a smile. "Fair enough. What's the second thing?"

"I'd be surprised and a little disappointed if you hadn't."

That seemed to surprise Aunt Sallie. "Oh?"

"I'm beginning to get an idea of the scope of this organization, or division or whatever it is. If I was on that side of the table I wouldn't hire anyone whose full psych records I didn't have."

"Invasion of privacy . . . ?"

"I'm all for privacy, hence my telling you to go fuck yourself. But at the same time I understand your needs. It's a gray area and I'm neither a philosopher nor political ethicist."

Aunt Sallie nodded.

"If you have my records, then," continued Bliss, "aren't you going to ask me about the suicide attempts?"

"It was going to be my next question."

"Yes, I tried to kill myself. Twice." She held out her arms, palms up, to show her wrists. There were two lateral scars. "Razor blades the first time, pills the second. Ask your question."

"Why do you want to die?" asked Aunt Sallie.

Bliss smiled. "I don't. If I did, I'd be dead."

"Explain."

"A determined suicide is nearly always successful. Countless studies show that. That's point one. Point two is how I went about it. Razors across the wrist."

"Right."

"Wrong. You've seen my IQ tests and all of my other test scores. Do you think that, even at thirteen, I was so unaware of human anatomy that I didn't know where to cut? Lateral wrist cutting does tendon damage, and I didn't wind up with much—if I had, I wouldn't have had the muscular control to cut both wrists. If I'd made a precise venous cut I would have suffered cardiac arrhythmia, severe hypovolemia, shock, circulatory collapse, and cardiac arrest. Clearly none of that happened."

Aunt Sallie said nothing. Mr. Church ate his cookie.

"And the pills . . . I took a fistful of tramadol between classes in school. I vomited and passed out in health class. Ask yourself, of all the teachers in a modern school, which one is most likely to know basic first aid? A health sciences teacher."

"So what are we talking," asked Auntie, "teenage angst? A cry for help?"

Bliss smiled. "No. Absolute boredom. I was in an accelerated school but I was miles above those others kids. I was smarter than all my teachers. And I hadn't yet had the offers from MIT, CalTech, and the other schools where my intellect would be cultivated and prized. I was screaming to be heard. And if I couldn't be heard, then I wanted to be locked away and medicated so I wouldn't be aware of how sucky my life was and how nowhere my future would be."

The room was utterly silent.

Without commenting on that, Aunt Sallie opened a second folder, consulted it, and said, "There's a lot of stuff in here about games. You play games, you hack them and design new levels, you share them with your friends."

"Is there a question in there?" asked Bliss.

Irritation sparked in Aunt Sallie's eyes, but there was none in her voice when she replied. "Games and game simulations are a big part of defense research. These simulations are used for everything from devising response protocols for various extreme threats to testing the security designs on new high-profile facilities."

Bliss nodded.

"Games are also being used for psychological screening," continued Aunt Sallie. "Put a bunch of candidates for spec ops or other classified jobs in separate rooms, wire them up so you can monitor everything from pupillary reaction to sweat glands, then let them play violent games, and you learn a lot. Like whether someone is going to freeze, to kill, to *want* to kill, to hesitate, whatever."

Bliss gave her another nod.

"We're always looking closely at that kind of research," said Hu. "We do a lot of it, and we want to do more of it."

"Building a better mousetrap," said Bliss.

"Building a tougher mouse," said Aunt Sallie. "Or spotting mice who are likely to become psycho killers if you put a gun in their hands and turn them loose."

Bliss shrugged. "A lot of it will depend on the quality of the test and how perceptive the people are who are interpreting the data."

There was a long silence. Church ate a cookie. Hu wrote some notes on a tablet. Aunt Sallie tried to stare holes through Bliss.

Finally, Church said, "How do you know we're not CIA?"

"I don't. But I'd be surprised."

"Why?"

Artemisia pointed a finger at Hu. "Because they wouldn't know what to do with someone like him."

Dr. Hu turned the color of a ripe tomato.

"And they wouldn't know what to do with someone like me."

Bliss gave Church and Aunt Sallie as flat a stare as she could manage. They gave it right back to her.

It was Aunt Sallie who broke what became a very long silence.

"She'll do," she said, grinning like a thief who had just stolen something of unexpected value.

Hu beamed.

Church ate a whole cookie before he gave a single, small nod.

Chapter Sixteen

Grand Hyatt Hotel
109 East Forty-second Street
New York City
Sunday, August 31, 6:38 a.m.

She didn't know I was watching her.

She thought I was still asleep.

She slipped out of the bed the way she did every morning, moving slowly so as not to wake me, moving across the bedroom floor on silent cat feet, reaching for her robe, ducking into the bathroom and closing the door.

It was a kind of modesty.

Not that she was coy about seeing her nude body. I have happily explored every inch of that beautiful landscape. I've mapped every pale freckle, paused to consider each tiny scar, paid my respects to each curve and plane, and become lost in the textures and tastes and scents of her.

No, her furtiveness in the first light of morning was because she did not sleep with her wig on. She wore a colored headscarf to bed and it usually came loose.

Junie Flynn did not like me to see her naked scalp. She'd never said so in words, but I knew her well enough to know that she did not want to start the day for either of us with so obvious a reminder that a clock was ticking down inside the cells of her body. We had no way of knowing how many days or weeks or months she had left. If the drugs in the experimental program she was on worked, then maybe it would buy her years.

If not . . .

Life is a cruel, cruel bastard. It's merciless and malicious.

Through the bathroom door I could hear her throwing up. Again.

When I'd met Junie last year she was already undergoing chemo, having already finished previous sets of drugs and radiation. The tumor in her head had been removed. Twice. But it was aggressive and sly. It hid little bits of itself from the doctors and then waited for everyone to take a deep breath for that sigh of relief before it snuck back into our lives.

At the moment, she was doing okay. She'd regained some of the weight she lost during the last relapse, with new padding to soften the edges of hip bones and ribs. I was doing my best to fatten her up with hot dogs and beer at every Orioles home game—and at the same time trying to convince her that baseball, not football, was the American national pastime. And we spent a lot of time with my best friend, Rudy Sanchez, and his new wife, Circe—both of whom could cook, and both of whom were medical doctors. Rudy was a psychiatrist and Circe had so long a list of credentials after her name that I'm not sure which profession most factually applied. Dinners with them always involved rich foods and appallingly rich chocolate desserts.

Junie had filled out to almost one hundred pounds. Twenty-five to go to hit the target weight for her height.

But her head was still pale and hairless and she didn't want it to be a statement in the morning. A reminder.

A threat.

So I faked being asleep and watched her out of the thinnest possible slit of eyelids. I saw her dart toward the bathroom, stepping over Ghost, who lay twitching, deep in a dream of flight and pursuit. Junie paused at the bathroom door and looked back to see if I was still asleep. I affected a soft snore. She bit her lip and there was an expression on her lovely face that was equal parts love for me and sadness for us.

No trace of self-pity even though, let's face it, it would be completely excusable and understandable. But that wasn't Junie. Her biggest concern was making sure those she loved could survive her passing.

Her death.

God.

The new experimental drugs were rough. They robbed her of energy, they gave her frequent nosebleeds, and they nauseated her.

But were they also saving her? Were they worth the suffering?

We all hoped and prayed so.

The bathroom door clicked closed and I waited until I heard the shower running before I sat up and swung my legs over the side of the bed. I sat there, flexing my toes in the carpet shag, staring at the closed door, feeling an ache throb in the center of my chest. It was so deep, so sharp, so powerful that it felt like a stab wound.

I would have preferred a stab wound. If that were the worst that we had to face, then I'd take the hit and go down smiling, knowing that she was safe and would live. Or I'd do what I do when someone tries to stab me for real. I'd deflect, defend, disarm, and destroy. If this were something I could confront and engage, then I'd be in the thick of it, teeth bared, eyes narrowed, a battle song in my head, blood singing in my ears. If this were some threat come to harm the woman I loved, then there would be no level of ugly to which I wouldn't go, no depth of crazy to which I wouldn't descend, to protect her.

I would win that kind of fight, too.

That's what I do. That's what people like me do. The trained killers. The shooters and fixers who work in the topmost level of special operations. Defeat is a rare thing for us because we train to disallow the probability of it, and we strive toward eliminating even the possibility of it.

And that's proof of the cruelty of this thing.

Among my friends who are doctors, my boss, Mr. Church, has the best of the best scientific resources at his disposal, and I'm top kick of the most lethal crew of shooters in the world, and none of us can really stand between an innocent woman and a monster so small that it has to be seen through a microscope.

It's all humbling in a vicious, mean-spirited way.

"Junie," I said, whispering her name.

She came out of the bathroom after a while, looking fresh and clean and wholesome and whole. Here wig of wavy blond hair was in place. Small touches of makeup applied to her face. Wearing a sheer white cotton blouse over a cream camisole and jeans. Lots of earrings, pendants, bracelets, and rings. Looking perfect.

Smiling at me.

"You're up!" she exclaimed happily.

"In many interesting ways," I agreed.

She cocked an eyebrow. "Morning wood or genuine interest?"

"Both."

"I'm already dressed."

"You got dressed before you checked the calendar."

"Why," she asked, "what's today?"

"It's National Romp Junie Flynn in the Ol' Sackaroonie Day."

"Elegant."

"It's early," I confessed. "Best I could come up with."

"*Romping* is sooo sexy a word."

"It's classier than 'banging my baby' day, which was in the running for a while."

She made a face. "I would have hit you with something heavy."

"Why should you be different from everyone else I know?" I held out my arms toward her. "It's an official holiday, ma'am. You wouldn't want to fly in the face of tradition."

"We both have important meetings today."

"Then let's start the day off with a bang."

She winced. "Ouch. That's bad, even for you."

"It's still early."

"I don't know," said Junie skeptically. "With a start like that, I don't know if your day is going to get any better. You'll be doing knock-knock jokes next."

"I never make jokes," I said. "I am a serious-minded kind of guy."

"Who wants to start the day off with 'a bang'?"

"That's serious."

She pretended to look at her watch, which she wasn't wearing. "Well . . . I have a few minutes."

Clothes went flying. Makeup was spoiled. My dog became disgruntled. And we did, in very point of fact, start that day off with a hell of a bang.

And through the laughter and gasps, the squeals and the insistent slap of hungry skin against hungry skin, we managed to forget to listen to the clock inside our world go tick-tick-tick.

Afterward . . . and after a second shower for her and a long, blistering crab boil of a shower for me, we kissed on the curb while the valet parking guys fetched our cars. Then I watched her drive off in her squatty little metallic green Nissan Cube.

As of three weeks ago Junie was deputy director of FreeTech, a brand-new think tank put together by Mr. Church and funded by private investors who were unnamed friends of his. Rich friends, too, because they put billions into the company. FreeTech's job was to find nonmilitary applications for technologies acquired from what they call "alternative sources," which included some of the weird science DMS teams take away from the bad guys. Understand, we trashed a lot of the really naughty stuff, but there was some radical science that could be repurposed in a way that would genuinely benefit humanity. Sounds corny, but isn't.

Church was the nominal director, though Junie was actually going to run things. I didn't know most of the other members of the board, but I suspected that some of them had checkered pasts and had been given the opportunity to redeem themselves. Not sure I agreed with that strategy, but then again, I don't remember Church asking for my opinion.

Circe O'Tree was a consultant, as was Helmut Deacon, a teenage supergenius who had become the unofficial "ward" of the DMS after the Dragon Factory affair. Spooky kid, but absolutely solid to the core. And one of the weird little kickers in all this was that Mr. Church had extended an invitation for Lilith, the head of Arklight, to join the board of Free-Tech. Lilith accepted, but sent a proxy to attend the meetings. Guess who the proxy was.

Yeah. Violin.

Junie and Violin working together.

I made a mental note to buy a very large bottle of Jack Daniel's on the way home from the office. I had a feeling I was going to need it.

I leaned against the wall of the hotel and watched Junie drive away. Ghost sat beside me, his brown eyes following the little Nissan Cube as Junie threaded it through the thick traffic with a combination of raw nerves, wild risk-taking, and deliberate aggression. She was a gentle soul but she drove like a New York cabbie.

When the car was gone from our sight, Ghost looked up at me and gave a small whine.

"Yeah," I agreed.

I closed my eyes and stood there for a while, trying not to be afraid of every single new moment in the day.

Junie, I thought. And I silently offered a prayer for her. Or maybe it was a plea to whichever gods were working the day shift, to look after her. To chase away the monsters in her cells and in her blood. To champion her in ways I could not, and let her live the life she deserved to have.

I doubt I have ever felt as profoundly helpless.

Then Ghost and I got into my car and we drove off to see if there were any monsters we could chase.

And catch.

And defeat.

Chapter Seventeen

Chanin Building
122 East Forty-second Street
New York City
Sunday, August 31, 7:12 a.m.

The sad-faced little man watched Joe Ledger and his dog get into the black Ford Explorer and drive away.

His name was Ludo Monk. Ludovico Monkato, according to his birth certificate, but he had it legally changed when he was old enough. Ludo Monk was simpler.

He was thirty-two years old and had once been told that he looked like a disappointed monk from a bad Renaissance painting. Monk did not disagree. Doleful eyes, receding mouse-colored hair, a hint of the jowls that would appear before another decade was out, perpetual five o'clock shadow, and a wide mouth that tended to turn down into a frown even when he was happy. He was, however, seldom happy.

Monk knew, with no margin for doubt, that he was more than a little crazy. The last time he'd hacked his therapist's session notes, the things he found only confirmed what he already suspected. There was a lot of jargon in the diagnosis, but the bottom line was that he was batshit crazy. He knew it and accepted it.

But he didn't like it.

There were drugs, of course. The ones that helped keep him stay steady, which he sometimes took. And the ones that helped him forget, which he kept handy all the time. Some others, too. Uppers, downers, and a few that moved him sideways. Right now he was running on empty, and the spiders were starting to crawl out of the doors in his head.

Being nuts was hard work and there was no payoff at the end of it except to either become so mad that he no longer cared—and he hadn't yet reached that point—or find a nice balance between his own damaged internal chemistry and the pills he popped. All that would give him would be a sharper awareness that he was damaged goods. And a clearer memory of every bad decision, every ounce of blood spilled, every scream.

Well, maybe there was one payoff. He was useful to Mother Night.

She said that she loved him. And he knew that she needed him.

Him and his weapons.

Whichever weapon she put into his hands. Guns, knives, whatever. So far Mother Night had asked him to kill thirteen people. Each kill had been important to her, important for the work she was doing.

For Ludo it was a way to shine a light into his personal darkness.

Burn to shine.

It was a thing Mother Night often said. It was a tenet of the religion of Mother Night, which was not a religion at all, because it was anarchy even though it used the structure of a religion and . . .

Every time he tried to make sense of it he just wanted to scream.

Actually, that would feel really good.

Nothing like a scream, he knew. Big ones, little ones. The kind you can feel building down in your testicles and that come out through the top of your head. The kind where you spit up some blood afterward. They were the best.

Of course, it mattered what he was screaming about.

When he played the video games Mother Night sent to him, he screamed and screamed and it was fun. In those games he killed thousands and thousands. With guns, with bombs, with germs, with fires. Sometimes he stomped people. He had the second-highest scores in all of Mother Night's family.

In games, that was.

When it came to pulling an actual trigger, he was second to none.

None.

Sometimes he screamed with pride at that. But they were private screams and he usually let them rip when he was in his favorite closet with a pillow pressed against his mouth.

He bit open a plastic bag of black licorice and watched the cars down in the street. They looked like insects. He wondered what they thought, or if they thought. If they could think. Lately, Monk had come to believe that all machines of war had some level of consciousness. Maybe cars, too. Motorcycles definitely did, anyone with half a brain knew that. And electric guitars.

He chewed the licorice slowly as the traffic closed around where Ledger's car had been. When the man was gone, Ludo lowered his binoculars and leaned against the window frame of the hotel room where he'd been waiting for just this eventuality. He tossed the field glasses onto the bed, fished his cell phone out of his jeans pocket, hit a speed dial, and waited through four rings.

"Yes, my dear," said Mother Night.

"They're on their way," he said. "The Flynn woman in a Cube. Ledger in his Explorer. I think he's going to pick up Dr. Sanchez."

"You didn't shoot anyone, did you?"

"You said not to."

"Good."

There had been a discussion about that. Ludo tried to explain to Mother about the right time and place for a kill shot. Morning rush hour was ideal. But Mother wanted it later, at a certain time and only if certain things happened in a desired order. Ludo privately believed that Mother was overplanning, but he would never dare say that to her. He would stab himself in the eyes before he told her that she was wrong. That her logic was flawed.

"What do you want me to do?" he asked. "I'm set up in both places. I can guarantee a kill for either of them but unless they go back to the hotel tonight I can't get them both."

"I only need one," she said, and gave him the details. "And, Ludo, it might not be a shot I'll need. Good chance I'll want you to use something else, so keep it in mind."

"Okey-dokey," he said.

"Ludo . . . please don't say 'okey-dokey.' "

"Yes, Mother."

The line went dead.

He sat on the edge of the bed and ate some more licorice while he thought about Joe Ledger, Rudy Sanchez, and Junie Flynn. He would have no regrets about killing Ledger—that brutal son of a bitch was a real killer.

Not the others, though.

Sanchez was a man of peace, a doctor. A psychiatrist. On most days, though, Ludo would gladly kill any psychiatrist. Free, no charge. Except on the days they wrote out the scripts. No way he'd want to interfere with a shrink who wanted to write a prescription for pills. Any color, any flavor. But on the other days, on days when the shrinks wanted Ludo to unlock the big box of spiders in his head . . . yeah, on those days he could kill one. Very easily. Wouldn't blink.

But what about Junie Flynn?

Ludo used to love her conspiracy theory podcasts and was sorry she didn't do them anymore. All that stuff about alien-human hybrids, reverse-engineered flying saucers, Men in Black. It was great stuff, and Junie seemed to believe all of it. It made him wonder if she was as batshit crazy as he was.

She was a civilian. And she was pretty. But there were two things that might make it easy for Ludo to punch her ticket. The first was that Mother Night wanted her dead, and that was about 75 percent of it. The second, though, was that Junie Flynn was being treated for a brain tumor. For malignant cancer. Shooting her might be kind of a nice thing to do for the pretty lady. Save her a lot of hassles and indignities later.

Again and again his thoughts revolved from Ledger to Sanchez to Junie Flynn. Three targets. Which one would Mother Night want him to kill today?

He breathed three words that were earnestly meant.

"God help you."

He had another piece of licorice.

Interlude Four

The Hangar
Floyd Bennett Field
Brooklyn, New York
Six Years ago

"They look like a gang of thugs," said Artemisia Bliss, loud enough for only Dr. Hu to hear. They stood together at the edge of a wide matted area in the new training center at the Hangar. The walls still smelled of fresh paint and there was a mountain of equipment still in crates from vendors ranging from sporting goods to weapons manufacturers.

The gathered men standing in a line on the mats were all hard-faced and battle-scarred. A few, she thought, were attractive in a brutal way. Like the way James Bond was described in the novels. They were dressed in baggy black pants, T-shirts, and training sneakers. None of them showed any emotion, not a flicker. They stood like robots, bodies straight but not tense, eyes focused on the three people who stood in the center of the mats. Mr. Church was there along with his aide and bodyguard, Sergeant Gus Dietrich; but the third person was a slender dark-haired woman Bliss had never seen before.

"Who's she?" asked Bliss.

Hu leaned close. "Major Grace Courtland. She's Church's pet killer."

"She's his girlfriend?"

"No. I don't think so. More like a protégée. She's apparently a superstar in the special ops world. First woman to join the SAS. Imagine the kind of harassment she had to deal with there."

"Joined as what? Field support or—"

"Shooter," said Hu. "Courtland went through the full training and rolled out with them a lot of times. Pissed a bunch of people off, but it also proved a point."

Bliss snorted. "It's not exactly news that women can fight, Willie." She was the only person who called him that, and she knew he liked it.

"Courtland's apparently more than that," he said. "Kind of a cross between Lara Croft and Alice from Resident Evil. Video game superbadass kind of tough."

"Lots of tough women in the world," said Bliss, already tired of the hype. "Go ask the Israelis and a lot of other armies. Hell, go ask the ancient Celts."

"I know. Look how long it took the U.S. Army to let blacks fight. Except in a couple of rare instances, it wasn't until the Korean War when they were fully integrated. It's stupid."

It was one of many points on which they agreed. Hu was a second-generation Chinese American, and Bliss had been adopted from China. The uneven pace of the American melting pot process was difficult to understand when viewed from any distance. It was impossible to accept when viewed from up close. The same damaged logic applied to gender, too, and that was going away even more slowly. Bliss was pleased to see a woman in a position of obvious power.

Under her breath, Bliss said, "God, I wish I were like that."

"What?" asked Hu.

"Nothing. It's just . . . that kind of power? In a woman? That's so . . . so . . ."

Even her vast vocabulary failed her.

On the mats, Mr. Church was addressing the line of men.

"Gentlemen," he said slowly, "congratulations for making it through the testing process. Welcome to the Department of Military Sciences."

The men said nothing, though one or two of them nodded. It occurred to Bliss that they might not all be military. Some had more of that bearing while others had the more streetwise demeanor of cops.

"You've been briefed on the kinds of threats that the DMS was formed to confront," continued Church. "There is no other domestic agency empowered or equipped to deal with that level of technological danger. You will be the front line in a new phase of the war on terror, and make no mistake—we are very much in the business of stopping terror. The fall of the Towers initiated a new era in Special Operations. Much will be expected of you. Everything, in fact, except the possibility of failure. And before you think that my last comment is glib, it isn't. The DMS is both a first-response and last-defense organization. We will accomplish both. Failure to stop the kinds of threats we know are coming will likely result in catastrophic loss of life and incalculable damage to America and its people."

All eyes were on Church. Bliss knew that each of these men could tell—as she could tell when she first met Church—that he was not given to exaggeration or swagger. He was not that kind of person, and that made his words far more chilling.

Church gestured to the woman who stood behind him. She was medium height, fit, with short dark hair and brown eyes. No rings, no jewelry. "This is Major Grace Courtland, late of Barrier and the SAS. Some of you will have heard of her record in the SAS."

Bliss watched the men appraising her. Most of the men's faces were wooden; one or two showed an unintentional sneer of contempt.

"Major Courtland has been seconded to the DMS and I have appointed her as the senior field agent. Henceforth you will answer to her without question. She will train you and together you will form the first DMS field unit, designated Alpha Team. Are there any questions?"

There were none but Church and Courtland watched their eyes. Bliss could see when Courtland spotted one of the sneers, even though the man in question—a bruiser with a row of fifty-caliber rounds tattooed around his massive biceps—tried to clear his face of all emotion. Courtland pointed to him.

"What's your name, soldier?" she asked in a clipped London accent.

"Staff Sergeant Ronald McIlveen, ma'am."

"Step forward."

His face was like granite as he took a single step toward her. He was well over six feet in height and loomed above the Brit.

"You don't want to take orders from a woman, do you?"

"Ma'am?" he asked, clearly trying to sidestep the question.

"I said, if I gave you a bloody order, would you take it?"

"Yes, ma'am."

"Any order?"

There was only a moment's hesitation. "Yes, ma'am."

"Really?"

"Yes, ma'am."

"I don't believe you," said Courtland. "In fact, I think you're a sexist prick who thinks women are for shagging and not fit to stand in the line of battle."

The man stood absolutely rigid, eyes locked on the middle distance.

"Well, answer me."

"I will follow orders, ma'am," he said, though it sounded false even to Bliss, who had never been part of the military.

"Will you indeed?" Courtland stepped close. The overhead lights threw his shadow across her, and she looked tiny and frail. "What if I ordered you to hit me?"

The soldier blinked. "Ma'am?"

"I didn't stutter, Staff Sergeant. I asked if you would follow my order to hit me."

"I cannot strike a superior officer, ma'am."

"So, then you're refusing a direct order."

"No . . . I mean . . ."

"Hit me, staff sergeant."

"I . . . . . ." began the sergeant, then he shut his mouth and froze into a statue. The other men in the line looked variously angry and amused.

Major Courtland snapped her fingers. "Sergeant Dietrich."

Church's bodyguard instantly stepped forward. "Major," he said crisply.

"Draw your sidearm."

He did it without question or hesitation.

"Did you hear my order for Staff Sergeant McIlveen to strike me?"

"Yes, Major."

"I will repeat that order, Sergeant. If he does *not* strike me, or if you believe his strike is either deliberately weak or deliberately misaimed, you are to kneecap the effing cunt. Is that clear?"

"As glass, Major." Dietrich raised his Glock and pointed it at McIlveen's left knee. Dietrich's hand was as steady as a statue.

"Ma'am," protested McIlveen.

Courtland looked up at him. "Prove to me you'll follow a woman's orders. I want you to punch me in the face. I want you to knock my effing teeth out. I want you to break my effing neck, you effing overgrown cock. Do it right now."

Bliss's breath caught in her chest. She grabbed Hu's hand and squeezed it.

The big sergeant had no choice, so in the absence of retreat he attacked and swung a punch that was powered by his entire body. All his mass and muscle, all his confusion and anger, all his training and skill. He threw it fast and he threw it well, right at Grace Courtland's jaw.

And then he was falling.

Bliss couldn't understand what had happened.

There was a confusion of movement and Major Courtland's left hand seemed to blur. The meaty after-echo of impact bounced across the floor a split second before the big man dropped heavily to his knees, his hands clamped around his throat, his face turning a dreadful red. Courtland stepped sideways and hit him again, the side of her balled fist crunching into McIlveen's skull just behind his ear. His eyes rolled up and he flopped face-forward onto the floor and lay as if dead.

Mr. Church sighed and brushed lint from his sleeve.

Gus Dietrich holstered his pistol, his eyes roving over the faces of the line of startled men.

Between them, Major Courtland straightened. She snapped her fingers again and a pair of EMTs came running from behind where Bliss and Hu stood. They crouched over the fallen soldier, who was now making hoarse croaking sounds.

Courtland walked over to a second man. "What is your name?"

The man stiffened. "Master Sergeant Mark Allenson, Marine Force Recon."

"Do you have any issues about taking orders from a woman," asked Courtland, "or about obeying those orders without question?"

"I do not, ma'am."

"Hit me."

Allenson moved like lightning, hooking a vicious short right into her ribs.

Courtland blocked it with a chopping downward elbow block. Allenson hissed in pain and stepped back, clutching his hand to his chest.

The major smiled at him. "Allenson, henceforth you are my second in command. The rest of you, fall out and hit the showers."

The men stared at her, their eyes darting from her to Allenson to McIlveen and back again. Then they began moving off, at first with slow and uncertain steps, and then nearly running to the exit that led to the shower rooms. As they passed, Mr. Church quietly said, "Welcome to the DMS, gentlemen."

Bliss was riveted, transfixed, her body flushed with an almost erotic electricity. The way those men—those huge, terrifying, powerful men—now stared at Major Courtland was so delicious.

There was so much power in the room, and so much of it belonged to that woman.

To a woman.

Artemisia Bliss studied Courtland and she wished she could stab her hands into the woman's chest and tear out that powerful heart.

And eat it.

Consume it.

Be it.

Her entire body trembled.

Chapter Eighteen

Starbucks
140 East Forty-second Street
New York City
Sunday, August 31, 7:19 a.m.

I made two stops on the way to work.

The first was the Starbucks on East Forty-second, where I double-parked in a tow-away zone. Coffee is more important than parking regulations. Ask any of my fellow caffeine addicts.

The barista flashed me a big smile as I came in and was already pouring my venti bold by the time I got to the counter. This was the Starbucks I frequented every time I was in New York. I was a confirmed regular, on a first-name basis with the staff and a nodding acquaintance to a bunch of frequent-flyer customers.

The barista set my cup down.

"Hey, Emily," I said as I stepped to the counter, "any chance you could put that in an IV drip?"

"Sorry, Joe . . . they still won't let us go intravenous."

"Barbarians."

"No argument," she said. "Is Rudy coming in today?"

"Heading over to pick him up now."

"Does he want . . . *the drink?*"

"Sadly, yes."

Emily half turned to another barista and rattled off the name of the unholy alchemical abomination Rudy Sanchez insists is the perfect morning cup of wonderful. "Iced half-caf ristretto quad grande two-pump raspberry two percent no whip light ice with caramel drizzle three-and-a-half-pump white mocha."

No one with testicles should be allowed to drink that.

No, check that, it's not a gender thing. No one with any self-respect should *want* to drink it.

"On it," said Jared, the boy who shared the morning shift with Emily. I could see him square his shoulders like a rat catcher about to leap into a nest of vermin.

I ordered egg sandwiches for us—not forgetting the fur monster in the car—and a paid with a scan of my smartphone.

Emily gave me a tentative smile. "How is Rudy? How's he doing?"

I knew that her question wasn't an idle one. Like everyone else who ever met Rudy, Emily was concerned about how his recovery was coming along. People cared about him. He was that kind of guy. I could have an I-beam through my chest and maybe I'd get a nod. Rudy gets a hangnail and everyone wants to mother him.

To be fair, Rudy was worthy of the concern, and he had been pretty badly mauled when the Warehouse was destroyed last year. He and Church were lifting off from the helipad on the roof when the bombs went off. The blast threw the chopper into the bay. Rudy now wears an eye patch and walks with a limp.

"He's auditioning for the role of Captain Jack Sparrow for the Broadway version of *Pirates of the Caribbean*," I told her.

She laughed. It took her a moment, though, because jokes like that can come off as insensitive. God knows I would never be insensitive. Ahem.

"Tell him I said hi," said Emily dubiously.

While I waited in line for Rudy's drink, I felt my phone vibrate, indicating an incoming text. A grin began creeping onto my face because I knew it had to be from Junie. Rudy is a borderline Luddite who has no idea how to text; Top and Bunny would call; and, let's face it, Church isn't the kind to text his BFF about last night's rerun of *How I Met Your Mother*. I'd only ever gotten texts from Junie and they tended to be pretty saucy. She loved doing that when she thought I was in some high-level meeting.

Oh, Junie, you vixen.

So I wore a wolf's smile when I unlocked the screen and read the message.

YOU COULD BE A WINNER!
OR A LOSER.
MAYBE BOTH.

There was no signature and instead of a sender's name there was only a capital letter A. That's it.

I think I said something like "What the fuck?"

The people around me waiting for drinks shot me looks. One lady in a fussy business suit actually made a tsk-tsk sound and shook her head in disapproval.

"Sorry," I mumbled.

I typed "Who is this?" into the reply box and sent it, but I got nothing back. So I forwarded the message to Bug with a request to trace the sender.

Back in the car I gave Ghost his sandwich, which he took apart and ate in pieces. Bread, cheese, turkey bacon, egg. I've never known another dog that eats like that. If he were a kid he'd be one of those who can't have his peas touching his mashed potatoes.

The dog will spend an entire evening licking his nuts, but when it comes to breakfast he's as dainty as a Bryn Mawr socialite.

Rudy was waiting curbside for me.

He was wearing khakis and a Polo shirt, Italian loafers with no socks, a gold watch, and Oakley sunglasses tucked into the vee of his shirt. Circe had begun to dress him like a Ken doll. But it was better than some of the outfits I've seen him pick, including his favorite electric-blue bike shorts.

He was smiling and I'm pretty sure it wasn't because he saw his best bud slowing to a stop. Maybe the newlyweds had enjoyed a morning wake-up call of the kind that kept putting a smile on my face. Rudy wiped his mouth, and I'll bet a shiny nickel he was removing a smudge of lipstick.

Rudy limped around to the passenger door, leaning heavily on a cane with a carved parrot head. It was one I'd given him. I figured anyone with an eye patch needed a parrot. I also bribed Bug to reprogram Rudy's phone so that the ring tone said, "Arrrrr, Arrrr." Rudy had so far not managed to remove the pirate sounds.

I leaned over and opened the door for him. As soon as he was in, he reached back to scratch Ghost on the head, earning a quick lick across his knuckles. Then Rudy fairly lunged for the Starbucks drink as if he were a man dying of thirst and this were the purest water.

"Not sure how you can tolerate that toxic waste," I said.

He took a sip, sighed, and cocked his eye at me. "Not sure why, after all these years, it still bothers you."

"Getting kicked in the nuts still bothers me, too."

"My masculinity is not endangered by my choice of beverage."

"How sure are you about that?" I asked. "It's not exactly a manly man drink, Rude."

"And a big cup of dark coffee is? Have you considered everything implied by *your* choice, Cowboy?" he asked mildly. His accent is cultured Mexican in a good baritone. Always reminds me of Raul Julia from the old *Addams Family* movies.

"There's nothing *implied*. I like a big cup of dark, strong coffee."

"Ah."

"Ah—what?"

"You like a 'big'—suggestive of size inadequacies; cup of 'dark'—an unintentional reference to your chronic disconnect from social normalcy, i.e., having a dark side that you are both proud of and fear; 'strong'— again we see fears of inadequacy and an infantile attempt to demonstrate strength through proxy; 'coffee'—said defensively as if all other forms of caffeinated drinks are somehow less so, and such a state only reinforces the fact that you want people to believe you're strong because your coffee is. Really, Joe, it's textbook, and it paints you as a weak, sad man. I pity you."

"I have a gun," I said, "I could shoot you."

"Intense feelings of male inadequacy often manifest as threats or acts of desperate violence."

"Ghost," I ordered, "kill."

Ghost looked up from his sandwich and gave me a pitying look.

I turned back to Rudy. "Yeah, well at least I'm not trying to get in touch with my inner tween girl with that drink."

"Perhaps I am," said Rudy, "but I, at least, will admit it."

"Fuck you.'"

"A cogent argument, very well put."

I put the car in gear and we drove off.

After we'd gone a couple of blocks, I said, "How are you doing, brother?"

"Good."

"The leg?"

"Meh."

"Meh?"

"I'm aware of when the weather is changing."

"Dude," I said, "after all the stuff I've had broken, I can tell when the weather's changing in the Dakotas."

"I defer to the human crash test dummy." He sipped his glop. "But to answer the question, the leg is about the same. We're discussing a surgical option, but it's unlikely to substantially improve things, so I'll probably opt out."

I nodded. "Sucks."

"It sucks," he agreed. "But it is what it is."

That was a big part of Rudy's philosophy. I was still juvenile to believe in the "cowboy up and walk it off" approach to pain and injuries. Rudy was more adult and he was a realist. His leg was never going to be prime again and no amount of personal rah-rah stuff was going to change that. The severity of the nerve damage also meant that he probably wouldn't drive a car again, not unless he got one that was modified for a left-foot driver. In that and other more fundamental ways, Rudy was permanently marked by the violence of our world.

In the rearview mirror I caught him checking me out, watching my eyes. Doing the kind of thing that made him a good shrink.

"How is Junie?"

"Doing good."

"The nausea, the disorientation——?"

"She's going through a phase. She says it'll pass."

"What about her latest panels?"

"We're waiting for those," I said.

Rudy gave me an assessing look. "Many people find waiting for the results of chemotherapy to be emotionally and psychologically corrosive."

"Kind of an understatement."

"Paranoia and doubt tend to crop up in a number of ways, Joe. Left unaddressed they can lead to bad decisions and poor judgment. They can do damage to each individual involved in the process as well as to the strength of the couple's relation——"

"Uh-uh. We're not having *that* kind of trouble, man."

As I said it I heard the unintentional emphasis I put on *that*. Rudy caught it at once.

"Do you need to talk about something else?"

With any other friend that would be an invitation to unload now, on the drive to work, or maybe later over a beer. But Rudy was more than a shrink, he was the senior medical officer for the DMS and it was his job to offer counseling to the staff. Just as it was his job to evaluate each field agent to determine whether we should go back out or hang up our guns. I have a rather long and complicated history of psychological and emotional trauma. Mentally, I'm paddling a canoe alongside the crazyboat. Rudy helped me find my balance and to use the dark, splintered fragments of my mind. But he kept his eye on me. We both feared the day when my inner demons would slam the door to lock him out, and trap me inside.

It took some effort to get it out, but I finally nodded and said, "Yeah, we could do an hour."

He looked relieved. "I'm free most of this afternoon. Two o'clock?"

"Two's fine."

"Tell me this much," he said, "is this a personal matter or is it *her*?"

"Her."

He nodded. We both knew that we weren't talking about Junie Flynn. Or Violin. This was about the Asian girl I'd strangled and drowned on a cold night in Baltimore.

"Two o'clock, then."

"Yup," I said.

With that settled, there was no need to talk about anything now. Nothing heavy, at least. It was a sunny, beautiful morning in the Apple. My day was likely to be a walk in the park, interviewing and evaluating potential new recruits.

Nothing stressful.

Nothing to worry about.

At two o'clock I'd unlock the Pandora's Box in my head and let Rudy clean it all out with Clorox.

Then I'd go home to Junie.

It was all going to work out, I told myself.

Everything was going to be fine.

So why did I suddenly sit upright and stare out the window of my car as two teenagers with hoodies and backpacks slouched by? They were skinny, and one had the skull from the Misfits on the back of his hoodie, and the girl had the A-for-Anarchy symbol stitched in sequins on the front of hers. Both of them had dark sunglasses. He wore Doc Martens and she had a pair of orange Crocs. They each wore iPods and mouthed silent words in time with whatever was blasting in their ears.

They began to cross just as my light turned green, making me and everyone behind wait. That was clearly intentional, and I began rolling down my window to growl something at them, but Rudy touched my arm.

"Don't feed it," he said mildly.

"Feed what?"

"Their desire to provoke you."

"If it's what they want, then I'm fine with—"

"Listen to yourself, Cowboy. They're a couple of kids who do something like this, dress that way and inconvenience people, for a very specific reason. They are forcing you to notice them and to acknowledge their existence by reacting to them."

"They could have done that by handing out flowers instead of blocking traffic."

"And maybe they would have felt silly or maybe it didn't occur to them. This is their way of spray-painting their name on the world." He shrugged. "Let them have their power. It shouldn't diminish us, Joe."

The kids passed, and the girl turned and smiled at me. It was a strength smile, almost a knowing smile.

My cell rang and I took the call. Bug.

"Hey, Joe," he said, "I had Nikki do a traceback on that text you got."

"And—"

"According to your phone provider's records, no such text was ever sent."

"Umm . . . how's that work?"

"Don't know. Glitch in the system?"

"If I were a normal guy working a normal job I'd buy that. Keep checking."

"Will do."

As I hung up, Rudy asked, "Problem?"

"Not sure," I said. Then laughed. "Nah. It's nothing."

Interlude Five

Beranger Sporting Equipment
Outskirts of Cheyenne, Wyoming
Five Years Ago

"Is it safe?"

It wasn't the first time Artemisia Bliss asked that question, but it was the first time someone took the time to answer.

"It is now," said the big man with the gun. Major Samson Riggs was tall, broad-shouldered, and handsome in a weathered Matthew Mc-Conaughey way. Older than her by almost two decades, but square-jawed, blue-eyed, and built like a fitness trainer. He offered her a hand that was tanned but crisscrossed with scars.

Riggs offered his hand to help her out of the armored SUV.

The air was filled with smoke and the rhythmic thump of helicopter blades. Various tactical vehicles sat at crooked angles in front of a four-story brick warehouse. A sign outside said that this place manufactured tennis rackets. It did not. Some of the things it did manufacture lay sprawled and broken in the tall grass. On paper their designation was rather bland, even by military standards. Enhanced drones. In reality they were terrifying.

Riggs led her past several of them. She paused to look down at one of them. Inside the shattered fiberglass-and-metal hull of the unmanned aerial vehicles were torn pieces of red and shattered spikes of white.

Meat and bones.

Bliss gagged and turned away for a moment, and Riggs placed a fatherly, calming hand on her shoulder.

"It's okay, kiddo," he said gently. "First time in the field?"

She nodded, not trusting herself to speak.

"Don't sweat it. Everyone has a moment like this. God knows I did."

She cut him a look to see if he was patronizing her.

"Seriously," he said. "My first gig with the Deacon was a dirty piece of business down in Guam. One of those damn supersoldier programs. Steroids, cybernetic enhancements, implants dumping hormones and stimulants directly into the bloodstream. Very nasty. We busted the place up pretty good, and that was just business, but then we crashed into the surgical labs. Lots of works in progress, if you catch my drift. It was like something out of a horror movie. All those poor bastards strapped to stainless steel tables or chained in iron cages. I don't think there was one single operator in that room who didn't toss their cookies. Not one."

"Even you?" asked Bliss in a croak of a voice.

"Hell, girl, I was the first one. Couldn't find a trash can, so I threw up into a desk drawer. Sounds like something from a bad comedy, but it wasn't funny."

"No," she said.

"No," he agreed.

He fished in his pocket and produced a tube of ChapStick, uncapped it, and held it out. She could smell the strong mint. "Here, rub this on your upper lip. Put a lot on. The mint kills your sense of smell and helps calm your stomach. Go on, take it. You'll feel better."

She reached out and tentatively took the ChapStick, screwed out the lip balm, and applied it liberally to her upper lip and around her nostrils. "Mind if I ask a personal question, Colonel?"

"It's Samson, and no, go ahead."

She looked up at him. "How did you become strong? I don't mean at the gym or good with a gun. I mean how did you, a human being like everyone else, become strong enough to do what you do? To go into battle? To kill. How? Were you born with it?"

She thought Riggs would blow the question off with the typical military trash talk, but he paused, giving it real consideration. "It's all about choice," he said. "If you have a calling, if you feel you know that this kind of work is what you want to do, or if you discover you're good at this and you let your talent pull you in a certain direction, then you have to make a choice. You have to look it in the face. It's like the way doctors do. The first day in Anatomy 101, when they wheel out the cadavers, half the med students pass out or throw up. Everyone feels sick, even the stoic ones, or the ones who believe they're stoic. And the reason they do is because it's a human moment and there is a very clear set of lines drawn in the sand. They have to cut into, dissect and therefore violate a human being. There are so many taboos, so many ancient dreads hardwired into our brains about not doing something like this that it feels perverse. However, the end goal is that the doctor learns things that will make him a good doctor and therefore a healer. Cutting into that corpse is like crossing the river Styx. Or maybe it's the Rubicon, I have my metaphors messed up. The point is that it's a rite of passage. You do what you have to do in order to be prepared for what you know will be expected of you later. It's the same in the military. We train to fight. We visualize and imagine killing the enemy. We learn the mechanics of it, the sociology of it, and the psychology of it. Those of us who want to be good at it also dip our toes into the philosophy of it."

"Which is?"

"Short version of that is we accept that killing is how we will survive, and it is through killing our enemies that we will guarantee the safety of those we love. Measure killing of that kind against the lives of those we hold precious, and the trigger is easier to pull."

"That can't be true for every soldier. Some of the men I've met in the DMS seem to be able to kill without emotion and maybe without remorse of any kind. It's part of their job."

"That's true, in the moment. And between jobs it's a useful mask to make. But we all take it home with us in one way or another. Hell, look at the current military, where there are more deaths from suicide than from combat."

"And for the bad guys? Like the Hutus in Rwanda who slaughtered nearly a million Tutsis. They hacked off arms and legs, butchered babies, killed nuns and missionaries. Are you saying that they went home and brooded over those killings?"

"Ah," said Riggs, "that's a different question. You asked me how guys like me reconcile killing. I'm a moralist as well as a shooter. I will pull a trigger but I damn well want a reason. But you're right when you say that there are plenty of people in the world for whom life is inconsequential. Ask a Nazi. Ask anyone in the drug cartels. The Russian Mafya. Yeah, there are coldhearted people out there. Some are sociopaths who have found their calling. Others have become dead inside because that is the culture in which they were raised. And maybe some are just plain evil."

"But they're powerful."

"Oh, yes. And there are a lot of them."

"Who is more powerful?"

Riggs laughed. "Ask the winners. In any fight, always ask that question of the winners."

"Last question," she said.

"Are you writing a paper or something?"

"No. I'm trying to understand how this all works. You know about the VaultBreaker software I'm writing? It's all about trying to get inside the heads of the bad guys in order to predict how they might attempt an intrusion. I need to know to what lengths someone would go to get what they want."

"That's your question? How far would someone go?" He grunted. "If they wanted it badly enough . . . if having it was more important than anything else in their life, then that person might do absolutely anything, cross any line, break any taboo, do whatever it took to have that thing."

Bliss nodded, letting it all sink in. She looked down at the dead baboon with all of the mechanical apparatus surgically forced into its flesh. The science displayed there was so radical, so cutting-edge. So powerful in its potential.

"It's unbelievable," she murmured.

"Welcome to the face of war," said Riggs, misreading her reaction. When she looked up at him, he added, "This is what the DMS is all about."

"You see this kind of thing in movies, in video games. I mean, I've played first-person shooter games where I've fought things as bizarre as this, but—"

"I know. The real world is always different." Riggs paused for a moment, studying her. Then he said, "I have two young nephews who play all those games. Sixteen and eighteen. Both of them plan to enroll in the army once they're out of school. They want to go into Special Operations, like their dad did, and like me, I suppose. I think they think that spec-ops is like Call of Duty or one of the games they play."

Bliss fought the urge to roll her eyes, expecting this to segue into one of those trite lectures where someone who's been there pooh-poohs the version of combat presented even in the edgiest games. She'd heard that rant a million times and wasn't interested. On one hand, she was well aware of the differences between real life and games; after all, didn't she design game simulations? On the other hand, her game simulations were the result of exhaustive interviews with shooters like Riggs, Gus Dietrich, Grace Courtland, and even Aunt Sallie. Plus she'd interviewed the counterterrorism expert Hugo Vox a dozen times, and had grilled more than a hundred operators at his Terror Town training facility. Bliss had built levels of realism into her simulations that were unmatched by anything on the current game market. And she'd played her own games, wearing earphones and goggles that gave her a massive 3D experience. She even co-created a simulator chair that provided smells—gunpowder, blood, sweat and dozens of others—so that the person playing the game had as real an experience as possible.

So, despite the "if it's a game, it's not real" diatribe, Bliss was pretty damn sure she knew what real felt like.

So to cut Riggs off at the pass, she nodded to the dead cyborg drone and said, "It's a shame it'll all get swept under the rug. We could repurpose this and—"

A shadow fell across the dead animal and Bliss pivoted to see Mr. Church. She hadn't heard him approach, but he was like that. Sergeant Dietrich stood a few feet behind.

"Oh!" she said, and it came out as almost a yelp. "Hi. Um . . . we were just . . ."

Riggs came to her rescue. "The site's secured, Boss. Nothing got out."

"Very well, Colonel. My respects and appreciation to Shockwave Team. You may stand down."

Riggs sketched a roguish salute, gave Bliss a wink, and walked off. That left Bliss smiling awkwardly at Mr. Church.

His face was impassive, a mask that told Bliss nothing about what he felt. She could never imagine him staggering off to vomit up his shock and disgust like the shooters in Shockwave had. Not him.

"What do we . . . um . . . ?" She didn't know how to finish the question.

"Everything gets cataloged," said Church. "Bag and tag all the bodies, human and animal. Secure all computers and records. Trucks will be here in a few hours to collect everything. It will all be flown to Brooklyn."

"No," she said, rising. "What I mean is, what will happen after that's all over? After we do our studies and dissections, after we run all of the data through MindReader, what happens then?"

"In terms of what?"

"In terms of the science."

Church removed a stick of gum from his jacket pocket, peeled off the silver foil, and put the gum in his mouth. He folded the wrapper very slowly and precisely.

"This isn't our science, Miss Bliss," he said.

She did not dare respond to that. He'd just put a big bear trap on the ground between them and there was no way she was putting her foot into it.

Instead, she nodded.

Church put the folded silver paper into his pocket.

To Dietrich he said, "Gus, when everything is cleared out, set charges and bring the building down. Remove the debris and have the foundation filled with dirt. Three days from now I want a field here and nothing else. Are we clear?"

Dietrich gave him a sharp nod. After a moment, Bliss imitated the nod.

Church lingered for a moment, looking at her, then down at the dead animal, then at the building.

"This isn't our science," he said again.

Bliss could not have disagreed more.

Chapter Nineteen

Vice President William Collins sat back against the cushions of the armored SUV and sipped his coffee as his motorcade rolled along the streets from his residence on the grounds of the United States National Observatory to his office at the White House. Coffee always tasted better after sex. Not after sex with his wife, of course, but always after sex with the wild woman he'd screwed twice last night and once again this morning. Coffee was the perfect after-passion taste treat. Good for the soul, good for the nerves.

And his nerves needed some help today.

Today of all days.

Beside him, his chief of staff rattled on about the affairs of the day. Bryan "Boo" Radley was a moon-faced Midwesterner with a computer mind and no discernible personality. A great number-two man, but he did talk a lot.

"Should I do that, sir?"

The question hung in the air and Collins had to fish around for whatever had preceded the question. But if it was there he couldn't grab it.

"Sorry, Boo, I was miles away," said Collins. "Give that to me again."

"It was the immigration reform bill. Were you able to look it over? Calvin has this morning blocked out to rewrite it before the press briefing and—"

"Ah, damn, I was so jammed up I didn't get to it. Put it on the top of my pile and I'll go over it first thing."

"Very well, Mr. Vice President."

Collins shot him a look. "Oh, don't sound so disapproving. Jeez, you're like my tenth-grade math teacher. She used to make me feel like shit if I forgot to do my homework."

"Not at all, Mr. Vice President."

"And here's how I know you're pissed at me, Boo."

"Sir?"

"You only call me 'Mr. Vice President' in that tone when I've been naughty."

"No, I—"

Collins laughed and reached over to clap Radley on the shoulder. "Christ, lighten up. It's a beautiful day in the capital. Take a breath. No, I'm serious, actually take a breath."

Bradley's mouth was pinched but then he drew in a deep lungful of air, pulling it in through his nostrils. He held it for a second and then exhaled, long and slow.

"There," said Collins, "now doesn't that feel better?"

"Yes, thank you."

Collins gave him a rueful shake of the head. "You need to get laid, Boo. I'm serious, you are in more dire need of getting your ashes hauled than anyone in the District of Columbia."

Radley made no comment.

"Okay, okay, I know, back to work," said Collins. He genuinely liked Radley and wished that he could bring him into his confidence. What did they call it in that movie, he mused. *Into the circle of trust*. But although Radley was absolutely ruthless in the prosecution of his duties as the chief of staff to the vice president, he was also a patriot. Worse yet, he was a Constitutionalist, one of those patriots who was a fierce proponent of the letter of the law rather than the spirit of what was really best for the future of America. The kind of patriotism that kept the lights on and provided for the general welfare. Blah, blah, blah. Not the kind who would take a risk and do what was necessary to change the game. The Boo Radleys of the world were always looking to get America "back on track," instead of taking America to the next level. That rather amazed Collins, too, because the Founding Fathers were innovative rebels before they created that restrictive piece of bad legislation called the Constitution. The Founding Fathers would never allow America to have fallen into the state of disgrace in which she currently wallowed. Escalating debt to China and other creditors. A continued off-the-books allegiance to old-money families like the Rothschilds. Allowing the bankers to constantly butt-fuck Congress. And a demonstrated fear of truly embracing the potential of radical new technologies.

In Collins's view it was a widespread problem. Republicans and

Democrats were both pussies, with maybe a few exceptions. Even though he was a party man according to the voters and election strategists, Collins privately considered himself to be a staunch, unflinching, and proud member of a much older party than either of those. The True American Revolutionary Party.

A party that, granted, existed only in shadows and private conversations, but which was growing very fast. It was gaining friends and power with every day.

And today . . .

Collins had to turn away to hide a smile. Today was going to be a very important day. A day of great social change. Not just for America, but for the entire world. Collins believed with his whole heart that by the end of today the world would be a different place. Public awareness would be tuned in to a newer and clearer frequency. Congress would no longer be allowed to remain complacent, or to put personal agendas ahead of the needs of what Collins prayed would be a renewed America. A reborn America.

"Sir?" said Radley, and once more Collins realized that his attention had drifted from what his aide was saying. He would have to watch that. Today was not a day to allow anything unusual to show, not even here in the relative privacy of his car.

"Sure, sure, Boo," he said expansively, "I'm all ears. What else do you have?"

The motorcade moved on, closing in on the White House in so many different ways.

Chapter Twenty

Dutch Trader Tavern
North Main and East Twenty-third Streets
Farmville, Virginia
Sunday, August 31, 7:27 a.m.

Colonel Samson Riggs leaned wearily against the wall. He held an empty pistol in his right hand, the slide locked back. Shell casings littered the floor all around him and blue-gray gun smoke clouded the air.

The unfinished brick walls were slimed with mossy dampness, and tendrils of creeper vines and the roots of weeds trailed down through the cracked mortar. Above him, the ceiling was a gaping hole that still smoked from the blaster-plaster they'd used to breach the wall into this place. The building had once been a mill in Colonial times, and a tavern for more than two hundred years. Eight years ago the economy crushed it into a silent and empty husk that waited for the sheriff to sell it for back taxes. Recently, someone else had moved in and taken possession of the extensive cellars. Perhaps "some *thing*" was more apt, because the hulking figures that lay sprawled around him did not look human.

They were massive, grotesquely muscled, and their faces had a distinctly simian cast. Riggs knew what they were.

Berserkers.

But that made no sense. The Berserker program had been shut down years ago by Joe Ledger and his team at a place called the Dragon Factory. That's where a group of fanatical scientists had used gene therapy to blend the DNA of silverback gorillas with that of a team of mercenaries. The result had been a kill squad who had all of the mass and muscle of the great apes and the total savagery of the world's number-one apex predator. Man.

It was a deadly combination, but it was damn well supposed to be past tense. All of the Berserkers had been killed. Every last freakish one of them.

So where did these monsters come from?

It was a question with no answer.

A rattle of gunfire made Riggs jerk out of his reverie. This fight wasn't over.

As he began running he slapped his pockets for a fresh magazine, found none. No grenades, either. All he had left was the fighting knife strapped to his combat harness.

"Never take a knife to a goddamn gunfight," he muttered as he tore it loose. He raced along the stone corridors.

A shape loomed up in front of him and Riggs nearly gutted it with the knife; but it was Wendig, the sergeant of Two Squad, the second of Shockwave's smaller teams. Wendig's face was as white as paste. The rest of him was bright red. He reached for Riggs with his left hand. Except there was no hand at the end of the reaching arm.

"I—I—" stammered the sergeant, and then he collapsed onto the ground.

Riggs had no time to do anything or offer any help. Someone else was screaming. A woman.

There were two women on Two Squad, a stocky Navajo named Mary Tsotse, and Star Phillips, a lanky black woman from Detroit. Ordinarily it was possible to tell them apart, whether whispering, talking, or even yelling; but that scream was so massive, so raw that it could have been either of them. Whoever it was needed him right now.

He leaped over Sergeant Wendig, ran down a narrow side corridor and burst into a larger room where old, broken beer barrels stood on wooden racks.

Two of his people were down. Both male. The rest of Two Squad. Jespersen and McPhail.

Down and either dead or badly wounded. They shared their pools of blood with three hulking forms who were indisputably dead, their heads blown apart by bullets. The brutes wore heavy body armor. Another body, Star Phillips, lay twisted into a madhouse shape, her spine bent backward so that her head touched the back of her thighs. Her sightless eyes were filled with a terminal wonder.

Only one member of Two Squad still stood. Still breathed.

Eighty feet away.

Two more of the Berserkers flanked her, closing in on Mary Tsotse. She fired at them, but the big men held a thick wooden table at head level and let the hardwood soak up the bullets. Tsotse tried for leg shots, but the body armor sloughed off the rounds, though the foot-pounds of impact slowed the approach of the killers.

Tsotse's body ran with blood from long, terrible gashes torn in her flesh by the steel-hard fingernails of the brutes. Her Kevlar and clothes were in rags, and the exposed flesh was ripped and bleeding. It was through sheer force of will that she was still on her feet, still firing, still fighting.

As Riggs ran into the room he saw the slide lock back on Tsotse's Sig Sauer. A look of abject fear and hopelessness filled her eyes. The brutes laughed in sudden delight.

She backpedaled while fishing for another magazine, but the brutes hurled the table at her, catching her in the chest with it. Riggs heard the meaty crunch as the table smashed flesh and broke bones.

Then Riggs threw himself at the brutes.

The men turned to meet his charge.

They grinned at the man who wanted so badly to die that he dared attack them with only a knife.

The closest one swiped at Riggs, trying to end it fast by crushing the man's skull. But Riggs changed his leap into a tuck and roll. He passed under the sweeping arm and hit the floor between them, rolling fast, coming up, spinning, cutting.

The blade caught the lunging mercenary across the back of the knee. Combat demands mobility and padding precludes it. The back of the knee was covered by thinner material that was far too thin. The edge of Riggs's knife passed through Kevlar and tendon in a tight arc that trailed rubies.

Before the monster could even buckle from the loss of structure, Riggs spun left, turning in a full circle to give mass to his motion, pushing weight behind his second cut. This time the blade sliced cleanly through the Achilles tendon of the second brute.

It was all so fast.

So fast.

The monsters' howls were filled with surprise as much as pain. Ordinary men did not move that fast.

As their legs buckled, they shifted to their uninjured legs and tried to dive atop him, to smother this man with more than a quarter ton of muscle and bone.

But Riggs came up out of his crouch, rising like a rocket, shifting toward the first brute, holding the Ka-Bar in both hands, shoving it edge upward, cleaving the simian face from chin to brow.

With a savage wrench, Riggs tore the blade free, pivoted into the rush of the second brute, and drove the point of his knife into the monster's screaming mouth. The blade punched into the soft palate, and Riggs instantly let go with his right hand and used the heel of his palm to pound on the flat pommel, driving the blade all the way through to the brain stem.

The ape-man reeled backward, aware that he was dying, seeing the cold and emotionless face of his killer rise above him as he fell.

Then Riggs turned to the other Berserker. The thing had fallen against the wall. One leg was limp and sheathed in blood. The apelike face was a ruin, cut in half to expose gums and broken teeth and gaping sinuses. It howled in agony.

Without a moment's hesitation, Riggs pivoted on the ball of one foot and drove his other foot in a brutal side thrust kick that shattered the Berserker's other knee. Riggs then turned, bent, and tore his knife from the second ape-man's mouth, turned back to the crippled first one, kicked flailing hands out of the way, and cut the monster's throat.

As the body collapsed, silence crashed down all around Riggs.

Nothing moved except his heaving chest.

Everyone around him was dead.

Two Squad. All of them. Dead.

Then there were shouts from far away as One Squad came pounding along the halls. Rico and Marchman and the others. The cavalry, riding to the rescue thirty seconds too late. They burst into the chamber and skidded to a halt.

Riggs heard gasps and curses.

And, from someone, a sob.

With a trembling hand, Riggs tapped his earbud to call this in, but there was nothing. There had been nothing since they came down here. Some kind of jammer hidden in the walls.

However, his cell phone vibrated in his pocket.

He frowned and dug it out, wondering why it had a signal when the earbuds did not. He expected it to be Bug trying some alternate way of contacting Shockwave.

It wasn't. Instead it was a text message, which was odd because he never used the message function. Ever.

The caller ID was only a capital letter A. The message read:

> THAT WAS A TASTE.
> NEXT TIME YOU'LL BE THE MEAL.

Riggs stared at the message.

"What the hell?" he murmured.

Chapter Twenty-one

World of Curios, Savannah, Georgia

The sign outside said 72-HOUR LABOR DAY SALE.

The boy who walked into the store did not look like the kind of customer who came to buy. He wore scruffy jeans, a black hoodie with the logo of the seventies band Crass silk-screened onto the back. His hood was up and he had sunglasses perched on a thin nose. Wires from an iPod trailed out from under the hood and disappeared into a pocket. The woman behind the counter spotted him right away and kept an eye on him as he moved from one display to another.

The boy stopped in front of glass display cabinets in which a dozen vintage French crucifixes were arranged with photos of the small towns from which they'd come. Then he moved sideways and stopped in front of an adjoining case that held hand-carved nineteenth-century walking sticks from Italy, Austria, and England.

A customer came to the counter and the saleswoman had to shift her attention to ring up a purchase, but a hissing sound made her jerk her head back to the boy. He had produced a can of spray paint from his pocket and was using it to spray a large letter A on the glass doors of the display case.

"Hey! What are you *doing?*" yelled the saleswoman as she began around the counter.

The boy ignored her and sprayed a letter O around the A. The legs and top spike of the A extended beyond the O.

The woman started to reach for the boy's arm with every intention of snatching the can away from him, but he suddenly turned toward her and sprayed the black paint full into her face.

She screamed and reeled back, bringing up her hands too slowly and too late to protect her eyes. The customer screamed, but she was an older woman and there was nothing she could do to help.

With dry contempt, the boy said, "Didn't anyone ever teach you the right way to think, you stupid bitch? The only action is direct action."

The saleswoman was totally blinded by the paint and she tried to back away, to flee, but instead she banged into a table covered with baskets of small sale items. The boy stepped forward and gave her a sudden and vicious shove, sending her crashing into the table so hard she rebounded and fell to the floor. The baskets and their contents—small guest soaps and specialty candles—rained down on her.

"Stop that!" shouted the older woman.

"Fuck you," said the boy, but he was laughing.

He was still laughing when he started kicking the woman on the floor.

The customer screamed and waddled out of the store as fast as her old, bad legs could carry her.

When she returned with the police, the saleswoman was still on the floor. She had been so comprehensively stomped that her face no longer resembled anything human.

The boy in the hoodie was gone.

No one—not the staff nor the police—noticed the small high-definition video camera attached at floor level near the crime scene. The camera shell was treated with photoreactive chemicals that sampled the background color of the wall and changed the thin layer of treated film on its outside to match. From five feet away it was virtually invisible.

Adams County Law Library, Gettysburg, Pennsylvania

The Adams County Law Library is maintained for use by the Adams County Court of Common Pleas, county officials, county attorneys, and the general public. The focus of the collection is Pennsylvania law. Along with thousands of books on case law, the collection also includes the Pennsylvania Statutes, Pennsylvania Code, and Court Rules.

Martyn Salinger ran the library with quiet pride, knowing it to be an excellent and accessible resource. The crucial information in so many important cases was found here. Maintaining and growing the library made Martyn feel like he mattered in the overall process of justice, and that was something he could take home with him every night. Something that made him want to go to work each day.

As part of a big Get to Know Gettysburg event that covered the whole Labor Day weekend, the library was opened at six in the morning and would remain open until midnight on Monday.

When the young woman came in that morning, Martyn assumed she was a law student. She had that underfed look. Too young to be a clerk, too poorly dressed to be a tourist, too into her own thoughts to be a messenger. She came in with a hooded sweater—he refused to use the term *hoodie*—and a heavy backpack, which she set down on a table. The girl wandered back into the rows of shelved books, apparently studying the titles on the spines with great interest.

"May I help you, miss?" asked Martyn.

She turned to look at him through the nearly opaque lenses of her sunglasses.

"No, thank you," she said politely. "I know what I'm looking for."

"Very well. Let me know if I can help."

She gave him a smile and returned to browsing, and Martyn returned to a LexisNexis search he was doing on his computer for one of the judges. When he looked up a few minutes later he saw that the backpack was still there, but he couldn't spot the girl. She must be all the way in the back.

A few minutes later she still hadn't come out.

Martyn frowned, wondering what it was she could be looking for back there. He got up and drifted down one of the rows, trying to make his approach seem casual.

But the girl wasn't there.

His frown deepened.

He made a circuit of the entire library and could not find her.

Realizing that she must have left and forgotten her bag, he hurried to the table where she'd left it to see if there was something in it that might have a name and phone number, or at least an e-mail address.

He unzipped the bag, which was fat and heavy.

Then he froze and his frown deepened even more.

Not a stack of heavy books, the contents of the backpack seemed to make no sense at all. Inside was a silver pot with a black lid. A pressure cooker. There was a small digital touchpad on the front and the maker's name: Fagor. When Martyn bent close to examine it, he heard a few short, spaced electronic sounds.

Beep . . . beep . . . beep.

He said, "What on earth?"

Those were the last words Martyn Salinger ever spoke.

The pressure cooker exploded. The tightly packed ball bearings, screws, and nails tore him to red rags in a microsecond. Small incendiary charges mixed in with the shrapnel lodged into tables, chairs, and row upon row of books.

By the time the first fire trucks arrived, the library was thoroughly involved. It would be six hours before fire investigators would be able to begin sorting through the rubble, and seven hours before they found the remains of the pressure-cooker bomb.

However, when the trucks rolled up, they could see the thing someone had spray-painted on the front doors.

The letter A surrounded by a rough circle.

Within minutes the fire blackened and then consumed the door. Just as it had the two small cameras mounted inside the library. The video feeds from the cameras had already been sent by the time the components melted.

The LexPlex Sports Arena, Lexington, Kentucky

Duke Hapgood and Cletus Hart were having a long damn morning, and they'd been at it since before dawn's early light. Their H&H delivery truck was too big to back up all the way to the service door, which meant they had to pick up each and every blessed folded gym mat and carry it from the parking lot, across a patch of grass, and into the event space. Ninety steps each way, and there were eighty mats.

"This is fucked up," muttered Cletus. It was probably the twentieth time he'd said it, but Duke couldn't argue with the sentiment.

Inside the event space, two of the other guys were unfolding the mats and laying them out on the floor. So far, thirty-six of the blue-and-tan mats were down, their sides trued up and secured with Velcro. Later those joins would have to be covered with strips of duct tape, and that meant a couple of hours with all four of them walking around on their knees.

"This blows," said Duke, which had become his go-to response every time Cletus made his comment. They were both puffing and bathed in sweat.

All around the edges of the event space, groups of people watched and offered no help at all. Duke wanted to say something smart-ass to them, but everyone was wearing a black belt. Some of them had swords and staffs and all that Jackie Chan shit.

The Kentucky Brawl was an annual Labor Day weekend martial arts tournament that drew competitors from eastern Kentucky, northwestern Tennessee, and the western part of West Virginia. Duke could throw a punch, but he didn't want to complicate the day by brawling with three hundred trained fighters.

Under his breath, he muttered, "Wouldn't kill one of these assholes to give us a hand for five minutes."

Cletus grinned. "They might break a sweat. Couldn't have that."

For some reason they both thought that was funny, and they laughed as they carried the next load in.

On the way out to the truck they passed a couple of kids heading in. Teenagers with hoodies and sunglasses. Cletus and Duke ignored them. The kids were carrying backpacks and had the slacker look, but they were both Asian, so the guys figured they were there for the tournament. They didn't look tough, but you couldn't always tell with kung fu and karate types.

At the truck, Duke stopped and stretched, bending backward with a grunt to try to pop his vertebrae back into place. Cletus opened a couple of cans of Mr. Pibb and handed one to Duke, who stopped stretching to knock back half of his can of pop.

Later, when reporters and police interviewed them, it was Cletus who first said that their lives were saved by Mr. Pibb. If they hadn't stopped to drink their sodas, they would have been inside when the bombs went off.

As it was, they were only flash-burned and bruised from the shock-wave that picked them up and flung them against the stack of mats waiting to be carried inside. They were not among the eighteen dead and ninety wounded.

In one of those public relations decisions that defy rational explanation, the Coca-Cola company, manufacturers of Mr. Pibb, gave the boys a lifetime supply of Pibb and hired them for public appearances. They became known as the Pibb Boys.

Even Duke and Cletus thought that was weird.

Their story went unnoticed, however, by the people who received the video feed from cameras placed inside the arena prior to the detonation of the bombs.

Chapter Twenty-two

The Hangar
Floyd Bennett Field, Brooklyn
Sunday, August 31, 8:38 a.m.

Rudy and I had just pulled into the cavernous hangar that gives the Brooklyn DMS headquarters its name. The hangar itself is mostly a parking garage. From the outside it looks like a dilapidated abandoned building. Lots of broken windows and obscene graffiti. But that was all for show. There was a double shell to the building, and directly behind those broken windows was a curved screen that projected a false interior view that reinforced the image of squalor. But behind that screen were walls of steel-reinforced concrete, sensors, alarms, and hidden guard posts. The guards who walked the perimeter were dressed to look like laborers working on restoring the building. They weren't. Most were former DMS field-team shooters who were either too old for active fieldwork or who'd been injured on the job and couldn't roll out for the kind of thing Echo Team faces down. Even so, it would be a serious mistake to mistake them for old guys or cripples. That would be bad in very messy ways.

My cell vibrated. I killed the Explorer's engine and pulled my phone out of my pocket. It was another text message from "A."

ONE OR THOUSANDS?
HOW DO YOU CHOOSE?

I showed it to Rudy.

"Nicely vague," he said. "There's no context to suggest a meaning."

I grunted something unpleasant and forwarded the message to Bug.

As we climbed out of the Explorer we were met by Gunnery Sergeant Brick Anderson, a massive and battle-scarred black man with a metal leg and hands that I'm pretty sure could crush a Volvo. When Gus Dietrich had been killed at the Warehouse last year, Brick had stepped up to take his place as Mr. Church's personal aide and bodyguard. He wasn't as tall as Bunny, but he had bigger arms and a broader chest. He usually had a genial smile, though he wasn't wearing one now.

"What's wrong?" asked Rudy as soon as he spotted Brick's troubled expression.

"The big man will fill you in," said Brick, "but the short version is that Shockwave Team just got cut in half on a routine look-and-see in Virginia."

"*Dios mio!*" gasped Rudy.

The bottom seemed to fall out of my stomach. "What happened?"

"They rolled on a tip that a Chechnyan extremist team was in-country to start some shit over the Labor Day weekend. Riggs and his boys kicked the door, but it wasn't Chechnyans waiting for them, and Riggs lost all of Two Squad."

I bared my teeth. "Who ambushed them?"

There was a queer look in Brick's dark eyes. "That's the weird part, man. Like I said, these weren't Chechnyans."

He pulled his smartphone and opened the image files. The picture he showed us was a dead man. The face was distorted, brutish, with a heavy brow, wide nose, thin lips, and teeth with overgrown incisors.

"Berserkers . . . ?" whispered Rudy. "I thought . . . I thought . . ."

"Come on," said Brick. "The big man will give you the full briefing."

Chapter Twenty-three

Office of the Vice President
The White House
Washington, D.C.
Sunday, August 31, 8:39 a.m.

"Sir!" cried Boo Radley as he burst into the office. "There's something on the news. You have to see this."

William Collins quickly closed his phone and hid it between his thighs, out of sight of his chief of staff.

"See what?" he asked.

Radley snatched the TV remote from the coffee table, aimed it at the flatscreen on the wall, and turned up the volume. The screen was filled with the face of a lovely Asian woman in a Betty Page black Dutchboy and opaque movie star sunglasses. Below her image was a banner: WHO IS MOTHER NIGHT?

The woman was speaking. ". . . are slaves only if we allow ourselves to be slaves. We are free if we take to the streets and *take* the streets back."

"Teresa Naylor at the President's office called to alert me about this," said Radley. "It's on every station. Some kind of computer virus that's hacked into all the news feeds."

Collins held a finger to his lips. "Shhhh, I want to hear this."

". . . That wasn't anarchy. The pigs in the system haven't *seen* anarchy. Not yet." The woman licked her lips "But it's coming. The only action is direct action."

It took every ounce of willpower the vice president possessed not to smile. Not to leer. That smile was delicious.

"Mother Night," he said softly.

The video ended and after a few awkward moments the face of the Fox News reporter blinked onto the screen, looking confused and angry. He immediately began jabbering, but Collins took the remote and muted the TV, then tossed the device onto his desk blotter.

"The White House needs to make a response," said Radley.

"That's the President's job," said Collins.

"But—"

"*But*," interrupted Collins, "whoever did this had to have hacked into the systems. That means it's a cybercrime. And that makes it ours and we have to jump on this. Right fucking now. Get the team on this and set up a conference call with the divisional leaders. Do it now."

Radley spun and nearly ran from the room, his eyes suddenly alight with purpose.

Then Collins sat back, laced his fingers behind his head, and stared at the ceiling, enjoying the way a smile felt on his face. He thought about the face of Mother Night. About her lips.

Those lips were incredibly sexy.

Full and ripe.

He remembered the way they looked when she kissed her way slowly up his thighs this morning.

Chapter Twenty-four

Mother Night arrived back in Atlanta courtesy of a private jet and driver. Her suite at the Westin was on the sixty-ninth floor, well above the motion and noise of the convention that sprawled among that hotel and four others here in the heart of Atlanta. She had other rooms—bolt holes, changing rooms, and staging areas—at the other four hotels that formed the loose quad used as a kind of convention center here in the heart of Atlanta.

Sixty thousand people thronged the streets and lobbies of those hotels. They were all very loud and everywhere you looked there was a dense crowd of people, more than half of whom were in costume. Mother Night had walked among them several times over the last two days, sometimes dressed as Lara Croft from Tomb Raider—and she knew she had the legs to rock that costume; other times as Jill Valentine from Resident Evil, Sophitia Alexandra from SoulCalibur, and the other night she danced herself blind at a party while wearing the full bat-wing costume of Morrigan Aensland from Dark Stalker. She'd had to glue her breasts into the costume to keep from flashing the fanboys. Though later, when she'd cut one guy out of the pack and dragged him off to one of her rented rooms, he'd been so eager to get her out of her bustier that he nearly tore her nipples off. It was very good glue.

The pain was a turn-on for both of them.

Just like it was with Bill Collins. She never once left his bed without bruises or the burning imprint of his open palm on her flesh.

She had a costume ready for later today—Lucy Kuo from Infamous 2—for the big event in the afternoon. The costume was perfect. She'd made it by hand and every attention to detail was paid. Her body was ready for that costume, too. Brazilian surgeons had given her bigger and better boobs, sculpted her cheekbones, thinned her nose, and puffed up her lips. With the ass and legs genetics had given her, she knew that she was a knockout, a knock 'em dead statuesque beauty, and when she walked out in a costume everyone noticed her. Everyone. Male, female, traffic cops, everyone with eyes.

That was fine. Mother Night wanted to be noticed.

Right now, though, she was dressed in a different costume, as a character from an entirely different game. She was dressed as Mother Night from the game Burn to Shine.

Her own creations. Persona and game.

In all of gaming, there was no more dangerous a female character. Not a shooter, not a sword-wielding killer of orcs and war machines, nothing like that. Mother Night was a different kind of power. She had others to do the killing for her, to crack the game levels, to rack up the points.

She had an army.

And as she sat there at the computer, she watched the first news reports about that army. None of it connected yet. Not event to event, or events to her. That was the next level of the game. However, on her monitor she watched the first fires being set in Lexington, in Gettysburg, in Savannah.

With so many more to come.

Her long, slender fingers danced over the keys, capturing the news feeds and sending them to recipients in a dozen countries.

She felt her heart racing.

Hammering.

With a start she realized that her whole body was trembling. Sweat was gathering under her clothes and in the hollows of her palms.

It *had* started.

Her children were going to war.

She suddenly felt so strange. Nausea churned in her stomach and she abruptly stood and headed quickly toward the bathroom, but suddenly the floor seemed to tilt under her. She staggered sideways and hit the wall next to the bathroom door. Her balance was so ruined that she hit hard, bruising her shoulder, knocking her head against the wall, sliding down, collapsing onto the floor. Her rump struck the polished marble hard enough to knock her teeth together.

"What . . . what . . . ?" she demanded of the moment.

The shakes started then, sweeping through her, running like cold fire through her skin, pebbling her flesh with goose bumps, striking sparks in her eyes.

"What's happening?" she screamed.

The shivers continued, wave after wave. Tears broke from the corners of her eyes and ran in hot lines down her cheeks.

"What's happening?"

This time the question was spoken in a tiny voice. Lost, and without hope of an answer.

But deep down she knew what was happening.

After all, it wasn't the first time something like this had occurred.

There were other times.

Three so far. Three she knew of, but she suspected there had been others. Fugue states that were wiped from her memory but which had left her asleep in strange places. The living room floor in her apartment. In the backseat of her car. Once on a bench by a river a hundred miles from where she lived.

It was all stress, she told herself.

Just that.

It had started years ago. The first had really been the worst, when a young woman who looked very much like her was murdered in a horrible way. Burned alive. Mother Night hadn't been there, but she imagined the screams and they echoed in her head for many nights after that. Drugs, alcohol, and hard sex with brutal men helped, but only when she was awake. Whenever she slept, those screams were there.

The death was necessary, of course. Mother Night knew and accepted that. If the girl hadn't died, then Mother Night could never have been born. When viewed as a problem in mathematics, of cause and effect, then it was easier to bear.

And the girl who'd died volunteered for it. Begged for it.

Of course she did. She'd been carefully picked and cultivated for that one purpose.

The woman who'd thrown the gasoline and match was less important, and her death two days later—her head was rammed into the shower wall a dozen times—meant nothing to Mother Night. The woman was a parasite who was going down for her third felony conviction on the three strikes rule. She'd thought the torch job was a payday, and that's all it was to her. The same went for the two dykes Mother Night paid to kill her in the shower. They, at least, were more or less human, and when they got out of jail they'd have money waiting.

But that burning girl.

God.

The shakes had been worse then.

They'd come again when the hit team she sent after Reginald Boyd had been slaughtered by Joe Ledger. It did not matter that their deaths were an almost foregone conclusion. Either they would die, or Boyd and Ledger would die, or some combination thereof.

When she heard that all of her people had died, and that Ledger had strangled pretty little Luisa Kan, the shakes came back. Very nasty, very intense. Mother Night had thrown up repeatedly and had diarrhea for two days.

It was nearly as bad when she'd helped torture a rogue scientist in Vilnius. Mother Night thought that it would be fun, that it would be interesting. Maybe even a turn-on. Instead it had been loud and ugly and smelly, and it had sickened her.

Even so . . .

That time wasn't as bad as the fiery death of the girl in prison.

Now the shakes were back.

Damn it, they were back.

Anger flared in her so intensely that it nearly pushed back the horror.

And that's what it was.

Horror.

Her people were out there killing people. With bombs, guns, knives, bare hands. On the news, the police were throwing out wild estimates of the dead in Lexington.

That was the tip of the iceberg.

There would be so many more deaths. Today. Tonight.

Tomorrow.

So many more.

Her teeth chattered as if she sat in a cold wind.

"Stop it," she snarled. She bared her teeth at the world, at whatever part of her was so weak, so feeble, so chickenshit that it rebelled against the reality of everything she had spent years planning. She was smart enough to know that this was her conscience fighting for its existence. Fighting as hard as it could even though the battle had been lost when that match touched the gasoline-soaked flesh of a young woman in a lonely prison cell.

"Fuck you!" she screamed at the air around her.

The echo of it punched her in the face, the ears, the heart.

But she drew in as deep a breath as she could and screamed it out again, tensing every muscle, balling her fists, straining the muscles in her throat, roaring it with black hatred at her own weakness.

"*Fuck you!*"

The shakes rippled once more. Again.

Then stopped.

Mother Night sat there on the hard floor, her back against the wall, panting like a dog, fingernails gouging the flesh of her palms.

"Fuck you," she whispered.

That whisper was as cold as dead stone.

She detested the weakness inside of her. The part of her who still *felt*. The part of her who wanted to put the barrel of a gun into her mouth and pull the trigger. The part of her that craved to punish and be punished for sins committed and pending.

"Fuck you," she said again.

She could hear the news reporters growing hysterical as they speculated on whether the bombings were connected. Was this another Boston Marathon? Was this something new? Was it terrorism? Was is Muslims? Was it militiamen? The rumors and theories flew and escalated with each new body added to the count.

The people to whom she'd sent these news links would be watching. They would be expecting her to call. Her, Mother Night, not a weeping suicidal fool who had no guts or backbone.

After a long while she clawed her way to her feet and shambled into the bathroom to wash away the stink of regret. She had important video calls to make and she was damn well not going to show any sign of weakness.

"Fuck you," she said one last time.

Chapter Twenty-five

Church wasn't available to see me, so I had to gird my loins to face Aunt Sallie.

She looked like Whoopi Goldberg but had the personality of an alligator with hemorrhoids. No, check that, a hemorrhoidal gator would be much nicer. It's my personal opinion that Auntie wasn't so much born as burst out of someone's chest like one of those creatures in those alien movies. Her opinion of me is slightly lower than that of used toilet paper stuck to her shoe. You'll be shocked to learn that we have failed to bond.

In the hierarchy of the DMS, she was the appropriately named "number two," and she ran the Hangar as if it were her private ring of hell. She and Church had history going back decades and there were rumors that once upon a time Aunt Sallie was one of the most feared shooters in the world. I believe those rumors.

Ghost disliked her as intensely as I did, but he stood behind me, out of her line of sight. Brave combat dog.

When Rudy and I asked her about Samson Riggs and Shockwave, her reply was pure Aunt Sallie. "He walked into a trap and had his ass handed to him. Fucking idiot got his people killed."

"That's hardly fair, Auntie," protested Rudy.

She ignored him. They get along once in a while, but on a day-to-day basis the only person who can actually stand Auntie is Dr. Hu. And there's a real surprise.

As for Colonel Samson Riggs, he was about as far away from being a "fucking idiot" as it was possible to get. He was the top team leader in the Department of Military Sciences, a real-life James Bond type who was smart, good-looking, suave, talented, inventive, and tougher than anyone I've ever met. Am I gushing like a fanboy? Maybe. Riggs was everything I wanted to be, and while normally natural human envy might dictate that I hate him, I didn't. Maybe couldn't. He was how I imagined Church might have been back in the day, except Riggs had a set of human emotions. I've done six missions with him, and each time I came away knowing more about how to do my job that I could have learned anywhere else. The fact that I had nearly as high a clearance rate as him meant nothing to me except that he set so great an example that I aspired to be like him, and maybe that brought my game up to a higher level. Hard to say.

His team were all heroes. No joke. Actual saved-the-world heroes.

To think that he'd lost four of them was appalling.

"Do we know where those Berserkers came from?" I asked.

Auntie shrugged. "That's being looked into."

"You want me to take Echo out there to—?" I began, but Auntie shook her head.

"You're supposed to be screening recruits, Ledger," she said sharply. "We need that done, so don't try to skip out on your responsibilities."

Ghost growled low and mean.

Aunt Sallie glared at him. "Growl at me again and yours wouldn't be the first nuts I've cut off."

Ghost did his best impersonation of a hole in the air.

I smiled at Auntie. "Do you spend time every night looking in a mirror and practicing how to scowl?"

She smiled back. "No, I look at a picture of you and practice gagging. Now get to work. If there's anything you need to know, you'll be told, so stop bothering me. I have grown-up work to do."

With that she turned and headed off to the TOC—the Tactical Operations Center—leaving Rudy and I standing in a pool of her disapproval. When she was well out of earshot, Ghost gave another low growl.

"That was refreshing," murmured Rudy.

"I know, chatting with her always validates me as a person."

He looked at his watch. "I'd better see if Samson needs me out there. His team must be in a great deal of pain."

"No doubt. Give them my best. I'll call Riggs later on."

Rudy nodded and head off.

"Come on, fierce descendant of wolves," I said to Ghost, who slunk along at my heels.

Chapter Twenty-six

Colonel Sim Sa-jeong sat at his workstation and watched a series of events unfold half a world away. Six separate windows had opened on his monitor, each one obscuring the face of the person with whom he had been communicating. One window showed a sports arena in Kentucky seconds before bombs exploded. Another showed a random act of brutal murder in a fine-arts store. The rest were similar. Brutality and explosions.

Sim reached for his cup of tea but it remained in his white-knuckled fingers for long minutes, the tea growing as cold as the blood in his veins.

Then, one by the one, the small windows winked out until only the original image remained. The smiling face of a woman.

She spoke in English, not bothering to provide a translation. Sim had been assigned as her contact here in North Korea because his English was very good. A similar arrangement had been made, he was certain, in other countries.

The woman said, "Do I have your attention?"

Sim cleared his throat. "You do," he said. "But of what value are these acts? Small bombs? Casual murders? Are we supposed to care about petty violence in America? We already know that it is a nation filled with corruption and—"

"Please," said the woman, "let us forgo speeches. They are trite and repeated by rote, and I do not care to hear them."

"Then—"

"These events are intended for three reasons," she said. "The first is to get your attention, which I believe I have."

Colonel Sim said nothing.

"The second is to make sure that the signals from the cameras are routed properly to you."

Sim again said nothing, waiting for what was surely the true point of this elaborate and highly dangerous contact.

"And the third is to inform you that the auction will commence on schedule. Five minutes before the bidding begins I will send a call-in code and a banking routing number. Each bidder will receive a separate routing number. Any attempt to use that routing number for any purpose except to make a bid will result in termination."

"Termination of what?"

The woman merely smiled and this time she did not answer.

Sim considered. "You ask a lot and yet we do not know this thing on which we are expected to bid? Do you take us as fools? Do you expect us to bid on crude bombs such as the ones—?"

"Of course not," she said smoothly, her smile never wavering. "You are bidding on something that will change the nature of the arms race. Something that will, in fact, end it. If you bid correctly, it will end the inequality of the arms race solidly in your favor."

"This is needlessly cryptic."

"Is it?" She laughed. The woman had a deep, throaty laugh that Sim found entirely unpleasant. "Make sure someone is watching this feed, Colonel. By the time the bidding begins you will have no doubts as to the value of what we are selling."

"What assurances can you provide that this is not an elaborate trick?"

"Beyond seventeen weeks of your own vetting process?" she asked.

"Yes. Beyond even that."

"Keep watching the feed, Colonel. By the opening bell you will have no doubts at all. I can guarantee it."

Before he could respond, the face vanished, replaced by a placeholder image of a sloppily painted letter A surrounded by a tight letter O. Even in China the symbol was known. It represented a concept that was totally antithetical to the strict Marxist social-political concept of the dictatorship of the proletariat.

It was the circle-A.

A for Anarchy. O for Order. And its polluted philosophy:

Anarchy is the mother of order.

Chapter Twenty-seven

I sat on a nuclear bomb, swinging one foot, cleaning my nails with the tip of a skinning knife. All around me people I liked were beating the hell out of each other.

Ghost lay at my feet, chewing on an arm.

It was a normal Tuesday for me.

The arm, by the way, was rubber. It's been a running gag with my crew to appease the fur monster by giving him toys shaped like human hands, arms, and legs. Occasionally they'd give Ghost toys fashioned to look like even more sensitive body parts. I took those away from him. Ghost sleeps on the foot of my bed. I don't want him to get ideas.

I sipped a cup of Death Wish coffee and watched the members of Echo Team go through armed and unarmed combat drills with a bunch of candidates sent to us by Delta, the SEALs, Force Recon, and FBI Hostage Rescue. These guys were the survivors of a group of ninety-two we'd started with two weeks ago, and this was why we were here in Brooklyn. The job would normally have fallen to the senior team leader at the Hangar, but he was still in the hospital recovering from injuries received on a bitch of a mission that had, among other things, landed him in a pit filled with genetically altered pit bulls. The smallest of those dogs had been 140 pounds. The rest of his team was in various states of recovery and rehab.

Very frequently our job sucks.

I'd brought the six remaining members of my own battered Echo Team with me to Brooklyn, and they were currently pitted against the last fourteen candidates. There was a lot of grunting, cursing, sweating, thudding, and groaning going on.

Very little of it from my guys, I was happy to see. Happy, but not surprised. Echo Team has walked a lot of hard miles through the Valley of the Shadow.

A wooden knife came sailing through the air, hit the mat in front of me, and bounced up to thud against the bomb. The resulting *carroom* was hollow. Most of the bomb was a shell; a Teller-Ulam case was enough to make a point during lectures. It had a dummy electronics package for disarming drills, but no fissile materials.

We're macho manly men, but we're not stupid.

As I watched, a Cro-Magnon-looking guy who'd been a first-team shooter for Delta grinned as he closed on the oldest man on Echo—Top Sims, who was pushing forty-five now. The Delta shooter saw an old man with gray threaded through his hair, a seamed brown face, and crow's feet. Easy meat. The Delta bad boy grinned and went for it.

The next thing the bad boy saw was the mat coming up to smack him in the face. I doubt he ever saw the punches and kicks Top used to knock a big chunk of ego off him. Next time maybe he'd fight the man rather than the assumption.

Ghost glanced up as the man hit the deck, and I swear to God I heard him snicker.

My guys—Top, Bunny, Lydia, Ivan, and Sam were dressed in black BDU trousers and T-shirts with the green Echo Team insignia on the chest. Someone—I suspect Bunny—had added a scroll of words around the insignia as an unofficial motto for the team: *If It's Weird and Pissed Off—We Shoot It.*

Crazy, but sometimes there is truth in advertising.

Besides, lately there was a lot of very bad stuff happening in the world. The DMS was stretched way too thin, hence the push to recruit some newbies. There was not one field team operating at full compliment. Not even Buffalo Team in North Dakota, which was nicknamed the "sewing circle" because they usually had twice the downtime of other groups. Not anymore. Buffalo Team had been chopped pretty badly in three successive gigs that left them with only two uninjured operators and four with moderate injuries who could still roll out at need. Hell, even our frequent collaborators in SEAL Team Six and the FBI's Hostage Rescue Teams were being run ragged. This wasn't a new war against a single enemy. It was everywhere. Cartels rolling with body armor and high-tech firearms, religious fundamentalists with bombs, splinter cells buried like ticks in the skin of society, and let's not forget a bunch of supposedly not officially sanctioned hit teams from China, Iran, Russia, and North Korea, neo-Nazis, and, yeah, even some secret societies. Everybody was cranky and the bad guys seemed bent on turning the whole world into a war zone. We needed to replenish all of our existing teams that had taken losses and put additional teams in the field, and we needed to do it yesterday.

I'd hoped we'd have more than fourteen left out of ninety-two. But one by one the candidates from that larger group had demonstrated qualities inconsistent with what we needed. Anyone who showed hesitation in a crisis was instantly cut. Anyone who couldn't switch from pack member to leader and back again was gone. Anyone who lost a step when mission parameters were changed was out. Anyone who couldn't take the bullshit, pain, and hardship we dealt was let go.

That left fourteen.

I set my coffee cup down and hefted my knife. This one was steel and it was sharp.

"Incoming!" I yelled, and threw the knife randomly into the mass of tussling bodies.

They all scattered, dodging and diving out of the way. All but one of them cut sharp looks at me as they moved. One guy, a wiry goofball with a shaved head, evaded the knife—which landed with a *thunk* in the middle of a training mat—but the way he did it pissed me off.

"Top," I said.

Top had caught it too. His eyes blazed as he rose to his feet and bellowed, "Ten-*shun!*" with his leather-throated drillmaster's voice. Everyone snapped to immediate attention, including the goofball. I picked up my coffee and sipped it while Top handled this.

He got up in the kid's face. Top is about six feet tall but when he's mad he's a roaring giant.

"Soldier," he roared, "what were you evading?"

"Knife, sir."

"'Sir'? *Sir?* Don't call me sir, goddamn it. You think I'm an officer? I *work* for a living."

"Knife, Sergeant Major."

"Did you look to *see* if it was a knife?"

"No, Sergeant Major, but I—"

Top got a little closer. "How did you know it *was* a knife?"

"It was a knife drill—"

As soon as those first words were out the goofball tried to put the brakes on, tried to keep the rest of that sentence in his own head. I heard a couple of the other guys hiss the way people do when someone else steps barefoot into his own shit.

Lydia and Bunny were silently shaking their heads. Sam sighed. I heard Ivan mutter, "Oh, hog balls."

No need to repeat exactly what Top said to the goofball. It was all bad, it was all nasty, and it was all deserved. In combat training you don't react to what you think the drill is, you react to what is actually happening. It was a worse mistake than when the Delta shooter had underestimated Top. It was the kind of mistake a Special Forces operator should never make. There is no margin for error, no allowing for those kinds of assumptions. It made me wish I'd thrown a flash-bang instead of a knife, because that would have hammered home the point.

"So you just assumed it was a knife because it was a knife drill," roared Top, "Your psychic powers eliminated every other possibility so that you did not even have to so much as turn your head to see what you were evading?"

"I'm sorry, Sergeant Major, it won't happen again."

"Tell me, son, who had the sheer audacity to send you to us?" demanded Top. "Who hates us that much?"

"Army Rangers, Sergeant Major."

"Bullshit, son," growled Top in a voice that shook the rafters. "I am an Army Ranger and Captain Ledger is an Army Ranger and the Army Rangers don't have a clown college, so you can't be an Army goddamn Ranger, now can you? I want you to get your shit and get the hell off of my training floor." Top paused for a millisecond. "Why am I still looking at you?"

It was harsh and it was humiliating, and usually neither Top nor I go in much for a public dressing-down. But it was such a rookie mistake that any operator who was here right now would have doubts about this kid when it came to real combat. That kind of split focus and weakened trust would get people killed. Not *could* get people killed—it absolutely would.

The Department of Military Sciences is a tough gig. Mr. Church built it around teams of operators who were not among the best, they *were* the best. The top men and women recruited from active service in Delta, the SEALs, and elsewhere. The best of the best without exaggeration. It wasn't an ego thing or a prestige thing. These soldiers had to be that good because of what we faced day in, day out.

However, while I was watching this incident I wondered how an ordinary citizen would react. They'd probably think that this was comical, or that it was needlessly cruel. That it was a bunch of macho thugs comparing dicks. From a distance, it looked just like that. But if that same citizen could see guys like Top in real combat, fighting the monsters we fight, then they might take a longer pause before passing judgment. This isn't a Sylvester Stallone flick and it's not a comic book. This is the world, and the world is a far scarier place than Joe Ordinary will ever know.

Ivan said, "Dog balls."

Most things were some species of balls to Ivan.

The room fell into silence as the Ranger, his face flushed to scarlet, gathered up his gear and walked to the locker room. His backbone was straight, though, I'll give him that. With luck, this incident will have burned out the last traces of slack assumption in him. He might go on to be the kind of soldier who would deserve his slot on our team. We'll never know, though, because there are no callbacks in this theater.

When the door closed, everyone turned toward me. My guys and the recruits. I looked at them, particularly the new guys, looking for resentment, for hostility, for accusing glares. Anyone who pinned his own emotion to what had just happened was going to split cab fare with the Ranger. All I saw were serious faces from the thirteen remaining candidates. I waited out a three-count and then gave them a single, curt nod.

"Any questions?" I asked.

There were none.

"Very well," I said. "New drill, Top—three to two, broken leg."

"Bite my balls," said Ivan, but he was grinning, enjoying what was coming. Lydia laughed and punched him on the arm.

Top gave me a curt nod. It was one of his favorite scenarios, too.

The group was divided into five-man teams. Three bad guys, two good guys; but the kicker was that one of the good guys was to simulate having a badly broken leg. Working together, the good guys had to fight their way past the three opponents, cross fifty feet of the mat, and cross a safe line Top had taped on the far side. The bad guys were allowed to have wooden knives and clubs. The good guys were not.

It was a bitch of an exercise. There were variations of it to simulate broken arms, being blinded, or in bigger groups having two soldiers protect a "shot" comrade from the whole rest of the team. There was nothing academic about any of this, most of the people in this room had already been in one real-life version of this kind of thing. And that's a damn sad fact to report.

Ghost, however, sat up to watch and was apparently entertained by the thuds of wood on skin and the sounds fighters made when their mock opponents weren't feeling all fuzzy and warm.

My phone rang. The screen display showed an icon of a steeple.

My boss, Mr. Church. Before I could get anything else out he cut me off. "My office. Now."

Chapter Twenty-eight

The Hangar
Floyd Bennett Field, Brooklyn
Sunday, August 31, 11:33 a.m.

Church was alone in his office and he gestured for me to close the door and sit. I dropped into a leather chair. Ghost sat in the corner, watching us both.

"Captain," Church said without preamble, "we are having an interesting day."

"I know. I heard about Riggs and the Berserkers."

"Before we get to that, where are we with the candidates? How soon before they're ready to roll?"

I sucked my teeth. " 'Roll' as in begin official training, or 'roll' as in go into the field?"

"The field."

"Ideally? Three weeks. Why, how much time do I have?"

"Almost none. We're having an interesting day."

"I hate the word *interesting*."

He snorted. "So far most of what's happening does not directly involve us, but I don't like the way the day is shaping up. If things move in a certain direction I would hate to lose a step getting into gear. To that end, we may have to dismiss anyone who needs hand-holding and assign the rest where they'll do the most good."

"That bad, huh?"

He merely grunted. There was a beautiful cut-glass water pitcher and two glasses on his desk. He poured us each a glass. In the middle of the desk, perhaps slightly closer to him than me, was a plate of cookies. Church always had cookies. If he had to jump off a sinking ship in only his skivvies he'd land in a lifeboat that was stocked with cookies. They were either his only weakness—or perhaps the only proof of his humanity—or maybe there was some kind of significance to the cookies. To which ones were on offer apart from his ubiquitous vanilla wafers; and to the times he offered one, or didn't, and how many he ate—and how often. Rudy and I have been trying to work it out for years. We were sure there was something there.

Or maybe Rudy and I had become batshit paranoid. Jury was still out.

Church took a vanilla wafer, tapped the crumbs off, took a small bite, and set the cookie down in the precise center of a paper napkin. "Have you watched the news this morning?"

"No. Been busy making life miserable for the candidates. Why? Are the Berserkers—?"

"No. We have no news on that situation. However, a bomb was detonated this morning at a sports center in Lexington, Kentucky. Initial reports suggest it was a backpack bomb similar to the Boston Marathon event some years ago."

"More Chechnyans?" I asked.

"Witnesses say that the suspects were two teenage boys, probably Asian." He described the situation. "This is breaking news, so you now know as much as I do. However, I rolled Moonshine Team to provide any on-site assistance, and I put them at the disposal of the ATF and local law."

"Okay."

"There was also an explosion at a law library in Gettysburg. One casualty, no witnesses. Nature of the bomb is unknown. So far no one is connecting the two, but I dislike coincidences. I sent Liberty Bell Team via helo to put eyes on that."

I nodded.

"We don't yet know if these are connected to each other or to the situation developing on the Net."

"Yeah, Bug sent something for me to watch, something about a hacker video, but I haven't had time to take a look. It didn't seem to be our sort of thing."

"Take a look now, Captain," he said. "I think you'll find that it's very much our thing."

He picked up a remote and pointed it at the flatscreen on the wall. The face of a pretty Korean gal appeared on the screen. Betty Page haircut, big sunglasses, bright red lipstick.

"Okay, monkeys," said the Korean girl, "pay attention, 'cause there are three things you need to know and Mother Night is here to tell you."

We watched the video. Twice.

"Crap," I said. "Mother Night? She's back? How old is this?"

"It's a combination of a brief prerecorded video loop used as a place-holder, probably to attract attention, followed by what appears to be a live feed."

"That girl . . . she looks like the one I . . ."

Church's eyes were dark marbles behind the tinted lenses of his glasses. He waited for me to continue. "Very similar," he said, "but we ran facial recognition on both women and they are not a match. This woman is likely as much as ten years older. And before this video began there was a second video, a loop of yet another Asian woman in an identical costume."

"What's that mean? Is Mother Night a *them* rather than a *her?*"

"Unknown."

"Jesus," I said. "We should keep a lid on this. Who's seen the video?"

Church sighed. "Too many people. This 'Mother Night' video, as it's already being called, appeared in an extraordinary number of places via a Trojan horse that contained some very sophisticated intrusion viruses. Conservative estimate is two hundred million computers have been infected, very likely over a period of weeks or months. Bug said you could position this kind of Trojan horse on search engines like Wikipedia or stream sites such as Netflix and Hulu. Naturally, every news network has broadcast it. Bug tells me that it has already gone viral on YouTube."

"Shit."

"There's more. Vice President Collins has been in touch with me."

"Of course he has," I said sourly. When Ghost heard the name Collins, he made one of his low growly noises. Not the kind of noise you'd want to hear when your name was mentioned. "Dare I ask what he said?"

Church pursed his lips. "He has officially informed me that his Cybercrimes Task Force is taking jurisdiction of this matter because he is convinced it falls under the umbrella of the VaultBreaker case."

"Really? 'Cause I think that whole attempted-murder thing in Baltimore dribbled the Mother Night case into our court."

"Not according to him," continued Church. "The Veep went on to say that we are to offer additional field support to the CTF."

"'Field support'?" I said, giving it the same inflection you'd give "nutsack pimple."

"Yes. He would like us to run down a few things for him."

I smiled. "Like what? Pick up his dry cleaning and walk his dog? I mean, did I miss the part where we became his lackeys?"

"If so, then I missed the same memo. And it's highly likely that task list will be misfiled." Church pursed his lips. "The Veep is a difficult man to admire. However, our immediate concern is Mother Night."

He replayed the video.

"What's the deal with the anarchist rant?" I asked.

"The phrasing is a bit glib," he said. "It could be a deflection. Nor does it give us insight to her real agenda."

"Oh boy." I thought about it. "And Labor Day's on Monday. Are we thinking that the anarchy thing and Mother Night's field trips to mad science labs are connected? It's a stretch, but I can see it. Maybe. Labor is work, working for a wage, working for the system, working for the Man, that sort of thing. Could be some kind of proletariat link there—"

"It's possible," Church said dubiously.

"Wouldn't be the first time some bonehead's confused anarchy with socialism or Marxism. Most people don't know the difference."

He made a noncommittal sound, unconvinced.

I changed direction. "Much as I really hate to do it, I could also make a case for the anarchist comment and the bombs in Gettysburg and Lexington to be connected."

"I agree with you on that much," Church said. "It's why I sent teams to each location. Dr. Sanchez and Circe are currently reviewing the video in hopes of decrypting any possible subtext. It's Circe's fear that if this is an anarchist matter then the 'burn to shine' reference may be a coded call to arms."

"That's the same phrase Violin said had been painted in blood on a lab full of dead people."

"Yes," Church said, nodding. He tapped a key on his laptop and Bug's brown, bespectacled face filled the big screen on the wall. "Where are you with the 'burn to shine' analysis?"

"I have a couple of things so far. Oh, hey, hi, Joe. And is that Ghostie? How's it going, pups?"

Ghost thumped his tail a few times. He likes Bug. He doesn't wag his tail around Aunt Sallie or Dr. Hu. Ghost is a very discerning dog.

"Bug . . ." Church prompted.

"Right, burn to shine. That's a very pop-culture phrase. Kind of a twist off the old 'candle that burns brightest burns half as long.' Or maybe the other one, you know, it's better to burn out than fade away."

"Specific examples?" asked Church.

"Sure. Burn to Shine is the name of a series of direct-to-DVD film projects created by Christoph Green and Brendan Canty—he used to be the drummer for Fugazi. Get this—for each DVD they select a house that's scheduled for destruction and then get a local band to curate the event. They do a rock concert as part of the daylong event to destroy the house. The DVDs document each house's history and so on. Not recent, though. Last one was in 2008."

"'Destruction of houses,'" I echoed. "Gettysburg and Lexington . . . ?"

"Possible," said Church, "or a general reference to destruction of any established structure or organization. Government, schools . . ."

"There's more," said Bug. "First off, a lot of musicians seem to grab that as a title or lyric. There was an album of that name by Ben Harper and the Innocent Criminals back in 1999. Rudy thinks that 'innocent criminals' could be one extreme interpretation of anarchists who cause destruction based on their beliefs that society needs to be torn down. If it's what society needs then it isn't criminal."

"Got it," I said. "Anything else?"

"Lots, but one more that Circe thinks might fit."

"Hit me."

"Remember that show, *The Sopranos*? The theme song was by a group called Alabama Three. There's a line, 'You're one in a million. You've got to burn to shine.'"

"Right," I said.

"Well, get this, in the context of that song that advice is given as a quote from the singer's mother. And, guys, remember, in the beginning of the song he wakes up and gets himself a gun."

Church said, "Ah."

"I'm compiling a list of all references in music, song, books, whatever. It'll be a long list, though, 'cause I'm including direct quotes and anything that kind of says the same thing."

"Good work, Bug," said Church. "Keep us posted."

"Wait," I said quickly. "Bug, did you get anywhere with those text messages I've been getting?"

Bug looked troubled. "Actually, Joe, Samson Riggs got one, too. Right after the fight in Virginia." He told me about it. "Same thing, though. No real caller ID and a dead end on a traceback."

"How's that possible? The only person who could block MindReader was Hugo Vox, and we now *have* that tech courtesy of that weasel Toys."

Toys, aka Alexander Chismer, was a wanted criminal who had first served as assistant and valet to Sebastian Gault and later to Hugo Vox and the Seven Kings. He was on the most-wanted list in thirty countries.

"What can I tell you, Joe?" said Bug.

"You can tell me where I can find Toys so I can park my car on him. If he's selling Vox's technology—"

"He's not," Church said. "In fact, Mr. Chismer was quite helpful to us since he resigned from the Seven Kings organization. He is not currently on our wanted list."

"He's on mine," I insisted.

Church gave me a long look through the tinted lenses of his glasses. "No, Captain, he is not. I believe you'll discover that Mr. Chismer has become quite a useful ally. He is, of course, under constant scrutiny. However, he is designated a friendly and that means all hands off."

It was not an invitation to a debate, though if there had been fewer things catching fire I might have pushed it. I wanted to know why Toys was no longer in the crosshairs.

Into the awkward silence, Bug said, "I have one more thing about 'burn to shine.' There are chat room rumors of an unlicensed video game called Burn to Shine that's being distributed through underground networks. We're trying to get our hands on a copy."

"What kind of game?" asked Church.

"That's where I think we're going to overlap with Mother Night," said Bug, "because from the chatter online it sounds like something that would appeal mostly to the real extreme anarchist crowd. Very edgy stuff. Rape, random murder of civilians, insurrection, and that sort of thing."

"Whatever happened to Pong?"

"Whatever happened to bearskins and stone knives?" replied Bug.

"Point taken."

"Find a copy of that game," ordered Church.

"Working on it. Apparently the CTF has tried several times to obtain copies but has not so far succeeded."

"The CTF couldn't find its ass with a GPS," I observed, and no one disputed me.

"Got to go," said Bug, but he paused and spoke quickly to someone off camera, then came back to us. "Wait . . . hold on . . . something just came in. We've been running pattern searches on how Mother Night could have uploaded that video, and I think we figured something out."

Church brightened. "Tell me."

Bug launched into an explanation of how he tracked the video to a source, but it was total gobbledygook to me. I grunted to give the impression that I understood what he'd said.

"Give me the bottom line," I said. "Where was the source file uploaded?"

"I'm about ninety percent sure it was done at a cyber café called the Surf Shop in Park Slope. Corner of Fifth Avenue and Garfield Street."

That was an upscale part of Brooklyn.

I smiled and stood. "I'll take Top and Bunny. Maybe we're about to catch a break."

"We could use one," Church said. "I have a call scheduled with the president in five minutes, and I'll be talking to State later this morning."

"Does that mean you think we're seeing foreign nationals blowing up our fellow citizens? Because that would be really fucking big. Like missiles-in-the-air big."

"We haven't reached that conclusion yet, Captain," said Church. "We don't yet know if Mother Night is a foreign agent or an American working with them. We don't yet know if her current actions are her carrying out orders given by foreign powers or if this is something else. Something internal. In short—"

"—we don't know. I've been using that phrase a lot lately."

"Anonymity is a very effective weapon in the terrorist arsenal."

"Yeah, and doesn't that suck?"

As I turned to the door, Church asked, "Did anything else stand out from Mother Night's message?"

"Sure," I said, nodding to the plate on his desk. "If I was superparanoid I'd think the cookie reference was aimed at you. Could be a coincidence, though."

Church studied me in silence as he took another bite of his vanilla wafer.

"Or not," I said after a beat. "But aren't we reaching pretty far to take that personally?"

"At this point we don't know how far to take anything."

I nodded, depressed by that thought. I clicked my tongue for Ghost and headed out to find Top and Bunny.

Chapter Twenty-nine

The Hangar
Floyd Bennett Field, Brooklyn
Sunday, August 31, 11:42 a.m.

Once he was alone, Mr. Church swiveled his chair to face the big flatscreen mounted on the wall. He hit some keys and the screen was filled with the Seal of the President. A few seconds later that was replaced by the face of the president, who was seated at his desk in the Oval Office. Paula Michelson, his chief of staff, came and stood behind him as they both stared into a laptop webcam.

"Deacon," said the president, "tell me something that will lower my blood pressure."

"I wish I could, Mr. President," said Church. "I have dispatched teams to Gettysburg and Lexington, and Captain Ledger is currently en route to a cyber café where we believe the Mother Night video was uploaded."

"That's something."

"We'll see." He then gave him everything from Circe, Rudy, and Bug. "We may be seeing the opening moves of something much larger."

"More bombings?" asked the president, his face grave.

"Impossible to anticipate, but I would not place a heavy bet on having a peaceful rest of the day."

"The ATF is coordinating with the FBI on the bombings," the president said.

"Apart from the oblique reference by Mother Night," asked Church, "has anyone stepped forward to take credit for those attacks?"

Paula Michelson fielded that. "I just got off the phone with Central Intelligence and they're as flummoxed as the Bureau. There wasn't a whiff of this in the pipeline. No warnings, no threats, nothing."

"Who's tracking threats from the disenfranchised?" asked Church.

"The FBI is combing through recent events by suspected anarchists," said Michelson. "So far, nothing jumps out as a connection."

The president said, "This is Labor Day weekend, Deacon. That's not a particularly political event."

"No," Church agreed. "However, it is one in which we have people gathering in crowds for parties, games, and events; which means that a great number of people are going to be in motion and away from homes or offices."

"What does that matter?" asked Michelson.

Church's expression was flat. "It means that bodies may be harder to identify."

The silence was fierce.

Church eventually added, "And our infrastructure is working on a vacation schedule except for police, who will be challenged with crowd control and traffic management. If there is some kind of coordinated terrorist action—either by a foreign power or something homegrown—this is a ripe opportunity."

Interlude Six

Artemisia Bliss sat in a car and watched a hospital burn.

Twenty-five minutes ago there had been more than one hundred and eighty-six civilians in the east wing of the hospital. Doctors and nurses, staff, patients, and visitors.

Now there was only flame and smoke. And a few fading screams.

Thirty-one minutes ago EMTs brought in a gunshot victim named Javad Mustapha, a suspected terrorist who'd been shot by a Baltimore police officer during a joint police/Homeland task force raid on a cell by the docks. Sergeant Dietrich told Bliss that several other terrorists were dead and some cops had been hurt. The E.R. was busy. But Javad Mustapha was definitely DOA.

Except that he wasn't.

Somehow he wasn't.

Impossibly, he wasn't.

The video-cam feed from the Baker Team agents who had intercepted Javad and accompanied him to the hospital was like something out of a fever dream. Horror show stuff.

Working on some sketchy intelligence that Javad might have been infected with some new kind of weaponized pathogen, Mr. Church ordered Baker Team to oversee the transport of his body to the hospital and the taking of all appropriate samples.

But something went wrong.

As the body was being transferred from a gurney, Javad suddenly *woke up.*

If that was even the right way to phrase it.

One moment he was slack, clearly dead from gunshot wounds, and then he sat up, grabbed the closest agent, and bit his throat. There was so much blood. Pints of red driven by that hydrostatic pressure, bathing Javad's face as he tore at the dying agent's windpipe and jugular.

The second agent drew his weapon and shot Javad in the side. Twice, three times.

But instead of collapsing, Javad turned and hurled himself at the agent. The Baker Team shooter fired twice more as he was borne to the floor, and the bullets punched all the way through Javad's stomach. One hit the ceiling and the other hit the pathologist in the chest.

The agent and Javad rolled around on the floor and for a moment the helmet cam showed nothing but wildly blurred movement.

The screams, though.

The screams.

They told what was happening with grotesque eloquence.

Aunt Sallie was in charge of the Tactical Operations Center at the Hangar and she immediately ordered backup into the hospital. The rest of Baker and Charlie teams raced inside. Twenty of the best special operators in the world.

Their helmet cams were all working.

Bliss and Hu watched all of this from inside a DMS SUV parked outside the hospital where they waited for the collected samples and also for the computer records from the task force raid. They were not even aware they were holding hands, but later each of them would have bruises on their fingers.

The car's TV monitors played the images from all of those helmet cams. They saw more impossible things. The two agents that had been bitten came surging out of a stairwell and fell upon their comrades. The incoming agents did not fire.

Not at first.

Instead they stared in total, numb, uncomprehending shock at what was happening.

Then they tried to help.

They slung their rifles and stepped in to try and pull the infected agents away from the newly bitten. It was an act of brotherhood, of fellowship, of compassion.

And they died for it as the infected turned on them. A small bite here, a bigger bite there. Men staggered backward from the melee, bleeding and screaming.

The other agents panicked.

Some retreated, totally unprepared for this, unable to respond, their training lost in the madness of the moment.

Others, either colder or hardier men, opened fire.

Aiming for legs. Shooting to wound. To disable that which could not be disabled.

The injured bled out.

Died.

And came back.

Javad joined the frenzy. Killing, wounding, and then loping down the hallway, gibbering and moaning, seeking fresh prey.

Some of the agents followed. Living and dead.

There was continuous gunfire for as long as ammunition and life remained.

And then, when there was no one left who looked or acted like a DMS soldier, the real slaughter began. There was so much life here. Even sickness was life. One hundred and eighty-six civilians.

Soon, one hundred and eighty-six monsters.

Then Alpha Team showed up.

By now the hospital was lost, overrun.

Mr. Church and Gus Dietrich were there. So was Major Courtland. And Bliss almost screamed as Javad and a knot of infected burst through a doorway and attacked the three senior DMS staff.

Dietrich drew his sidearm and began firing double-taps to the chest. Infected fell from the impact of the bullets, but they did not stay down. He and Courtland stood side by side, firing, reloading, firing.

Javad ran around them. Dietrich twisted and hit him twice with rounds in the side of the chest. It should have exploded the man's heart and lungs. But Javad drove straight for Mr. Church, hands reaching, red mouth wide to bite.

Church stood his ground, his face grave but without fear. As Javad lunged at him, Church slapped the reaching arms to one side and fired a Taser point-blank into Javad's mangled face. The flechettes buried themselves in the dead terrorist's cheeks and the gun sent two joules of electrical power into what remained of the central nervous system of the infected.

Javad Mustapha fell, immediately and with all the grace of a toppled mannequin. Bliss watched Mr. Church evaluate that and then study the gunplay unfolding around him. In her earbud, Bliss could hear him ordering everyone back, recalling the remaining DMS troops in the building.

Church stood by the open door until the last stragglers—some of them bleeding from bites—staggered out into the parking lot. By now a sleek DMS Black Hawk helicopter was in the air above the lot.

"Kill all cell phone feeds," Church ordered. "Cut all phone lines and jam the signals from the press. Do it now."

Bliss took her hand back from Hu and immediately began hitting keys. Bug said that he was doing the same, both of them using the Blackout software package they'd written to Church's specs. Maybe there was an Executive Order on file to approve this kind of thing, but probably not. Church needed it done and they did it.

"Done," said Bug.

"Done," said Bliss.

Then she heard Church address the pilot and speak two words that sent a thrill through her entire body.

He said, "Burn it."

A moment later the Black Hawk launched its full complement of Hellfire missiles at the hospital. In seconds the entire place was burning.

A pyre.

Bliss stopped typing and leaned slowly forward to study Mr. Church. The massive fire was reflected in the lenses of his tinted glasses and for a moment Bliss had the irrational feeling that she was seeing inside his mind, that behind his stony face real fires burned.

Something shifted inside her own mind. Gears were stripped as she thought about everything that had just happened.

A designer pathogen so dangerous and sophisticated that it killed everyone who was infected—killed them and then raised them from death to become vectors for the spread of the disease. That was something military scientists had discussed since the Cold War. It was science fiction stuff. Horror story stuff. But now . . .

Real.

Right here.

Such power.

And Church himself. In the heat of the fight he was cool, efficient, his actions uncomplicated by any acceptance of his own emotions. Whatever he felt about what was happening Church kept chained in his head. It made him seem inhuman. Not less than human.

More than human.

Bliss felt heat flash through her body as if she could feel the fire that was reflected on Church's glasses, and on his skin. Her own cheeks grew hot and she was glad they were inside a darkened vehicle.

Church was unlike anyone Bliss had ever known.

Completely in control.

So powerful.

With a word he'd called down hellfire and destroyed the entire hospital. At once stopping the immediate spread of the plague and demonstrating a level of personal power that was greater than anything Bliss had encountered. And she'd met generals and presidents.

Burn it.

That's what he'd said.

"God . . ." she breathed.

Beside her, Hu said, "I know, right? This is fucking nuts!"

She nodded, but it was in no way a response to his comment or enthusiasm. Hu was already excited, happy in his own way, that there would be new puzzles to solve, new toys to play with. He was a genius sociopath, and as such he was less evolved, less interesting than Church.

No, Church was no sociopath. He *did* care about people. He cared quite a lot. So much that he was willing to take a scalpel to the skin of the world in order to carve out the cancers. He was willing to burn the sick and dying, the helpless and the desperate in order to save the city, maybe the world.

That was power.

That was real goddamn power.

Bliss felt a wave of erotic need surge through her and she almost moaned.

It was not completely a desire to hold someone that powerful in her arms or between her thighs. No . . . she imagined what it would be like to touch her own flesh and to know that the person inside that body was *this* powerful.

To be as powerful as Church.

To be more powerful.

"God," she said again.

Chapter Thirty

Corner of Fifth Avenue and Garfield Street
Park Slope, Brooklyn
Sunday, August 31, 12:19 p.m.

"There it is," said Bunny, nodding toward the intersection just ahead. He angled the black Crown Victoria toward the curb and parked near a bistro on the corner of Garfield and Fifth. It was a lovely area, with leafy green trees and moderate car and foot traffic. The Surf Shop was catty-corner.

We were in a nondescript Lincoln Town Car. Well, by nondescript I mean it pretty much shouted "federal agents," but it wasn't an armored personnel carrier. No rocket launchers mounted on the hood. I was in the front seat with Bunny, and Top was in the back with Ghost. Despite all regulations to the contrary, Top was slowly scratching Ghost between the ears, and my dog was, from all indications, floating in a lazy orbit around Neptune. His eyelids fluttered and occasional shivers rippled down his back.

There was a bing-bong in my earbud and then Church's voice. "Deacon to Cowboy."

"Go for Cowboy," I said.

"There have been eleven additional acts of random violence in different parts of the country. In four cases crimes were committed by young women wearing the same glasses and wig as Mother Night. It's likely this is being done to foil facial recognition, and probably to send a message, a reinforcement of the anarchist model."

"Ah," said Top, "black bloc?"

"That's our guess," agreed Church.

Bunny frowned at Top and mouthed the words *black bloc*, clearly unsure of the reference. Top held up a finger.

"Whatever is happening appears to be heating up. Proceed with caution," warned Church.

"Copy that," I said and disconnected.

Bunny turned off the engine. "What's a black bloc? Or is it a hip-hop thing?"

Top gave him a pitying look. "Don't you ever read the damn newspapers, Farmboy?"

"I read Yahoo news sometimes."

"A black bloc is a protest thing," explained Top. "It's a tactic some groups use, including anarchists. Bunch of people show up to make a protest and they're all wearing black hoodies, dark glasses, scarves, ski masks, motorcycle helmets. That sort of shit. Trying to be anonymous, like ants in a swarm. No individuals, just a faceless mob, which forces the target of their protest to react to the mob as a whole. No way to focus countermeasures like discussion or negotiation on a single person, because they're all the same. Get it?"

"Yeah, okay, maybe I did hear about something like that. Started somewhere in Europe?"

I nodded. "Sure, Germany, places like that. People making protests against squatter evictions, war involvement, nuclear power. All sorts of stuff, and some of it's legit. Sometimes they have a good point."

Top's expression was sour. "But the tactic's for shit. Building barricades, setting things on fire, throwing rocks at cops."

"Not to go all Occupy on you, old man," said Bunny, "but some of those cops deserve it. Tear-gassing unarmed protesters."

Top leaned on the seat back between Bunny and me. He gave Bunny a hard look. "So you're saying there are assholes on both sides of a conflict? Really? That's brand-new news for the whole world? Damn, Farmboy, you're smart."

"Okay, okay, you know what I'm saying. Sometimes you have to make a lot of noise to get heard."

"No doubt. Sometimes you have to pull a trigger, too. But I don't believe Mr. Church sent us here to debate political ethics."

"Point is," I said, leaning into their conversation, "the big man thinks Mother Night's wig and sunglasses might be a black bloc costume. Emphasis on 'costume.' Doesn't mean she's an anarchist or a protester. Means she and her people are maybe trying to look like them."

"Can't rule it out, though," said Top.

"Can't rule anything out," I said.

"So," said Bunny, "we're not sure this is a real anarchy thing? The hacking thing, the bombings."

"You heard Mother Night's rant," said Top. "Pretty much right out of the anarchist textbook."

"Exactly," I said. "So textbook it's generic."

They nodded and Bunny said, "Wonder if her name has some kind of meaning to it. Some kind of symbolism."

Top shrugged. "Comes from the title of a novel by Kurt Vonnegut. 'Bout a guy who becomes a Nazi propagandist. Ends up in an Israeli prison."

Bunny half smiled. "Have you read *every* damn book in the world? I mean, when the fuck do you have *time* to read?"

"Maybe you'd have time to read if you weren't playing video games all the damn time," murmured Top, "and following Lydia around with your dick dragging on the ground."

"Hey."

Top shrugged. "Mother Night. Might be something in the name, in the book reference. What do you call it? A metaphor. Propaganda and that shit. We should keep it in mind, Cap'n. Been too many cases already that have one coat of paint over something else."

"Yup," I said, nodding. "Okay, street looks quiet. Let's go do this."

"Hooah," said Bunny dryly. "Hoo-frickin'-ah."

He opened the glove box and sorted through a stack of official identification wallets, selected two, and handed one each to Top and me.

I opened mine, saw the letters FBI, nodded, and tucked it into the inner pocket of my coat. We checked our weapons, nodded briefly to one another. Ghost wagged his tail like we were going to play.

We got out of the car and walked toward the cyber café.

Interlude Seven

The Liberty Bell Center
Independence Mall
Philadelphia, Pennsylvania
Four Years Ago

Dr. Artemisia Bliss stood with her back to the wall, keeping out of the way as EMTs and DMS field techs carried in armloads of body bags.

Armloads of them.

Ninety-one people died at the Liberty Bell Center today. A few were part of a terrorist cell run by the legendary El Mujahid. Fourteen of the dead were members of Congress. The rest were civilians. Tourists, press, children.

Dead.

Dead twice, she corrected herself.

Killed by the *seif-al-din* pathogen delivered either by the explosive device that was hidden at the center or by the vectors.

Vectors.

Such a strange little word for so dreadful a thing.

The truth was much more horrible. Infected people whose bodies had been hijacked by genetically modified parasites, driven by unstoppable urges and specifically triggered brain chemicals to attack. And bite.

And devour.

Many of the bodies were no longer whole.

There was blood everywhere.

Everywhere.

Bliss wore a yellow hazmat suit and held a forensic collection kit in one hand.

"It's safe," said Dr. Hu as he came over to join her.

"'Safe'?" she echoed.

"It's not airborne," he said, unfastening his hood and pulling it off. "Just don't touch anything without gloves."

She removed her hood and looked around at the devastation. The new DMS shooter, Captain Ledger, sat on a bench next to another recent recruit, the psychiatrist Dr. Rudy Sanchez. They both looked shell-shocked.

Bliss had watched videos of Ledger in action.

She could understand why Church liked him. The man was utterly ruthless, brutal and efficient. A nearly perfect killer, except for a psychological profile that read like it was written by Stephen King. Lots of people inside Ledger's head, and none of them very nice.

Which did not at all change the fact that Bliss liked him.

No. *Wanted* him. That was closer to it.

She wanted the power that was in him to be inside her.

Sexually, sure, but that still wasn't it. It was at times like this that she wished she were a vampire so she could drink his power and take it for her own. If she had that power, she knew she would use it. No question. She'd take Ledger's power. And Church's, of course.

Who else?

Samson Riggs—now *Colonel* Riggs; Aunt Sallie. A very few others.

Maybe even a weasel like Hu. He was as sexless as a broken dildo—and in bed he was all talk and very little else—but he had that brain. That sexy, sexy brain.

At times like this she felt that old familiar shift inside her head. As if something was changing. The first few times it happened, it felt like a loss of control, but an unspecified loss over an unknown area of control. Like something was happening in a closet somewhere in the back of her mind.

Now she understood it a little more.

It wasn't a loss of control. Not a loss at all.

It was a process of removal.

Cutting away restraints. Removing the chocks from beneath the wheels of potential.

It was all about power.

Wanting it.

Deserving it.

Getting it.

Having it.

And . . . using it?

That part was still unformed in her mind, and she wasn't at all sure she wanted to attach an agenda to the process. That felt somehow limiting. It was like the quantum phenomenon of light photons. A photon can behave as a wave or a particle, depending on how you measure it. To measure it restricts its infinite possibilities.

Bliss knew that she was changing, evolving, but she had no idea where that evolution would go or what form it might take. To predict is to attempt to measure, and that felt wrong.

These thoughts flowed through her brain as she moved into the Liberty Bell Center, knelt by one corpse, opened her kit, and began to collect samples. The protocol was simple enough: take three vials of blood, scrapings of skin from around the mouth and cells from inside the cheek. Bag and tag each set of samples along with a fingerprint card and digital photo of each victim and then place them in a plastic bag marked with a biohazard symbol. Later, at the Hangar, the science team would run a massive battery of tests.

But as she collected samples, Bliss felt as if that evolving part of her gently but firmly took over the controls that drove her hands. She filled three vials with blood. And then a fourth. A fifth. A sixth.

She took two sets of skin samples.

Two cheek swabs.

Two of everything.

Into identical biohazard bags.

One bag went into the evidence pouch. The other . . .

She glanced around to see if anyone was watching her.

No one was, although the vice president was in the room, and he glanced her way, then glanced away.

When she was sure no one was looking, she unzipped a tool pouch on her hazmat suit and slipped the duplicate bag out of sight.

Then she paused there, letting both aspects of her personality—the upstart science geek girl she'd always been and this more evolved personality—stare at each other across the fact of what she'd done. Like gunslingers.

However, only one real gunslinger had come armed to this confrontation.

She felt the smile that reshaped her mouth as she began taking two sets of samples from a second victim.

Why am I doing this?

Both parts of her mind asked that question.

The geek had no answer. Or was afraid to answer.

The evolved aspect whispered an answer that was couched inside a single word.

Power.

She rose and moved to another body, and another, and another.

When she was finishing with the eleventh body, she rose and yelped in surprise to find a man standing directly behind her.

A tall man. Good looking in a desk-jockey way but with big hands that Bliss knew came from blue-collar work in his youth. A square jaw and intense eyes. And a smile that she'd seen on TV and the cover of *Time*. A smile everyone in the country knew. A smile everyone in the world knew. The supremely confident smile of a truly powerful man.

She said, "Oh—Mr. Vice President . . . I didn't see you there."

"Yes," he said, "you did."

"W-what?"

His smile was very handsome, but not at all the same one from the cover of *Time*. This wasn't the smile you wanted on the face of a man kissing babies at a rally. This smile, she knew, was meant for her to see, and to interpret exactly as it was meant.

"You're the Deacon's wonder girl," he said.

"I, um, work for Mr. Church."

"Church, Deacon, whatever the fuck he calls himself. You work for him."

She nodded, wondering where this was going.

"Your team's always wired in to each other. Did you see the way that bitch Courtland treated my wife?"

Bliss had. The Second Lady was a notorious loudmouth and a legendary bitch. When the outbreak started, Collins's wife tried to take charge of the moment and boss everyone around, and even if she was well-intentioned, she went about it the wrong way. Things went south from there and Major Courtland had dropped Mrs. Collins with some kind of karate chop. The Second Lady was ambulanced off once the whole thing was over. She never stopped screaming threats up to the point where the beleaguered EMTs slammed the doors.

"I . . ." began Bliss, and didn't know where to put her conversational foot.

But Collins leaned close and, in a voice pitched only for her to hear, said, "Between us, sweetheart, I was kind of hoping Courtland would have busted my wife's fucking jaw."

The statement was a showstopper.

Bliss stared at him, totally unable to react or respond in any useful way.

Collins laughed. "God, you should see the look on your face."

"I . . ." Bliss said again, and once more her vocabulary failed her.

"That bitch'll be in the hospital for a day or two. Longer if I can arrange it."

"Um . . . yes, I suppose."

He took a step closer. She could feel the heat of his breath on her face. "If the Deacon ever lets you off the leash, I know a great place for Kobe steaks. You're Japanese, right?"

"Chinese."

"Whatever. Steaks as thick as your wrist."

She said nothing.

He removed a business card and a pen, scribbled something onto the back of the card, and then tucked it into the pouch on her hazmat suit. The same pouch where she'd dropped her duplicate samples.

"Call me if you want to get your hands on an expensive piece of meat."

He turned and walked away. Almost sauntering. But as soon as he saw some officials, his posture instantly shifted from that of smug asshole to man of action. It was immediate, like throwing a switch on a nuclear reactor. Very smooth, very practiced.

And, despite everything else, including the man's absolutely offensive comments, it was impressive. Appealing.

It was power.

Artemisia fished the card out of her pouch, turned it over, and saw that he'd written his cell number in a sprawling hand. The geek in her wanted to tear the card up. The professional and accomplished woman in her wanted to spit on the card before tearing it up.

However, that other part, the other self, the evolving self, smiled and tucked the card back into the pouch.

Chapter Thirty-one

Corner of Fifth Avenue and Garfield Street
Park Slope, Brooklyn
Sunday, August 31, 12:22 p.m.

We were still a few doors down from the Surf Shop when my phone rang. I expected it to be Rudy. It wasn't. I held up a hand to the guys and stepped a few paces away to take the call. I smiled and punched the button.

"Hello, Junie."

"Hello."

When Ghost heard me say her name he brightened and made a happy *whuff* sound.

"How's your day?" she asked.

"Oh, you know. Just another day in the D. of M. S."

"I can only imagine."

She could, too. Last year, she was there when we took down Howard Shelton and his team of superfreak killers. She'd pulled the trigger on one of them. She knew that my job did not involve shuffling papers or sneaking out of the office for a quick nine holes.

"What's cooking, darlin'?" I asked.

There was a beat before she said, "I know you can't talk about work stuff, Joe, but *is* everything okay? For real, I mean?"

"Why do you ask?"

"I was on the Net looking at something on YouTube and suddenly this woman's face popped up." She described the Mother Night video.

"Yeah, we saw that. It's a computer hacker," I said. "Nothing you have to worry about."

"Don't patronize me, Joe. I can hear something in your voice."

"Sorry," I said quickly, lowering my voice and stepping farther away from Top and Bunny. "I wasn't patronizing you. That video popped up all over and, sure, we're looking into it. So far, though, it looks like what it is. A smart-ass hacker with more talent than common sense using the Internet to shout to the world that she's there. It's the cyberworld equivalent of spray-painting your name on a wall that everyone has to pass. Forced attention."

"You're sure that's all it is?"

"No, of course not. That's why we're looking into it."

"What about the backpack bomb thing? They're saying it's another Boston."

"I'm not on that."

"Is it connected to that video?"

"I don't know."

"Will you tell me what you find out?"

"I'll tell you what I can."

"Joe, I'm not asking you to break protocol. I'm just . . ."

"Just . . . what?" I asked.

"It's nothing."

"No, tell me."

"Okay, you know how you joke about your 'spider sense' tingling when you think something's wrong but can't quite put your finger on it?"

"Sure. It's one of my many superpowers."

"Well . . . I guess my spider sense started tingling."

"Because of that video?"

"No," she said. "I've been having weird premonitions all day, ever since I got to work."

I grunted. "How weird?"

"I don't know. Weird. Nonspecific. Just . . . bad feelings."

A whole bunch of very ugly questions jumped into the front of my brain and I had to bite down to keep my foolish mouth from giving them voice. The process took too much time, I was quiet too long, and Junie caught it.

"Joe . . . ?"

"Yeah."

"I know what you're thinking."

"Are you undressing, then?"

"I'm serious, Joe. Don't joke."

"Sorry."

"These feelings I'm having . . . they're not about me. They're not about the test results."

I did not trust myself to respond to that.

"But *something* is wrong," she added. "I can feel it."

Before I met Junie my tendency was to dismiss that kind of comment as too New Agey, too space cadet. I have since learned that my knee-jerk dismissal of that kind of perception was a fault in me rather than a fault in others.

There are, after all, more things in heaven and earth.

So I don't laugh it off when Junie has a premonition or a "feeling." I don't wave it away like cigarette smoke.

At the same time, I don't always know what to do with those kinds of things. It's not like I can ask Bug to do a MindReader search on a feeling.

Instead, I said what I say when these things happen. "Okay."

"Okay," she said, accepting that she'd made her point and I'd got it. She knows as well as I do that there wasn't anything specific I could do other than to make sure my awareness and reaction time was at high bubble. It had become a rhythm with us. A useful one.

"Come home to me," she said.

"Always," I replied.

I knew that she was smiling, as I was smiling.

As I went to put the phone back into my pocket it vibrated. Another text message from A.

YOU ALWAYS HURT THE ONE YOU LOVE

I glared at the screen. Was it a threat or was I being stalked by someone in a fortune cookie factory? Either way, I sent it to Bug with a rather terse note to find whoever was sending this. Foul language was involved.

I clicked off and shoved the phone into my pocket. A few yards away Top and Bunny were pretending to look at the birds in the trees. As I joined them a chill wind blew up my spine and made me shiver. Ghost looked up at me and whined faintly.

"You okay, boss?" asked Bunny.

"Someone walked over my grave," I said, making a joke of it.

Neither of my guys laughed. Come to think of it, it wasn't all that funny to me, either.

Chapter Thirty-two

The C Train

Near Euclid Avenue

Brooklyn, New York

Sunday, August 31, 12:23 p.m.

The man in the yellow raincoat looked out of place, even on the C train. It was hot in the swaying subway car, and he wore a black hoodie under the raincoat, the hood pulled all the way up. He was sweating heavily. Beads of moisture ran down his cheeks and throat and vanished inside the humid darkness beneath the slicker. The smell that seeped out from under the yellow rubber was intense.

The woman seated next to him was named Maria Diego. She was billing secretary for a firm of dentists, and next Thursday would be her fifty-seventh birthday. A thickset, quiet-mannered, plainly dressed woman with a Heather Graham novel open on her lap and Marc Anthony crooning to her through earbuds.

When Maria was sure the man in the yellow raincoat wasn't watching, she removed a bottle of perfume from her purse, put a drop on her finger, and covertly dabbed her upper lip with it. The car was crowded, there was nowhere else to sit, and she was too tired to stand. The smell from the sweating man, however, was like the stink of an open sewer.

He's probably a junkie, she thought, but that didn't bother her very much. Maria slipped one hand into her jacket pocket and closed it gently around her can of pepper spray. As long as the man sat quietly, she was content to mind her own business, read her book, and make her way home. This was the New York subway system, so body odor was nothing new. The perfume always made that easy to manage.

The man's smile, though . . .

That bothered Maria.

It was not a happy smile.

For six stops Maria tried to understand the smile. After thirty-four years of riding this line she'd seen everything, every kind of person, every frequency of expression. However, she'd never before quite seen an expression like the one carved into his face. It was so intense, so constant, that it was like a mask. His mouth was set in a huge jack-o'-lantern grin that stretched his cheeks so wide it had to be painful. His teeth were yellow and dry. His eyes stared forward and slightly upward with such intensity that when he'd first sat down Maria darted looks at the ads on the other side of the car, above the heads of the commuters, to see if the man was drawn to something in particular. But no. He stared with a fixity that made her wonder if he was obsessed with some thought that hung ten inches in front of his eyes. She tried not to look at him too often, but if he ever blinked then Maria hadn't seen it.

Definitely a junkie.

The train rattled on underground. The lights flickered the way they often flicker. The train was old, the rails were old. And this was the C train.

The man kept staring at nothing Maria could see, so she turned back to her book and was soon lost in mystery and suspense.

The train made another stop and then headed into the tunnel, rattling along the rails, jostling its passengers, causing Maria to bump sideways into the smiling, sweating man. It was nearing the end of the line at Euclid Avenue.

The lights flickered again. Off. On.

Off.

And this time they stayed off.

The train slowed to a squealing halt. Not fast. Not at all once. And not at Euclid Avenue station.

The passengers did not fly into an immediate panic. Of course they didn't. This was New York. This was the C train. This was Brooklyn.

When the car settled into stillness, the passengers were quiet for a moment as they listened for the kinds of sounds that would provide information.

There was no sound.

So they collectively moaned in soft irritation, sighed, rustled as they set themselves into comfortable positions to wait it out. There was not one person on that train, not one in that car who hadn't been here before. Stopped, stalled, delayed, and in the dark.

The darkness was total.

And then one by one passengers began punching buttons on their cells phones, spilling the glow of screen displays into the car.

There were some laughs.

A couple of jokes. The MTA and the mayor had their names taken in vain.

Laughter rippled through the crowd.

Maria closed her book and accessed the e-reader app on her cell, found a different book—a mystery by Hank Phillippi Ryan—and began reading. Unperturbed. Undisturbed.

Unsuspecting.

Something brushed her side and she half turned to watch as the man in the yellow raincoat stood up. His face was illuminated by the glow of cell phones. His mouth was moving as if he was saying something, but by now half the passengers on the train were calling people who weren't on the train to talk. The buzz of chatter was loud, and Maria didn't catch a word the sweating man said.

Then she felt herself frowning as her mind began evaluating what her eyes were seeing. The man wasn't speaking. His mouth was moving, jaws working, the way someone does when they're eating. But she could see that he wasn't really eating anything. There was nothing in his mouth. It was like he was pretending to eat.

Muy loco, she thought.

The man turned slowly in place, his unblinking eyes seeming to take in everything and everyone around him. Maria watched with an odd and inexplicable fascination. It was like watching one of those YouTube videos her son sometimes sent her without including a clue as to what it was about. She had to watch to find out.

The man completed his turn and then slowly closed his eyes. Maria felt strangely relieved that the man had finally closed his eyes. Her eyes had begun to feel dry and sore.

The train still did not move. The chatter of the crowd grew louder, more cell phones glowed to life. More rude jokes were swapped. There was almost a party atmosphere. Everyone was laughing, joking, smiling.

Except Maria.

What was this man doing? Standing there, eyes closed, sweating in a heavy yellow raincoat, pretending that he was chewing.

Then the man abruptly stopped chewing, drew in a deep breath, squared his shoulders, and in a voice that was as fractured and raw as it was powerful, shouted at the top of his lungs.

"I have a message from Mother Night!"

It was so shockingly loud that for a moment everyone froze, silent, staring.

"The current administration of the United States government is acting in opposition to the will of the people and the laws of the Constitution. The American people are cattle to them and we will remain so unless we take action, take to the streets, take the country back."

After another moment of awkward silence, a tall black teenager in jeans and a Yankees shirt lowered the cell phone into which he was speaking and said, "The fuck you talking about, man? Some kind of Occupy the C Train bullshit?"

A couple of people laughed, but none of them was seated close to the man in the raincoat and hoodie. The teenager who'd spoken out, though, was three passengers back from where the sweating man stood. The intervening people began shifting out of the way, not wanting to be a part of anything.

Maria couldn't blame them. She slipped the pepper spray out of her pocket and held it in her lap, covered by both hands. Ready.

The sweating man pointed at the teenager. "Tell everyone. The only action is direct action."

"The fuck's with you?" asked the teen in a tone of rising belligerence. "You high or some shit?"

What the sweating man said in reply meant nothing at all to the black teen, or to Maria.

"*Sometimes you have to burn to shine.*"

And then without warning, without the slightest hint, the sweating man leaped at the teenager and slammed him back into the laps of a row of people seated against the wall. The scream he made as he pounced did not sound human. To Maria, it sounded like the hunting shriek of one of the big cats, like the mountain lions who hunted the canyons in Mexico where she'd lived until she was twelve. It was inhuman, and filled with fury and hate.

And with hunger.

But it was almost immediately drowned out by the high, shrill screams of total agony from the teenager as the sweating man bit into the flesh of his throat and tore it out. In the glow of the cell phones the geysering blood was as black as oil.

Then everyone was screaming.

Maria screamed, too.

It took two minutes and nine men to subdue the sweating man. They crowded him into a corner and hammered him with kicks and punches. People hung from the straps for balance as they stomped him. Breaking his face, breaking his bones, knocking out teeth.

Through all of that, the man kept fighting. Keep trying to bite.

He never grunted in pain. Never begged for mercy.

He stopped fighting back only when one of the kicks caught him just right and his head struck a pole so hard that skin and bone burst.

The kicks continued for ten more seconds.

Then the crowd froze again, caught in a tableau, shocked by what had happened, calculating the degree of their involvement in any police action that might follow.

Cell cameras flashed, flashed, flashed.

Someone said, "Jesus Christ."

The sound of panting—from exertion and fear—filled the car.

Maria hurried over to the teenager, but she could tell that he was already gone. His windpipe was exposed and ragged, the arterial blood pulsed once more, weakly, then settled down to a dying bubble.

She felt for his pulse, felt the last throb, and then . . . nothing.

"Jesus Christ," said someone else, loading it with a different meaning. Then Maria herself said it. *"Jesus Christ!"*

Because the teenager opened his eyes.

And his mouth.

And he lunged for her.

The last thing Maria saw was a glaring eye inches from her own as the teenager—the dead teenager—darted in to take his first bite.

Chapter Thirty-three

FreeTech
800 Fifth Avenue
New York City
Sunday, August 31, 12:24 p.m.

Junie Flynn watched as each of the newest members of her board settled into their chairs. It was a strange mix of people, and Junie knew that each of them had secrets that the others at the table did not necessarily share. Each brought their own unique skills, knowledge, connections, and motives to FreeTech. They came to help and to share in the benefits of an organization with a structure like DARPA but which had no military agenda. It was, to Junie's experience, a unique organization.

After thanking them each for attending this closed session, Junie addressed the group. "We will operate with two levels of disclosure. Each of you has requested and been granted a public identity that has been crafted by MindReader. No one outside of this group and the upper echelon of the DMS will know who you are."

The people seated around the table nodded, some with less enthusiasm and more suspicion than others.

"However," said Junie, "everything else we do at FreeTech will be available through the Freedom of Information Act. All benefits will be shared equally with the public, without reservations. Since none of ⌐ research or development is intended for military use, that freed⌐ cess will extend beyond U.S. borders. Agreed?"

Another round of nods.

However, one person, a young woman with olive skin and dark hair, raised her hand. "As much as I can appreciate altruism on this scale," said Violin, "it is expensive. Surely, whomever is financing this venture will want the lion's share of any profits."

"Actually," said Junie, "if any profits are generated they will be used for further research and to fund foundations tasked with distributing the fruits of that research."

"How? This will take many millions . . ."

Junie smiled. "We are operating with a start-up bank of seventy billion dollars."

It was a shocking amount. An absurd amount. Everyone gaped at her.

"How?" demanded Violin. "Your congress could never pass an appropriations bill of that size."

"Private donation," said Junie. She was intensely aware that the challenge in Violin's voice spoke to issues beyond FreeTech. Violin had been Joe's lover and Junie suspected that the strange woman still had strong feelings for Joe. They'd gone into combat together on multiple occasions and shared a kind of intimacy that was unique to them. Even though Junie knew that Joe was faithful to her, she was adult enough to realize that there were unresolved issues hanging fire between him and Violin. Issues that might never be resolved.

Although her trust in Joe's fidelity was ironclad, Junie had less faith that this beautiful, exotic, and powerful warrior woman was the kind to simply bow out without a fight. Junie had been mentally preparing herself for that fight, and she dearly hoped it wouldn't involve actual knives.

"Donated by whom?" Violin's brow was knitted with doubt and concern. "Who has that kind of money? And why would they give so much? Is this part of the Bill and Amanda Gates Foundation or—"

"No," said a sad-eyed young man seated across from her. He was in his thirties, thin, handsome, and he spoke with a British accent. "I donated the money. All of it."

"You?" asked the thin, dark-haired teenager seated to Junie's right. His name was Helmut Deacon. "And how do you have that much money?"

"I suppose you could say I inherited it," said the Brit.

"Oil money?" asked Helmut.

"No."

Suspicion flickered in Violin's eyes. "Inherited from where?"

The Brit turned to Junie and raised inquiring eyebrows. She nodded.

"No secrets between us," Junie said. "That's our rule. Besides, Free-Tech is your idea."

"Bloody hell," said the Brit. He took a breath. "Well, buckle up, kids, because this is going to be a bumpy ride. The funding for this was appropriated on my behalf from the Seven Kings. I was made steward of the money on the condition that I find a way to do the best possible good with it. I proposed the creation of FreeTech as a way of fixing some of the damage the Kings did. Damage that I am partly responsible for."

Everyone at the table stared at him in stunned silence.

"And before I give you those details," said the Brit after taking a steadying breath, "I want one favor from you. No matter how much good we do, even if we cure the common effing cold, I don't *ever* want to hear the words 'thank you' aimed in my direction. Ever. This isn't about me and it never will be."

One by one the others nodded, though they all looked suspicious and mystified.

"Very well," said the Brit. "I'll start by introducing myself. My name is Alexander Chismer, but everyone calls me Toys."

Interlude Eight

Four Seasons Hotel
1 Logan Square
Philadelphia, Pennsylvania
Four Years Ago

"Take it, you bitch!"

Bill Collins snarled the words as he thrust into her from behind. She was on elbows and knees; he stood beside the bed. Her buttocks flared red from where he'd slapped her over and over again with each thrust.

She snarled back at him from between clenched teeth. Goading him on, demanding that he go harder and faster, that he hit her.

Demanding it.

When they came they howled together like night creatures. Like wolves.

The iPod played very loud opera. If anyone else in the hotel heard them, no one called the front desk.

The Secret Service men outside the door were paid a lot of money under the table to pretend to be as deaf as they were blind. As far as they were concerned, they worked for Bill Collins, not for the vice president. That distinction was expensive and paid for in cash.

Collins collapsed on her by slow degrees, his sweaty chest falling onto her back and bearing her down to the sodden and tangled sheets. They panted loudly, unable to speak, spent and aching, lost in the exhaustion and pleasure and an afterglow that burned their skin.

This was the tenth time they'd met in private, and it was always like this for them.

Genuine tenderness formed no part of their relationship, though they went through the motions of it over dinner and before clothes were off. Once they were naked, each of them knew that they could be their real, true selves. They were not nice people, and that was part of the fun for each of them. They were rough and mean to each other, and that was a turn-on. And they both knew that they were trying through physical extremity to try and fuck each other's mind. To do that, in fact, would have been their only goal, their only act; but in the absence of that possibility they drove each other toward the edge of the cliff every time.

And every time it was good for them.

Bliss had never allowed herself to be like this with anyone with whom she'd ever slept. Not even her foster father. In all other situations she'd made sure to dial it down, to play a borderline virgin, to be the good little geek girl who—oh my god!—has sex. None of that was her, or if any of it was, then it belonged to that lesser, unevolved self whom Bliss left farther behind every day.

As the sweat cooled on their skin, they gradually fell apart, him rolling off her, Bliss shifting toward the center of the bed. They were totally unabashed about nakedness or preference, and that was such a liberating thing.

After a while, he said, "The president has been having some heart problems."

Bliss turned and looked at him. Collins was staring up at the ceiling, smiling.

"Really? Like what?"

"He nearly had a heart attack at Camp David. It was kept out of the press, but the doctors are freaked. They ran all the tests and his arteries are for shit. They're going to try him on some statins to see if that will clear things out, but if not . . ."

"What? You think he'll have a heart attack for real?"

Collins barked out a sour laugh. "I'm not that lucky. No . . . they're talking bypass surgery."

"Oh."

There was a moment of silence and then Bliss realized that Collins was waiting for her to say something. She replayed the conversation and then realized what it was.

"If he has surgery and they use a general anesthesia," she said, "wouldn't that mean that you'd be president?"

"Short term . . . but abso-fucking-lutely."

She turned and propped herself up on her elbow. "Bill—that's so exciting."

"It does not suck," he agreed.

"Now, all we need is an allergic reaction to the anesthesia."

"Or a surgeon with the hiccups."

They were silent for a long time, and she pulled the sheet over herself. The room was getting cool. "Bill . . . while you're acting as president, I mean . . . you'll actually *be* the president, right?"

"Yes."

"With all of the powers of the president?"

"Yup." He stroked her hair. "Why?"

"Oh, I don't know. It's just that it seems like a great opportunity. There has to be something you can do with that chance."

"Yeah," he said. "But what?"

Bliss smiled. "I don't know. But let me think on it."

Chapter Thirty-four

Ludo Monk was playing a video game while he waited to kill people. It was a great way to unwind one kind of tension—ordinary, everyday stuff—and an equally great way to ramp up for the trigger pulls to come.

He was on level sixteen of Burn to Shine, and he'd just completed the second Virus Vault level. He'd burned through two lives to do it, but the game gave you an unlimited number of replays.

The hit itself was of little concern to him. The target, location, angle, weapon, and escape route had all been worked out to the smallest detail, a process that included consideration of many hundreds of variables. Ludo had spent weeks getting it all set up the right way. He did not believe in haste. He never took a job that did not permit at least a month of planning, and preferred to have more time than that.

It was all about the variables.

Time of day, weather, wind conditions, location, angles, access and egress, distance to resources, traffic congestion at different times of day, frequency of police car and air patrols, access to multiple vantage points, availability of additional assets, reliability of those assets, training of same, events on that day's calendar for any venue within a mile, even the particulate count in the air quality report.

He was aware that some of the variables he considered were requested by parts of his brain that were less orderly and reliable than the part that generally drove the car. But that was fine. The frequency of his own madness was also a variable and it had to be considered.

Had to be.

Things went wrong only when planning was weak. The hit on Joe Ledger and Reggie Boyd in Baltimore was a prime example. That was rushed, built on poor intel, and it relied on some of Mother Night's goofy suicide flunkies. Henchmen, as Monk thought of them. Henchmen were notorious for flubbing things. Ask anyone. Read a comic book.

Monk never used henchmen. He would occasionally use a lackey, but they were different. Lackeys were for fetching and carrying, not for wet work in the field. Lackeys picked up supplies for him, had his vehicles serviced, delivered packages, and made sure he had licorice, Coke, and plenty of pills. They were good at that sort of thing.

It was the henchmen who fucked things up. Attacking someone like Ledger with a car and then trying to outgun him. Seriously? Ledger had killed more people than smallpox. Monk knew, he'd read the files. Ledger was a psychotic killing machine—or at least that's the phrasing Monk used in his head, and he figured he was not very far off. Monk would have handled that whole thing differently.

For one thing, he'd have picked a secure and dry shooting position, ideally in one of the buildings across the street from the Warehouse. Then he would have used explosive rounds and parked six shots through the windshield as soon as Ledger pulled up to the security exit. There was a three-second window of opportunity there while Ledger showed Boyd's transfer papers. It would have been a clean kill. Three shots into Ledger, and then three into Boyd, allowing the explosive rounds to turn the inside of the Explorer into a fireball. Then he would have abandoned his gear, set a ten-minute explosive charge in the room he was vacating, and been halfway across Baltimore before the debris stopped falling.

That's how it should have gone.

But Mother Night had decided to let the clown college handle it, and that resulted in zero targets being eliminated while the entire so-called kill squad was butchered by Ledger and his dog.

As he thought about that he felt something shift inside his head. The colors of the paint on the walls started shifting in tone.

"Uh-oh," he said and made a grab for his pills.

He stuffed a few into his mouth, reminded himself not to chew them, washed them down with warm Coke, and waited for the colors to return to normal.

"Fucking henchmen," he said to the air around him.

Monk returned to the window and settled himself down. His elevated shooting position was inside a hotel room that had two banks of elevators and excellent stairwells. Six runners—all reliable lackeys—were positioned to flee down the stairwells, each of them wearing a ski mask. Monk would simply walk down the hall, enter a room booked under a different name, and take a bath. All of his equipment and clothing would be collected and disposed of by a woman seeded into the maid staff two months ago. The equipment would be placed in a barrel filled with hydrochloric acid, sealed, and stored in the basement among three other similar barrels, each marked as diesel fuel for the back-up generator.

Monk's cover was ironclad. He was in town for a business meeting, and was, in fact, enrolled. A superb double would attend the meetings wearing a mike so Monk could hear the lectures. He'd already watched videos of yesterday's sessions, and he would attend the closing session tomorrow. In the unlikely event that he was questioned, his alibi would hold water.

And polygraphs are virtually useless with the insane. He knew that from experience.

His team of lackeys had already prepped the shooting room before he arrived, but Monk chased them out and spent two hours going over everything. Obsessively. Multiple times. The only thing he did not do was disassemble the rifle. In the movies snipers did that, but it was silly. When you took apart a gun, no matter how carefully you handled it, you disturbed the settings. Those settings could not be perfectly duplicated without sighting it again on a range. He'd arranged to have the fully assembled gun wrapped loosely in bubble wrap and brought here by two lackeys who understood his rules.

Those two were replacements for a team who'd made an error on a previous job. Monk regretted what he'd done to them, but you couldn't put people back together after they'd been hacked apart. He knew, he'd tried.

The new team was very, very careful, so it was really an opportunity for them all to grow together.

The rifle was a Dragunov sniper rifle, which was not his weapon of choice, but its use in this hit—and later discovery—would send a nicely conflicted message. It had mechanically adjustable back-up iron sights with a sliding tangent rear sight and a scope mount that didn't block the area between the front and rear sights. Very useful and a nice piece of design work. *Bravo for our Russian brothers,* he thought. It fired 7.62 by 54 millimeter rounds at 2,700 feet per second, fed from a ten-round box magazine.

He decided to name it Olga.

Monk sat with Olga for a long time, explaining to the rifle what was expected of her and why it was important.

Olga listened without comment.

That was not a given. Monk had engaged other weapons in long and complicated back-and-forth conversations. His meds had changed since then, and he thought wistfully of the subtle insights of the German PSG1 and the wacky humor of the Beretta .50.

When Monk realized that he was falling into a depression because Olga wasn't speaking with him, he got up and crossed to where he'd hung his jacket, dug his blue plastic pillbox out of the pocket, sorted through all the colors, made a selection, and swallowed two pills. He crouched in the closet until talking to a rifle seemed ridiculous.

He was grateful there were no cameras here in this room. His employer knew that he was mad, but she probably did not know how thin the ice was beneath his skates. Most of the time he didn't, either.

It frightened him to realize that he was probably slipping. Or maybe had already slipped. At least a notch or two.

The woman he worked for was always looking, always watching. If he slipped in her eyes, then he would be dead. Two in the back of the head and his body run through a wood chipper. He'd seen that done to others. He'd helped do it to others, so he understood that it was standard operating procedure.

He was sad, he was crazy, but he didn't want to die.

And he definitely didn't want to become mulch.

Monk squatted inside the closet until he was sure that the meds had kicked in. As much as they could or would kick in. He'd have to up his dose soon, and that was going to change him. It would sand another layer from his mental sharpness. Dull him. Make him less of what he was.

When he opened the closet door he had to avoid looking at Olga until he was sure there wasn't more he needed to say to her.

No, he warned himself.

Not Olga.

Not like that.

Just a gun.

A tool.

Nothing else.

"Fuck," he said aloud. He permitted himself five curses or obscenities each day. This was his first for today, so he repeated it. "Fuck!"

The gun remained a gun.

He closed his eyes and breathed a sigh of relief.

He accessed an app on his smartphone that asked him a bunch of pop-culture questions. Monk was excellent at trivia, and appearing on *Jeopardy* was the third item on his bucket list. He took time to consider the answers. Who was the current speaker of the House? Who played Radaghast the Brown in *The Hobbit*? How many Americans walked on the moon?

Like that.

He answered all his questions and got each right. Weird answers raised flags and made him want to reach for his pillbox.

He took a breath and smiled a little as he let it out. The pills he'd taken seemed to have bolted him to the ground very nicely. It was a relief.

His phone vibrated. The screen display said "Mom," which was not true. His mother had died in a fire when Monk was fifteen. It was the first fire he'd set that had taken a life, and as such it was sacred in his memory.

Nevertheless, when he answered it he said, "Hello?"

"Things are moving," Mother Night, "but we're not ready for you yet. You need to be patient and wait for the signal."

"Okey-dokey."

There was a pause.

"Monk . . . ?"

"Yes, Mother?"

"Don't say 'okey-dokey.' "

"Oh. Okay."

Another pause. "How are you doing?"

He suspected that Mother knew about his problems, though not about their severity. The question was layered and it contained traps both obvious and subtle.

Ludo Monk was mad, but he had been managing his damage for too long to make that kind of mistake. On reflection, though, he wondered if Mother knew that about him and was giving him a gentle nudge toward self-management.

"I'm doing well," he told her, and at the moment he meant it.

"Good," said Mother Night.

She disconnected.

Monk moved a chair across the room and positioned it behind the tripod-mounted Russian sniper rifle. He did not check the box magazine. It had been preloaded by another member of their team. Someone who had fingerprints that would be consistent with Russian intelligence.

The tripod was set up well inside the room, away from the window. There was no chance of anyone spotting a gun barrel sticking out, no chance of sun glare on the blued steel. He turned the room lights off, made himself comfortable on the chair, and bent his eye to the scope.

It took very little time to find the big picture window on the third floor. The glass was clear, the angle of the sun was perfect to allow for a crystal-clear view of the boardroom at FreeTech. Several people sat in big leather chairs around a blond wood table. Four women, three men, and a teenage boy. Monk knew little about most of them and cared even less. Mother Night had specified only one target, and Monk knew everything about her. She had a very specific outcome in mind. Actually, Monk appreciated the effect she was going for. It was so deliciously subtle.

He tucked the stock into his shoulder and closed his hand around the gun, laying his finger along the outside of the trigger guard. Across the street, 206 yards away, one of the women began passing blue file folders to the others at the table. She was a very pretty woman. Tall, but not too tall. A bit on the thin side. With masses of curly blond hair and a lovely spray of sun freckles across her nose and cheeks.

Monk looked at that hair. At how light seemed to move through it and change. How it framed so beautiful a face.

He wondered if a bullet would knock that hair off her head.

It was, after all, a wig.

Chapter Thirty-five

Surf Shop 24-Hour Cyber Café
Corner of Fifth Avenue and Garfield Street
Park Slope, Brooklyn
Sunday, August 31, 12:49 p.m.

"Tell me about the girl," I said.

Caleb Sykes, the nerdy kid who ran the cyber café, was sweating bullets. He was seated on a backless stool with the three of us ringed around him and Ghost sitting like a hungry wolf ten feet away. It wasn't exactly thumbscrews and the rack, but that's how he was taking it. I think if I'd yelled "Boo!" he'd have fainted dead away.

"I already t-told y-you," said Sykes. Nerves were bringing out a repressed stutter. I felt bad for the kid and believed that he really had nothing to do with anything. Had to go through the motions, though.

"You said she was Korean," I prompted.

"Yeah. I th-think so."

"Not Chinese? Not Japanese?" asked Top. "You're sure?"

"I used to date a Korean girl. They don't look Chinese or Japanese. They look Korean. But later, on TV . . . she looked Chinese. I d-don't th-think it w-was the s-s-s-same g-g-g—"

He couldn't get it out. I told him it was okay, we understood.

"Did she touch anything in the store?" asked Top.

"Like wh-wh-what?"

"Like anything. Can you remember any specific surface she might have touched with her hands, her fingers."

Caleb suddenly brightened. "Oh! You m-mean f-f-for fingerprints."

"Exactly. Take a second, son, and think about it."

"Um . . . just the c-counter and the m-money she handed me."

"Did she bring her own laptop in?" I asked. "Was she just using your wi-fi, or did she—?"

"She r-r-rented an hour on D-D-Dell Three."

"Show us," said Top.

We stepped back to allow Sykes to rise, but the kid did it carefully as if expecting us to swat him back down in the chair. We didn't. Instead we followed him from the small office we'd been using for the interrogation and into the store. A CLOSED sign was hung in the window. Sykes led us to the table on which was the laptop used by the Korean girl who claimed to be Mother Night.

"This is it?" asked Top.

He nodded.

"You're sure?"

"S-sure I'm sure. It w-w-was on the r-receipt."

Top fished through the receipts and found the right one, read it, and handed it to me. "Station eleven."

Sykes nodded again.

He reached out to touch the closed lid of the laptop for emphasis, but Top caught his wrist.

"Don't do that," he said. "Fingerprints."

"Oh . . . r-right . . ."

We all stood there and considered the laptop. A two-year-old Dell. It was open but turned off.

"How many other people used this computer after the girl?" I asked.

Sykes thought about it. "S-six . . . ?" he suggested.

Top bent over it and grunted. As he straightened he nodded to the machine. "See that?"

I did. It was small, but it was there. And it looked to have been carved into the tabletop with a pin. A capital A surrounded by an O.

I waved Bunny over. "Dust it and bag it."

Bunny produced a device that looked like a department store pricing gun. When he aimed it at the laptop it produced a cold blue laser light.

"What's th-that?" asked Sykes.

"Digital fingerprint scanner," explained Bunny. "Uses a laser to take microfine pictures of fingerprints. There's special software to separate overlapping prints. Does it by determining the orientation, finger pad size, and so on, then it assembles the pieces into as clear a whole as possible."

Sykes said, "W-wow. I watch suh-suh-*CSI* all the t-time and I never saw anything like th-that."

Top smiled at him. "Our boss has a friend in the industry."

My cell phone buzzed again and I nearly tore my pants snatching it out of my pocket. I wanted to smash the damn thing. The message this time was

NO ONE LIVES FOREVER

Ghost suddenly whuffed, and I glanced over my shoulder as a shadow fell across the front window. There were two people standing outside, peering in through the big plate glass.

They were both young. They were both wearing black hoodies and black sunglasses. They were smiling.

They each held a machine gun.

Sykes had played enough video games to know what AK-47s were.

He said, "Wh-what . . . ?"

Then the world exploded into a terrible storm of shattered glass, bullets, screams, and blood.

Chapter Thirty-six

FreeTech
800 Fifth Avenue
New York City
Sunday, August 31, 12:51 p.m.

Toys was winding up his presentation about projects he wanted to fund in the more economically depressed areas of Central and South America, particularly of research into diseases of poverty that were doing incredible damage there. When he realized that Junie Flynn was no longer listening, his words trickled off and stopped.

The others at the table were also studying Junie.

"Is something wrong?" asked Toys.

Without answering, Junie got to her feet and slowly crossed to the big picture window. She stood there, staring out, though it did not appear to Toys as if she was actually looking at anything.

Violin rose, too, and came around the table to stand by Junie. And Toys could see a lot of dangerous potential in the catlike grace with which she moved.

"What is it?" asked Violin.

Junie crossed her arms and hugged herself as if she stood in a cold wind.

"I don't know," she said.

Violin hesitated for a moment, then placed her hand on Junie's shoulder. Junie flinched, then shivered, but she didn't shake off the touch.

"What is it?" Violin repeated. "Is it Joe?"

Junie shook her head. "I don't know," she said softly. "Something's wrong."

Interlude Nine

He caught her looking at him.

"What?" asked Joe Ledger. His tone was rough, all sharp edges.

"Nothing," said Bliss quickly.

"No, it's not nothing. You've been giving me the stink-eye all afternoon," muttered Ledger. He wore a sling and had small bandages taped to almost every visible inch of skin. There was a haunted look in his eyes. Across the street was the blackened hulk of what had been the offices and labs of the Koenig Group, a billion-dollar think tank linked to DARPA. It had been shut down by the DMS after it was learned that—despite contracts, agreements, and laws—the senior management had buyers outside the U.S. government. Ledger had gone in to investigate possible intruders into the supposedly sealed building. Things had apparently gone badly wrong and now the place was a pile of ashes. Bliss had been sent to see if there was anything that could be salvaged. Computers, records, lab equipment, anything. But it was ashes.

A team from the coroner's office was pulling bodies out of the place.

"I'm not giving you the stink-eye," she said.

"Then what's on your mind?"

"They . . . won't let me read your after-action report."

Ledger smiled. A strange and unpleasant smile. "Yeah, well."

"Well . . . what?"

"Well, it wouldn't make good reading."

"Come on," she pleaded. She'd known him for months now. Had even been to a barbecue at his father's place in Baltimore. But Bliss didn't know if she understood Ledger. In his time with the DMS he'd risen to equal Colonel Riggs as the go-to guy for impossible jobs. Dr. Hu hated and feared him, but that didn't matter to Bliss. She'd cooled on Hu, realizing that he was in no way a pathway to power.

"The report is sealed for a reason," said Ledger.

"But *why*?"

His response was a flat stare.

They sat in silence for a while, watching the forensics team pick their way carefully through the still smoking debris. He drank coffee, she sipped from a Diet Coke.

"Joe—?"

"What?"

"Can I ask you something?"

"You did, and I told you I couldn't talk about it."

"No," she said, and she leaned closer to him, dropping her voice, "I want to ask you something else. It's something I've wanted to ask someone for a couple of years but I never knew who to ask."

"I'm probably not the right guy."

"I think you are."

He studied her for a few moments. Then he said, "What's the question?"

"I've read most of your other reports. I've been to a lot of the places you've been to. After you've been there, I mean. You know what I'm saying?"

"Yeah, I guess I do."

"What's it like?"

"What do you mean?"

"Joe . . . come on. They send you in only when they need something *handled*. You know what I mean by that." She didn't ask it as a question.

"So?"

"What's it like?

He sighed. "You're asking what it's like to kill people, right?"

She paused, then nodded.

"It's a lame question."

"Sure, and it's probably offensive," she said, "but my hands aren't exactly clean. The science I help create puts weapons in your hands and you use them to kill people. That means I share some of whatever is there. I'm not going to call it guilt because that's not what it is, is it?"

"Not exactly. Not in any textbook way."

"You're a soldier, a special operator," she said. "You were trained for this sort of thing. You had the mental training for killing as well as the physical, which means you're better prepared for it than I am. I'm a scientist, a geek. Until I joined the DMS the only trigger I ever pulled was in first-person shooter games. I guess it still is. But that doesn't change the fact that my science is being used as your weapon. That means when you kill, I'm part of that process. But I don't understand it. And . . . and I need to."

Ledger said nothing.

"I'm afraid that if I don't understand it," continued Bliss, "then it's going to fuck me up. It's going to do something to my head."

"You talk to Rudy about this?"

"Yes," she said. "He suggested I talk to you."

"Ah."

She waited.

He drank more of his coffee and looked everywhere but at her.

The forensics people pulled another twisted shape out of the rubble.

"If you're sane," he said softly, "you find ways of disconnecting your actions in the field from their context in civilized society. We're a predator species, Bliss. Maybe we're moving toward a point of spiritual peacefulness and grace, but we're not there yet. We have a long damn way to go. Evil is not an abstraction. It's a reality. And there are hundreds of variations on greed and corruption. Anyone who says different is a fool."

She waited, almost holding her breath.

"Killing is necessary in this line of work. The bad guys want to burn down the world. Like the Jakobys. They wanted to kill everyone who wasn't white according to their definition of white. That's evil, and that has to be fought. That kind of evil doesn't give up easily, either. They fight all the way, and they want to rack up as much of a body count as they can on the way down."

She knew he was talking about Grace Courtland, but she didn't say her name. An assassin working for the Jakobys had killed her. There was a rumor that Ledger had hunted the man down and murdered him somewhere in Europe. Courtland's ghost seemed to stand with them, eavesdropping on his words.

Ledger kept watching the forensics techs. "There was a time when I could remember the face and name of everyone I ever hurt. Everyone I ever killed. But since I joined the DMS, I can't even remember how many dozen people I've killed. In a war you don't count the dead and invite them into your head like that. You do that and you lose your shit, you wander into the darkness and you don't come back. That's what happens to some guys who come home from the war. They make the error of taking stock of what they had to do while the war was going on, as if the things done in war could be assessed by a civilized mind. They can't. War is war. The best you can hope for is to have a clear understanding of who the enemy is and what it is you're fighting for. If you can hold that in your head, then you can continue to do whatever needs to be done."

"How do the bad guys do it?" she asked. "How are they able to kill and kill and stay sane?"

"Who says they do?" he asked, shaking his head.

"I've watched some of the tapes of Rudy interviewing some of the people you and Colonel Riggs and the others have arrested. Some of them seem so ordinary. How can they commit those atrocities if they have a conscience? Is it their nature? Or is it a nurture thing, are they from an environment that makes it okay for them?"

Joe grunted. "I asked Rudy that same exact question once."

"What did he say?"

"He said that the nature-versus-nurture argument is fundamentally flawed because it assumes that there are only two possible forces at work on a person. Sure, a person's nature is a factor—and that could be a product of their brain chemistry, or whatever makes a person a sociopath or a psychotic or a hero. Just as the forces at work in a person's life have to be taken into some account. Some abused children grow up to abuse, there's math for that. But neither viewpoint covers all the possible bases."

"So what's missing?"

"Choice," said Ledger. "Rudy thinks that choice is often more important than either nature or nurture. Some people grow up in hell and *choose* to let others share in that hell. Some people grow up in hell and they make damn sure they don't let those in their care even glimpse those fires. It's a choice."

"Not everyone can make that choice."

"No, of course not. But a lot more people can than you might think. Like the Jakobys. Like some of the people we fight. They want to be what they are. They groove on the power and the perks that come with it. It's how they paint the world in the colors that please them."

"Choice," she said.

"Choice," he agreed. "It's what defines us. And it's probably the most underrated power in the world."

"What about conscience?" she asked. "Where does that fall into the equation?"

"It's a factor. If I were naïve I'd tell you that conscience is what steers us toward a good choice instead of a bad, but that's bullshit. Conscience can be kicked to one side, it can be locked away, and in some people I think it can be killed."

"Killed?"

"Yeah. Hate will do it. When you can get to the point where you despise someone else, you can do all sorts of things to them. Look at how white folks treated blacks from the beginning of the slave trade. Those assholes had to convince themselves that blacks were subhuman in order to treat them the way they did. That was hate, sister, and it lasted for centuries."

"You're saying hate killed their conscience?"

"No. It edited their conscience. I imagine the slavers cared about their family and about white folks. They went to church and kissed babies. But they hated their slaves enough to brutalize and dehumanize them. Torture them. You know the drill. Happened to a lot of people in a lot of places. Still happens. There are a lot of sweatshops with women and kids more or less acting as slave labor now. You think the owners have sleepless nights thinking about how their employees feel? You think slumlords give a wet shit about the squalid living conditions in their tenements? And look at the Nazis and . . . well, you see where I'm going with this. My point is that conscience isn't as powerful a force as we'd like it to be. If it was, we'd all be perfect. I sure as hell don't put 'spotless Christian hero' in the blank for 'occupation.' No . . . at the end of the day it's choice. You are what you choose to be. Good or bad, saint or sinner."

She thought about it. "Conscience isn't unbreakable, that's what you're saying?"

He snorted. "I've looked into the eyes of a lot of very bad people, Bliss. I've seen the damaged ones and the insane ones, I've seen the hurt ones and the asswipes who hate anyone that doesn't look like them. Most of them are caught up in the nature, nurture, choice thing. But there are a few—not many, but a few—who don't have a conscience anymore. I'm not talking about sociopaths born without one, if such a thing is really possible. I'm talking about people who, when you look into their eyes, you know you're not looking at through windows of the soul. These are people who have no soul. No conscience. No nothing. They're dead inside."

"Sounds like you're describing a zombie."

"No, zombies are dead meat driven by nerve conduction. You science geeks told me that. No, sister," said Joe, "I'm talking about people who deliberately take a scalpel to their own psyches and carve out their conscience."

Bliss saw dark lights flare in Ledger's eyes.

"That's how evil is born," he said.

Chapter Thirty-seven

Surf Shop 24-Hour Cyber Café
Corner of Fifth Avenue and Garfield Street
Park Slope, Brooklyn
Sunday, August 31, 12:56 p.m.

The innocent and inexperienced often die because they are simply too shocked when violence sets into their lives. The possibility of violence is so foreign to the day-to-day reality of most people that even if they possess good reflexes there is no built-in protocol for how to react. So they hesitate, they stand and stare.

And they die.

In the split second before the smiling killers with the AK-47s opened up, Top hooked an arm around Caleb Sykes and was already in motion, halfway through a brutal diving tackle, when the bullets exploded the glass.

Bunny and I were also in motion. He was diving left, I was falling right and dragging Ghost with me. As we fell, Top, Bunny, and I tore at our jackets, pulling them open, grabbing for our guns.

We are not the innocents; and when it comes to violence and killing we, sadly, are not inexperienced.

The thunder of gunfire was impossibly loud. The huge picture window broke with a sound like all of the glass in the world shattering at once. Bullets tore into wooden desks and exploded the hearts of laptop computers. Chunks of plaster leaped from the walls.

I hit and slid toward the wall and floor, shoving Ghost with me, and I tried to cram us into the woodwork. Debris rained down on us. The razor edges of glass slashed at my clothes and skin. I could feel the bite as splinters sliced me. Blood was hot on my face and limbs. Ghost yelped and whined.

Then I was firing.

Firing.

Firing.

My rounds punched holes in the clouds of gun smoke and flying wreckage. Outside, one of the grinning killers suddenly spun away, but any cry of pain was lost in the din. Blood splashed the other killer, and there was a momentary pause as the second figure turned to watch his partner fall.

In that moment, Bunny put four rounds into his chest and face and blew him apart.

There was a second of silence so deafening I couldn't even hear the echoes of the gunfire. My head felt like it was inside a drum. Ghost scrambled out from under me, his coat glittering with glass splinters, teeth bared in a snarl of pure rage.

Then someone else opened up on us.

Heavy-caliber automatic fire, but muted. Distant. Bullets struck the front door, which disintegrated into meaningless fragments. The CLOSED sign was whipped around and seemed to dissolve into confetti as it was struck over and over again. I saw Bunny, who had begun to rise from the floor, suddenly jerk backward and fall as bullets struck him as other shooters opened up from across the street.

"Ghost—down!" I snapped, and I had to repeat the order to break through his shock and anger. Then he flattened to the floor, out of range of the bullets.

I dropped my magazine, fished for a new one, and slapped it in place, praying that Bunny wasn't dead. In that heartbeat of time it took to swap out the mags I cut a look across the room and saw Top and the kid, Sykes, lying under a blanket of silver and red debris. Silver from the glass, red from blood that ran from dozens of wounds in each of them.

"Green Giant!" called Top, using Bunny's combat call sign. There was fear and desperation in Top's voice.

Bunny didn't answer. I raised my weapon and began firing.

Bullets chopped into the frame around the window, but there was enough of it left to give me a bit of protection. Enough so that I could stand and return fire.

They had assault rifles and they capped off a lot of rounds, but it was wild, the bullets sawing back and forth. They were hosing the place but not really aiming. I found the pattern of their gunfire and took my moment, leaned around the bullet-pocked wall, and fired with every ounce of skill and precision that I've learned as a Ranger, a cop, and a special operator. One of the guns went instantly silent.

But there were four more shooters.

They were arrogant because they thought we were nothing.

They walked toward the front of the store in a loose line, firing, dropping spent magazines onto the blacktop, reloading, firing.

Then I sensed movement behind me and Top was on his feet, cutting low and forward to take cover behind the other side of the ruined window frame. He carried a Glock 34 with a nineteen-round extended magazine. I swapped out my magazine again and gave Top a nod. Then we emptied our magazines into the four men. They had the numbers and the better weapons.

We had the skill.

Even as their bullets continued to chew at our protection, we aimed with precision, forcing down the panic, keeping our heads in the moment, letting all of our training carry us through the insanity. We conserved our ammunition, picked our targets, and killed them. Their bodies juddered and danced, blood erupting from terrible wounds. The slide on my gun locked back.

"I'm out," I said.

"Got this," said Top as he swapped in his last magazine.

But there was nothing left to do.

No one left to fight.

Outside, the street was littered with the dead. Shell casings by the hundreds twinkled in the bright sunlight. Just as it gleamed from the bright blood that flowed out from beneath the bodies. A pall of gun smoke polluted the afternoon air of this quiet part of Brooklyn. In the distance I could see the heads and shoulders of people hiding behind bullet-riddled cars and benches.

Ghost staggered to his feet, furious for having no one to attack. He snarled and showed his fangs, but the only audience left was the dead.

With Ghost beside me, I stepped through the shattered window and scooped up a rifle that lay by the slack hand of one of the first two men I'd killed. I tore a magazine from his pocket, dropped the half-empty one, and slapped the fresh one into place. The echo of thunder still hammered in my head.

Seven bodies were collapsed in ugly heaps.

Smoke ghosts haunted the air above them and drifted between the store and the open doors of a now-empty white panel truck.

The first two shooters were on the pavement just outside the window. One lay in a twist, arms reaching toward the truck as if imploring help that could never arrive. The other was splayed like a starfish.

All of the corpses were dressed in black hoodies.

All of them were young. Twenties. Late teens.

Kids.

Except for the smoke, nothing moved.

The only sound was the fading echo of death and the soft moans from Caleb Sykes.

Then I remembered Bunny and wheeled around, but I saw Top helping him to his feet. There were two holes in Bunny's shirt, but the Kevlar had done its job. Even so, Bunny looked gray and sick and in pain. They stepped through the gaping window, fanning their gun barrels left and right, eyes tracking, looking for more targets.

But there was nothing.

This storm had raged and raged, but now it had passed.

Slowly, almost reluctantly, we lowered our guns.

Far away was the promise of complications as sirens began to wail.

Top looked down at the shooter who lay dead at his feet, arms and legs splayed wide. With the sunglasses blown away, the revealed face was slack in death. It had been a pretty face. A woman's face.

Young. Asian.

"Mother Night?" murmured Top.

But I shook my head.

"I don't know."

Somewhere back inside the store my cell phone lay amid the debris, and I recalled the last text message I'd received. "Nobody lives forever."

Maybe the woman on the ground wasn't Mother Night, but I was now absolutely certain who was sending me messages.

A police car rounded the corner at the end of the block and screamed its way toward us.

Interlude Ten

The Hangar
Floyd Bennett Field
Brooklyn, New York
Three and a Half Years Ago

On a cold November morning Artemisia Bliss trudged into the Hangar, lightly hungover from too many dirty martinis and exhausted from a night with Bill Collins. The man was inexhaustible. She suspected he took something. Viagra and maybe some kind of energizer. Whatever it was, he could go all night like a horny, well-hung version of the Energizer bunny. It was worse than screwing a college boy—and college boys were notorious for having no off button when it came to sex. For her own part, Bliss had a lot of appetite, but she didn't have the staying power she once had.

When she looked into the bathroom mirror before leaving her apartment it was like looking at a zombie movie.

"Yeah," she told her image, "you're ready for that *Vogue* cover shoot."

Dark glasses and a Starbucks drive-through helped.

It was going to be a tough day, too, because she had to finish proofreading the code for a video game simulation she was designing to help test the new VaultBreaker software. It was her idea to hire a bunch of gamers from outside the Defense Department to play the simulation without knowing what it was. She'd convinced Church—and Collins—that only real gamers could test the limits of the software. Her argument had been compelling enough to get approval. Collins had gone to bat for it, too, but from his own direction, and so far no one knew about her relationship with the vice president.

The simulation was a matter of pride for Bliss. It was one of the most elegant and sophisticated game modules in existence, a claim she was certain was true. It really burned that there was no way to take VaultBreaker and turn it into an actual commercial game. It was so devious and crazy, and so damn much fun to play, that she was absolutely positive it would make a hundred million easy. Video games were big business—often pulling in more cash than big-budget movies.

The delicate work of proofreading game code, however, was not going to be a picnic with her head feeling like it was filled with spiders.

But as soon as she walked into the lab complex she knew that her day was about to get worse. Sergeant Gus Dietrich stood beside her desk, and instead of his usual benevolent bulldog grin he wore an expression of pinched disapproval.

"Hey, Gus, what's—?"

"Doctor Bliss," said Gus in a strangely formal way, "you need to come with me."

It was one of those moments when every guilty action ever taken, from jaywalking to screwing her college roommate's father, flashed on the movie screens in her mind.

Do they know?

That was the real question.

Did they know about the duplicated files and all the samples she'd taken while collecting evidence at more than thirty DMS crime scenes?

Did they know?

How *could* they know?

Oh God, what did they know?

"Wh-what's going on, Gus?"

He shook his head. "Aunt Sallie's waiting for you."

Dietrich refused to say anything else as he escorted her down hallways and up a flight of stairs to Auntie's office. The face of the woman behind the desk was locked into a grim scowl.

Bliss began to tremble, but she fought to keep it from showing.

"Sit," ordered Aunt Sallie. She jerked her head for Dietrich to leave.

When they were alone, Auntie leaned back in her big leather chair and studied Bliss through narrowed, suspicious eyes.

"You know why you're here?"

"N-no."

"Really? No idea?"

"No!"

Aunt Sallie lifted a sheet of paper from her desk. Bliss couldn't read it, but it looked like an interoffice memo on the pale green paper used by Bug's computer division. Auntie put on her half-moon granny glasses and read from the memo.

". . . between 3:51 p.m. and 7:18 p.m. MindReader recorded nineteen separate intrusion attacks. These attacks were targeted at bypassing the cycling encryptions. Four attempts were made during that time to bypass the password protection; and three attempts to clone the intrusion software. All attempts were made from the same workstation." She slapped the memo flat onto the desk. "Three guesses whose workstation was used for those attacks?"

Bliss couldn't even speak. The world seemed to have frozen solid around her, turning her blood to slush and freezing her vocal cords.

"Goddamn it, girl, you fucking tell me what's going on right fucking now or by God I will have you arrested and I'll ram the Patriot Act all the way up your tight little cooze." Auntie was so furious that spit flew with every word. Her brown face darkened to a dangerous purple.

"But I—"

Aunt Sallie jabbed a warning finger at her. "Be real careful, girl. You tell me the truth, the whole truth, and nothing but the fucking truth, so help you God."

Time ground to a halt as Bliss's evolved self stepped back from the moment to take a cold, hard look at the situation. There were a lot of ways to play this, most of them bad. She could burst into tears and pretend innocence, claiming that she was just curious. That was even partly true, though it sounded lame enough to walk with a limp. Bliss dismissed it with a mental sneer.

Or she could act genuinely surprised that what she'd done was in any way improper. Aunt Sallie might buy that on the grounds that the policies about not trying to hack MindReader were not so much written as generally understood, and it was impossible to prove the extent to which something like that was grasped. But that was likely to be a long and acrimonious tug-of-war, and Bliss didn't like her chances of winning. It would also never remove the stink of suspicion.

Then there was the way her evolved self wanted to play it. It was totally out of character with the Artemisia Bliss who'd been working here for three and a half years, but not entirely out of character for the Bliss who'd been interviewed by Dr. Hu. Surely that interview had been recorded. Her attitude and self-possession had to be part of her record, even if since then she'd played the role of a dutiful team member.

Yes, that felt like a good card. Maybe the only real card she could play without going bust.

Auntie's eyes seemed to exude real heat.

So Bliss untangled her fingers, leaned forward, and placed her palms down on the edge of the desk. She deliberately shifted her posture forward in a way that was a borderline physical threat.

In a voice as flat and cold as a reptile, she said, "Excuse me, but who the fuck do you think you're talking to?"

Aunt Sallie, veteran of a hundred violent field encounters, blinked. She said, "What?"

"You heard me. Who the fuck do you think you're talking to here? You drag me in here and accuse me of impropriety. *Me?* I bust my ass all day, every day to make sure the DMS is cutting-edge. With my skills and my brains I could be a billionaire by now, filing patent after patent, kicking Bill Gates in the nuts with my designs. I could have made fortunes designing video games. Instead, I work for salary night and day to make sure that every threat we face is assessed and defeated as quickly as possible. I wrote the code for two thirds of the tactical software packages every one of our teams relies on when they go into battle. I *designed* the security simulations that keep every DMS facility secure from cyberattack and I co-designed most of the physical security systems. My programs are built into every workstation, every MindReader field kit, and even into some of the counterintrusion software Bug installed into MindReader itself. And who do you think came up with the idea for VaultBreaker? The fucking Easter Bunny? Shit. You want to know why I tried to get into MindReader? Because I need to be prepared for when someone tries it for real. I need to understand the safety measures so that I can be ready with backup, with stronger and fresher systems, with new designs no one has ever thought up. That's why you hired me and that's what I do, and fuck you, but I do that better than *anyone* else."

Her voice was never once raised above an arctic snarl.

The moment held as the two women glared across the width of the desk and a frozen wasteland at each other.

"Making modifications on MindReader is not part of your job," said Auntie, but her voice had lost some of its edge. "All modifications are overseen by—"

"By Bug, I know. So what? He's smart, sure, but he isn't the smartest person in this building by a long stretch. You don't believe that, look at our last performance evaluations. Hell, look at our scores on game simulator speedruns."

Aunt Sallie did not reply, and Bliss knew that she'd scored big with that. Either Auntie already knew those scores or she hadn't checked. In either case she was short one card.

Bliss's heart was going a million miles an hour but she'd be damned if she'd let it show on her face. Instead she played her next card.

"Tell you what, Auntie," she said, her voice about twenty degrees colder, "why don't you go through the field reports of the last forty missions. Pick any teams at random, any missions. Then do the math to see whose software contributed most to preserving the lives of our operators and insuring the success of the missions. Match that against Bug or *anyone* else, then if you have anything to say to me we can do it as part of my exit interview. Otherwise I'm done with this bullshit and I have work to do."

She stood up, intending to use the objectivity of the height of a standing person over one sitting to put Aunt Sallie in a defensive position. Instead, Aunt Sallie smiled and folded her hands primly on her desk.

"Sit your ass down," she said. Her voice was on the cold side of dangerous.

Bliss gave it a moment, then sat. Slowly, and with control.

"You spoke your mind, and it's nice to know that you have a backbone. After all these years I was beginning to wonder. And maybe you're being straight up and not simply wiping your ass with the flag, but I have two things you need to hear."

Bliss said nothing, knowing that any response would weaken her hand. Instead she arched one eyebrow. Half interested, half mocking.

"First," said Aunt Sallie, "you do not have full clearance on Mind-Reader, and that means you will attempt no further intrusions into the system. I don't care if there are missiles inbound and that's the only way to save the day. You. Don't. Hack. MindReader." Aunt Sallie spaced those last four words like gunshots.

Instead of replying or acknowledging that, Bliss asked, "And what's the other thing?"

"Don't ever get in my face again," said Aunt Sallie.

Bliss leaned back in her chair and crossed her legs. She gave it a moment while she composed the best response, given the nature of the implied threat, the nature of her own faux pas, and the echo of her own words which still hung in the air.

"A lot of people are afraid of you, Auntie," said Bliss, her tone conversational. "Maybe they have reasons. There are a lot of tall tales floating around about you. And even if half of them are true then once upon a time you were hot shit. Well, here's a news flash, that's not even yesterday's news. It's last century's. You're a bitchy, foul-mouthed, and disgruntled old woman who likes to bully people and you probably get some kind of contact high every time you verbally bitch-slap someone. It's all very interesting and maybe it would make a good movie. But in the real world, in the world of right now, I'm more valuable to the DMS than you are. You're not a scientist and you're long past being a field agent, and this organization's entire effectiveness is built on geeks and shooters. I'm worth ten of you. Now either fire me or fuck off."

Later, back at her desk, Bliss tried not to smile.

An official reprimand went into her file. And that wasn't worth the paper it was printed on, since she worked for a secret organization. Besides, she could take her skills anywhere—even outside of the Department of Defense, DARPA, or any related group—and if she couldn't file patents on what she'd done as part of the DMS, she knew that she had a lot more game. She'd come up with something brand new. Something that would kick the ass of everything else on the market.

That evening she lay in the warm circle of the vice president's arms in a hotel room guarded by Secret Service agents who were totally owned by Collins. The vice president's wife was on yet another charity trip. Bliss told Collins everything that had happened.

They both laughed until they cried.

Chapter Thirty-eight

Surf Shop 24-Hour Cyber Café
Corner of Fifth Avenue and Garfield Street
Park Slope, Brooklyn
Sunday, August 31, 1:17 p.m.

I tapped my earbud for Bug but got Nikki instead.

I told her about the attack and ordered her to put it into the system with A-clearance priority.

"God, are you all right?"

I had glass splinters in my hair and a case of the shakes I was sure would never go away. I wanted to curl up on my couch with a pint of Ben and Jerry's and watch daytime TV until I no longer believed that there was a real world.

"Sure," I said, "I'm just peachy. Listen, kid, have you guys made any progress on those text messages? 'Cause I got one right before the hit."

"Not so far, but—"

"Put more people on it," I barked, and told her about the one I got right before the attack. "These have to be coming from Mother Night. Which means she knows my cell number and she can bypass MindReader. I don't care what you have to do, but get this solved."

Then my brain shifted gears so fast that I nearly hurt myself.

"Wait a goddamn minute. The message before that last one. *You always hurt the one you love.* Christ, it sounded stupid at the time but it sure as shit doesn't now. It sounds like a threat. Junie is at FreeTech. I want two security guards bookending her and I want it right fucking now. And call her to let her know they're coming. Don't talk to me. Make it happen."

She was gone.

I stood trembling in the street, but now the shakes had nothing to do with gun battles or flesh wounds.

"No," I said to the day—to this awful, awful day. "No."

Chapter Thirty-nine

NYPD transit officer Maureen Faustino stared into darkness.

"What happened to the damn lights?" she asked as she reached for her flash.

A few feet away, her partner, Sonny Dawes, clicked his light on. The beam reached twenty yards down the subway tunnel before being consumed by the intense darkness. Faustino turned her flash on and swept it along the ceiling and the damp walls. Rows of security lights in wire cages were dark.

With her other hand, Faustino clicked her shoulder mike and reported the power outage. The dispatcher noted it and told them to proceed with caution.

Use caution walking into a pitch-black tunnel? thought Faustino. *No shit.*

"How far's the train?" asked Dawes.

"Dispatch says six hundred yards."

They looked at the utter blackness beyond their flashlight beams.

"Well, fuck a duck," said Dawes.

They glanced at each other for a moment, nodded, and drew their guns.

Faustino and Dawes were down here responding to a call from the conductor. There had been some cell calls from people trapped on the train, but those calls were badly distorted by some kind of interference, and then they all abruptly stopped. To prevent a collision, the transit company halted all other trains on that line, so now people were in stations all along it, getting impatient, getting pissed, demanding answers.

No further contact had been established with anyone on the train.

Faustino swallowed nervously. Nothing about this felt right.

"Think we should call for backup?" asked Dawes.

"For what?" answered Faustino. Though, in truth, she wanted to do just that. She didn't, though. The transit authority had begun installation of cellular carrier boosters in the subway system, but there were still cell phone dead spots, and they seemed to be in one. Hardly justification to ask for additional units when everyone was already stretched thin because of Labor Day. Besides, they were both experienced at this sort of thing—the New York version of tunnel rats. Faustino had lost track of how many times she'd had to walk through these stone veins beneath the city.

"Let's go," she said, and together they moved single-file along a narrow concrete service walkway.

The smell was damp and electrical, with undertones of rot and waste.

The tunnels were bad enough when the lights were on. Vermin of every kind. Cockroaches big enough to mug you. Shit from homeless people coming down here to take a dump. Syringes and crack vials underfoot—though Faustino could never imagine anyone coming down here to get high. And the constant drip of water and puddles that never seemed to evaporate.

Dawes pointed. "There's a light up there."

She looked past him and saw something. Not a train light or a service light. This was small and red. And as they approached they saw that it was a small security camera of a kind they'd never seen before. Very compact and brand new, stuck to a pillar with some kind of adhesive.

"Since when are they putting CCTV down here?" asked Dawes. "And what for? To watch rats fuck each other?"

"Hey, watch your language," cautioned Faustino in a whisper. She pulled him away from the camera. "You don't know who's watching. Don't want to get written up."

He nodded and they pressed on, but soon found a second camera. And a third.

"Must be something new," decided Faustino. "Quality control or something."

"Not our problem," said Dawes. Then he stopped and squinted into the shadows. "Wait . . . you hear that?"

Faustino listened.

She heard nothing.

And then she heard something.

Very faint, very far away. Soft. Distorted by distance and . . .

"You hear that?" asked Dawes.

"Yeah. But I can't . . ." Her words trailed off as the sound came again, a little louder now.

It wasn't a scream or a yell for help. Nothing like that.

But it was a human sound.

Almost like . . . singing. Faustino frowned, trying to understand what she was hearing. No, not singing. This noise was not musical. Not humming either, though that was a little closer to the quality of the sound that drifted on the fetid breaths of bad air.

It was like someone was keening.

The way old women do sometimes at funerals. The way her aunt Maria used to do. A steady, keening sound that chilled Faustino to the marrow.

Whatever it was, it was wrong in ways she could not identify.

Something worse than any malfunction of motors or generators.

"Call this in," whispered Dawes. "We need someone else down here."

This time Faustino did not argue. She keyed her mike for dispatch.

And got a burst of sharp static.

Faustino adjusted her squelch and tried it again.

More static, but this time she could hear a voice.

". . . at . . . ituation . . . all back and . . ."

Just pieces.

Then nothing as the signal faded and died.

Faustino could feel Dawes's breath on her cheek and throat. As close as a lover, the exhaled air warmer than anything down in this tunnel.

"What *is* that?" she asked.

They both knew she wasn't asking about the message from dispatch.

The sound filled the tunnel, rolling in waves, rising and falling.

Human voices.

Not singing.

Not humming.

They were . . . *moaning*.

Chapter Forty

Bug perched on his chair, eyes darting from screen to screen as his slender fingers danced like hummingbird wings over the keys. A lot seemed to be happening in the world, and none of it was good. Bombings in Kentucky and Pennsylvania, a bizarre spike in random violence ranging from gang attacks in upscale neighborhoods in five states to eight separate attacks on salespersons in stores in different parts of the south, and arson in three sporting goods warehouses in Indiana. Individually, they were the kind of events that would make headlines and be top stories on any news broadcast. Collectively, they were likely to make this the most violent day in the country in a decade. News services were already slanting their coverage that way.

Bug and his team were running it all through MindReader's pattern-recognition software. There was no known connection and no reason to believe that these events were connected, but Bug didn't like coincidences any more than his boss did. Also, the Mother Night cyberhacking had everyone on edge. Her message used anarchist rhetoric, and the craziness sweeping the country felt like things were falling apart. So Bug created a search argument for anarchistic behavior and asked MindReader to create a list of possible connections. Sadly, this being America, the list of apparently random acts of violence grew too rapidly to read.

Sighing, Bug let that compile and worked on ways to refine the search so it didn't include everything from road rage to jaywalking.

His intercom buzzed and he hit a key to take a call from his senior assistant, Yoda—which, sadly, was his real first name. Yoda's parents were ultrageeks even by Bug's standards.

"Bug!" gasped Yoda. "Jesus, man, you have to see this."

"See what?"

"It's from my friend at the NYPD. He sends me stuff when there's something hot. This is direct from the subway in Brooklyn. You have to see this shit to believe it."

"I'm really swamped here, Yoda, and . . ."

Bug's words trailed off as a video feed filled the main screen with dozens of smaller windows, each one showing a crowd of civilians crammed into a tight space. It was clear that the crowd was standing in darkness and lit only by the glow from cell phones and tablets. The pictures were erratic. People were screaming, yelling for help, shouting at one another.

Then one by one most of the phones fell or were knocked from the hands of the people making the calls. Instead of normal angles, the phones lay on the floor or on seats of what was obviously a subway car.

"What the hell . . . ?" whispered Bug.

The people on the subway car were tearing one another to pieces.

They were *eating* one another.

Chapter Forty-one

Joseph Curseen, Jr., and Thomas Morris, Jr., Processing and Distribution Center

900 Brentwood Road, Northeast

Washington, D.C.

Sunday, August 31, 1:21 p.m.

The mailroom at the Brentwood processing center receives tens of thousands of pieces of mail each day addressed to the White House and Congress. It operates twenty-four hours a day and rarely pauses for holidays. Items marked for the personal attention of select individuals in the succession of powers were culled from the mass and sorted separately, put in sacks and sent by cart to a senior sorter for screening.

On Sunday morning, Jorge Cantu loaded the fourth mail sack onto the conveyor belt that fed the sacks through a high-tech scanner. There were several sections of the scanner, including an X-ray, a metal detector, an explosives detection system—EDS—and a bio-aerosol mass spectrometer typically called a BAMS unit. If any of these machines so much as coughed, Cantu stopped the belt and hit an alert button. Different alerts resulted in different kinds of responses.

The nitrite sniffer never, in Cantu's experience, beeped, because there were similar explosives detection devices used by the Post Office and Secret Service before the bags were ever sent to the mailroom. Ditto for the metal detectors. Once in a while something like a bolo tie from a western resident or a tin of chocolates from a sewing club in New England would make it as far as the White House mailroom, but never any farther. No matter how well-intentioned, gifts of that kind sent through the mail seldom made it even as far as the president's staff. Never to the desk in the Oval Office.

The same scrutiny was afforded to the vice president, Speaker of the House, and other notables. There had been enough problems, even before 9/11, that no one took chances. And there were so many stages of screening that Cantu seldom encountered anything more dire than junk mail. Once, though, a load of dog crap sealed in plastic made it to the desk of the press secretary's assistant before it was discovered. The package included a note that said, "At least this shit is honest."

No return address.

There was a rumor that the press secretary had the letter framed.

Otherwise, the mailroom at Brentwood was busy but not particularly interesting.

Until the morning of August 31.

A warning light flashed red and a small bell suddenly started ringing.

Not the bomb alert.

Not the metal detector.

This bell was one that had never rung once in the seven years Jorge Cantu had sorted mail for this administration.

It was the warning alert for the mass spectrometer.

The device whose sole purpose was to detect dangerous particles. It had four colored lights. Green for normal. Yellow for suspicious. Orange for likely toxins.

And red for a verified hit on one of four possible threats.

Spores.

Fungi.

Bacteria.

Or viruses.

Cantu stared at the light as the bell jangled in his ear. He said, "Oh my god!"

He hit the stop button and stumbled backward from the scanner, kicking his chair over with a crash, heels slipping on the floor in his haste.

"*Red light on four!*" he yelled. "*Red light on four.*"

There was instant motion, the slap of shoes on the hard floor, shouts as Secret Service agents hustled in his direction.

"Step back from the scanner," ordered the lead agent even though Cantu was already as far back as he could go.

Within minutes the mailroom was cleared as were adjoining offices in that part of the mail processing center. Dozens of people flooded in, however. Police first, then within minutes agents from Homeland arrived. Soon techs in hazmat suits descended on the center accompanied by squads of supervisory personnel.

The bag was removed from the scanner and placed very gingerly into a portable steel biocontainment unit. The scanner was draped in chemically treated cloth and the entire area was sprayed with a ferociously dangerous antibacterial, antiviral agent.

The biocontainment unit was loaded onto a specially designed truck, and it roared off with heavy support from Secret Service and Homeland officers in riot gear. The motorcade went lights-and-sirens to a facility in Arlington where scientists and technicians waited.

The bag was offloaded, scanned again for explosive devices, and when it was conclusively determined that nothing was going to blow up, the bag was opened and the contents each placed in a separate biohazard container. The pieces were then scanned by a much more acute BAMS unit, and although several pieces of mail were deemed to have secondary contamination, the techs quickly identified an envelope that they separated out. It was a standard white greeting card envelope sealed with clear adhesive tape. No bulges, no metal or plastic components. The envelope was moved to a special containment chamber and a scientist used Waldo gloves to slit the envelope open and remove the card. A Hallmark card.

On the front of the card was a photo of a field of flowers that rose up to the crest of a gently sloping hill. Beyond the hill were trees and puffy white clouds. In flowing script across the top of the card were the words *So sorry for your loss*. It was obvious that the sentiment was printed as part of the card's professional design.

The card had no preprinted message inside. Instead there was a handwritten note.

Payment in kind.
Seems only fair.
Hugs and kisses,
Mother Night

Inside the card, compressed between the cardboard covers, contained by the heavy grade envelope and tape, was a fine-grained white powder.

High-res digital images of the card, envelope, and message were sent to the Secret Service and Homeland. Laser scans of the card were initiated to capture any fingerprints. Small samples of the card, the envelope, and the tape were taken for separate analysis.

But that was secondary to the rush to analyze the white powder.

The BAMS unit had provided a preliminary identification, but the techs at the Arlington lab were able to discover much more about it. So much more that the BAMS reading was later viewed as "inadequate."

Yes, the BAMS unit correctly identified it as *Bacillus anthracis*.

Anthrax.

But that description did not and could not fully describe the bacterium in that powder. It was like nothing the Arlington lab had ever seen. A mutation of anthrax so virulent that it was terrifying.

Data and samples were flown by armed couriers to military laboratories at Fort McNair in D.C. and Fort Myer in Virginia, next to Arlington Cemetery.

The information about the terrorist attempt was shared with the national security advisor, who requested an immediate audience with the president and vice president. When the president's chief of staff asked why the vice president's presence was requested, the answer was simple, though frightening and inexplicable.

The letter had been addressed to the vice president.

Chapter Forty-two

Officers Faustino and Dawes stood listening to the darkness. Listening to how wrong it was. The moans came rolling down the line, louder now. Stranger.

They were not moans of passion or disappointment. Not moans of defeat or frustration.

The moans were filled with hunger. Faustino knew that, even though she could never explain to herself or anyone else *why* she knew it. Her reaction and the understanding that came with it was purely primal. This was the sound of a hunger so deep, so vast that it could never be assuaged.

The two officers pointed flashlights and guns into the darkness but did not take another step toward that sound.

No way.

"What *is* that?" said Dawes in a voice that trembled with fear.

Faustino took several long, steadying breaths before she reached for her shoulder mike. She keyed the button and called for dispatch.

Got static.

Got nothing else.

The moaning was continual.

"Shit, shit, shit," whispered Faustino. She glanced up at one of the small security cameras with its steady red light. It reminded her of a rat's eye. "I wonder if anyone's watching."

Dawes waved at the camera. "Hey! Anyone there?"

Of course there was no answer.

Faustino stepped in front of the lens. "This is Police Officer Maureen Faustino and Officer Sonny Dawes. We're down in the subway tunnel near Euclid Avenue. The lights and power are off down here and we're not getting radio reception. If anyone is watching this, please contact our department and tell them officers are requesting backup."

She gave some additional information, including their estimated position in the tunnel and their badge numbers.

The red light remained fixed and uninformative.

In the darkness the echoes of the terrible moans were growing louder.

"Oh, man," complained Dawes, "what the hell *is* that?"

"Shit," muttered Faustino. "C'mon, Sonny, we have to find out."

They stood where they were for another minute. The hungry moans bounced off the walls and were amplified by distance and fear and cold concrete.

"Fuck this," said Dawes. "I think we need to get our asses back to Euclid Station and see if we can get a signal. Or use an emergency phone. Something."

"Yeah," she agreed.

They didn't move.

"Shit," Dawes said after another minute.

"Shit," agreed Faustino.

They began moving forward. Not toward Euclid, but farther down the tunnel. Toward the moans.

Their feet crunched softly on the walkway, the sound battered to insignificance by the moans. The tunnel curved around, and from the intensity of the sounds they knew that the train had to be right there, no more than twenty yards away. There were more of the small security cameras mounted on the wall. Faustino had a weird feeling about them, but right now they were the least of her concerns.

The officers paused again, whispering to each other the way cops do, stating proper procedure, assigning right-and-left approaches, reminding themselves that they were in control of the moment.

It usually worked.

It didn't work now.

Like a pair of frightened children they crept around the bend in the tunnel, keeping their flashlight beams low so as not to signal whoever was inside the train. They saw their light gleam on the silver rails and then reflect dully from the steel body of the last car. The blocky lines of the train, the letter C in the window.

There was no one outside the car.

But there was so much noise coming from inside.

The moans.

Those terrible moans.

And other sounds they hadn't heard before. Dull thumps. From inside. Like weak fists pounding on the doors and windows.

Inside.

Faustino slowly raised the beam of her flashlight and the glow climbed over the metal skin to the big panes of glass on either side of the rear door. The glass was cracked. Spiderweb faults were laced outward from multiple impact points. Behind the glass, darkened figures moved. The pounding sounds continued and Faustino realized that the people inside were banging on the glass.

Cracking it.

Breaking it.

Trying to get out.

"Jesus Christ," yelled Dawes, "they're trapped."

He suddenly broke and ran forward, leaping down from the service walkway.

"Hey!" he called at the top of his voice. "New York Police. We're here to help you. Just calm down and we'll get you out."

Behind him, Faustino stood her ground. Her flashlight beam still covered the rear of the car, sparkling along the fissures that continued to spread out from the damaged glass.

There was color on the inside of the glass.

Red.

Blood red.

For a moment she thought that the people had injured themselves trying to break out of the crippled train. But that made no sense. The rear door wasn't locked. Anyone could open it.

Anyone.

The pounding continued, despite Dawes's yells.

The moaning got louder.

More insistent.

Hungrier.

As Dawes raised his leg to climb onto the back of the train, Faustino shouted a single word.

"No!"

Chapter Forty-three

Bug lunged for the phone. Not the regular phone, or the one connected to the Tactical Operations Center. He grabbed a slender black one that automatically made a call when the handset was picked up. Bug waited through two rings that seemed to take an interminable time, then the call was answered.

"Bug," said Mr. Church.

"It's happening again!" cried Bug. "*Oh sweet Jesus they're back!*"

"What's happening? Calm down and—"

Bug pounded the keys that would send the feed to Mr. Church.

"They're *back*," Bug said in a strangled voice.

There was a profound silence on the other end of the line.

Then, "Where did you get this? Where is this happening?"

Bug told him.

"Spin up the system," growled Church. "Put all teams on maximum alert, recall all off-duty personnel. Do it *now*."

"Already doing it," Bug said. His fingers flew across the keys.

Chapter Forty-four

Boo Radley laid several folders on the vice president's desk.

"These are the latest reports on the Mother Night video," said Radley. "As you'll see, the task force hasn't locked anything down yet, but they're following some promising leads. We reached out to the DMS for assistance, hoping that they'd do some deep searches for us with MindReader."

"Is the Deacon stonewalling us as usual?"

"Actually, sir, they're not."

Collins raised an eyebrow. "Oh?"

"They've been unusually cooperative today, and it's because of their help that we've gotten as far as we have."

"Hm," grunted Collins. "Keep that back-and-forth going, Boo, but make sure that when we get something solid we have the first men through the door. I want our cuffs on these hacker assholes, not the DMS's, you hear me?"

"Loud and clear, sir," said Radley with a cold little smile. "I took the liberty of passing along a similarly worded message to our division heads."

"Nice." Collins set the top folder aside and opened the second. "What's this? The anthrax thing?"

"Yes."

"Where are we with that?"

"It's too soon to be anywhere, sir, but the president has thrown his full support behind the investigation and that's greased the wheels a bit."

"As well he should."

"Agreed, Mr. Vice President."

Collins leafed through the file, then slapped the cover shut. "Christ, I want this psycho bitch found. I want her head on a pole."

In his private thoughts, he smirked and rephrased that as *I want her on my pole . . . again.*

Collins was aware that his inner self was often a twenty-year-old frat boy, but he was fine with that. Kept him young.

Radley's cell rang. He looked at it, arched an eyebrow, and excused himself as he stepped a few feet away to take the call. Collins listened to one side of the conversation.

". . . I'm with the vice president," said Radley. "No, I haven't heard—Wait, what—? What channel?" With the phone still pressed to his ear, he suddenly crossed to the table, picked up the remote, and jabbed it toward the TV. "It's on now. Get me everything you have on this. No . . . I'll stay here with the vice president. C'mon, get your ass in gear. Get moving on this and give us regular updates."

He lowered the phone, looking dazed and sweaty.

"Now what?" demanded Collins.

Radley swallowed. "Sir, there's been an incident on a subway train in Brooklyn."

They both turned to the television, which showed a grainy, jumpy, and badly lit image of what looked like a brawl. Radley turned up the volume, and the shrill sound of screams filled the office.

The voice of the commentator from the local ABC affiliate was rattling on in a tone that was partly normal shock and partly the malicious delight of a news reporter.

"If you're just joining us, we have exclusive coverage of what appears to be a deadly riot on the C train in Brooklyn, New York. We must warn you that these images are streaming live. We have not watched them and the content may be too intense for some viewers."

On the screen a portly Latina grabbed the arm of whoever was filming the melee with his cell. There was a flash of white teeth, a terrible scream, and then bright red blood spurted from a vicious wound. The cell fell to the floor and a moment later the signal was cut as someone stepped on it.

The news reporter was caught in a moment of shocked silence, then he dived right in, taking his own bite out of the story. The screen divided into two smaller windows as the footage was replayed while the reporter commented on it.

"Details are still sketchy but reporters are en route to the C train to bring you up-to-the-minute coverage of this unfolding situation. To re-cap what we know, there appears to be a deadly riot aboard a stalled train near the Euclid—"

Radley stood with a hand to his mouth. "My god . . . what's happening?"

Vice President William Collins could feel the shock tightening the muscles of his own face. It was, indeed, shocking to see something like this.

It was so much more *real* and messy than he'd imagined.

Though, he mused, it was every bit as impressive as Mother Night said it would be.

His mouth said, "Dear God in heaven."

His mind said, *Nice!*

Chapter Forty-five

Ludo Monk's phone rang and he sat back from his rifle with mixed emotions. Part of him was suddenly disappointed because he wanted to pull the trigger and see what kind of red splash patterns he could paint on the walls. The woman with the blond wig and the others at the conference table were just waiting for his bullets, begging for them, really.

The other part of him—the part that was responding to the pills he'd swallowed—did not want to pull the trigger. That part of him wanted to find a church and talk to a priest and see what it would take to buy a ticket back from the outer rings of hell. He had money and was willing to make significant donations to have a reasonable priest apply a fresh coat of whitewash on his immortal soul.

However, the call was from Mother Night, so he sighed, picked up his phone, and answered.

"Yes, Mother?"

"You haven't taken that shot, have you?"

"No," he said sulkily, "you said not to."

"Good boy. We're moving some pieces around on the board. The target may return to her hotel or go to another location. Possibly the Hangar. If so, I want you to use one of the fallback locations for the shot."

"Why not now? I can do her right now."

"The timing is wrong, Ludo. How many times have I told you, it's not the target, it's the timing."

He grumbled something to himself. Not loud enough for her to hear.

"This is a tweak on the model," said Mother, "and it's within the operational plan we discussed, so stop bitching. You'll get your shot. Stay ready and I'll call back in a few minutes to give you the go order."

"Okey-dokey."

A sigh on the other end of the line. "Ludo . . . don't say okey-dokey."

"Sure."

The line went dead.

Ludo lowered the phone. The room was awash in brown shadows intercut with bars of light that sliced through the gaps in the blinds. The rifle waited on its tripod. Calling to him. Flirting with him. Daring him to touch it. Wanting him to.

Across the street heads waited for bullets.

Wanting them, he was sure of it.

"Okey-dokey," he said to the empty room.

Chapter Forty-six

Fulton Street Line
Near Euclid Avenue Station
Brooklyn, New York
Sunday, August 31, 1:27 p.m.

It was a burst of squelch that saved the lives of Officers Faustino and Dawes.

A static rasp and then a voice.

"*. . . your location . . .*"

"Sonny," cried Faustino. "Don't. We got the radio."

Dawes stopped with his leg raised to climb onto the back of the car. A few feet above him, darkened figures moved behind the cracked glass. Dawes looked from his partner to the milling shapes, and he lowered his leg and stepped back.

Faustino plucked her radio from her shoulder and keyed the mike to call dispatch. The connection was bad and polluted by static, but she reported the situation and asked for orders. The delay in response was so long that Faustino was worried that the connection had been lost. Inside the train, the pounding was getting louder, more urgent.

Dawes stared up at the shapes like a man transfixed.

"How come nobody's saying nothing?" he said.

Faustino held the radio to her ear to hear what the dispatcher was trying to say.

"*. . . ordered to return . . . station . . .*"

"How come none of them people are saying nothing?" demanded Dawes.

"Dispatch," growled Faustino, "you're breaking up. Repeat message."

The reply was almost totally garbled. Faustino was able to pick only four words out of the mess, but those words were enough to chill the blood in her veins even more than the sound of that awful moaning.

"... *biohazard* ... *do not approach* ..."

"*Dawes!*" she shrieked as she holstered her gun, grabbed her partner by the arm, and dragged him backward.

"What the fuck—?" he barked, surprised by the violence of her grab.

"Sonny, they told us to get back."

"There are *people* in there."

"*They said it's a biohazard situation.*"

That shut him up and he allowed himself to be dragged back to the midpoint of the tunnel's curve.

Suddenly he was backpedaling, scrambling as fast as he could to get away from the train. "Oh God oh God oh God!" he said in one long continuous breath.

They retreated all the way around the bend and then another hundred yards, both of them panting like dogs, running forward and then backward, too scared to really think.

"What . . . what is it?" gasped Dawes as they slowed to a trembling stop.

She shook her head and once more the radio was filled with useless static. "I don't know, I don't know. Some kind of toxic thing. They didn't say what it was. The connection's fucked."

He gripped her sleeve. "Christ, you think it's a terrorist thing? Anthrax or some shit?"

Faustino shook her head. Not in denial, but in fear that he might be right. Now it all seemed to make sense; a brutal and broken kind of sense. The moans, the lack of verbal communication.

Then they froze as they heard new sounds. Not from the train. Behind them. They whirled, guns up and out.

These sounds were different. Loud, insistent. Boots crunching on the ground, splashing through water. The creak of leather, the rattle of metal, the whisk-whisk of clothing.

And shouts.

Human voices.

The a dozen figures came pelting out of the darkness. A full SWAT team in Kevlar and body armor, helmets and guns, lights and shouting voices. They spotted Dawes and Faustino. One of them—a man with sergeant's stripes—stopped and pointed his rifle at them.

"Holster your weapons," he shouted. "Do it now."

Numbly, Faustino and Dawes slipped their Glocks into the holsters at their hips. They identified themselves and stood with their hands well away from their guns.

The SWAT team surged past, running at full speed down the tunnel toward the train, which was still hidden by darkness farther along the track.

"Officer Dawes," said the sergeant, "Officer Faustino, did you approach the train?"

"What?" said Faustino. "No, we—"

"Did you go inside the train?"

"I told you, we didn't—"

"Did you encounter anyone else down here?"

"What's going on?"

The man pointed his rifle at her head. "Did you encounter anyone down here? Anyone at all?"

"Get that rifle out of my fucking face."

The sergeant's hands were rock steady, the black eye of the gun barrel relentless in its stare. "I won't ask again, officer," he said.

Faustino and Dawes exchanged a look.

"Don't look at your partner, officer," warned the sergeant. "Look at me, and tell me if you encountered anyone or spoke to anyone since you came down here."

"No," said Dawes hastily. "No one, man. Just us. And this is as far as we got."

The gun barrel moved from Faustino to Dawes. "Be sure, officer."

Faustino swallowed a lump in her throat that felt as big and rough as a pinecone.

"What's happening?"

The sergeant studied her for a moment, then lowered his gun. "Listen to me," he said in a more human tone, "we received a call saying that a biological agent had been released on that train. It's happening."

"What's happening?"

The SWAT sergeant shook his head. "We've been hit again."

Neither Faustino nor Dawes had to ask what that meant. This was New York. It would take a lot of years before the events of 9/11 had to be explained.

The sergeant pointed a finger at the two cops. "Get the fuck out of here now. Get back to Euclid Avenue Station. Make sure nobody comes down here. Do you understand me? *Nobody*."

He did not wait for their answer, did not flinch or respond to their outraged protest. Instead he ran into the tunnel, and a few moments later they heard another gun open up.

Faustino drew her pistol.

So did Dawes.

And for a moment they stood facing the direction of the gunfire.

"What the hell's happening?" asked Dawes. He sounded absolutely terrified.

All Faustino could do was shake her head.

Together, guns raised and pointing, they began backing away. Soon they turned and ran for the lights of Euclid Avenue Station.

They hadn't gone two hundred feet before a new sound tore through the chatter of gunfire and the dreadful moans. These sounds were sharper, higher. Far more horrible.

It was the sound of men in great fear and great pain . . . screaming.

Chapter Forty-seven

The Hangar
Floyd Bennett Field
Brooklyn, New York
Sunday, August 31, 1:28 p.m.

Rudy Sanchez came running into the Tactical Operations Center just as all hell was breaking loose. He spotted Aunt Sallie and Mr. Church, who were each speaking hurriedly into telephones. He rushed over to them, and as Church disconnected a call, Rudy touched his arm.

"*Dios mio*, is it true?" cried Rudy. "Is it true?"

Church gave him one moment of a hard, flat stare.

"I pray that it is not, doctor."

"But—?"

"But I fear that it is."

Church turned away to make another call. And another.

Rudy, helpless and impotent, could only stand and stare.

And pray.

Chapter Forty-eight

Surf Shop 24-Hour Cyber Café

Corner of Fifth Avenue and Garfield Street

Park Slope, Brooklyn

Sunday, August 31, 1:28 p.m.

I stood in the street, watching the police and paramedics do their job. I was shirtless, and the left leg of my trousers had been slit from ankle to hip. Bloody bandages were wrapped and taped in place. I felt sore, angry, and older than my thirty-odd years. Someone had brushed the glass out of Ghost's fur and wrapped some gauze around his legs and chest to staunch the flow of blood from a dozen shallow cuts.

A dozen yards away, Bunny sat in the open back of an ambulance while a nervous EMT picked glass and wood splinters out of his back. Top stood watching, his face an unreadable stone. The EMTs had argued with them both, wanting to transport them to the local E.R. instead of doing much on site, but we flashed the right ID and pulled rank and they stopped arguing. Apparently, calls had been made to hospital administrators, the fire commissioner, and the police commissioner. Resistance crumbled, wheels were greased, but no one was happy about it.

I'd recovered my cell phone, but there were no new messages from "A." Nothing from Junie either. I kept fighting down the urge to scream.

I wanted to grab my woman and hit the ground running. Take off for some tropical spot that was ten thousand miles away from gunfire and explosions and senseless death.

Instead, Top, Bunny, and I were watching forensic techs take photos of people we'd killed.

Young people.

Kids.

My earbud buzzed and Nikki was there.

"Cowboy," she said quickly, "we have assets at the desired location. Bookworm is okay. Repeat, Bookworm is safe and sound."

Bookworm was the codename Top had given Junie last year.

I sagged against a parked car and actually had to fight back the tears. "Thank God."

"Everything's okay there. She's fine. Really."

I was so dazed that I had to scramble to remember Nikki's call sign. "Thanks, Firefly."

"But I have to tell you, Cowboy," she said, "there's a lot of crazy stuff going on."

"I know, I know. Gettysburg and Lexington . . ."

"That's the tip of the iceberg. There's stuff going on all over the country. Lots of weird violence. Vandalism and arson. Stuff like that. And the phrase 'burn to shine' keeps showing up everywhere there's something bad happening. It's on walls, spray-painted on the street. They even brought a guy into an E.R. in Akron with it carved into his skin. They think it was done with a razor blade. We're still trying to make some sense of it. If this is terrorism, then no one's taking claim except indirectly. There was that Mother Night video and now all this."

"Burn to shine," I said. "A call to action."

Circe was right.

"Everything's chaotic. And even if it is Mother Night, then we can't find a pattern to it."

"Keep trying. Look, what about the digital prints we sent from here? You get any hits on our shooters?"

"Only two of them are in the system, Cowboy. Serita Esposito and Darius Chu. Both have juvenile records. Esposito was arrested twice for hacking. First offense was an intrusion into the computers belonging to her bank in order to add funds to her debit card. She was fourteen at the time and the intrusion went unnoticed for eleven months. Two-year suspended sentence and community service, plus appropriate fines and restitution. A couple of years later she hacked Delta Airlines to obtain first-class tickets to Paris for her and five of her friends. She was arrested upon her return to the States and is—or rather was—awaiting trial."

"Only seventeen," I said, feeling even older.

"She fired on you, Cowboy," Nikki said.

"Small comfort."

Nikki sighed. "I know."

She didn't know. Like all of Bug's team, she was support staff and never once set foot in the field. But she meant well.

"What about the other one?" I asked. "The boy? Chu, was it?"

"Let's see . . . he's a Canadian citizen and, according to Montreal police, is in custody awaiting trial for armed assault."

"I can pretty much guarantee he's not in prison," I said, watching them zipper him into a body bag.

"The prints match a suspect arrested in Montreal following the nonfatal shooting of a member of the Canadian Parliament. However, the photo you sent does not match the person in jail, and apparently neither do that person's fingerprints. The Canadians are trying to determine how the swap was made, and the person in custody as Chu refuses to talk. I'll have to go deeper and—"

Suddenly, Nikki's voice vanished and was replaced by a three-note alarm signal. Then Church's voice was in my ear.

"This is Deacon for Cowboy, do you copy?"

"Go for Cowboy."

"What is the status of your team?" he said, and he sounded stressed and hurried. "Give me the short answer."

Now was not the time to complain about cuts and scrapes. Even a lot of cuts and scrapes.

"We're still at the cyber café, but we're good to go," I fired back. "What've you got?"

Seemingly out of left field, Church said, "Have you heard about the event in Brooklyn?"

"Other than this one?"

"In the subway," he said. "The C train."

"No."

I could hear him take a breath.

"Scramble your team," he said. "We have a Code Zero."

Chapter Forty-nine

Surf Shop 24-Hour Cyber Café
Corner of Fifth Avenue and Garfield Street
Park Slope, Brooklyn
Sunday, August 31, 1:31 p.m.

Code Zero.

There are no words more terrifying to me, either in my private lexicon or in that used by the Department of Military Sciences.

Hearing those words punched me in the solar plexus.

It stabbed me in the heart.

A big, dark ball of black terror expanded inside my chest.

We have different codes for the various kinds of threats we face.

Code E is an Ebola outbreak.

Code N is a nuke.

But Code Zero . . .

God.

That was used only for a specific kind of horror that I hoped was gone forever from my life and from this world.

"Wh-hat?" I stammered. "*How?*"

Church told me about the C train and the SWAT team that went down into the tunnel. I held my phone up so I could watch the video feed. It was herky-jerky and tinted green from night-vision equipment. The ghostly shape of the big silver train rose out of the darkness as the SWAT officers swarmed toward it. I could see that the windows of the train were cracked and some of them had been smashed outward. People wriggled through the shattered windows and filled the tunnel.

I call them people, but I knew that it was a term applicable only in the past tense. They were streaked with blood, their clothes and skin torn. Their mouths biting at the air, their eyes black and dead.

The SWAT team reacted to them the way compassionate people will. They tried to help. But I heard the helmet radio feed from command telling them to fall back, to make no contact. Warning the cops of a biohazard threat.

Some of the cops held their ground, caught by indecision. Some retreated a few paces. A few could not let their compassion for injured fellow citizens outweigh personal safety.

And that is the horror of warfare in the twenty-first century. Terrorists view compassion as a weakness and they attack it as a vulnerability, making the benevolent pay for their own humanity. The SWAT officers who stepped forward to help were buried beneath a wave of the infected.

I wanted to turn away from the images, I wanted to smash the phone so I couldn't hear the screams. There was too long a delay in responding. The gunfire—the awful, necessary gunfire—came much too late.

The feed ended abruptly when the camera was smashed.

It brought me all the way back to my first day with the DMS. To the first of horror of this world in which I now live. Code Zero indicated an outbreak of a very specific kind of disease pathogen. A bioweapon of immeasurable ferocity. The people who designed this weapon called it the *seif-al-din*.

The sword of the faithful.

It was nothing that could have ever developed in nature, though each of its components was, to a degree, natural. The core of the *seif-al-din* was a prion disease known as fatal familial insomnia, a terrible variation of spongiform encephalitis from which a small group of patients worldwide suffered increasing insomnia resulting in panic attacks, the development of odd phobias, hallucinations, and other dissociative symptoms. In its original form it was a process that took months, and the victim generally died as a result of total sleep deprivation, exhaustion, and stress. But Sebastian Gault and his scientist-lover Amirah rebuilt the disease and married it to several parasites and a radical kind of viral delivery system. The infection rate of this designer pathogen is absolute, and it triggers an uncontrollable urge in the infected to spread the disease. It is spread primarily through bites.

The infected host lapses into a nearly hibernative state, with most body systems shut down and all conscious and higher mental functions permanently destroyed. Stripped-down parts of the circulatory, respiratory, and nervous systems remain in operation—only enough to keep the host on its feet and able to attack in order to spread the disease.

Unless you used very precise medical equipment it is impossible to detect signs of life. Heartbeat is minimal, respiration is incredibly shallow. And those tissues that are not necessary to the parasitic drive are not fed by blood or oxygen and therefore become necrotic. What is left is a mindless, shambling, eternally hungry killing machine with an infection rate of nearly one hundred percent.

A walker.

A *zombie*.

No one had survived a bite; no one came back from infection.

That was the *seif-al-din*.

That was a Code Zero.

We stopped an intended mass release at the Liberty Bell Center in Philadelphia four years ago. All of our computer models predicted that an outbreak in a densely populated area would result in an uncontrollable spread. If this got out, the world would consume itself.

Totally.

Completely.

Ravenously.

Dear God.

All of this—the science, the memories, the horror—flashed through my brain in a hot microsecond after the video ended.

"*Where?*" I demanded.

Church told me. "The infected are still in the tunnel, but it's only a matter of time before they find their way to the station and then up to the streets. I have a chopper in the air. It will pick you up in Prospect Park. Echo Team will rendezvous with you at Euclid Avenue station, and I've called in the National Guard. Every subway exit is being sealed, but I need you to go down there, Captain. I need you to stop this." He paused for a terrible moment, then added those dreadful words. "No matter what it takes."

But I was already pushing past cops and EMTs, yelling for Top and Bunny. Ghost barked as we ran. All four of us were bleeding and hurt but we ran like we didn't care, like we didn't have time to be hurt. I could hear the distant beat of the heavy rotors of a military Black Hawk. Prospect Park was only a few blocks from here.

We piled in the car. I hit lights and sirens and we broke laws as I kicked the pedal all the way down, scattering civilians and emergency personnel in every direction.

There are times to stand there with your jaw slack and your pulse hammering, and there are times to get your ass into high gear and run over anything in your way.

Chapter Fifty

Pierre Hotel
East Sixty-second Street
New York City
Sunday, August 31, 1:34 p.m.

Ludo was masturbating when the phone rang.

He was sitting on the edge of the bed, his pants and boxers puddled around his ankles, staring at the rifle on its tripod as his hand moved with feverish speed.

Nearby, the rifle gleamed. Oiled and curved and so lovely.

Olga.

The phone began jangling with the same shrill outrage that was in his mother's voice when she'd caught him doing this. There had been no gun that first time, but that didn't matter. She'd dragged him out into the hall in front of his younger brother and older sister, his underpants still down, and had beaten him to the edge of unconsciousness. Calling him a freak, a pervert. Telling him that God was watching. Saying that God would punish him.

Ludo had tried to cover his shame with hands over his groin and face, but his mother slapped those hands away and rained blows on every inch of him. Even when his siblings started screaming for her to stop, she kept hitting.

Ludo did not remember how it had ended. He'd begun screaming, too, and he'd screamed so long and so loud that it opened a big, dark trapdoor in the floor of his mind, and he'd plunged downward into shadows.

There had been other beatings, of course. And his mother had removed the locks on the bathroom door so she could barge in to try to catch Ludo doing something disgusting. Something worthy of a beating.

The others got beatings, too. His sister, Gayle, lost hearing in her left ear because of a beating. And Bobby, who was a bleeder, had tiny scars all over his body. Mother always found something they were doing wrong. Always.

She hadn't ever caught him masturbating again, but that didn't matter. She searched his belongings and found things that gave her fists their purpose. A copy of *Playboy* Ludo had stolen from a drugstore. Pictures of naked girls Ludo downloaded from the Net. Then, later, as Ludo spent more and more time swimming in the shadows beneath the floor of his mind, the things she found were different. Gun magazines. And then guns.

That was when the beatings stopped.

As Ludo grew, he sometimes walked in on her in the bathroom. While she was on the toilet. Ludo would stand there with a gun in his hand, saying nothing while his mother tried to hide her shame.

That's when his mother started drinking.

She never could find his guns after that. She looked everywhere. When he was out, either at school or bagging groceries at the Acme, his mother looked. Every once in a while Ludo would leave a bullet for her to find. The lead tips were bright with dots of her lipstick. Ludo wished he could have seen her face when she found those.

A few weeks later, after his mother died in an unexplained fire, Ludo snuck into the cemetery the night they buried her. With shadows swimming around him, he dropped his pants and masturbated on her grave.

It was the fastest he ever came. And it removed so much of the tension in his soul. Even so, it was oddly asexual, despite the necessary mechanics of the process. He never fantasized about his mother. He didn't think about seeing her naked—a thought that deeply disgusted him. And he never thought about having sex with her. He'd rather stab his own eyes out. What turned him on was the thought of maggots and worms wriggling their way through her skin. The mental picture of cockroaches and beetles feasting on her flesh and shitting on her bones was deeply erotic.

Today, though, it was the gun.

Olga.

So pretty.

So saucy.

Sitting there in the hotel room, waiting for the kill order, he kept glancing at her. Kept remembering what it felt like to slip his finger inside her trigger guard. To let his fingers glide ever so lightly along the length of her barrel. He stuck the tip of his tongue into the opening of the barrel, licking and tasting the gun oil.

That was when he knew he had to rub one out, and his pants were down in a moment.

And then the damn phone rang.

Mother Night.

Another mother.

Fuck.

Catching him at the wrong moment, catching him in a shameful act.

His penis went instantly soft and he grabbed for his pants as quickly and desperately as if Mother Night had banged the door open right here.

He was panting when he snatched up the phone.

"Yes," he gasped.

"Ludo—?"

"Yes."

"What's wrong?"

"Nothing."

"Why are you out of breath?"

"I—"

"What were you doing?"

The moment froze around him. God! Did she see him? Did she have this room bugged? Were there cameras in here? Oh God, oh God, oh God.

"I-I-," he stammered. "I was doing push-ups."

A beat.

"Push-ups?"

"Yes."

"Why?" asked Mother Night.

"Um . . . trying to keep my muscle tone."

Another beat. "Uh-huh," she said slowly.

"Seriously. You can't do what I do with flabby, um, muscles. Killing requires core strength." He winced at that, believing it to be the single silliest thing he'd ever said.

"Okay," she said.

"Okay," he said.

There was a final beat.

Then, "Ludo, are you feeling okay today?"

He paused before answering, taking a moment to make sure his voice and tone were perfectly normal.

"Sure," he said. "Absolutely tip-top."

"I can get someone else in there if you want me to."

"No."

"You'll still get paid," she insisted. "It won't be a problem."

"No," he said again, leaning on it. "I'm right as rain."

"Okay," she said dubiously.

"Okay."

"Now listen to me. I want you to rest. I don't think I'll need you today. Maybe tonight, though. Or early tomorrow."

Ludo felt his flaccid penis suddenly jump to new hardness. He glanced at Olga, who waited there for his touch.

"Oh," he said, deflated.

"Proceed to the other location and wait for my call or a text. And Ludo—?"

"Yes, Mother?"

"No more push-ups."

The line went dead, but he barely noticed. He tossed the phone onto the bed and, with slow steps and a beating heart, he approached the lovely, lovely rifle.

Interlude Eleven

The Dragon Factory

Dogfish Cay, The Bahamas

Three Years Ago

The place was called the Dragon Factory, but that was a conceit. There was only one dragon there and it was a pathetic little thing that had been cobbled together from other animals in an attempt to make it look like a Chinese dragon. The wings of an albatross, the mustache from the barbels of a Mekong giant catfish, the horny crest from the Texas horned lizard, and the slender body that was mostly an immature Komodo monitor. From the records Artemisia Bliss found on the recovered computers, the creature had been made to impress Chinese investors. But it was a fraud. A chimera born of radical surgery and ill-conceived transgenics.

It lay dead, its neck broken from repeated impacts with the glass wall of its cage as it tried to flee the sounds of gunfire and slaughter. Most of the other animals were dead as well. Faux unicorns and griffins and basilisks. And some things that were almost sad—midgets surgically altered to look like leprechauns or satyrs. Sad, pathetic things that were insane from pain, humiliation, and the horror of what had been done to them.

Bliss kept expecting some kind of outrage to soar up inside her. Or empathy. But there wasn't even much sympathy flickering in her heart as she moved through the complex, day after day, collecting samples, weighing and measuring corpses, and sitting in on the endless dissections.

The only thrills of any kind, she felt, were when she cracked another level of the encryption the Jakoby twins had built into their computers. Sadly, the code writers who created the system for the twins were dead. Most of the staff was either dead or keeping mum per their attorneys' instructions.

That meant each level of the encryption had to be cracked.

That, for Bliss, was fun.

Every time she bypassed a firewall or disabled a self-delete subroutine, Bliss felt a genuine thrill. A tingle at first, but one that grew and grew.

And grew.

There was so damn much here.

The Jakoby twins—Hecate and Paris—were geniuses on a par with Dr. Hu and, she had to admit, herself. That rare group of supergeniuses whose nature suggests an evolutionary leap forward. Granted, the Jakobys were sick, twisted, murderous sociopaths whose father was attempting ethnic genocide on a global scale—a genocide that would have wiped out those of Asian blood as well—but Bliss had to admire the science. It was so vast, so ballsy.

So damn sexy.

As she worked, she wished there was someone she could talk to about it.

Someone who was not William Hu or Bug or anyone even remotely related to the Department of Military Sciences. With every single passing day Bliss felt less able to open up to them, to share her thoughts with them.

Though even she had to admit that sharing those thoughts would make for one very awkward conversation. Quickly followed, she was certain, by emergency phone calls, a psych evaluation, and her walking papers. She'd be out the door so fast that it would make her head spin.

Out, or maybe worse. Aunt Sallie watched her like a hawk, and Bliss was positive that the old bitch was waiting for the first opportunity to strike.

Let her wait. Caution was part of Bliss's skill set. When you helped to crack systems designed to counterattack, you learned caution. When you helped design security protocols for the highest level of ultrasecure facilities, you learned caution. Bliss knew that her old, unevolved self had been smart but not necessarily sharp; whereas her evolved self was as sharp as a scalpel and intensely sly.

She wondered what Aunt Sallie or Church's actual reaction would be if they suspected that she was duplicating every bit of evidence, each file, each report on genetic design, each computer program.

Would they have her locked up?

Or would Bliss wake up one night and find Colonel Riggs or Captain Ledger standing over her bed, dressed all in black, with a pistol aimed at her head.

She rather thought the latter was a more likely possibility.

Though . . . what could they prove?

She sighed. Depends on where they looked.

There was nothing at her apartment, of course, except some deeply encrypted stuff hidden inside video games. Not even her games. She'd built dozens of "libraries" into new game levels she'd hacked onto the existing software of popular games. She concealed petaflops worth of data in the virtual game world, all of it disguised as something else, all of it protected by what she was absolutely certain was the most sophisticated can't-beat-them levels of game play.

To her, it was like hiding diamonds in the sand at the playground. No one would think to look there, and anyone who found them by accident wouldn't believe they were what they were.

Bliss sat hunched in front of Paris Jakoby's personal workstation computer as a steady stream of data was flash-downloaded onto dual drives. That dual-drive system was her own design. Bundled flash drives feeding off a single rebuilt USB plug. Since the data was being downloaded only once—albeit in two exact and simultaneous copies—the system only registered a single download.

She paused and looked around.

Paris Jakoby's office was built onto a balcony and it had a glass wall that looked down onto the main lobby of the facility. The last of the corpses—human and otherwise—had long since been removed, but the tiled floor and carpeted areas were still stained with dried blood. She'd watched the battle on the big screen back at the TOC, her lip caught between her teeth, fingernails digging into her palms. Major Grace Courtland had led the first wave of DMS agents onto the island, followed by Captain Ledger's Echo Team and others. And then a wave of Navy SEALs. That should have been overwhelming force, but there was a shocking amount of resistance, the core of which were the Berserkers—mercenaries with silverback gorilla DNA. The men were massive, enormously strong, and filled with a nearly uncontrollable rage. She rewatched the videos of them in action a dozen times. So much power.

But there were other horrors on the island, and Ledger's team encountered those first. When Bliss saw those she nearly screamed. Monstrous mastiffs that had been surgically and genetically altered so they had the chitinous armor plating and deadly arching tails of scorpions. It was like something out of an old Michael Crichton novel. Or one of those corny monster movies on Syfy.

The main part of the fight was recorded on helmet cams until Church ordered an E-bomb to be detonated over the island. The electromagnetic pulse knocked out all electronics and ended the show.

It became fun again for Bliss only when the science team was sent onto the island with orders to catalog everything. Absolutely every single thing.

Weeks of work.

Weeks of fun.

They were to be sequestered on the island during the forensic collection and initial analysis period, and then would be debriefed once they returned to the Hangar. That, however, was still many days away. The first part of the job was rebuilding the power systems and replacing those components necessary to make the computer systems functional again.

Still plenty of time to continue the process of copying everything. Of duplicating samples. Not everything, of course. But everything *she* was assigned to collect. It was too dangerous to interfere with what other techs and scientists were doing.

One of the most fascinating things she found was the complete record, including all research and procedures, for the Berserkers. Although intensely complicated and enormously expensive, it was a step-by-step guide to creating the transgenic mercenaries. There were even samples of all of the chemicals, drugs, and genetic materials necessary, stored in biosafe bins.

All of the data was on an external hard drive stored in Paris's closet. Not one byte of it was on the main computers.

On a whim, Bliss took the hard drive, duped the data onto her own laptop, and destroyed the original. Obtaining samples of the genetic material would have to wait until her team was ready to leave the island. She would, however, manage it, even though she had no idea what she was ever going to do with it.

Not yet.

It was late on a Sunday night when Artemisia Bliss made the single most significant discovery while she was decrypting a series of files labeled BULK DATA—MISC UNSORTED. The encryption was particularly difficult, and Bliss opened a fresh Red Bull and dived in with gusto. So far, the encryption on all of the Jakoby files was exceptionally tough, some of it so mind-bogglingly complicated that it felt like pulling nails out of hardwood using only her mind. But it was so damn much fun. This was what she lived for. Each layer she peeled back, each level she cracked made her feel more powerful, more alive. Naturally, the encryption on the Jakoby main research files was devious, but after two weeks Bliss found her way in, which opened the system to her whole team.

That Bulk Data file was something, though.

The encryption was many layers deep and had some very strange traps built into it, including a counterattack tapeworm that was strangely familiar. The tapeworm tried to intrude into her MindReader substation and rewrite the software. That stunned Bliss. MindReader was unassailable. It was the ultimate intrusion monster and even Bliss had never been able to hack into its programs. But this program attacked in the way MindReader typically did.

Ultimately, though, MindReader slapped it down. Bliss was able to remove the attack programs with some effort and then began rooting around inside the data files.

What she found at first startled her, because there were monstrously large files hidden inside the nondescript "misc unsorted" folder. Massive files, including hundreds of subfolders filled with computer code.

As she scanned through them, Bliss felt her pulse quicken. Then her heart began racing. Sweat popped out along her brow. She couldn't believe what she was seeing.

She simply could not.

The files contained a complete schematic for a computer system. A system with ultrasophisticated intrusion software. A system with multiphasic pattern-search capabilities. A system with a subroutine designed to erase any trace of its footprint after it hacked other systems.

A system labeled "Pangaea."

But one that she knew under a different name.

MindReader.

Chapter Fifty-one

The Hangar
Floyd Bennett Field
Brooklyn, New York
Sunday, August 31, 1:35 p.m.

Everyone snapped to attention as Mr. Church came hurrying into the training hall. Lydia cut a surprised look at Sam. Neither of them had ever seen Mr. Church hurry. The world usually waited for him. His aide and bodyguard, a monstrous gunnery sergeant known as Brick, was right at his heels, keeping up despite an artificial leg.

They came right over to where Echo Team formed up at a right angle to the line of candidates.

"Chief Petty Officer Ruiz," said Church, "Captain Ledger says that there are three candidates he likes for Echo Team. Call them out."

Lydia did a neat half-turn. "Sergeant Duncan MacDougall, Sergeant Noah Fallon, Special Agent Montana Parker, step forward."

The three named candidates did. A short, squatty man with no neck and Popeye forearms, a tall, ascetic man with a poet's face and shooter's eyes, and a tanned blond woman with cold gray eyes.

Church gave them one full second of appraisal. "You three now work for me. Welcome to the jungle." They saluted, but he turned to the others. "You are dismissed and may return to your units."

Once more he turned, this time to Echo Team.

"A Black Hawk is smoking on the roof," he said. "You will be on it four minutes. It takes off in five. Weapons and equipment are already being loaded. Hammer suits and BAMs for everyone. Full kits for the new team members."

"Sir," began Lydia, but Church cut her off.

"No time. You'll be briefed en route and will rendezvous with Captain Ledger. This is a Code Zero."

They did not argue or hesitate.

A few blurred minutes later they were in the air.

Interlude Twelve

The Barn
DMS Special Teams Field Office
Near Houston, Texas
Three Years Ago

Dr. Bliss sat next to Dr. Hu, both of them sipping Diet Cokes and swinging their feet off the side of an open Huey. The big helicopter was a rebuilt holdover from a war that ended before either of them was born. It was also the personal property of Colonel Samson Riggs. It was parked on the side of a runway behind the Barn, the massive former dairy farm that had been recommissioned as the field office for the DMS's new "special teams" division. Riggs ran two teams out of the Barn, Shockwave and Longhorn. The latter was used as backup for whenever the ATF ran up against something coming over the border other than cartel gun thugs and drugs. Bioweapons and teams of foreign terror squads trying to use the Mexican pipeline as a conduit. That sort of thing. The former, Shockwave, was a go anywhere, do anything all-purpose team. Freed from normal duties as a regional team like those at the Warehouse in Baltimore or the Hangar in New York.

A few feet away, leaning a muscular shoulder against the Huey's frame, was Gus Dietrich. He was pretending to look at something on his smartphone, but Bliss knew that he was listening. Dietrich was always listening, always watching. Because he did such a stellar job of fading into Mr. Church's shadow, and because he looked like a muscle-bound mouth-breather, people tended to regard him as slow. He wasn't. No one who worked for Church was slow. No one who worked for Church was even ordinary.

Bliss and Hu were at the Barn to take possession of boxes of scientific research records Riggs and his shooters had taken from a biological war-fare lab in Bucharest. That lab was supposedly closed during the last days of the Cold War, but Interpol had discovered otherwise. Sadly, the Interpol team had been wiped out. Riggs brought Shockwave in and got some useful backup from Echo Team, which had been in Europe anyway. Echo was the only other team authorized to go anywhere.

Beyond where the tech people were offloading the boxes of records, two figures stood together, talking and laughing. Colonel Riggs and Captain Joe Ledger.

"They seem to have bonded," observed Bliss. There had been a run-ning bet at the Hangar that the two team leaders would do nothing except butt heads. Instead they'd developed a quick and, apparently, deep friendship. Their combined teams had mopped the floor with a much larger force of mercenaries in Bucharest. A four-to-one fight, and every member of Shockwave and Echo Teams had come home, alive and whole.

Hu sniffed. "Cut from the same cloth," he said in a way that implied no compliment.

She looked at him. "What is it with you and them? You can't stand ei-ther of them."

"They're at the wrong end of the evolutionary curve," sneered Hu. "Useful when we need something dead, but otherwise they're meat. And arrogant meat at that."

"Oh, come on, Willie," she countered, "that's not fair. If you combine their clearance rate for high-profile jobs it exceeds the rest of the DMS combined."

Hu made a small, disgusted noise. "So they can pull triggers. Big deal. Hugo Vox has compiled a list of men—and some women—with the same potential. Same military and martial arts background, same psychopathic tendencies. Same lack of intellectual refinement. Don't fool yourself, Artie, they're entirely replaceable."

There was another sound, equally disgusted, but not from Hu. The two scientists leaned out to look at Dietrich.

"Excuse me," said Hu with chilly contempt, "did *you* have something to add?"

Without looking up from his cell phone, Dietrich said, "For a smart guy, Doc, you do say some stupid shit."

"What did you say?" The chill in his tone turned to arctic ice.

Bliss jumped in. "What do you mean, Gus?"

He glanced up at her. Pointedly at her. "You think that Riggs and Ledger have such a good clearance record because they're lucky? You think shooters of their quality are interchangeable? If that's what you think, then you either don't understand them or don't understand how the DMS works."

"As if you do?" demanded Hu.

Bliss elbowed him lightly.

"Ow!"

"Go on, Gus. What were you saying?" she asked.

Dietrich put his cell phone into a pocket and folded his arms. He had a bulldog face that was scarred and weathered. "I've seen Hugo Vox's list. I recruit from it all the time. I'd have any of them at my back in a fight. Any kind of fight. But none of them have a certain thing that Riggs has and Ledger has. Major Courtland had it. I mean, don't get me wrong, all of the operators on Hugo's list are top-notch, best of the best, but they don't have that thing, that X factor."

"What X factor?" asked Hu belligerently.

"Well, Doc, if I knew exactly what it was I wouldn't call it an X factor, would I?"

Bliss had to bite down to keep a laugh from bubbling out. Hu went livid.

"Can you explain it at all, Gus?" Bliss asked.

He nodded, shrugged, shook his head. Shrugged again. "If you understand combat from a spec-ops perspective, then you know there's a lot of variables. You guys, the science team, and Bug's team, do a great job providing real-time intel so that the field teams can adjust to the variables and react in the right way. Without the science and computer teams we'd have lost a lot of fights, no doubt and no joke. But sometimes, deep in the heart of something, there comes a point when things are going south so fast there isn't time to ask for or use additional intel. Not just the heat of battle," he said, "but times when everything is totally crazy, shifting inside the firefight, with radical new elements being introduced that no one could foresee. Like when Echo Team ran into the Berserkers the first time. No one could have predicted mercenaries amped up with DNA from silverback gorillas. I mean, seriously, who could have seen that coming? It wasn't part of the game as we understood the game at the moment. The first DMS team that ran into them was slaughtered. So was a Russian kill team. Then Ledger, Top, and Bunny got ambushed by them. They should have died right there and then. No doubt about it. Do a statistical-probability assessment of it and it comes out with them dead ten times out of ten."

"But they didn't die," said Bliss, fascinated by where Dietrich was going with this.

"No. Joe Ledger changed the game. It wasn't exactly *what* he did, 'cause from a distance it was just him using a knife. But it was how he did it in the moment. The lack of hesitation, the choice of target, the way he reacted, the fact that he attacked rather than retreat, that he wasn't trapped by how freaky and fucked-up everything was. It was his X factor that changed it from a certain loss to a win that just pissed all over the odds. The same thing goes for how Riggs dealt with those cyborg baboons. I mean, shit, cyborg baboons. Most guys, even top shooters, would be like, 'holy fuck, those are cyborg baboons, what the fuck?' And they'd have died. Riggs just adapted to it because in his mind it wasn't Freaky Friday, it was how things were in the moment. I'll bet those frigging baboons where thinking 'what the fuck' when Riggs went apeshit on them."

Bliss nodded, seeing it.

"If those were the only instances, you could throw statistics at me again and say it's a fluke. But go browse their files. Those two. And look at how many times they've thrown Hail Mary passes and won a game that everyone—every-fucking-body—said was lost. Time and time again, and those are numbers that do not lie."

Hu sniffed dismissively, but he said nothing.

Bliss was still nodding. "So . . . this X factor is what defines them."

"Yeah, I guess so."

"And they're the only two who have it?"

"So far," said Dietrich. "The big man is always scouting for others, but guys like that are pretty scarce. And believe me, we *are* looking."

"Gus," she said, cocking her head to one side, "have you ever played games?"

"Games? Like what? Poker?"

"Video games, board games. Ever play Dungeons and Dragons?"

"Nope. Never much gone in for wizards and dragons and all that shit. Not fake ones. Why?"

"There are a lot of qualities that make up your characters in D and D, and it's all based on how you roll the dice. You can be good, evil, neutral, or chaotic."

"Chaotic?" Dietrich thought about that and a slow smile grew on his face. "Yeah, Doc, you might have put your finger on it. It's not an X factor—"

"It's chaos," said Bliss, finishing it for him. "Chaos resists computer models, it can't really be predicted. What Joe Ledger and Samson Riggs bring to any fight is a chaos factor."

Dietrich nodded. "Yes, ma'am, and that's what makes them so damn dangerous. Understand something, I'm good—I'm real fucking good—but if it came to it, I would never want to go up against either of them."

"Sure, sure," said Hu, breaking his own silence, "and what are we supposed to do if we ever encounter this 'chaos factor' in one of our enemies?"

"If it was someone like that, we'd throw Ledger or Riggs against him."

"And if they weren't available?" asked Bliss.

"God help us if that ever happened, doc," said Dietrich. "Because we would stand no chance at all."

Chapter Fifty-two

We jumped the curb and drove straight into Prospect Park and tore deep furrows in the dirt of the baseball field as we raced to meet the Black Hawk. The big helicopter's wheels touched down at the same time that I slewed us into a bad skidding, turning stop. We left the doors open and ran bent over through the rotor wash, Ghost ranging ahead. The bay door opened and we dived in.

"Go, go, go!" I bellowed, and the helo rose straight up into the afternoon air.

By car, it's twelve congested miles from Park Slope to the subway entrance on Euclid Avenue at Pitkin, and by now the streets around the station would be jammed with civilians wanting a peek at a disaster. The Black Hawk helicopter tore above the traffic at nearly two hundred miles an hour. We were there in minutes.

It still felt like too long.

During that short flight, Top, Bunny, and I shucked our torn and blood-stained suits and pulled on black BDU trousers and tank tops. Then the tech crew helped us into Saratoga Hammer suits. These are two-piece, lightweight overgarments consisting of a coat with integral hood and separate trousers. The suit incorporates a two-layer fabric system consisting of liquid repellent cotton fabric and a carbon sphere liner. The double layers protect against chemical warfare vapors, liquids, and aerosols. The ones Mr. Church bought for us were not the standard off-the-rack variety but a special grade designed by a friend of his within the company. They were tougher and they had spider-silk fabric woven into what is normally Kevlar sheathing. Very tough and tear-resistant.

Not tear-proof, but tear-resistant. The difference mattered and it was never far from our minds.

Our suits were black and unmarked. No agency patch or rank insignia of any kind. With the helmets on and balaclavas in place we looked like high-tech ninjas. We strapped gun belts around our hips and equipment harnesses to our torsos. These harnesses had pouches for lots of extra magazines and hooks for flash-bangs and fragmentation grenades.

They don't make Hammer suits for dogs. "You're staying on the chopper," I told Ghost. He gave me a wounded and baleful glare.

The weapons tech from the Hangar, a moose named Bobby Cooper—Coop to everyone—handed out lots of useful gizmos and additional equipment, including various-sized blaster-plasters, knives, strangle wires, and everything else a psychotic kid might have on his Christmas list. The last thing Coop did was strap a tactical computer to each of our forearms. When he was done, he patted me on the shoulder. "You're good to go."

"Thanks, Coop. Take care of my dog, okay?"

He grinned. "With all the shit that's going on today, Joe, I think Ghost and I should go the hell out and get drunk."

"He'd like that."

Coop's grin was fragile and it eventually slid off. "Is it true? Are you going after walkers?"

"We'll see," I said to Coop. He didn't press it.

Bunny clipped a sturdy fighting knife handle-downward onto his rig, ready for a fast pull. He said, "Is this more Mother Night stuff, too?"

"Don't know," I said.

"It is," said Top. We didn't argue. We couldn't be sure, but the day had a certain feel to it. A lot of things were sliding downhill, but it seemed to be one hand doing the pushing.

"How'd they get this shit?" asked Bunny. "I mean, we have it secured, right?"

"Yes, at the Locker," I assured him.

"You sure?"

I wanted to tell him that of course I was sure. Instead I contacted Nikki. "Have someone run a security check on the Locker. Let's make sure that—"

"We already did," said Nikki. "As soon as word came in about the subway, Aunt Sallie initiated a system-wide security lockdown and status check. All the lights at the Locker are green."

That was a tremendous relief. Keeping that place safe was always number one on any security to-do list. Always.

The Locker is the nickname for the Sigler-Czajkowski Biological and

Chemical Weapons Facility, located three quarters of a mile beneath a wooded hill in a thinly populated corner of Virginia. There are other similar facilities scattered around the country and the world, places where dangerous things like chemical weapons and VX nerve gas and other monsters are stored. Domestic and international agreements have shut a lot of them down, but we still have a few, some being closely monitored by congressional watchdog groups and teams of independent observers composed of members of NATO, the U.N., and others. And there are facilities squirreled away in places no one would think to look for them. Places funded by obscure allotments in black budgets; places you might pass every day and never know what insanity was stored behind nondescript stone walls and meaningless signs.

But there's no other place exactly like the Locker.

In the six years since its inception, the Department of Military Sciences has gone to the mat with the world's most extreme terrorists. Not just al-Qaeda fanatics wearing explosive vests or Taliban fighters with shoulder-mounted RPGs. I'm talking about actual mad scientists who put vast amounts of money and their own towering but fractured intellects to the task of creating the most dangerous bioweapons imaginable. Things like quick-onset Ebola, mutated strains of anthrax, radical new forms of ultra-contagious tuberculosis, weaponized HIV, and even genetically engineered contagious forms of diseases like Tay-Sachs and sickle cell, which had previously been purely genetic disorders. And, not that this shit had to get any scarier, but there were also a slew of designer superpathogens in there, each of them constructed as doomsday weapons, either as threats in the postnuclear covert arms race or as kill-them-all-let-our-version-of-god-sort-'em-out holy war weapons, or retaliatory devices for use as a Hail Mary pass if their side was losing a war. Stuff like Lucifer 113, Vijivshiy Odin-Vasemnartzets, Reaper, and the *seif-al-din*. Stuff no sane human, however politically or theologically motivated, should be capable of dreaming up, let alone making. All of these things were out on the bleeding edge of science.

In my four years with the DMS I've taken my fair share of these toys away from people like the Jakobys, Sebastian Gault, the Cabal, the Seven Kings, the Red Order, the Hebbelmann Group, and others. Too many others. I've had to do some terrible things to keep those weapons from creating the misery for which they were created. Things that have ruined any chance I will ever have of sleeping peacefully through an entire night.

I told Nikki to make sure Church called me as soon as he was free and then disconnected. In my pocket my cell phone vibrated. I removed it and all three of us looked at the message window.

ALWAYS REMEMBER: AIM FOR THE HEAD

"Well, ain't that damn interesting?" said Top sourly. "Nice of someone to give us advice in our time of trials and tribulations."

"Amen, Reverend," said Bunny. His tone was light, but his eyes were bright with tension.

I said nothing. It was getting harder and harder not to smash the phone against the metal wall of the helo.

"Those texts have to be from Mother Night," said Top. "This new one proves that she knows what we're about to step into. It proves that she has the *seif-al-din*."

Bunny licked his lips. "Okay, but how the hell did she get her hands on it?"

"I don't know," I said. "But we're going to find out."

"Hooah," Bunny agreed.

Without taking his eyes from mine, Top Sims said, very softly, "And then we are going to kill her and everyone working with her."

I added two extra magazines to my pouch. "Yes, we damn well are."

"Hooah," they both said.

"Coming up on it," called the pilot.

Interlude Thirteen

Terror Town
Mount Baker, Washington State
Three Years Ago

When Dr. Bliss heard the news it rocked her.

Hugo Vox was a traitor.

Worse than a traitor, he was a terrorist and mass murderer.

And, worst of all, he was a founding member of the Seven Kings. A faux secret society that borrowed the myths and legends of other secret societies—real and imagined—to make itself appear ancient and vastly powerful.

Only some of that was a lie. They were not ancient . . . but their power was beyond dispute.

The Twin Towers had fallen according to their plan. As did the London Hospital. The Seven Kings used bribery, manipulation, and other means to inspire various fundamentalist groups to commit acts of terrorism. The Kings, knowing that such atrocities always impacted the stock market, made hundreds of billions of dollars. Most of that money would never and could never be recovered.

And Hugo Vox was at the heart of the whole thing.

A man trusted by everyone in the U.S. government, from Mr. Church to the president. A man who had access everywhere. A man who was tasked with developing the most elite counterterrorism and antiterrorism training programs.

Bliss stood in Vox's office at Terror Town, the training facility in Washington State where America trained its agents, and where teams from the nation's allies came to learn the best ways to combat terror.

The irony seemed to scream at her from every molecule of air in the place.

Vox was a bad guy.

The news seemed to hit Bliss very hard but from several different angles. On one hand, as a DMS team member, the betrayal was huge. It rocked the foundations of the whole organization and damaged the previously iron-hard credibility of Mr. Church. There were some angry murmurs in congress that Church already had too much freedom of action, and that his judgment no longer warranted that level of trust or authority. Bliss thought this was a little unfair. She had no love for Church or that harpy, Aunt Sallie, but Vox was a master manipulator. Maybe the smartest and most subtle of his kind that ever lived. He hadn't just fooled Church, Vox fooled everyone. Including the president and every member of Congress, including the grumblers. They'd all been cheerleaders for Vox for years. Church was merely a handy target. That rankled Bliss.

On a more personal level, she was hurt. She liked Vox and had worked closely with him and his protégée, Dr. Circe O'Tree, on dozens of cases.

She'd gone to him to vet nearly every employee she hired for her division and every contractor she used when designing security systems for top-secret facilities like the Locker. Many of those people had been personally vetted by Vox.

Just as she had been.

Until two weeks ago, "vetted by Vox" was the highest stamp of approval you could get. It was a badge of honor. Grace Courtland had been vetted by Vox. So had Top Sims, Captain Ledger's right-hand man. And dozens of others in the DMS, and hundreds within government service.

Clearly not all of them could be villains. But how to tell which ones were Vox's creatures?

But the news hit Bliss in another way.

She found that she admired Vox even more for all of this.

Admired him a lot.

Thinking about it sent a thrill through her veins. This was real power. Bigger power than anything she'd ever glimpsed. Eclipsing Church by miles, in her estimation. Power that changed the entire world. 9/11 was a point around which the future history of everyone on earth turned, and Vox had done that.

Vox.

She sat at his desk and looked at the computer he'd left behind. Vox had somehow constructed some technology that could fool MindReader. He had untraceable cell phones. His plotting was accomplished through some means MindReader could neither detect nor control.

Power.

So much power.

Bliss booted up the computer and, when it was ready, removed two devices from her bag. One was a micro MindReader substation. The other was something neither Aunt Sallie nor Bug nor Mr. Church knew she had. A device Bliss had painstakingly constructed from the schematics she'd found in Paris Jakoby's computer.

He'd called it Pangaea, and from his records it was clear that the system was not only designed and built by a now-dead Italian computer pioneer, but it was without doubt the forerunner of MindReader. There were far too many similarities for it to be coincidence. Bliss did a little digging, and from bits and pieces of information gleaned from Bug, Captain Ledger, and Dr. Hu, it seemed that in his pre-DMS days, Church had run with an international team of shooters. They'd torn down a group called the Cabal, which in turn had been built on the philosophical and scientific bones of the Third Reich. Pangaea had been allowed the Cabal—and later the Jakobys—to steal information from hundreds of other research programs around the world. Steal it without leaving evidence of the theft. By combining research from so many sources, the Jakobys were able to make what appeared to be freakish intuitive leaps in various fields related to genetics.

Captain Ledger and Grace Courtland had torn their empire apart, killing Paris and his sister, Hecate, in the process. That Grace Courtland had also died was something Bliss thought she'd feel bad about, but found that she did not.

Several Pangaea workstations had been bagged and tagged by the DMS forensics team, but the schematics in Paris Jakoby's desk were known only to Bliss. She'd copied them and then deleted them. Then she spent months handcrafting a new system that including many of her own upgrades. Although she had great respect for the man who designed Pangaea, she knew that she was smarter. Her knowledge base, in terms of programming, hacking, and cyberwarfare, was decades fresher. That meant that the computer she built was as unlike MindReader as it was similar. A cousin rather than a twin.

It was no longer Pangaea, and it was definitely not MindReader.

She gave it a new name.

Haruspex.

That was far more suitable, considering how she'd built it. A haruspex, in terms of ancient Etruscan and Roman culture, was a person who could divine the future and unlock the mysteries of the fates by reading the entrails of sacrificed sheep.

Very appropriate. She'd read her own future in the entrails of Pangaea. Haruspex had been born in the blood of devastation left behind by the slaughter at the Dragon Factory and the fall of the Jakoby empire of twisted science.

Now she had a computer that was nearly as powerful as MindReader, and more important, one that was invisible to Church's system.

Invisibility was a kind of power.

She smiled at the thought. It was like a superpower. Bliss had enough geek genes to actively wish that she could be a superhero.

Or even a supervillain.

But this was the real world.

She sighed and began her assault on Hugo Vox's computers using Mind-Reader and Haruspex.

Firewalls and anti-intrusion programs rose up to challenge her, but with the deftness of a pagan priest of the religion of cyberscience, she eviscerated them and thereby divined their secrets.

Chapter Fifty-three

Euclid Avenue Station
Euclid and Pitkin Avenues
Brooklyn, New York
Sunday, August 31, 1:52 p.m.

I leaned my head and shoulders out of the open bay door. The area was cleared of everything except official vehicles, and per instructions the actual intersection was cleared. Police were erecting barricades and working crowd control. A half dozen news vans were already there, their satellite towers rising like metal trees above the crowds. News choppers were in the air, but police birds were establishing a no-fly zone for anyone but cops, Homeland, and us.

I tapped my earbud.

"Cowboy to Warbride."

"Go for Warbride," said Lydia.

"What's your twenty?"

"Right below you, boss. In the lee of the SWAT van. There's not enough room for the helo to land. We had to rappel in. You will, too."

"Copy that."

"Cowboy—we are Echo plus three. Deacon made the call, but they're locked and loaded."

"The three we talked about?"

"Affirmative," she said. "See you on the ground."

Top and Bunny had listened in and were already setting up the fast-ropes for our drop to the street. I explained the situation to the pilot and then rejoined my guys.

"Duncan, Noah, and Montana?" asked Bunny.

"Yup."

Of all the candidates we'd tested, three were solid standouts. A SEAL, a Boston brawler turned ATF agent, and an FBI agent who looked like a country cowgirl but who was one of the most vicious unarmed combat fighters I've ever met. I had good feelings about them, both in combat ability and in the likelihood they would fit into Echo Team. It remained to be seen if it was their bad luck they joined the DMS today, or my good luck that they were adding useful skills to my team.

I spotted Lydia standing with the rest of Echo Team. They were between two white-and-blue NYPD SWAT trucks parked crookedly by the subway entrance. A dozen men and women in body armor and helmets stood looking up at us. Even from that distance I could feel their anger and tension. Their friends and colleagues were down in the tunnel and they felt it was up to them to go charging to the rescue.

Bunny was next to me and must have been reading my thoughts. "We going to have trouble keeping them off the dance floor, Boss?"

"Let's hope not."

We dropped fast-ropes toward the street, clipped on, and flung ourselves into the air. Normally any kind of jump scares the shit out of me. I am not a heights person. Today I had other things to be afraid of. I plunged toward the ground, one gloved hand on the rope, the other behind my back to work the brake. We touched down one, two, three, unclipped, and saw the ropes rise like magic snakes as the Black Hawk climbed away, dragging its wind and noise with it. We hurried over to meet Lydia and the team. Sam nodded to us. The newbies did, too, but they were far more wary. Ivan wasn't there.

"Where's Hellboy?" I asked.

"Down on the platform with the first responders, a pair of transit cops, Faustino and Dawes," said Lydia. "The station's been cleared. We have National Guard units on their way, ETA eleven minutes. SWAT is positioned at the stations down the line, but they've been told to stay at street level. Deacon ordered that no one goes down there but us."

We were all dressed in Saratoga Hammer suits and helmets, and under the August heat it was boiling hot. I caught a brief exchange of micronods between Bunny and Lydia. It was an open secret that they were a couple, but they were professional enough to keep it to themselves. They didn't let it spill over into the job.

"What do we know about the SWAT team that went in?" Bunny asked.

Lydia shook her head. "No contact with them. Faustino said she heard gunfire. *Mira, jefe*," she added, "the transit cops said that their radios didn't work in the tunnel. From what she described, it sounds like a jammer. Said there were cameras down there, too, mounted on some of the pillars."

"Ain't that interesting as shit," mused Top.

"Whatever it is," I said, "we'll figure it out on the fly."

Without another word we then ran down the stairs into the subway.

Down into hell.

Chapter Fifty-four

Fulton Street Line
Near Euclid Avenue Station
Brooklyn, New York
Sunday, August 31, 1:56 p.m.

Officer Faustino stared at us with big eyes in a white face. She held her Glock in one hand, the barrel pointed to the ground. Her partner, Dawes, stood nearby, looking equally scared and confused.

"Officers," I said, pulling down the lower half of my balaclava as I stepped onto the platform. Sweat ran down my face. "I'm Captain Ledger, Homeland Security."

A lie, but a useful one.

Beyond the cops I saw Ivan squatting on the edge of the platform, pointing a combat shotgun into shadows. The rest of Echo swarmed past me, moving quickly to double-check that the station was secure.

"C-Captain," said Faustino, tripping over it a bit. "What's happening?"

Instead of answering, I said, "Holster your weapons, officers. Do it now, please."

They did so, but reluctantly. The two cops looked to be about one short step away from losing their shit. The male cop maybe more so. I could sympathize. Control is not a constant or a given, even if you have a badge pinned to your chest.

However, Faustino forced herself to straighten and chased the tremolo out of her voice as she asked, "How can we help?"

A good cop. I gave her a smile.

"We can't let anyone down those stairs," I said, "and we sure as hell can't let anyone go up. Not unless you get an all-clear directly from me or my superiors. Can I trust you and your partner to hold this line?"

She forced herself to straighten. "Yes, sir. We got it."

I kept eye contact for a few seconds longer, then spun away to join my team. This was a "life sucks" moment for everyone. I dearly hoped this would be the worst moment of all of our days.

At the edge of the tracks I hunkered down next to Ivan, who was studying the tunnel through a night-vision scope.

"What are you seeing?"

"Seeing nothing, boss," he said, quietly, not looking at me. "Hearing some weird shit, though, and its making my balls want to shrivel up and hide."

I held my hand up for silence and bent my ear toward the tunnel entrance. I didn't hear anything. Until I did. It was soft, distant, like a breeze blowing through a cracked window on a stormy night.

"Those are human voices," said Sam quietly. Lydia and the others clustered around us and they listened, too. They all heard it. Some sooner, others after a few seconds, but they all heard it.

The moans. Plaintive and hungry.

"Fuck me," whispered Bunny.

"Okay," I said as I went over the edge and down onto the tracks, "form on me." We moved quickly and quietly into the tunnel, but a hundred feet in I stopped and turned to the others. "Listen up," I said, facing the newbies, "there wasn't time before and I didn't want to say this in front of those cops, but here's the deal. This is the point where I'm supposed to make a speech to the new recruits. But I don't like speeches and we don't have time, so this will be short and sweet. You three are jumping in ankle-deep shit. You're doing that without being properly briefed or trained. All of that sucks, but there it is."

Three sets of eyes studied me. Everyone pulled down the lower shrouds of their balaclavas. Easier to have a conversation that way. Ivan stood apart and kept his shotgun pointed down the tunnel.

"We're heading into a situation that is probably going to be worse than anything you've dealt with," I continued. "Get used to that because this is what we do. The DMS usually doesn't put boots on the ground unless the shit is already hitting the fan. Sucks but there it is." I cut a look at Lydia. "You tell them what's down here?"

She nodded. "As much as I could. Wasn't a lot of time."

To the newbies I said, "So you know. This is the real face of terror, kids. Not guys in turbans and not homegrown assholes with fertilizer bombs. As far as the DMS goes, it's mad science and monsters. You three good to go or do I send you back to babysit the cops? The appropriate response is 'hooah.'"

"Hooah," they said. If there wasn't overwhelming enthusiasm, who could blame them?

"Good. Combat call signs from here out."

"Sir," said the bullet-headed ATF shooter from Boston, Duncan Mac-Dougall, "we don't have call signs. At least I don't."

The FBI woman, Montana Parker, shook her head. "Me neither."

"I do," said the Navy SEAL, a tall, ascetic man with a poet's face. "Been called Gandalf since OCS."

"Gandalf," I said, nailing it in place.

MacDougall, I remembered from the training sessions, had a tattoo of a snarling wolf on his left forearm. I pointed to him. "You're Bad Wolf."

He grinned.

"What about you?" I asked the FBI woman.

"Most of the guys I've ever worked with have called me 'that bitch,' but I don't think that's going to play."

Despite everything, I laughed.

Ivan shifted to stand next to her. He was six four and she came to well below his shoulder. Five three, tops. "How about Stretch?"

She gave him a smile that was softer and brighter than I would have expected. She hadn't smiled once during the training sessions, and I had the feeling that no one had ever accused her of having an overly sunny disposition. I'd been leaning toward a call sign of Genghis or Harpy, but I was glad I hadn't said anything.

"Welcome to the DMS, Stretch. I'm Cowboy." I pointed to Top and Bunny. "Sergeant Rock and Green Giant."

They'd already learned the call signs of the others. Lydia was Warbride, Ivan was Hellboy, and Sam was Ronin. And for a weird little moment I thought I heard other call signs whisper through the shadows. Names of comrades and friends long gone, and others who'd taken injuries that had pushed them off the firing line.

Dancing Duck.

Chatterbox.

Trickster.

Scream Queen.

So many others.

Too many others.

"Now pay close attention, and that goes for everyone," I said. "We're stepping into a world of wrong here, and if we come to a worst-case scenario then we are going to have to make hard choices without hesitation. The first two DMS teams who faced people infected with the *seif-al-din* were overwhelmed and destroyed because they hesitated. They let ordinary human feelings get them killed. We can't repeat that. The reason you three made the cut is because you never hesitated, not in any of the drills. Well, this isn't a drill. This is as real as it is ever going to get. We are going to face walkers. You understand what that means?"

MacDougall—Bad Wolf—said, "What Warbride told us seems unreal. This is World War Z stuff. I mean . . . are we really talking zombies here? It's hard to believe."

"Tell you what, son," said Top in a slow drawl, "how about you cover yourself with steak sauce and walk point for us. Let's see if it feels like hazing when those fuckers tear a flank steak off your ass."

The other members of Echo laughed. Not nice laughs.

Bad Wolf stiffened. "No, that's not what I meant. It's just . . ."

Top laid a hand on his shoulder. "Son, you're fishing for a context that just ain't there. We've all been through it. You'll get through it, too."

"It's what we do," murmured Lydia.

"She's right," said Bunny. "You know that line from Shakespeare? The one about there being more things in heaven and earth?"

"Sure," said Bad Wolf. "*Hamlet*."

"Pretty much our job description."

It chilled me to hear that line used now when I'd thought it less than two hours ago.

I said, "Look, guys, here's the bottom line. These walkers—they're not supernatural, nothing like that. This is a weaponized disease that turns innocent people into mindless killers. It isn't pretty and it isn't curable. Anyone who is infected is a time bomb because he or she can and will try to spread it. If we don't stop it, those movies—*The Crazies*, *28 Days Later*—they won't be horror flicks, they'll be historical documents. That is not a joke and it's not an exaggeration. Tell me you hear and understand."

The horror in their eyes was total now. But they said, "Hooah."

I pulled my balaclava into place. "Then let's go to work. Ronin, you have our backs. Hellboy, you're on point. Nobody gets out of visual range. Be sharp and be professional."

We moved on. It did not help my peace of mind knowing that Euclid Avenue Station was the end of the line. I hope we didn't cut ourselves on that kind of irony.

Interlude Fourteen

Four Seasons Hotel
Philadelphia, Pennsylvania
Two and a Half Years Ago

"I think they know."

The vice president propped himself up on one elbow and placed his other hand on the naked back of Artemisia Bliss. She sat on the edge of the bed, a wineglass cradled between her palms, head bowed, black hair falling to hide her face.

"Who knows?" he asked.

"Aunt Sallie," she said. "Church."

Collins snorted. "I doubt it. If they had a clue you'd be out on your ass."

She shook her head. "I might be out on my ass. I'm not sure."

"What makes you think that?"

"I tried to do a remote login to my workstation from my laptop and it said that the system was down for repairs."

"So?"

"The system is never down for repairs. There are too many redundancies."

He grunted and stroked her back, running his fingers slowly up and down the knobs of her backbone, circling them one at a time as he went.

"What could they know?" he asked.

Bliss pushed her hair out of her face and took a sip of wine. "It's possible they may have discovered that I copied Hugo Vox's records."

"Vox? Not Paris Jakoby?"

"I deleted all traces of what I took from the Jakobys. No, Aunt Sallie has been retracing all the stuff we took from Terror Town. And I saw that there were special eyes-only requests for any files I accessed."

"I thought that Haruspex thing could hide from MindReader."

"It can . . . but this was right after I started using it. I've upgraded it a lot since then."

He stopped caressing her and sat up. "You erased your tracks, though, right? Haruspex is just like MindReader, right? It doesn't leave a footprint. That's what you told me."

"Yes."

"Then what's the problem?"

She shifted to look at him. "I know everything Pangaea could do, and I think I know everything MindReader can do . . ."

"But—?"

"But what if I'm wrong? What if MindReader can somehow track erasures, even ones made by software that does what it does?"

"Is that even possible?"

She was silent for a long time.

"Bliss?"

"Maybe."

Collins launched himself off the bed and walked across the room, then wheeled on her. She could feel his anger. It filled the whole room.

"And you're fucking telling me this now?"

"I—"

"You do know that Deacon wants my head on a pole," he growled. "After the NSA dropped the ball in shutting them down last year, Deacon all but tore me a new asshole. Came right up to the edge of threatening my fucking life, you know. He came right out and told me that he had his eye on me, that if he discovered any impropriety he would bury me. His words. Bury me—and knowing him I don't think that was a metaphor."

Bliss shook her head. "He can't touch you."

"He can if he gets inside Haruspex and sees what we're doing. Jesus fuck, Bliss. There's enough there to have me arrested and jailed."

"No . . ."

"Yes there is and you damn well know it."

"I . . . I'll wipe the files. Demagnetize the drives and wipe everything," she insisted.

He came back and squatted down in front of her. "Can you dupe everything and hide it?"

"Hide it?"

"Yes. Make a master copy and put it somewhere safe. Somewhere Mind-Reader can't find it. No Internet connection."

"Sure, I can copy it to a master drive and—"

"How long will that take?"

"I don't know, Bill. A day . . . ?"

"Do it. I'll have one of my guys come by your place. We need that data. All of Vox's notes, the security game modules, the pass-code interpreter . . . we need all of it. If we lose it then we lose any chance of doing some real good."

Bliss said nothing but she gave him a token nod. Bill Collins had a different worldview than she had. He was, in his own way, a patriot. She was genuinely apolitical. He wanted the presidency so he could rebuild America into a form that he believed would approximate the way the country would have been had politicians not spent two centuries wandering in the opposite direction of what the Founding Fathers intended. Bliss wanted to publish file patents, and revise the current definition of what "filthy rich" meant. So far, though, both paths led through a landscape she thought of as "deliberately chaotic." Funny how fanatical idealism and rampant greed sometimes look the same from a distance.

"I can make the copies," she said, "and I can blank out my own laptop. But what happens if they hit me with a warrant? Think about it, Bill, if they really think I hacked and copied those files, a warrant would be a no-brainer."

He nodded. "Yeah, damn it."

"So what do I do? I could get arrested."

That was a big ugly truth and it hung in the air, leering at them. Collins refilled their wineglasses and they sat next to each other, naked and slumped, thinking it through.

Collins said, "We have to stop using Haruspex, that's for certain. At least for now."

"I know."

"When I send my guy to get your drive, let him have that, too. I have places to hide it where no one can find it. Believe me."

She gave a weak little laugh. "I'll feel naked without it."

He touched her face, then trailed his fingertips down over her chin, her throat, her breast.

"Bill—?" she asked, her voice small.

"Yeah, babe?"

"What will happen to me if they really arrest me?"

He didn't answer. Not at first. Long moments drifted past them like burning embers.

"We'll think of something," he said. It sounded weak.

"If they find out," she said, her voice even smaller, "we'll never see each other again."

Collins put a smile on his face. Bliss wanted to believe that it was real.

"Sure we will," he said. "We'll find a way."

And then he took her wineglass and set it on the night table next to his. Then he took her in his arms and they fell together onto the tangled sheets.

When Bliss arrived at the Hangar the following morning, Aunt Sallie and Gus Dietrich stood beside her workstation. Their eyes were ice cold. Harsh. Angry and unforgiving.

Before Bliss could say a word, Dietrich tossed a pair of handcuffs onto her desk.

Chapter Fifty-five

We moved through darkness that had never seen sunlight or felt rain. Our footsteps sounded strangely muffled. With the lights off we used night-vision goggles, which painted everything in eerie shades of green and gray.

For the first hundred yards we saw nothing. Not a rat, not even a cock-roach.

The original members of Echo each carried a BAMS unit clipped onto their shoulder straps. Ivan kept checking his, murmuring the comforting "Green" every few dozen yards.

We ran around puddles and long steel rails, guns in hand. Ivan was on point, leading the way with a combat shotgun fitted with a heavy drum magazine. Bunny had an identical shotgun. Lydia had our backs. I knew the newbies knew their jobs, but they didn't yet know ours, and I needed someone I could trust without supervision.

Suddenly, Ivan stopped with his fist raised, the universal signal to stop.

We stopped.

He unclenched his fist and pointed to something attached to a pillar. A small high-tech camera with a burning red eye.

I tapped my earbud. "Cowboy to Bug."

"With you, Cowboy."

"What do you know about this?" I tilted my helmet cam toward the device on the wall.

"It's not regulation," he said.

I snapped my fingers. "Green Giant."

Bunny moved past me, pulling a small scanner from a pocket. He reached up and swept it past the camera. "It's not a bomb," he said, then pressed a button to switch the nature of the scanner. "Not sending a signal. What-ever it is, it's not doing anything."

"Getting the scanner feed," said Bug. "Wow, that's a nifty toy. Mucho expensive and it should not be there. Since company policy is that we don't like coincidences, my best guess is that it was put there by our bad guys."

"Is it safe to touch?" I asked, stepping up beside Bunny.

"Yeah. It's just a camera."

I reached up and punched it with the side of my fist. Very damn hard. "Fuck it."

We moved on. There were more cameras. Bunny scanned each one, and once the bomb detector gave a green light, he smashed them.

"That's like eight thousand dollars a pop," said Bug.

"Not anymore," said Bunny.

We kept going, running through darkness as quickly and quietly as we could.

Then we crossed a line.

It wasn't something you could define, nor was it an actual line on the ground. But within the space of a few steps the world suddenly changed. It no longer felt like we were running through an empty tunnel toward something. No, all at once it felt like were *in* something.

Something ugly.

Something wrong.

That fast, Ivan's pace slowed from a careful run to a wary walk.

I could see it in his body language, in the tightening of his shoulders, the hunch of his back as if following a primitive instinct to shield his vitals against an unseen claw.

We slowed, too.

And then Ivan held up a fist again.

We froze. Nobody was stupid enough to ask what was wrong or if Ivan actually saw anything. Even the newbies knew better than that. In that polluted darkness we stood as still as statues in some lost and forgotten tomb of ancient warriors.

Then Bunny raised his BAMS unit and showed me the display. The warning light was no longer green. Now it was a faint orange. There was something in the air and I didn't need the digital display to tell me what it was.

Seif-al-din.

Although the pathogen was a serum transfer, traces of it could be carried in moist air. Not enough to infect on inhalation but enough to scare the living shit out of me.

Something ahead of us moved. It was a soft step. Faint, dragging. Around the bend in the tunnel. Coming our way.

I signaled the others to hold their positions as I crept forward to stand with Ivan. We stood shoulder to shoulder in the center of the tracks, guns up and out. The sound grew louder. A shuffling step, a scrape of rubber soles on the wet concrete. Footsteps without emphasis. Listless. The way a dazed and injured person walks.

The figure moved around the bend in the tunnel and into our line of sight. Behind me I heard Noah whisper something.

"Jeez, it's one of our boys. Good . . . maybe they have everything contained."

The figure was dressed in full SWAT gear. Limb pads and body armor, a helmet, weapons. Sergeant's stripes.

No mask, though.

That was gone.

Beside me Ivan gagged. "Oh . . . balls . . ."

Behind me I heard a sharp intake of breath. Maybe Noah, maybe one of the others. The SWAT sergeant moved toward us without haste. Limping, dragging one foot. He stopped for just a moment, head coming up, eyes seeming to flare with green light because of the night-vision distortion. But I knew that the SWAT man could not see us. And it wasn't because the tunnel was so dark.

You need eyes to see.

He had none.

No eyes.

No nose.

No lips.

All we could see was raw and ragged ends of muscle and chipped edges of white bone.

There was no way this person could still be alive. His throat had been savaged, his clothes were drenched with blood that was as black as oil in the green night-vision light. I thought that it might somehow be easier for me because I'd seen this before. The walking dead, the violation and perversion of the body that was the hallmark of the *seif-al-din* pathogen. I'd fought these walkers before. Fought them with guns and knives and my own hands. I believed that having defeated this horror before that I was somehow immune to the soul-tearing sight of it again. That the reality of it would be less real to someone like me.

That's hubris. That's the kind of thinking that only a fool can manage and I hated myself for my blindness and my weakness.

The man—the wreck of what had been a man—opened its jaws and from between rows of broken teeth he uttered a moan of such aching and indescribable hunger that it made me want to weep. Or scream.

Instead, I pointed my gun at his ruined face and pulled the trigger.

God help us all.

Chapter Fifty-six

Grand Hyatt Hotel
109 East Forty-second Street
New York City
Sunday, August 31, 2:06 p.m.

He checked into the hotel under the name Thomas T. Goldsmith, Jr. It was a nice choice, Monk thought. Goldsmith had co-created the very first interactive electronic game—a missile simulator—back in 1947. One of Mother Night's little jokes.

Monk took the elevator to the thirteenth floor and entered his room. A gift basket stood on the table by the window. Wine, fruit, cheese, chocolate. And at the bottom a plastic pill case filled with the right goodies, and also keycards for three other rooms at the hotel. Those rooms were booked for Estle Ray Mann, Goldsmith's partner for the missile game; Alan Turing, inventor of the first computer chess game, also in 1947; and his colleague Dietrich Prinz.

Each room had an identical suitcase and bag of golf clubs. In each golf bag was a twin—or a sister, as Monk viewed it—of his darling Olga. The suitcases also contained handguns and explosives. Better to be prepared for all eventualities.

He unwrapped a chocolate bar, bit a piece, and sat down to wait for Mother Night's call.

"Hope it won't be too long," he said to Olga's sister.

Interlude Fifteen

Her lawyers told her to wear a pretty suit and show a little leg, maybe a hint of cleavage. Bliss spent a lot of time on her makeup, and when she stepped into the courtroom she was sure that no one even noticed the handcuffs. They were looking at the prettiest woman in the room, and that was a tactic. It was, the lawyer assured her, the last card they had left to play.

The judge had spent a lot of time during the trial looking at Artemisia Bliss's legs. The judge was a well-known hound dog and had a useful track record in light sentencing for pretty women.

She smiled at him—not too overt a flirtation, of course—as she sat down at the defense table. Her lawyers—both attractive women—sat on either side of her. They, too, were showing a little skin. Skirts and tailored jackets. Probably push-up bras, too. Anything that would work.

Bliss was well aware that nothing much else had worked so far.

Eighteen separate charges had been brought against her. Her lawyers had gotten four of them tossed on technicalities and the jury had decided in her favor on six more. That left eight in place, and the jury didn't let her slide on those. Standing there, listening to the foreman delivering eight guilty verdicts, was the toughest thing Bliss had ever done. She wanted to cry. She wanted to scream. Before that day she'd been certain that it wasn't possible to feel more completely vulnerable and afraid than she already had. Through the booking phase, that awful first night in jail, the arraignment before a grand jury, the months in federal custody, the endless nights in jail where predators abounded and her looks and breeding were no protection at all. Feeling abandoned by Bill Collins, who could not risk even the most tenuous connection to her. The trial itself, burning away days, then weeks, and finally two months of her life.

And the endless deliberation. Four and a half days of it.

Guilty of cybercrimes.

Guilty of wire fraud.

Guilty of unauthorized access to protected computers. Notably those belonging to federal agencies.

Guilty.

Guilty.

Guilty.

Including the big one. Guilty of human rights violations.

That was not actually true. Not as such. But she had copied all of the information in the computer systems of the Jakoby twins and their father, Cyrus. The elder Jakoby had devised a number of pathogens designed to target different ethnic groups. Her theft of that science painted her with the same brush. No amount of argument from her lawyers could convince a jury that any innocent person would want the formulae for ethnic genocide for any reason other than to use or resell it.

Hence the conspiracy charges for which she was convicted.

Which brought her to today.

The sentencing.

Her looks and the judge's poor personal judgment when it came to women. One card left to play.

The judge sat behind his bench and listened to prosecution and defense make their elaborate arguments for and against a harsh sentence. Bliss thought her lawyers were particularly eloquent, and the judge even smiled as he watched the younger of the two attorneys jiggle her way to the lectern. The cuffs had been removed before the proceedings began.

The judge then turned to Bliss.

"Would the accused like to make a statement?"

"Yes, your honor," said Bliss, rising slowly to her feet. Exactly as she had been coached.

He gestured for her to continue.

"Your honor," began Bliss, "I understand the gravity and consequences of what I did. I really do. But I meant no harm. I've been a loyal and dedicated member of the *team* since its inception." It had been agreed by all parties that the DMS would never be named and would instead be referred to as the "team." "I've done everything I could to help strengthen our country against all threats." Her use of *our* was deliberate and she leaned on it ever so slightly. "Everything I've done since joining the team was to make sure that we were prepared for anything that could pose a threat to us. Collecting and collating data, analyzing it, disseminating it to the proper groups within the team was my only concern. Everything else was part of that goal. Everything. I love our country. And I want to continue to serve it and to help protect the American people." She paused and gave him a brave smile. "Thank you."

There was a frown on the judge's face. Was it doubt about the convictions? Was it doubt about whatever sentence he'd already decided before today? As she sat down, each of her attorneys took one of her hands. When she cut a look at the prosecutors, they looked worried.

The judge was silent for a long time, his lips pursed, chin sunk on his chest. Finally, he looked at Bliss and nodded.

"Very well," he said. "Bearing in mind your record, the evidence, and the remarks made here this morning, I am prepared to pronounce sentence."

He cited the verdicts and the applicable laws and statutes.

Then he smiled at her. "Dr. Bliss, you are a very attractive and charming woman. You are a brilliant scientist and perhaps one of the most intelligent people I have ever met. Your skills and your potential are, as has been pointed out, a powerful weapon capable of doing great good for the American people in these troubled times."

Bliss brightened, and both of the hands holding hers tightened.

"However," said the judge, "when a person puts self-interest in front of patriotism, and personal gain before the general welfare, then that person has thrown away any grace or consideration she might otherwise have."

Bliss did not hear anything else the judge said.

Her mind simply shut down.

There were only vague memories. She remembered screaming. Weeping. People putting hands on her. The coldness of handcuffs. Shouts.

Red madness.

It was only later that she was able to assemble the facts. The horrible, impossible facts.

The judge had given her the maximum sentence for each separate charge.

One hundred and sixty-five years.

Life.

And death, because she would never get out.

They had to drag her from the court.

Chapter Fifty-seven

Sometimes a gunshot is a small, hollow *pok*. Sometimes it's a sharp crack.

In the damp blackness of the subway tunnel, my pistol boomed like thunder. Too loud, too harsh, the echo slammed off the wall and boomed into my eardrums.

The SWAT officer's head snapped back and he fell.

It was that quick.

There was no intermediary phase of a body slowing down from the chemical urgency of life into the stillness of death. This was as immediate as throwing a switch. Like cutting the strings of a puppet. The strange blend of misfolded proteins, chemicals, and genetically modified parasites that made up the *seif-al-din* kept only a part of the brain alive. The motor cortex and some cranial nerves. Everything else was already dead. So when my hollow-point bullet punched through his forehead and exploded his brain, that entire process simply stopped. On one side of a broken moment the man was a walking, ravenous monster, and on the other he was simply dead. Totally, finally, tragically dead.

I watched the officer fall.

A SWAT operator.

A cop.

A person.

Gone.

I heard Ivan say something. No joke about balls in this moment. He called on God, needing and wanting some mercy down here. Some grace. But then movement around the bend proved that we were closer to hell than heaven as several figures shambled around into view.

Four.

Six.

More.

The rest of the SWAT team. Their Kevlar armor ripped and yanked aside to reveal flesh that was no longer whole. We saw dreadful things.

They were twenty feet away and moving toward us. Their moans rose from the cry of the lost to a more urgent and hungry tone.

"Hellboy," I said, using Ivan's combat call sign.

He did not move.

"*Ivan,*" I barked, my voice as sharp as a gunshot.

He flinched and jumped. For one brief, wretched moment he looked away from them and into my eyes. With the night vision he could not have seen much, and maybe it wasn't a visual connection he was looking for. Maybe he needed to see the living, to remember that he, too, was alive, before he could bring himself to fight the dead. I don't know. I'm a soldier, not a psychologist, not a philosopher.

"Ivan," I said again. Just that. His name.

I saw the exact moment when he regained himself. He jerked as if I'd shocked him with an electrical cord, and I think that's when he realized that this was how so many of our comrades had died in the past. Charlie and Delta Teams, who were devoured the first time any of us encountered this disease. This was how the SWAT team died. Ivan's mouth became a hard line and he bared his teeth as he brought his gun up.

He carried an AA-12 assault shotgun and the big drum magazine loaded with twelve-gauge rounds. He had the selector switch set to full automatic, and the gun fired five rounds per second, filling the tunnel with thunder a hundred times worse than my Beretta. The walking dead men were caught in a maelstrom of destructive force. Ivan was aiming at them but not aiming for their heads. His first thirty rounds tore away arms and legs, blew torsos apart, tore heads from necks, but he wasn't destroying enough of them.

Then Lydia was there and with her were the new members of Echo Team. More and greater thunder filled the tunnel. Lydia had her rifle snugged against her shoulder, shooting on semiauto, taking time to hit the head. To end the unlife of these monsters. Duncan, Montana, and Noah hesitated for only a moment, and then they crossed the line that the moment demanded we all cross. They opened up on fellow officers, on men and women in uniform. On victims of terrorism who had been forced to embody the very concept of terror.

There were screams stitched into the thunder.

They did not come from the walking dead.

The screams came from the living.

From us.

From all of us.

The SWAT members fell, but the fight did not end there. We stepped over torn pieces of bodies and rounded the bend. Knowing what we'd find.

The train was there.

The tunnel was filled with the dead.

Hundreds of them.

Some dismembered, some dragging twisted limbs. Others achingly whole, their death wounds hidden from our eyes.

All of them dead.

Walkers.

Zombies.

Coming for us. Moaning, aching for our flesh.

We stood there in a shooting line. Lydia, Sam, Ivan, Duncan, Montana, and Noah. And me. Echo Team.

We fired and fired and fired.

We covered one another as we reloaded.

Our guns bucked in our hands, the barrels growing hot. The air was thick and toxic with gun smoke and cordite.

The dead walked into our gunfire. They did not—could not—evade or duck away. They came into the bright muzzle flashes and the lead. They flew apart like broken toys.

We used every bullet, every grenade, every magazine.

And they still kept coming.

In the end, when the last bullets were fired and the empty magazines dropped, when we were ankle-deep in blood and spent shell casings, the dead still came.

A few left.

Civilians.

The ones from the last car.

Old and young. Some children among them.

They came.

Ivan was weeping openly. So was Noah. Lydia's face was stone and I feared for her. She was way, way out on the edge.

"God, please," said Duncan. He was breathing too fast, his whole system teetering on the edge of shock as he slapped his pockets for fresh magazines that weren't there. "I'm out. I'm out."

I felt a sob break in my chest as I drew my knife.

What followed was unspeakable.

Chapter Fifty-eight

Westin Hotel
Atlanta, Georgia
Sunday, August 31, 2:15 p.m.

Mother Night watched the video feeds.

There were six cameras mounted at different points around the subway train. Each one had a lens that provided a panoramic view of the slaughter. Three of them showed close-ups of the infected, and she took them offline, not wanting to send a mixed message. One camera had a tight view of a line of DMS agents, and Mother Night was almost positive that the second man in that line was Joe Ledger. Even with the helmet, a balaclava covering his nose and mouth, and night-vision goggles, he had the right build, the right carriage. He looked like a video game character. She could have sampled him and built him into one of her own games. Maybe she would. She'd already established a network of dummy corporations and technical obfuscation that would allow her to bring games to market under a variety of false names so that nothing could be traced back to her.

It would be hilarious to have Joe Ledger, Top Sims, and that hunky Bunny as characters. Maybe Lydia, too, though Mother Night did not know her very well. The others were strangers to her except as names on covert reports hacked by Haruspex.

The two remaining cameras showed the whole line of shooters from a distance, and as the walkers shambled forward they were torn apart. Nice. From that angle and that distance, and in that shitty light, it was impossible to tell that they were infected. Or how badly they were infected. They looked like frightened people reaching out for help. And being killed by government troops.

Absolutely perfect.

She took a sip of Diet Coke, drew in a calming breath, let it out slowly, and then tapped the keys that would send this video feed to its various targets.

First was YouTube, with links automatically placed on six hundred preset Twitter pages and fifty Facebook group and event pages, as well as on thousands of blogs into which Haruspex had intruded.

Bang, bang, bang.

Using reposting services modeled after Tweetdeck and Hootsuite, the link was posted over and over again every few seconds. Tiny changes in wording and URL kept the antispam programs from blocking her out.

The number of hits began sluggishly, but within three minutes it had jumped, and then soared.

The thought of it going "viral" was an irony not lost on her.

She took another sip of Diet Coke.

Then she sent the YouTube, Twitter, and Facebook links to the media.

To every network news desk. To more than six hundred global news agencies, from the Associated Press to Al Jazeera. And then Haruspex took over, sending the links to local affiliates, newspapers, and Web news editors.

Within minutes the slaughter in the Brooklyn subway system had hit sixteen thousand news sources.

"Burn to shine, motherfuckers," she murmured.

Chapter Fifty-nine

The Oval Office
The White House
Washington, D.C.
Sunday, August 31, 2:19 p.m.

Vice President William Collins stood with a group of top advisors as they clustered around the president's desk to watch the horror unfolding on the TV screen. The image was that of American troops in unmarked black combat gear firing continuously on a group of unarmed civilians.

The bullets tore into the people.

The soundtrack was filled with shrieks and screams as the people begged for mercy. Threaded through the gunfire was the sound of gruff laughter.

Nice touch, thought Collins; and he wondered from which video game or movie Mother Night had lifted that soundtrack. In all the confusion it was impossible to match those cries for help to any actual mouth on the screen. Maybe one day someone would discover that the soundtrack didn't match the video at all, but by then it would be a different world.

And a different president.

Maybe a president whose last name began with a C.

It was hard not to smile, so he took the urge and made it look like a grimace.

The gunfire began to dwindle as the last of the civilians staggered and fell. Collins knew that the staggering movements were as much to do with the nature of the *seif-al-din* pathogen as they were from bullet impacts, but millions of TV watchers wouldn't know or suspect that.

The secretary of state said, "Oh my god."

The president was pale with shock. "How did this get on the air?"

Collins pushed through the crowd. "Did you authorize this?" he demanded. "Did you send troops in to kill those people? My god . . . these are Americans!"

The president shook his head, dazed and apparently lost. "How did this get on the air?" he repeated.

Collins had to bite his tongue to keep from smiling.

Chapter Sixty

Fulton Street Line
Near Euclid Avenue Station
Brooklyn, New York
Sunday, August 31, 2:22 p.m.

We stood there, wrapped in a shroud of gun smoke, haunted by the echoes of our guns, ankle-deep in blood, filled with horror.

Everybody was panting. Hands shook with a palsy that was born of the realization that this moment was both unreal and yet sewn into the fabric of our lives. No matter what else happened, no matter how hardened we got, or how insane we became, in one way or another we would each re-visit this place in dreams. In those dark times we would stand in the fetid darkness and do awful things, knowing that we must and knowing that with each bullet fired we were blasting away at those precious human qualities that defined us. In a very real way, we all died a little that day, and we would be less alive from here on.

Behind me I heard someone quietly weeping. Maybe one of the newbies, maybe one of the regulars. I didn't know and didn't want to find out.

I understood, though.

If this had been a regular battle between us and the bad guys—terrorists, criminals, soldiers in a foreign army—then there would be some kind of natural path along which we could walk from here back to the world.

These were civilians. They hadn't been driven by an ideology to attack us. It wasn't politics or religion or even greed.

They were victims.

They had been murdered twice.

Once by whomever had released the *seif-al-din* pathogen aboard that train; and then again by us.

My earbud buzzed.

"Deacon to Cowboy," said Mr. Church, "I need you to listen to me very carefully. Do not say anything. Not a word. Switch to my private channel. Only you."

I raised my hand and snapped my fingers. Everyone fell silent.

Church said, "This action has been filmed. Look for cameras."

I did. And I found them. Same as the ones from the tunnel, but we'd missed them as we'd closed on the train. There had been no time to look for cameras at that time. Now I saw all the little red lights shimmering like rats' eyes in a sewer.

"Disable the cameras," ordered Church.

But before I could even reach out the red lights flickered off. They all went dark.

"Cowboy, the feed has stopped," said Church. "Locate and collect those cameras. Bug will want to examine them."

Top instantly organized everyone into a search.

Church switched to a private channel. "Just listen. We have a situation developing. The feeds from those cameras were streamed to the Internet and all major news services." He quickly explained about the soundtrack of people screaming and begging for mercy. The president just called me and demanded that I pull your team and order you to stand down pending an investigation. The media is exploding with this, and a great deal of that heat will be directed toward the president. It's likely to damage or destroy this administration."

I cursed very quietly.

"Do not exit at Euclid Avenue," Church continued. "Proceed along the tracks three stops to Liberty Avenue station. It's a mile and a half. I'll have people down there with decontamination equipment and fresh clothes. We'll extract you from there."

"How much shit are we in?" I asked.

Instead of answering he said, "Get moving."

The line went dead. I called my people over and gave them the short version of what was happening.

Ivan said, "This sucks dog balls."

"Hooah," muttered Top darkly.

"Nobody knows who we are," I told them, touching my balaclava. "We're soldiers in unmarked black. Trust Deacon to protect us."

"Can he?" asked Montana.

"If anyone can," I said, which did not sound as comforting as I hoped it would. "Clock's ticking, so let's haul ass."

We hauled ass.

We ran as if monsters were chasing us. Which they damn well were.

Interlude Sixteen

Metropolitan Detention Center
Brooklyn, New York
Two Years Ago

Artemisia Bliss sat in her cell and waited for her life to end. Wished, in fact, for it to all be over. They had her on suicide watch, though. Fair enough. If there was any chance for a quick way out, she'd take it.

Living in hell was not living.

This was going to be hell. Of that she had no doubt. The judgment against Artemisia Bliss had been so severe.

One hundred and sixty-five years.

The joke was that there was a chance for parole after seventy years.

By then Artemisia Bliss would be ninety-seven years old. Even in the unlikely event that she was still alive, freedom would not be freedom at all. No, the judge had given her a death sentence. Soon they would come and take her from this holding cell at MDC and transfer her to a medium-security prison whose location was still to be determined. Her lawyers were still wrangling with the judge about placement. They wanted her in a minimum-security facility like Waseca in Minnesota or, better yet, the one in Danbury. The judge wanted her in supermax. The only reason for the delay in his orders being carried out was the scarcity of women's cells in supermax. It gave the lawyers a little time and it kept her in Brooklyn. It was much easier to influence the destination of a new prisoner from an administrative facility than it was to effect a transfer from one long-term prison to another.

A small and very cold comfort.

Every time she heard a footfall outside her cell, Bliss dreaded what it could mean. Lately there was bad news and worse news.

The only blessing, however small, was that the cliché of aggressive sexual abuse in the showers hadn't happened. But Bliss always mentally tagged "yet" onto that.

She had few illusions about what would happen to her.

She was young. She was very pretty. And she had lost all of her power.

All of that wonderful power. To her it was losing her heart and all the blood that ran through it. She felt dead inside.

Almost dead.

The fact that there were still some very small options kept her from finding a shortcut out of the cell and this—whatever it was. She couldn't call it "life" anymore, even though that's what the judge called it.

Cosmic jokes like that she did not need.

She knew she could try to play the card of her affair with Bill Collins as a way of getting a new trial and the protection of becoming a high-profile witness against a sitting vice president. That card was all that was really left to her, and with every passing moment she drew closer to playing it.

What would he do, she wondered.

Would he have her killed?

She had absolutely no doubts that he could. Collins, for all his passion and words of love, was a vicious man who had layers upon layers of friends in very low places. He was enormously wealthy and his friends were wired in everywhere. Bliss suspected that Collins had been more directly involved with the Jakobys and the Seven Kings than anyone—even the DMS—ever guessed or could prove. He owned people in the Secret Service, the FBI, the ATF; and nearly everyone in his Cybercrimes Task Force belonged to him heart and soul. If he ever became president, which was becoming a real possibility, then he would build an empire whose corrupt roots dug down into the deepest levels of big business and the military-industrial complex.

So, yes, she decided, he could have her killed. If she could be certain that he would find a way to do it without pain or humiliation, then Bliss would have welcomed it. It would get the job done. She just didn't want to suffer in the process. She was okay with death, but not with pain.

No matter how she died, she didn't think Collins would shed any real tears.

Well, she thought bitterly, maybe one.

They'd had a lot of very good nights. There's only so much passion you can fake before your true heart shows through. She knew Collins had glimpsed her inner self, her evolved self. Just as she had seen his true face.

There was love there.

There was a genuine connection there.

Whether any of that could buy her a splinter of mercy was another thing.

After her conviction and sentencing, Bliss had given a sealed envelope to her lawyer with instructions to mail it to a certain address. The letter was coded, so that if anyone read it all they'd see would be a lot of prayers for forgiveness. The real message was hidden in references that Bill Collins could read using the key they'd worked out years ago.

Had he ever received the letter? It was filled with words of love, genuinely meant. And with pleas for help. In all this time he hadn't reached out to her in any way, not even using contacts so many times removed that they could never implicate him.

Nothing.

The silence was deafening.

Soon they would come for her and she would descend into hell, with the only grace being the certain knowledge that it was impossible to prevent people from killing themselves if they truly wanted to die. That seemed to be all that was left to her.

Bliss put her face in her hands and began to weep very quietly. She was too afraid to let her sobs be heard. Not in this awful place.

Broken minutes crawled past.

Then she heard the clang of cold steel as the security doors rolled open.

A moment later there was the distinctive sound of shoes on the concrete floor. Not the clickety-click of the heels her lawyers wore. No, these were solid, flat sounds.

Bliss cringed, tried to shrink into herself, to become small and invisible.

The footsteps approached with the unhurried and measured pace of someone with purpose and confidence. Jailor's footsteps.

A shadow moved along the floor, long, distorted by lights behind whoever cast it.

Not a man's shadow, though.

But mannish.

A few moments later a large woman stepped into view. She stopped outside the cell and stood there for a while, shadow-shrouded eyes fixed on Bliss.

"Prisoner Bliss," said the woman. Not as a question, but in a flat statement. "On your feet."

"Wh-what?" stammered Bliss.

"Now."

The woman's voice was hard, certainly not inviting debate.

"But . . ."

The guard stepped into the cell, towering over Bliss. And now Bliss could see that the woman held something. A garment bag. "Get dressed."

Bliss frowned, not understanding. The garment bag was the one in which her courtroom clothes were stored. She wasn't due in court again. Unless . . .

Oh, God, she thought, sudden hope flaring in her chest. *The request for change of facility came through!*

She leaped up, smiling, wanting to shout for joy. A minimum-security prison was bearable. It was a lesser ring of hell. One she could possibly endure. Cable TV, Internet access, no brutality . . .

Was this her lawyers? Or had Collins pulled some covert strings?

The guard held the garment bag at arm's length.

"Time's running out."

Bliss took the bag with a fumbling thanks. The guard did not turn away or leave her to change in private, but Bliss didn't care. She stripped off the orange jumpsuit issued to her at the holding facility and dressed quickly in her charcoal skirt and coral blouse. Her shoes were in there, too.

And other things. She looked at them and then frowned at the guard.

"I don't . . . understand."

The guard said nothing.

After a long moment of hesitation, Bliss finished dressing. She reached for her books and possessions, but the guard interrupted. "No. Leave everything here."

Bliss straightened, her joy turning to doubt. Fear began once more to eat at her.

However, without another word she followed the guard out of the cell.

TWO HOURS LATER, an unsmiling woman in a charcoal skirt and coral blouse was led into the cell.

"Give me those clothes," said the guard.

The woman changed and put on the orange jumpsuit. Tears cut long channels down her face. Her gleaming black hair fell like a veil as she sat down and hung her head as she wept.

The guard was smiling as she stuffed the nice clothes back into the garment bag.

The weeping woman listened to the sound of the guard's shoes echo on the hard floor.

Then there was another sound.

A softer footfall.

She looked up.

Another woman stood outside the cell. Not the guard. This was another inmate, a hatchet-faced white woman with cornrowed hair and old blue prison tattoos on her neck.

"Artemisia Bliss?" asked the woman.

The weeping woman nodded.

"They say you have to burn to shine," said the woman.

Then she hurled something in through the bars. A gleaming, stinking pintful of golden liquid. It slapped the seated woman in the face, blinding her, gagging her, choking her with gasoline fumes.

The weeping woman never heard the strike of the match.

Never saw the flames.

Her screams filled the whole of the prison.

Part Four
Fun and Games

Turning and turning in the widening gyre
The falcon cannot hear the falconer;
Things fall apart; the center cannot hold;
Mere anarchy is loosed upon the world.

—WILLIAM BUTLER YEATS, *"The Second Coming"*

Interlude Seventeen

"I can't believe this," said Hu. It wasn't the first time he'd said it. He looked younger than his years and shock had stripped away his arrogance, revealing a far more vulnerable person than he generally revealed. Rudy placed a comforting hand on his shoulder.

They stood in the corridor outside the cell. Aunt Sallie stood slightly apart with Joe Ledger and Ghost, while Jerry Spencer was inside the cell, crouched over the blackened, withered husk that had been a person hours ago.

"God," Hu said, shivering, "it doesn't even look human."

Joe Ledger opened his mouth to say something, almost certainly a sarcastic jab of some kind, but Rudy gave him a quick shake of the head. Joe looked disappointed. He went back to the quiet conversation he'd been having with Auntie and Jerry.

"What I don't get," said Hu, "is why anyone would do something like this."

"Prison violence is common. Until the staff and other inmates are interviewed we won't know the details."

"But why *her?*"

Rudy shook his head. The warden and guard shift supervisors were conducting interviews under the supervision of Gus Dietrich. Answers would emerge. One of the female guards said that she thought she heard Bliss arguing with a couple of other women prisoners who had reputations for harassing the more vulnerable detainees. Rudy wondered if this would turn out to be a punishment for refusing sexual advances, though that sounded a bit cliché to him.

They watched as the forensics ace Jerry Spencer moved around the corpse, taking small samples of burned flesh and clothing. More extensive samples would be taken once the body was transported to the coroner's office, but Jerry exercised the authority allowed him under the DMS charter to take his own samples first.

Hu was angry with what he described as a violation of Bliss's person. "Why can't he just leave her alone?"

"Because," said Spencer without looking up, "right now I'm not seeing Artie Bliss. I'm seeing a charcoal briquette. And I won't believe this *is* Artie Bliss until DNA, tissue comparisons and dental records prove it."

"That's ridiculous."

Spencer glanced up at him. "This is my crime scene, doc. Shut up or fuck off. No, better yet, shut up and fuck off."

"Gentlemen, please," said Rudy, pushing the air down with calming hands. "We're all upset by this—"

"I'm not," said Aunt Sallie.

Spencer gave her one of his rare smiles and returned to his work.

Ledger just spread his hands.

"You're all a bunch of assholes," growled Hu. "Artemisia used to be part of our family. Show some respect."

"Family?" said Auntie. "Yeah, as I remember it, Cain was part of a family, too. So was Judas."

That shut Hu up.

There was no more conversation. Spencer continued his work and everyone else stood and watched him.

Rudy stayed by Hu's side. Despite the animosity between Ledger and Hu, and the more recent tension between Hu and Auntie, Rudy liked the scientist. Per DMS requirements, Hu had spent hours in therapy sessions with Rudy, and that allowed Rudy to see a more three-dimensional person. A man with vulnerabilities, with layers.

Although Rudy had become fond of Hu, he found that he did not entirely trust the man. And for the same reasons that Rudy had liked but not entirely trusted Bliss. Both of them were cut from similar cloth. Brilliant on a level that made life awkward in many ways. Both socially inept, though Bliss managed it better, partly because she'd known how to use her looks to advantage and because she appeared to have some consideration for how her words affected people. Joe had confided to Rudy that he thought Bliss was much more manipulative than she appeared.

"It's crazy," Joe had told him last year, "but I'd find myself telling her the damnedest things. Really opening up to her."

"Why?" asked Rudy.

"Beats the crap out of me. Maybe it's that she looks so earnest. And she listens. She's like you in that regard. She really listens. When someone listens with that much focus and attention, it's . . . I don't know, it's somewhere between an ego stroke that says 'damn, but you're one interesting son of a bitch' and a validation that what you have to say matters. Does that make sense?"

It had.

Rudy had noted that about Bliss. She was always paying attention. Her brain was never cruising on autopilot. Another of Joe's phrases. But she was like Hu in another way. Both were ambitious, and if they'd been in the private sector they would probably have set up competing shops and battled each other while making vast fortunes. As it was, within the confines of the binding security and nondisclosure agreements of the DMS, their ambition had been mostly channeled into bringing the edgiest science into play so that the organization was second to none in the world. More than once Rudy had cautioned Mr. Church about that arrangement. He felt that Hu, Bliss, Bug, and the other experts should be given some opportunity to profit from their work, even if only in the form of accolades from publications. The generous bonuses—which Rudy was certain came from Church's personal bank account—were nice but they couldn't match the enormous wealth his people were passing up in order to do their jobs. Church was adamant, however, believing that this would open a door beyond which was a slippery slope.

"People need reward," said Rudy during one conversation. "As much as we would both like patriotism, humanism, and idealism to be their own rewards, we have to accept that these are *people*. They're not characters from a heroic ballad."

"Yes, doctor," Church replied with a faint smile, "I am aware of that. However, I won't apologize for holding a high standard for people who are doing work as important as this. And I won't lower those standards to accommodate personal agendas. If we do that, then the focus becomes personal gain. The work we do requires the best efforts and actions from those few people with minds and skill sets that are truly exceptional."

"It's a lot to ask."

Church nodded. "I know. And because so few can rise to that standard the DMS is—and will likely remain—a small organization."

Rudy could understand Church's rationale, but in his professional experience he'd met only a precious few people who could live within those restrictions. Joe Ledger was one, and Samson Riggs. Bug was another. And there were a few dozen within the DMS. Top, Bunny, Lydia. Each answering the call with varying degrees of personal commitment. Rudy knew that some of those people would burn out and fall away.

Church, of course, was the icon, the role model for that level of total dedication to this war, but he was a very hard act to follow. Likely an impossible act. Like Lancelot without the emotional flaws. There were few people answering his call, relative to the vast sea of available military and paramilitary operatives, scientists, and support staff; the world rarely coughed up someone like Church. Rudy knew more about him than anyone except Aunt Sallie, but even with the privileged insights from staff-required therapy sessions, Rudy was certain he'd merely scratched the surface of who Mr. Church was.

Rudy wondered what Church was thinking now; how the news of Artemisia Bliss's murder had affected him. Even though Church had never been her biggest supporter, had hired her only on the strong recommendations of Hu and Auntie, he had worked with her for years. Rudy knew that her criminal activities had hurt and angered him. Would he grieve over her death?

"We're done here," said Spencer as he got to his feet. They all took a moment longer to look down at the blackened corpse.

"Such a waste," Ledger said.

He, Aunt Sallie, and Spencer left. Hu lingered for a moment longer, and Rudy stayed with him.

"I can't believe it," said Hu.

Rudy thought he caught the edge of a sob in his voice.

With his hand still on Hu's shoulder, the two men turned and left the cell.

By the end of the day the dental records had been compared and matched. Within three days the DNA comparison was done and that, too, matched.

And that was the end of Artemisia Bliss.

Chapter Sixty-one

We were met at Liberty Avenue Station by a small DMS field team. The techs sprayed us with some noxious shit that smelled like moose piss, then we stripped out of our Hammer suits right down to our skivvies. The suits, our gear, and even our weapons were stuffed into big oil drums and filled with more of the smelly stuff, then sealed. Permanently sealed, I think. The bag of cameras went into a biohazard bag for immediate transport to Bug. The only things we kept were our earbuds and cell phones. I told everyone to stay offline. Now was the not the time to be texting our BFFs or playing Angry Birds. Silence was genuinely golden.

There were clothes for us to change into, and we variously became Con Ed, water department, subway techs, or cops. Not a whiff of anything federal. I was a transit cop, which is okay because I used to be a cop and could talk the talk if it came to it.

My cell buzzed and I looked at it warily, expecting something bad.

Getting it.

The message read:

> ROLL OVER AND HAVE A CIGARETTE, HONEY,
> BECAUSE YOU'VE JUST BEEN FUCKED.

I showed it to Top and Bunny.

"Shit's not funny anymore," said Bunny. The strain of the shooting and now the knowledge that we were being labeled as monsters had etched deep lines into his tanned face.

I said nothing.

As we all changed there was a noticeable lack of the usual rough humor and trash talk. Lydia didn't make jokes about the way Ivan looked in boxers. Bunny didn't flirt with Lydia. Sam didn't flirt with the new gal, Montana. They all looked at me, though. Hard eyes from hard people who were as deeply afraid and confused as I was. My own snarky sense of humor seemed to have shriveled up and crawled off to hide under a rock.

Usually, I could joke my way out of most tense situations. A defensive reaction, sure, but a useful one because at least I kept myself amused. Now all I had inside my head were growls and questions.

The lead tech from the Hangar was a guy named Rasheen who'd once run with Broadway Team before he got hit with almost enough bullets to kill him. Now he ran logistics for the New York office. We were old friends and we shook hands in the troubled darkness.

"Must have been some shit back there," he said. "You holding it together?"

"For the moment." I said, accepting a police utility belt. "Give me some good news, man."

"They don't have your names on the news. That's something."

I grunted.

"But otherwise the goddamn Net's gone ass-wild on this shit."

"Tiny midget balls," grumbled Ivan. Not one of his better choices but not bad in the moment.

Rasheen handed me a set of car keys. "The big man wants you at the Hangar a.s.a.p. Can't risk a military helo or regular DMS transport. They got every news helicopter in North America up there, and you wouldn't believe the crowds we're drawing. You'll have to go out in ones and twos. Get in your vehicles and get out of here nice and slow. Don't draw attention."

"What about my dog?" I asked.

"Big Fuzz is already at the Hangar."

"What about *us*?" asked Noah Fallon. He and the other newbies, Montana Parker and Duncan MacDougall, stood together in a kind of defensive cluster. "Are we supposed to go to the Hangar or what?"

The logistics man turned to them. "That depends," he said. "Y'all are new, right? Just signed on?"

They nodded.

"But you signed on? You rolled out with Captain Ledger?"

A pause, then another nod.

"Then what do *you* think you're supposed to do?"

The rest of us gave them a few moments to work it out. It was Montana who answered. "I guess we get our asses back to the Hangar and circle the wagons."

"Hooah," said Rasheen.

The rest of Echo Team said it, too.

With the goggles and masks off I could see their faces. After several days of training with them I could tell you everything about their service histories and combat capabilities, but I had no idea who they were.

Still strangers.

And yet not so, because we had just shared an event together that connected us in ways no one else could possibly share. This massacre and the media firestorm that it had ignited were ours. We were the family that lived on that plot of land in that dark country.

It was an odd connection, like passengers on a crashed airliner working diligently side-by-side to pull total strangers out of the debris. Or folks who might otherwise pass on the street without even a nod to the existence or humanity of the other suddenly striving together to save the injured after a bomb goes off.

I hoped I would get to know them, to have them become fully rounded people in my mind instead of ciphers, though part of me resisted that thought. Some cops and soldiers never form close connections, even to someone they've gone into battle with or kicked in the door with at a gang-bangers' clubhouse. They despise the attachment, the connection to a human personality, because of all the potential for grief, for loss, for personal hurt. They think it's better to keep their own emotional plugs pulled than to risk sticking their fingers into the fan blades. Maybe that's a better way, a safe and sane form of professional detachment.

But I've never played it safe and no one has ever accused me of being sane.

Chapter Sixty-two

On the Road
Brooklyn, New York
Sunday, August 31, 2:45 p.m.

I took Montana Parker with me. I drove; she road shotgun. She sat so far from me that she was crammed against the passenger door.

Traffic was almost totally snarled. While we inched along I tapped my earbud and surprised myself by getting Church. I gave him my location and ETA.

"Where do we stand right now?" I asked. "How much shit is hitting the fan?"

"The intensity varies but we haven't caught any breaks today," he said. "Circe estimates that the video is having exactly the effect Mother Night intended. The world press is galvanized and public outcry hasn't been this intense since the planes hit the towers. Every reporter with an audience has begun a personal witch hunt, and that is being reflected within the government. Not merely party polarization, but even within the president's party a lot of people are distancing themselves from him in case he is complicit in some illegal act."

"He isn't."

"No, but considering how many levels of secrecy are involved, including those which both charter and protect the DMS, there isn't a lot of wiggle room for the president to come clean to the American people. Virtually anything he could say would either endanger or substantially weaken Homeland. It could potentially cripple our fight against global terrorism. It's not unlikely that the DMS will lose its charter and be shut down. It would be difficult to imagine a more effective attack on our nation's apparatus for counter- and antiterrorism."

"Is that Mother Night's endgame?" I asked him.

"Difficult to say. Not everything she's done appears to serve that goal, but we don't yet know the scope of her plan. We are rich in suppositions but wanting in facts."

"Meaning that we have nothing."

"Deliberate and well-crafted obfuscation is clearly part of her agenda."

"Meaning," I repeated, "that we have nothing."

"As you say."

"Is she a she or is she a them?"

"I asked Dr. Sanchez to speculate on that earlier today. It's his considered opinion that Mother Night is an individual who is using stand-ins for certain high-risk activities. He says it fits with a certain kind of megalomaniacal personality subtype."

"Sounds like Rudy."

"However, it's clear that she fronts a large organization," added Church.

"Of what?" I asked. "Is she the poster child for National Anarchy Day?"

"Remains to be seen," said Church. "Dr. Sanchez has some doubts as to whether this actually is anarchy, and I agree with him."

"Why?"

"He'll discuss that with you when you get here," said Church.

"Are we anywhere on the text messages?"

"No, although it's interesting that only you and Colonel Riggs are receiving them. Circe and Dr. Sanchez are working on ways to attach specific meaning to that."

"We're the cool kids in class."

"You are of a kind," said Church, but he didn't explain. "Bug is working on some things and believes he might be able to crack the block on the tracebacks. In the meantime we have a few other things to cover first."

"Hit me."

I was aware that Montana was watching me like a hawk. She had an earbud in but she wasn't on the same channel as my conversation with Church; she had only my side of things. Fine for now.

Church said, "Vice President Collins is among those who have distanced himself from the president since the video went live."

"What a guy. I'd hate to be next to him on a sinking ship. Pretty sure he wouldn't want to share the lifeboat."

"It's unlikely," conceded Church. "He hasn't gone public with anything, but he made some challenging remarks in the Oval Office in front of the senior staff members. Word has already begun leaking."

"So much for top secret."

Church made a small sound that might have been a laugh. "The Speaker of the House and several other key members of Congress have begun demanding information about the team shown in that video. Some of them unofficially know about the DMS but they are reluctant to reveal that knowledge until they sort out how it might reflect on them. That buys us a little time."

"Which is all well and good, but how close are we to knowing anything at all about Mother Night?"

"I wish I could say that we were close to putting her in the crosshairs, but we are no closer now than we were when she first surfaced in April."

"That's not making me feel good. How much more has to blow up in our face before we can put a name at the top of our hate list?"

"We are working on it, Captain. If there's a method of discovery you know about that you feel we've missed, I am all ears."

"Yeah, sorry. Just feeling a bit frustrated."

"Is that all you're feeling?" he asked, and I nearly snapped at him before I realized what he was asking. I took a moment then said, "It was a bad scene down there."

"I imagine it was."

With most people a comment like that is lip service. Not with Church. I don't know much about his history, but from what I've been able to put together he's waded through more blood and fire than I've ever imagined.

"You had three new members on the team today," he said, and for a moment I had an itchy feeling like he could see me and Montana in that car. But I dismissed it, sure that Rasheen or someone else told him who drove out with whom. In either case he knew that I wasn't alone and was feeding me a cue. So I took it.

"Echo Team performed superbly," I said, but I made sure I wasn't looking at Montana as I did so. "Everyone did their jobs."

"Any casualties?"

I knew Church well enough to know that he wasn't asking about KIA or physical injuries.

"Unknown but I don't think so," I said. "A lot will depend on how things play out today. I would hate to see anyone's name surface in either a news report or in congressional testimony."

"You have my word on that, Captain," he said. It was a hell of a promise to make, but then again, I'd like to see the son of a bitch who could force or bully information out of Church. On his weakest days Church scares the cat piss out of me.

The line went dead.

The traffic moved at a glacial pace. Montana kept staring at me. It felt like a couple of lasers burning on the side of my face. I let that slide for a few blocks.

Finally I said, "It'll be okay."

"Really?" It came out sharp and sarcastic. In any other circumstances it would have been insubordinate, but let's face it, we were miles past that kind of policy.

"No," I said, "actually I don't know how this is going to play out."

She stared at me, appalled. "Then why did you say that?"

"Had to say something."

She turned away so I wouldn't see her mouth the word *fuck*. Or maybe it was *fucker*. Could have been that.

"It's okay if you want to call me an asshole."

"Wouldn't dream of it," she said, then added, "Sir."

I had to grin. "Lose the 'sir' bullshit. We don't use it in the DMS and I don't like it."

Montana said nothing.

"The first time I met Mr. Church," I said, coming at her from left field, "he put me in a room with one of those walkers. No gun, no knife, and no clue what I was facing. He gave me a pair of handcuffs and told me to go in and cuff a prisoner."

I paid attention to the traffic but I could feel her eyes on me. "He didn't tell you what it was?"

"Nope."

"Just sent you in there?"

"Yup."

"Bullshit."

"God's honest truth."

"What happened?"

"I got bitten and turned into a zombie, and now I have my own reality show—*Real Zombies of Baltimore*," I said. "What the hell do you think happened?"

"You cuffed him?"

"Actually, I beat the shit out of him and then broke his neck."

"Bare-handed?"

"I was in the moment."

"Damn," she breathed.

We sat in heavy traffic for a while. I debated using my lights, but the street was gridlocked. All that would do was add noise.

After a while she said, "They never told us any of this when we were invited to try out for this gig."

"Well, they wouldn't, would they? I mean, how many of you would have showed up if the recruiters said hey, join the DMS and fight zombies, supersoldiers, and vampires."

She smiled at the word *vampires*, but then she took a better look at my face and went dead pale. "Oh . . . come *on* . . . don't even try to tell me that there are vampires . . ."

"Not the sparkly kind," I said, "but, yeah, vampires."

I told her about the *Upierczy*, the Red Knights. Then I told her about some of the other things Echo Team had come up against. Several different kinds of enhanced supersoldiers, including a group of men given gene therapy with insect DNA that resulted in a kind of freakism that still gives me nightmares. All of those soldiers are, I hope, dead. I told her about the Berserkers and what they did to Shockwave Team this morning. Her face went dead pale under her tan.

"Can we *do* that?" she demanded. "I mean, can science really go that far?"

"Science is all about pushing back boundaries. If you're willing to sidestep the restrictions about testing on human beings, or disregard all safety precautions, then it's possible to make huge jumps forward."

"That's horrible."

"Pretty much why we call them the 'bad guys.'"

She thought about that as I shifted into a lane that had started to move. "What about us? Do we do that kind of thing? Off the radar, I mean?"

I sighed. "I wish I could say that we don't, but that would be a lie. But here's the thing . . . the DMS doesn't approve of it. Mr. Church doesn't approve of it. He has a bit of a hard-on for people who misuse science like that. That's why he hires shooters like us."

"How can he do that if some of this is government-sanctioned?"

"First off, a lot of what goes on inside the government isn't sanctioned. There are levels and levels of secret research going on funded by black-budget dollars. We're talking about stuff the president never hears about. All of it's supposed to be—and pardon me if I throw up while saying this—in the 'best interests of America.' Some is. A lot isn't."

That's when I told her about what happened last year with Majestic Three, the T-craft, and the general feeling it left us that we are *definitely* not alone in this big ol' universe. Even then, recounting the details of that investigation, I felt like it was something that I'd seen in a science-fiction movie rather than a series of events I'd lived through. It had taken a hell of a lot of effort to keep the main details off the public radar and to find acceptable explanations for those events that played out where everyone could see them.

Montana said nothing for quite a while as we inched through another traffic snarl. When I glanced at her I could see that she was sweating. She kept shaking her head.

"It's a lot to process," I said. "I wish there was a better way to do this than to dump it on you."

"No," she said. "No." I waited to find out what *no* meant in this context. Eventually she said, "All this is going on all the time? The DMS is fighting this kind of war all the time?"

"All the time."

"Alone?"

"Mostly," I said. "But we have a few friends. There's Barrier in the U.K. They were actually the first group like ours. Church helped build that and used its success to sell the idea to Congress here. And there's Arklight. You'd like them. A bunch of totally bad-ass women warriors."

"Are you saying that because I'm a woman?" she asked sharply.

"Yes, I am. You have a problem with that?"

"I . . . guess not."

"Good. You might get to meet them. They were in on a part of this." I told her about the stuff in Poland and Lithuania. "One of their operators is in New York right now. Combat call sign is Violin. She's top of the line."

A hole appeared and I steered through it. Soon we were away from the congestion that was turning that part of Brooklyn into a parking lot for rubberneckers. Above us the thrum of news agency helicopters was constant.

Montana had gone into her own head and seemed content to stay there while she worked some things out. That was fine. I put the radio on and listened to the news. The story of the Subway Massacre, as it was now being called, dominated everything. No one knew who the soldiers in black were, but on the news we were being labeled "monsters."

I'm not sure if I objected.

You see, there are really three people living in my head. They are the result of a psyche that was fractured when I was fourteen. A group of older teens trapped my girlfriend, Helen, and me in a deserted place. They stomped me almost to death and then, while I lay there, dying and unable to help, they destroyed Helen. We both survived the day and later, after surgeries and rehab, we went back into the world; but in a lot of important ways we were only pretending to be alive. I found that my mind began splitting off into separate parts, and it was only through intensive therapy that I found my footing again. Later, when I met Rudy Sanchez, he helped me pare away the inner voices until only three remained, and those three became more or less stable. They didn't go away, though, and I've learned to accept that my life is always going to be shared among the Civilized Man, the Cop, and the Warrior.

The Civilized Man is closest to who I might have been if life had been kinder. He is the idealist, the humanist, the optimist. He also gets his ass comprehensively kicked every time I go to work. The Cop is pretty much my central personality. He's balanced, astute, precise, and cold in a useful, detail-oriented way. He's the puzzle-solver, the investigator, and, in many ways, the protector.

The other aspect is the Warrior, or as he prefers to be known, the Killer. That's the part of me who was truly born on that awful day when Helen screamed and I bled and innocence died. The Warrior is always vigilant, always ready to go hunting in the jungles of my life, always aching to bring terrible harm to those who in any essential way resemble the people who destroyed Helen's life and changed mine. That part of me grieves most for Helen, because he could not save her when she went looking for a permanent way out of her personal darkness—and found it.

As I drove back to the Hangar, the Civilized Man was too numb to comprehend the enormity of what was going on. The Cop kept trying to make sense of something that refused to be understood. The Warrior wanted to find Mother Night and everyone who worked for her or with her, and he wanted to do red, wet things to all of them. As punishment for bombs and murders, and—I have to admit it—for putting me in that subway tunnel with the wrong people walking into my spray of bullets.

I—*we*—drove on, thinking some of the darkest thoughts I have ever had.

Chapter Sixty-three

Guitar George's Tavern and Grill
Nashville, Tennessee
Sunday, August 31, 3:01 p.m.

A priest and a rabbi walked into a bar.

The priest was a tall man with lots of red hair and intensely blue eyes. The rabbi was shorter and dark, with intensely black hair and blue eyes. Their eyes were the exact shade of blue. An improbable electric blue with a metallic glitter.

The bar was packed with a Sunday holiday-weekend crowd and a five-piece band was playing down-and-dirty swamp blues. In what little space was available more than fifty people were dancing. Some well, some not, all happily. The priest and the rabbi stopped at the edge of the dance floor. They each carried a bulging plastic shopping bag on which INTERFAITH MINISTRIES was printed in a blue that matched the eyes of the two clerics. The bags were heavy and the men carried them with some effort.

Some of the crowd—those that noticed the two men—reacted in a variety of ways. Some gave them sober nods. Some raised glasses to them. A few avoided eye contact with one or the other and shifted away to be outside of whatever implied field of guilt emanated from the men of the cloth. One very drunk woman curtsied to them with all of the elaborate grace of a tipsy lady of the court.

The priest and the rabbi smiled at her. They smiled at everyone.

They smiled and smiled and smiled.

A waitress came up to them, approaching with a nervous and tentative smile.

"Um, can I get you a table or . . . ?" Her words faltered as she noticed their eyes. Working in a bar, she'd seen a thousand kinds of false contact lenses, everything from bright green lenses on ordinary brown eyes to Marilyn Manson glaucoma chic to slit-pupiled cat's eyes. She'd even seen eyes as metallic and blue as those of the priest and rabbi. But she had never seen novelty contacts *on* a priest or, for that matter, a rabbi. It was a kind of freaky that wasn't funny and wasn't cool, and wasn't even nerdy comical cool. What it was, was weird.

It was a funny day to be weird.

That's how she saw it.

What with all that was going on in Pennsylvania and Kentucky and New York. The day had enough freakiness in it already. It was probably why so many people were out getting hammered. Not merely drinking, but guzzling the stuff.

She tried on a smile, hoping that it would somehow let her in on the joke.

But their smiles were bigger and brighter and totally . . .

Well . . . *weird* was the word that stuck in her head.

Another word occurred to her, too.

Those smiles were *wrong*.

The rabbi opened his big shopping bag and for a moment the waitress thought he was reaching for a gun. The news reports were still running through her head.

But then she saw what the rabbi had.

It was a water balloon. Bright red. With a happy face on it. He showed it to her and his grin widened.

Her smile flickered on again, though uncertainty kept it at a low wattage. She thought she understood what was happening.

These guys weren't real. They weren't a priest or a rabbi. No way. They were a little too hunky anyway. What with the contacts and the water balloons . . . this was some kind of college stunt. A frat thing. These were a couple of guys from the University of Tennessee. And, oh God, they had two bags filled with water balloons. They were going to throw them and get everyone wet and then get their asses kicked and there would be a big fight and the cops would come and . . . and . . . The waitress's mind raced on and on at warp speed, working it out all the way to the point where she was out of work because the place was closed by the police and there were lawsuits from injured customers.

"Sir," she said, stepping close to the rabbi to make sure he heard her over the band's cover of "Down on the Bayou," "you can't—"

And the rabbi hurled the water balloon high over her head. It struck the whirling blades of one of the bar's six ceiling fans and exploded, showering the dance floor with water.

There were shouts and screams.

And laughter.

None of the laughter was from the people who were spattered with water. But there was a lot of it from the people seated and standing around the dance floor.

The priest set his bag down and removed two more balloons. A yellow one and a blue one.

"Here!" he said brightly, handing them to a pair of brawny college jocks in UT shirts. The jocks looked at the balloons, at the priest, at each other, then they grinned and hurled the balloons, which burst against the ceiling and rained clear water onto the crowd. The crowd yelled and shouted, and some of them laughed.

The waitress was yelling, but the rabbi ignored her as he pulled another balloon out of the bag and hurled it at a different ceiling fan. The priest handed out more balloons.

That's how it started.

In seconds the whole place was wild.

Water balloons were flying everywhere. The waitress was shrieking now, but no one was paying attention to her. Bouncers were trying to fight their way through the press. The people were getting into it. Water balloons hit women and burst without doing harm, but the effect was an impromptu wet T-shirt show.

It spiraled upward into a massive prank that toppled off the ledge of order into a loud, laughing chaos.

Until the screaming started.

It came from one of the dancers who'd been splashed by the first balloon. She wiped water from her eyes but her fingers came away red. Bright, bright red.

The man she had been dancing with stared at her in white-faced horror. Except that his face was white only where it wasn't red.

They stared at each other, caught in a fragment of reality that was chipped off the craziness of what was going on. Blood ran from their eyes and noses and ears. When they screamed they sprayed blood at each other. Blood darkened their clothes as it ran from every opening in their bodies.

The people nearest them screamed, too. Not because of what was happening to that couple, but because it was happening to them. To everyone.

Everyone.

The laughter was gone, replaced by shouts and screams.

Some of the people bolted for the door as if they could flee what was already happening to them. However, as they crashed against the double doors they rebounded. Someone had looped a heavy chain through the wrought-iron handles set in the big wooden doors. The rear door was blocked by a Jeep that had been backed up against it. No one was getting out. Bloody fists pounded on the doors.

When the two jocks from UT grabbed a table and tried to heft it through a window, the rabbi drew a pistol and shot them both. The priest took a Glock from under his vestments and began firing indiscriminately into the crowd.

The priest and the rabbi were both bleeding from every orifice, every pore. They used their last two bullets on themselves, tucking the hot barrels under their chins and blowing off the tops of their heads.

Dying patrons collapsed slowly onto the floor as their tissues melted and ruptured. Blood boiled out through their pores. They vomited it onto one another, onto the floor, onto themselves.

In the distance the first sirens wailed, but no one in the tavern could hear them. And never would.

In all the panic, no one noticed the small boxes affixed to the walls, high up near the ceiling. The devices had been planted in the middle of the night and were hidden among decorations and beer posters. Six tiny red eyes watched the death below. The video feed from the cameras was compiled into a single streaming signal, at the bottom of which was a continuous text crawl. It read: *Quick onset* Bundibugyo ebolavirus *suspended in distilled water. Bidding starts at fifty million.*

Chapter Sixty-four

The Hangar
Floyd Bennett Field
Brooklyn, New York
Sunday, August 31, 3:03 p.m.

"Boss," said Bug from the view screen, "I think I have something."

Church had a phone to his ear and others lighting up on his desk. Into the phone he said, "Excuse me for a moment, Mr. President." He muted the call. "What is it?"

"The forensics team just called. They've been collecting evidence at the apartments of two of the shooters from the cyber café. At both locations they found portable game consoles. Like Gameboys, but off-market stuff. A runner just brought them in to me. They're loaded with games, and—"

"Cut to it, Bug," snapped Church. "What have you found?"

"The most recent game played is Burn to Shine. It's a massive program and heavily password-protected. Here's the kicker, though. MindReader is having trouble hacking it."

"Keep on it and keep me posted."

"No, listen, boss, this is scaring the crap out of me."

"Why?"

"The reason MindReader is having trouble cracking it is because it's fighting back exactly the way MindReader would. I think Mother Night has our technology."

Chapter Sixty-five

The Hangar
Floyd Bennett Field
Brooklyn, New York
Sunday, August 31, 3:04 p.m.

We reached the Hangar without incident. Bunny, Ivan, and Noah were already there; the others would arrive soon. Ghost was there and he let out a series of furious barks as he came bounding over to me. I couldn't tell whether the barks were because he was happy to see me or to scold me for leaving him behind. I didn't care, either. I dropped to my knees and gathered the fur monster into my arms. He licked my face with enough enthusiasm to remove a layer of skin. Then he began nosing at my pockets, but I was wearing borrowed clothes.

Brick came to my rescue. He was almost as big as Bunny and looked like the actor Ving Rhames except for some shrapnel scars on his face and a high-tech artificial leg. He held out a hand and pulled me to my feet then gave me an up-and-down appraisal. "Damn, son, normally a guy has to get mugged in an alley to look as bad as you."

"Getting mugged would be a step up for my day, Gunny."

"Yeah, so I hear." He clapped me on the shoulder hard enough to loosen some fillings. "The big man is in the big conference room."

"We anywhere yet?"

"We are exactly between a rock and a hard place."

"Ain't that just fucking peachy?" I grumbled.

I left Montana with my team and headed to the conference rooms, which were on the next level down. On the way I got a phone call and stepped into an alcove to take it. Junie.

"Hey, beautiful," I said. "We have to make this fast."

"Are you okay?"

"Define *okay*."

"Are you hurt?" she asked.

I had cuts and scrapes all over my body from the flying glass at the Surf Shop, and I had a gaping wound in my soul from the subway. "Nothing a couple of Band-Aids and a change of career wouldn't fix."

"Oh, Joe," she said, breathing it out with a lot of pent-up frustration and concern. There was an old saying about how the people who sit at home and wait are also serving. But it goes deeper than that. They're also taking fire in their own way, and they're being injured as surely as if shrapnel pierced their flesh. It is a phenomenon as old as war and as horrible as all the pain in the world. Nothing that I could say could make it right because "right" had so little to do with my world.

"I will come home to you," I told her. And I meant it.

"You have to."

"I will," I swore. "In the meantime, I have a couple waiting in the lobby at FreeTech. Things are getting really weird, so I want you to go with them back to your hotel. Stay there until this is over."

"Violin's here. I'm quite safe—"

"Please," I said.

She said, "Yes. Okay." A reluctant acquiescence, but enough to keep me from having a heart attack. We hung up a few seconds later and I stood there for a bit, allowing myself to dwell in the oasis of understanding that came from knowing there is a world beyond the one in which I generally traveled. There were clearer skies out there somewhere, and suns that did not shine on spent bullet casings and spilled blood.

I leaned back against the wall, looked up at the ceiling as if I could see those unpolluted skies.

"Junie," I said.

Like a talisman.

Like a lifeline.

And then I pushed off the wall and went to find Church.

Chapter Sixty-six

Across America

Sunday, August 31, 3:17 p.m.

Passage to India Restaurant, San Antonio

Donald Crisp sat across a food-laden table from Amanda Shockley and wondered if he was going to get anything this afternoon. A kiss? Sure, she kissed him every time they went out for food. Once she even let him get a little grabby. But when he tried to go from outside her tight-fitting blouse to under it, the flag went down on the play. Five times now he'd dropped serious cash on her and so far he'd gotten tongue action and maybe felt a nipple under her padded bra, but wasn't sure.

He was losing confidence in his own charm.

Back in high school it was different. He was always smooth and had that brooding man-of-mystery thing because he was the new kid in town. He milked that for a lot of ass. Even got a BJ from a teaching assistant, and for a while that was a personal highlight. In college, ass was easy. There was a lot of it and everyone seemed to want to prove that they were consenting adults—emphasis on the adult part, so they consented a whole damn lot.

After college, though, it all slowed down. He went into insurance and discovered that there was nothing less sexy than insurance. There were no stud insurance reps. Stud real estate guys, sure; Donald's best friend, Chico, sold condos and got more ass than a public toilet. It drove Donald nuts.

When he did score, he had to work for it.

Like with Amanda. She was a junior account executive. Half Swedish and half something else that gave her a permanent tan, black hair streaked with brown, and a body that would not let him have a moment's peace. The ass-kicker was that she didn't seem to give much of a hot shit that she was built. She dressed in expensive clothes, but the stuff she chose made her look like an upscale librarian. On the hot side of dowdy. Never any-thing low-cut, but she did like things tight.

Over the last few weeks, Donald had asked Amanda out for dinner, drinks, and music, followed by a romantic stroll along the River Walk and then . . .

And then it was some kissing, a little touch, and he was watching her walk to her doorway while he sat in the car with a restless trouser lobster.

Today, maybe, things would go a different way.

Today, maybe, he'd get to explore the undiscovered country of Amanda Shockley's upper torso, sans blouse and Wonder Bra.

They'd worked their way through a spicy samosa and into chicken tikka masala, with naan and a bottle of really expensive wine. He sprang for a bottle of Gewürztraminer, a dry aromatic wine with a tangerine and white peach nose, and lychee flavor. Donald knew his wines and this one was perfect for Indian food. He pretended not to see how much the fuck-ing restaurant charged for it, though, almost three times what he would have paid at a liquor store, but if it loosened some of those buttons and undid the hooks on her bra, then it was worth it.

"Let me fill your glass," he said, smiling what he knew was his best smile, the one that got him so much ass in high school.

"Just half a glass," said Amanda. "I'm already feeling it."

He poured her a full glass.

They smiled as they clinked and her eyes met his in what Donald was absolutely sure was "the moment." That point of connection when the internal conversation switches from trivialities to okay-let's-do-this. Her smile changed, too. He'd seen that before, too. The lips relaxed in some indefinable way, becoming softer, fuller, less defensive and more inviting.

I'm so getting laid today, he thought.

And then her eyes slid away and looked past him. Too soon, too soon, he thought.

Her expression immediately changed again. Soft mouth parting into an O of surprise, eyes clouding with confusion, a narrow vertical line form-ing between her brows.

"Is something wrong?" he asked quickly, beginning to turn, begin-ning to look.

He heard it before he saw it.

It was a sound that did not belong in an Indian restaurant. Or on the River Walk. Or anywhere in San Antonio.

It was a roar.

Not like a big cat. Donald had heard cougars roar, and this was lower, deeper, more powerful than that. This was like the gorillas he'd seen when he visited the zoo in Philadelphia.

But the San Antonio Zoo didn't have gorillas.

All of this flashed through his head in the time it took to twist around in his seat and look.

There were no gorillas there, of course. This was a restaurant. That would be silly.

But the man who stood in the doorway looked kind of like an ape. Massive sloping shoulders, huge chest and arms, thick black hair standing stiff and wiry on his head. And there was something clearly simian about his face. It was very . . . well, apelike.

The man wore a black tank top with a symbol printed on it that Donald didn't know. A capital letter A surrounded by a circle. A for what? What team was that? Was it a school? He didn't know.

Donald's thoughts were falling all over one another, trying to find an exit from confusion into understanding. Everyone in the restaurant sat in shocked stillness, each of them struggling to make sense of it, too.

Two other people stood behind the ape-looking man in the tank top. A couple of girls. Chinese or something, Donald couldn't tell. They each held a small portable video recorder.

The big man opened his mouth and roared again.

The sound was so ridiculously loud that it shook the whole place. And it jolted the diners out of their shocked silence. Some of the women screamed. Some of the men cried out in surprise.

One man got to his feet. He was big, too, though well dressed in a very expensive summer-weight suit. Donald thought the man had the air of someone who was used to handling things. Tough-looking.

"Okay, pal," said the man, "time to dial it down and hit the road."

The guy in the tank top said nothing. He smiled, though, and to Donald that smile was every bit as scary as that freaking roar.

Then the ape-guy swung a punch at the diner in the summer suit. Donald saw the look of surprise on the diner's face, but also saw him whip an arm up to block the punch. The incoming blow hit the blocking arm—and bashed it aside like it was nothing. The punch struck the diner on the side of the head. Even from twenty feet away Donald heard the wet-sharp sounds of bones breaking inside the diner's arm and head. The diner's head jerked sideways and lay almost flat on his opposite shoulder; it stayed there as the man's knees suddenly buckled and he fell like a bag of disconnected pieces onto his table. The man's date screamed.

Everyone screamed.

The ape-man reached out and grabbed the screaming date by the throat, tore her out of her seat, lifted her above his head, and threw her across the room.

The last thing Donald saw was the screaming, flailing, flying woman slam into Amanda Shockley with so much force that another wet-sharp crack filled the air.

Then a shadow fell across Donald.

He never saw the hands that grabbed him.

All he saw was Amanda falling, falling, her lovely eyes rolling up, her soft lips open.

And then the world dissolved into red and black and then nothing.

Morro Bay, California

Three men who surviving witnesses later described as "looking like gorillas" got out of a Humvee that had been driven all the way up to the front doors of the Morro Bay Aquarium. A fund-raiser was under way to raise money and awareness of sea lion conservation. A trio played light jazz, and two hundred people with checkbooks and an interest in conservation mingled, drank, ate little crab puffs, and chatted.

Until the three men showed up.

They piled out of their Humvee and without a moment's pause barged through the doors and attacked the crowd. They did not have guns or knives. They used no conventional weapons at all. Instead they picked up people and used them like clubs to batter anyone they could hit. They tore arms and legs out of their sockets—a feat the medical examiner would later argue in court as a physical impossibility—and beat people to death with them. This was refuted, of course, by video footage to the contrary. The exact source of the footage was never determined.

Of the two hundred people at the fund-raiser, one hundred and sixty-one escaped. The others, including all three musicians and seven wait staff, did not.

Chapter Sixty-seven

The Hangar
Floyd Bennett Field
Brooklyn, New York
Sunday, August 31, 3:23 p.m.

Rudy intercepted me as I approached the conference room. He shook my hand and held it as he asked, "How are you, Joe?"

"Shaken, not stirred," I said.

"This isn't a time for jokes."

"No," I said and sighed. "It really isn't. But I got nothing else right now."

He studied me with his one dark eye. "No, don't do that. Tell me how you are."

My instinct was to bark at him like a stray dog and tell him this wasn't the time or place for a therapy session. But I understood where he was coming from. He was the DMS house shrink and I was a senior operator. One who had just come back from two gunfights and might have to do more violence tonight or sometime too damn soon. So I took a breath and nodded.

"I'm halfway to being freaked out," I said quietly. "There's enough adrenaline in my bloodstream to launch a space shuttle, and I don't know if I'm ever going to sleep again. All I can see are the faces of ordinary people as I gun them down—women and children, old people, civilians with no part in this."

"You do know that—"

"Yes," I interrupted, "I know that they were infected, that they were already dead. I know that, Rude, and you know how much that helps? It helps about as much as a fresh can of fuck you."

"Take it easy, Joe."

"Don't tell me to—"

He placed a hand on my chest. It was such an oddly intimate a thing to do that it snapped the tether that was pulling me toward rage. He stood there, fingers splayed, palm flat, one eye fixed on mine. And I heard it then, like an audio playback. There was a note of genuine panic in my voice. Not quite hysterical but close enough to feel the heat.

I closed my eyes and nodded. Rudy removed his hand.

"It must have been dreadful down there," he said quietly.

"Everyone keeps saying that."

"I imagine so. Have you spoken with the others on your team?"

"We weren't feeling all that chatty."

"Joe, look at me," he said, and I opened my eyes. There was compassion in his expression, but also something harder, sterner. "Have you, *Captain* Ledger, senior DMS field commander, spoken with the members of *your* team?"

I sighed. "Fuck."

This wasn't the first time someone had called me on this, on being so wrapped up in my own reaction to the horrors of the war fought by the DMS that I forgot that this wasn't a solo drama. Everyone was feeling it, being changed by it. I'd even thought about that fact while we ran, but I'd stumbled right past the moment where leadership—real leadership—might have made lasting difference to my team. Especially to the three newbies.

"I'm an asshole."

Rudy shook his head. "We're all experiencing shock. When you have a chance, do what you know you have to do to ameliorate this. As I will when this is over. Like most things, Cowboy, psychological survival is as much an inexact science as it is a work in progress."

"I will," I promised. "And when we have time I'm going to give you full permission to crack my head open and start swatting flies."

Aunt Sallie seemed to materialize out of nowhere. "When you two fellows are done with your circle jerk, would you mind joining us for the briefing?"

With that she blew past and entered the big conference room.

Rudy smiled and smoothed his mustache. "What a charming woman. Haven't I said it a hundred times?"

"Yeah," I said, "she's a peach."

But before we followed her I asked, "Rudy—you've been here all day.

Can you tell me what's going on? Is this all Mother Night? If so—what does it mean?"

He shook his head. "We've been wrestling with that all day. Nearly everything that's happened indicates that these events are connected, but no one has been able to establish a pattern. Even MindReader hasn't come up with a clear picture and that's what it was designed to do, look for patterns."

"Well, Mother Night's rant on the Net this morning seemed to be about anarchy . . ."

"Seemed to be, yes," he said.

"What's that supposed to mean? If there's no pattern then wouldn't that pretty much fall under the heading of anarchy? From what Nikki told me on the way over here, that A and O anarchy symbol is popping up all over the place. Maybe we can't find a pattern because there isn't one to find."

"Perhaps," he said, "but the fact that she seems so organized argues against the anarchy model."

"Yeah, fair enough, Rude, I've been wondering about that since the jump. So, what label do we put on her?"

"Definitively?" mused Rudy. "I really wouldn't want to commit to anything. But on the level of intuition, assumption and the kind of paranoid cynicism I've been cultivating since we joined the DMS . . . ?"

"If not anarchist, how does the label 'terrorist' fit?"

He gave another shake of his head. "That's too easy and too broad. Knowing Circe has taught me a lot about how inexact a word that is. We've come to use it as a blanket term in much the same way that during the Vietnam War we called the indigenous people 'gooks' and in Somalia everyone was a 'skinny.' They are dehumanizing and demonizing labels that help to engender an aggressive-responsive attitude, but there is no genuine political insight in their use. To our enemies in al-Qaeda we are terrorists. Except in instances of psychopathy, terrorism is a biased view of a tactic that is implemented to achieve an end."

"Noted. So, what does that make Mother Night?"

"I don't know. To determine what she is requires that we know something about her, and I confess, Joe, that I don't. Is she an extremist prosecuting an agenda? If so, for which political party, nation, religion, or faction? Is she a criminal, or part of a criminal empire? Is she a charismatic psychopath or a cult leader? We simply don't know."

"Got to be political," I said. "We know about her connections with the cyberhackers from China, Iran, and North Korea."

"We know that she was interacting with a cell, Joe, and the members of the cell were from those countries. However, I spoke to Mr. Church about this at length today and he said that neither the State Department nor the CIA have been able to definitively connect those nine men in Arlington with active operations in their native countries. And remember, those nations denied involvement in their actions."

"Which they would."

"Certainly, but that might just as easily suggest that Mother Night knows and understands the political process, the habit of denial, the subtleties of communication through diplomatic channels . . ."

"If that's the case, Rude," I said, "she'd have to be really well versed in behind-the-scenes politics, and I'm not talking about what she could crib from old DVDs of *The West Wing*."

"I don't think we can discount that possibility, Cowboy. Since this whole thing began I've developed quite an appreciation of her intelligence."

"You said there were two reasons you didn't buy this as pure anarchy. What's the other?"

"It's sideways logic, so you'll think I'm losing my marbles."

"That's a past-tense observation, brother."

His smile was small and fleeting. "Well, anarchy is by nature a lack of structure, correct? It's an attempt to separate life from structure and procedure, allowing the infinitely creative potential of chaos to dominate."

I nodded.

"So why isn't Mother Night creating chaos?"

"Christ, Rudy, I thought you said you were following the fucking news. The whole country is going ape-shit out there and—"

"Is it? In its strictest philosophic form, anarchy is less about bomb-throwing and abandonment of rules and more about social justice, a breaking down of current corruption in order to allow a new and just system to emerge. In spirit, both the French and American revolutions fit that view. And if there was even a hint of a true political agenda in Mother Night's actions, I might buy that that's what we're seeing. An attack on a dystopic political landscape. However, things as they are today *appear* to fit the more popular interpretation of anarchy as the absence of government, a state of lawlessness, a society of individuals who enjoy complete freedom without a governing body. And yet Mother Night is a leader figure, and to do the things she's accomplished necessitates a well-formed and well-run organization. In order to maintain the kind of secrecy needed to have avoided a MindReader search or detection by the CIA, her organization must be tightly administrated, and the members need to follow precise sets of rules. That is not anarchy, Joe. That's not chaos."

"So . . . what is it?"

But before he could answer, Aunt Sallie leaned her head and shoulders out of the conference room doorway. "Now!" she growled.

Chapter Sixty-eight

FreeTech
800 Fifth Avenue
New York City
Sunday, August 31, 3:26 p.m.

Junie Flynn and the other members of her board did no work at all on matters pertaining to their new organization. Instead they sat around the conference table gaping at the spectacle unfolding on the big-screen TV.

So much death. So much pain.

And Joe was out there, in the middle of it.

At one point, Violin got up, walked around the table, took a fistful of Toys's shirt, and hauled the young man out of his chair. She then raised him completely off the floor with one hand, something Junie didn't think even Joe could do.

"Convince me that this isn't the Seven Kings," said Violin in a voice filled with quiet menace and frank threat.

"I—I—"

Junie launched herself from her chair and grabbed Violin's arm. She tried to pull Toys from the woman's grip but it was like attempting to unlock a steel trap. Violin flicked a single, dismissive glance at Junie.

"Don't," she said.

Violin made a sound of deep annoyance and thrust Toys back into his chair, where he landed in a tangled and disheveled heap. Toys sprawled there, making no attempt to straighten his clothes.

Very slowly and clearly he said, "I am not with the Seven Kings. I haven't been for years. I don't know who is doing this, and if the Kings are involved I don't know anything about it."

It barely mollified Violin. "Do not let me discover that this is a lie," she warned.

"I will definitely make a note of that. And if it turns out I'm lying, you have my blessing to rip out my fucking lungs. Fair enough?" said Toys. He sat straight, jerked his shirt into some order, and turned away from her. He did not ask for an apology.

Violin sneered at him and turned back to the television. There was a knock on the door and two men came in without waiting for a reply. Junie recognized them as security personnel from the Hangar. Reid and Ashe.

"Ma'am," said Reid to Junie, "we're here to escort you to your hotel."

Junie turned to Violin. "Joe sent them. Do you . . . I mean, would you like to join me?"

Chapter Sixty-nine

Frontierland, Disney World
Orlando, Florida
Sunday, August 31, 3:34 p.m.

Sammy Ramirez always thought he'd either end up in Hollywood or end up in prison. He had that kind of life. Two of his brothers were in jail. Ishmael was doing three to five for armed robbery after he used a plastic gun to steal sixty-two dollars and a can of Red Bull from a 7-Eleven in Miami. Jorge was on his second fall for grand theft auto. The sad part of that was, the car he boosted was a piece-of-shit Chevy Suburban. He couldn't even get respect for having stolen an Escalade. A Suburban. Jesus.

Sammy had done a few small crimes, but always stupid little things. He sold some weed in high school. He shoplifted a cell phone charger from a strip-mall CVS. Like that. Peer pressure from his brothers or his friends had been involved every time.

It wasn't who he was, though, and it wasn't who he wanted to be.

Who he wanted to be was the first major Latin action hero. He had the speed, the reflexes, a little bit of tae kwon do, and the best smile in the neighborhood. He had no trace of an accent and was sure that with a little training and the right breaks, he could be to Latinos what the Rock was to whatever the fuck ethnicity he belonged to.

That was what Sammy thought about every day. He thought about it when he woke up, he thought about it before he went to sleep. He even prayed about it sometimes. And he thought about it all day at work.

Sammy Ramirez, star of his own series. *Legal Aliens*, a cross-border science fiction thing. Yeah, that would not suck. Or maybe something generic where none of it was based on race. Just on good looks, the ability to kick ass on screen, and charisma. Sammy knew he had bags of charisma.

That's why the kids loved him so much.

After all, he wasn't the only one dressed as a cartoon dog here at Disney, but goddamn it, more kids wanted their picture taken with him than any two of the other Goofys combined.

Booyah, motherfucker. That was star power.

Working at Disney was not exactly the most direct route to an action franchise of summer blockbusters, but it was technically acting. Disney called its staff "cast members." He was working on getting into one of the shows, which was a shortcut to getting an Equity card. That was the plan. Get into Actors' Equity and then leverage that to get some screen time, enough at least to get a SAG card. That would get him an agent, and an agent could get him some auditions, which would in turn allow him to fire his charisma guns on full auto.

Neither his friends nor his brothers knew he earned his pay as a cartoon dog. Specifically as a mentally challenged cartoon dog dressed in a cowboy outfit. You couldn't lay that rap on your homies and ever walk it off. They all thought he worked maintenance at Epcot.

Sammy was posing with a bunch of fat little German tourist kids when he spotted the two men in hoodies. They both wore dark hoodies on a hot Florida night in August. Sammy was boiling the pounds off in his Goofy suit, so he knew how hot it was. But he had to; why were these kids in hoodies, with the hoods up? That seemed odd to him.

And they both had backpacks.

Not uncommon in Disney. People walked all day long. A lot of them carried water, souvenirs, and other stuff.

But Sammy knew what was going on today. Everyone did. That's why all of the off-duty security had been called in.

The guys in the hoodies were drifting along behind a large group of girls dressed in cheerleader costumes. There were always cheerleading contests and events at the park. Had to be fifty, sixty girls in three or four different school colors, all of them laughing. None of them paying attention to the men in the hoodies. The whole group melted into the lines waiting to take photos with him. There were more than a hundred people in line. The park was jammed, even this late, and the costumed staff was working overtime. Fireworks were exploding in the sky. And Sammy did not like those two fuckers in the hoodies.

There was something about them.

Maybe if Sammy had grown up in the richer parts of town he might have looked right through those guys. But he'd grown up hard in Washington Shores. He was used to seeing trouble coming long before it ever got up in his face.

So, when the two men stepped out of line, moved to stand by a trash can near the heaviest part of the crowd, and shrugged out of their backpacks, Sammy knew that something bad was about to happen. The men did it together, smoothly, like it was something they had rehearsed. The men set the packs down and started to turn to walk away.

That's when Sammy knew for sure. For absolute goddamn sure.

He was running before he knew he was going to do anything. In his huge, ungainly costume and floppy oversized feet, he blew past the startled German kids, shoved a Korean tourist with a video camera out of the way, drove right through the suddenly shrieking gaggle of cheerleaders, and threw himself into a flying tackle that slammed him into the two men. He hooked an arm around each one and drove them forward and down onto the hard concrete. They landed with a muffled thud and yelps of surprise.

Instantly the two men tried to get away.

Not to struggle with him. Not to fight him. Not to demand to know why a cartoon dog had just tackled them. They wanted out of there.

They clawed at the ground to get out from under him.

Sammy wore big, fuzzy gloves, so he had no fists. So he raised an elbow and drove it down as hard as he could between the shoulder blades of one of the men. Sammy was not a big man—only five ten—but he was all muscle. He was lean to a rock hardness from sweating in that suit. And he was madder than he had ever been in his whole life.

The elbow hit with so much force, the first man's head snapped back and then nodded nose-first into the concrete. The second man twisted under Sammy and simultaneously tried to shove him away and pull something from a pocket. A gun, a knife, Sammy couldn't tell.

He raised himself up and dropped down full weight on the man, crushing the air from him. Then he elbowed the man's face into a red mess. The item the guy had been reaching for tumbled to the ground.

Not a gun.

Not a knife.

It was a cell phone.

In a flash of clarity, Sammy understood.

It was like Boston and those other places. He tore off his mask and at the top of his lungs yelled one of those words you are never supposed to yell in a crowded theater, on an airplane, or in a theme park.

"BOMB!"

Sammy heard the screams, felt the tide of panic swirl around him. This was America and most of these kids had been born after 9/11. They understood bombs. Even the tourists from other countries. America didn't own terrorism; that belonged to everyone everywhere.

They ran.

Sammy didn't.

The two men, bleeding as bloody as they were, were still game, still struggling. One of them kept reaching for the cell phone.

Later, when the reporters interviewed Sammy about what he did then, his initial answer was "Fuck, man, I just went ape-shit."

He would be asked to give them a new sound bite. Many hundreds of times.

However, in all fairness, he did go ape-shit. He beat the two men into red pulp. Putting one into a coma, maiming the other. Then he picked the cell phone up and threw it into a pond.

The two backpacks did not blow up.

Bomb squad crews came and took them away. Sammy later learned that there were enough explosives in each to kill dozens. But that wasn't the worst threat. Mixed in with all the screws and nails and other shrapnel were tens of thousands of tiny pellets filled with ricin. A dose the size of a few grains of table salt can kill an adult human. Each pellet had twice that amount.

In all of Mother Night's dozens of orchestrated attacks, it was the only one in which no one died.

No one.

All because of a cartoon dog.

Sammy Ramirez did not become the first Latino star of summer blockbusters. Instead Disney cast him as a Jedi in their ongoing series of Star Wars movies. They would later hire actors to play Sammy Ramirez at their theme parks, so kids could get an autograph with him.

Sometimes the good guys actually win.

Chapter Seventy

The Hangar
Floyd Bennett Field
Brooklyn, New York
Sunday, August 31, 3:36 p.m.

We met in the big conference room. Church was at the head of the table, Rudy and Circe to his right, Dr. Hu and Aunt Sallie on his left. I grabbed the seat at the other end.

"What's the good news?" I asked.

"Your optimism is an inspiration to us all," said Church dryly. "Today's events are accelerating downhill."

I sighed.

"There's no good place to start," he continued, "but let's begin with something Bug has worked out. He's analyzed the video cameras from the subway and several others obtained from other attacks. Even though some are different brands, they're all of a type and each has received an aftermarket upgrade from Mother Night. Bug was able to determine that the reason we haven't been able to interrupt the video feeds is that some of the technology being employed is strikingly similar to certain elements of MindReader."

That had the effect of tossing a flash-bang onto the table. Heads jerked up, eyes bugged out, and if anyone said anything, I was unable to hear or process it.

"How the hell is that possible?" I demanded. "Do we have a leak?"

"Unknown. Bug says the technology is similar, but there are some subtle differences."

"What differences?" asked Hu. "Our systems are constantly being updated. Can we compare the software in the cameras to versions of ours? If so, we could probably put a date on when it was stolen."

Church nodded approval of the question. "The software matches ours at two points, both a little over two years ago. Nikki is preparing employee lists from that time and matching them against team members with access to the software."

"You said that 'some' of the technology was ours," I said. "What's the rest?"

"That opens up an entirely different can of worms. The cameras have a chip specifically designed to make traces impossible via a random and encrypted rerouting process. That chip was designed specifically to foil MindReader searches."

Another kick-in-the-teeth moment.

"Wait a goddamned minute," I said, "we *know* that chip."

"Yes, we do," said Church, tapping crumbs from a vanilla wafer.

"Hugo," breathed a stricken Circe.

She'd been Hugo Vox's protégée for years and he'd been like family to her. The revelation that he was a world-class traitor and terrorist damaged something in her. It was like discovering why your beloved uncle Adolf didn't like your Jewish friends. It left a huge, ugly hole carved in her life. During our battle with Vox and the Seven Kings, he'd stymied us with technology that had been, at the time, impossible to trace. The key to that tech was a certain chip.

"Son of a bitch," I said. "Does that mean Vox is a part of this?"

Church nibbled his cookie and stared at nothing for a moment. "Hugo Vox is dead."

"How do you know that?" asked Rudy. "He was never—"

"Hugo Vox is dead," repeated Church. "There is no doubt."

The silence was big and filled with unspoken conversation. I wondered if Church would ever share the details. Probably not.

"Then someone has his science," said Hu.

Church nodded. "At least as far as the chip goes. It's reasonable to assume the chip is being used to block all traces of the text messages being received by Colonel Riggs and Captain Ledger."

"Excuse me," said Rudy, "but we've had Vox's chip for a while now. Surely we've figured out how it works . . ."

"We have. This new chip has some upgrades, and yes, we'll figure those out as well. Unfortunately, Bug and his team have been stretched pretty thin with this case. However, I've made cracking that chip a priority."

Hu made a face. At first I thought he was having gas and needed to be burped, but as it turned out he had a thought. "This is going to sound very weird, but there are very few DMS people I know of who had access to MindReader and the Vox chip and who had enough knowledge and technical sophistication to take that science further. Actually, only three people occur to me. Two of them are in this building—Bug and Yoda. And the third is . . . well . . . the third is dead."

"Yes," said Church, "and isn't that an interesting line of speculation?"

I held my hand up. "At the risk of being mocked by Dr. Frankenstein, what the hell are you talking about?"

Rudy turned to me. "They're talking about Artemisia Bliss."

"Yeah, I got that part. But she is actually dead, right? So why the fuck are we wasting time talking about her?"

"Because," said Hu with asperity, "we have to be open to the fact that she sold this technology to someone."

"Ah," I said. "Okay, putting my dunce cap on and shutting up now."

Hu actually grinned at me. Maybe the way to his heart was through self-mockery.

"Circe," said Church, "where do we stand on the subway video?"

"It's not good," she admitted. Circe was a beautiful woman with a lovely heart-shaped face framed by intensely black hair that fell in wild curls to her shoulders. Her eyes were so dark a brown they looked black, and in those eyes glittered a steely intelligence. She had advanced degrees in a variety of fields including archaeology, anthropology, theology, psychology, and medicine with a specialty in infectious diseases. But her principal area of expertise was as a world-class expert in counterterrorism and antiterrorism, and specifically in how the terrorist mind works. "The video from the subway has gone global. It's everywhere, and everyone is reacting to it. In a way, we have to admire the finesse by which Mother

Night primed the pump for it. First there was the cyberhacking this morning. That alone was a massive media event, and it dominated the news until the bombs went off. Then public attention was shifted there, with some reporters speculating on a connection."

"How did they make that connection?" I asked, breaking my self-imposed silence.

"That's the right question," said Circe, nodding, "and we're looking into that. We can't say for sure if it was because the reporters are cynical and suspicious, or if they speculated on the connection in hopes that there was one—thereby giving them a scoop while insuring that they appeared savvy and insightful—"

"So young to be so jaded," I murmured. She ignored me, as was appropriate.

"—or if they were in some way tipped off. Because the coverage was so widespread, it's taxing our resources to try to pin that down."

I said something like "Hmm."

She glanced at me. "What?"

"Mother Night seems pretty savvy herself, and she's clearly using the media as a weapon. But at the same time we have to consider whether she knows how the investigative system works. If she's the computer genius she appears to be—"

"She is," said Bug.

"—then she might have counted on investigative agencies targeting the media for deep background checks and thereby allocating resources that might otherwise be useful in hunting her."

"What else could we do, though?" asked Rudy. "Don't we *have* to make those background searches?"

"Absolutely," I agreed. "I'm not saying we're making a wrong move. What I'm saying is that she may have played a good card and we have to accept it."

Church nodded. "In light of her other moves, I think that's a fair assumption." He nodded to Circe to continue.

"I don't think Mother Night's ultimate goal is terrorism," she said, and held up a silencing hand as we all started to speak. "Hear me out. Rudy and I have been wrangling with this all day. Most of you have heard this already." She recounted what Rudy had said to me before the meeting regarding the elements of anarchy. "If she was using bombs in order to create chaos then her picks were clumsy and moderately ineffectual. A law library and a martial arts sporting event? Don't get me wrong, those bombs were devastating and there was terrible loss of life, but this is Labor Day weekend. There are parades, mass gatherings, ball games, concerts. If she'd wanted to rack up a body count to create genuine chaos, she could have picked a thousand more useful targets."

"So what was the point?" asked Aunt Sallie. "To get the media's attention? She already had that."

"No," said Circe, "I think we can call the hacking phase one, with the goal being to energize the media. Phase two was the bombings, and that effectively brought every law enforcement agency to point. Bombings will do that in post-9/11 America. The way the media covers it and the pervasive buzz of social media only serve to reinforce that conditioning. It's very Pavlovian."

"And phase three is the subway?" asked Aunt Sallie.

Circe nodded. "Sure. Phases one and two nicely set up phase three so that the false message conveyed by the altered soundtrack—that the government is using illegal force on ordinary citizens—was something the media helped sell to a willing audience. It's really very smart. Get the media and everyone in the country watching, then bring all emergency response teams to a state of high alert so that armed cops and soldiers are in the streets in certain places. It doesn't matter that they're not in every street, but the sensitized, ratings-hungry media will make it seem that way. Prior to the subway the media rolled footage of SWAT teams, cops, and other emergency responders as part of the message that 'America is responding to terrorism'; but once that video went out, the message automatically changed to 'America responds to a threat by using lethal force against its own people.'"

"The logic doesn't hold," said Hu.

"It doesn't have to hold. It has to be big. In media terms it has to dominate the conversation, and right now that is the *only* conversation."

I said, "I can see it, Circe, but then I hit a wall at high speed. What's Mother Night want from all of this? Now that she has everyone's attention, what's she selling?"

"Ah," said Circe, "that's where I hit a wall, too."

Rudy said, "If, as we agree, the logic does not hold, then we have to wonder if that is a known variable. In other words, does it *need* to hold? Mother Night would have to know that this would eventually be picked apart and, to some degree, defused. That would suggest that this is a plot of limited duration, yes?"

We all nodded.

"Then," concluded Rudy, "if we can predict the time it would take for the story to crumble, then wouldn't that give us an idea of the timetable for whatever Mother Night's larger plan is?"

In the thoughtful silence that followed, everyone began nodding, first to themselves as they worked it through according to their own insights, and then to the group.

"That's very good, doctor," said Church. "Circe . . . public perception and reaction is your field. Can you project a timetable?"

She chewed her lip. "With the prevalence of social media everything is faster. Action and reaction. Ballpark guess? I think whatever Mother Night is doing—providing she needs the social and media disruption she's created as a cover—then I think we have twelve to twenty-four hours to figure it out and stop her. And maybe not even that long."

That was not good news. It took the clock that was ticking in my mind and bolted it to the wall in front of us. Twelve hours to make sense of the senseless, to solve a puzzle whose shape and meaning was completely unknown to us.

Swell.

Right around the time I wondered if we were doing any damn good at all, like maybe we should turn jurisdiction of this case over to a more competent group—say, the Cub Scouts or a group of mimes—Bug interrupted with a news update.

"What do you have?" asked Church.

"Nothing good."

"Can I go home?" I asked. Church ignored me.

Bug said, "Our field lab in Virginia finished their preliminary examination of the mercenaries Shockwave ran into this morning. There's absolutely no doubt about it . . . they're Berserkers."

We'd all been expecting that. Absolutely sucked, though.

"But here's the kicker," continued Bug, "we had a molecular biologist and two pathologists examine the bodies, and our field investigators did a load of interviews with family and known associates of the dead Berserkers. And . . . these guys are new to the whole mutant supersoldier job description. They were all normal eight to ten months ago, but there's no way they were part of the Berserker team at the Dragon Factory. We're running background checks on them, and so far we've proven that three of them were in the military on overseas deployment during the raid on Dogfish Cay. So . . . bottom line? Someone's making new Berserkers."

Chapter Seventy-one

Grand Hyatt Hotel
109 East Forty-second Street
New York City
Sunday, August 31, 4:17 p.m.

Violin had accompanied Junie back to the hotel and followed the DMS agents from room to room, making sure that everything was secure. Then, when they were positioned out in the hallway, Violin checked the suite again, this time scanning it with a small electronic device she produced from her bag. Once she determined that the room was truly secure, she and Junie sat on the couch and watched the news. They had some food sent up, which Violin again checked using a small chemical analyzer. They drank wine. They watched horrors on TV. They did not hear from Joe Ledger.

Finally, Violin stood up and reached for her bag, removed her cell phone, went into the bathroom, turned on the shower, and called her mother.

"What is it?" That was how her mother usually answered the phone. Lilith was not known for social graces.

"You are aware of what is happening in America?"

"Of course I am, girl," snapped Lilith. "Do you think I've gone blind?"

Violin let that pass. "The Deacon's people are being stretched dangerously thin."

"So?"

"So, I would like to offer them our help."

"*Our* help or *your* help?"

"Mine, if we have no one else here in the States."

Lilith paused. "It is my understanding that Captain Ledger is in love with another woman."

"Yes," said Violin.

"Make sure that your motives are quite clear, girl."

"Yes, Mother."

"Don't 'Yes, Mother' me."

"Sorry."

"And don't say you're sorry. If you truly want to help then I will clear it with the Deacon. But you'll go where he needs you, not where you think you should be."

"Of course, Mother."

"'Of course.' God, save me from fools in love."

Lilith ended the call.

Violin waited until the burning red was gone from her face before she left the bathroom. Junie was right there and she pushed abruptly past her and swung the door shut. Violin could hear the woman gagging and then the flush of the toilet. Water ran in the sink for a long time, and when Junie came out her face was flushed.

"Chemo?" asked Violin, realizing at once how awkward a question it was.

Junie shook her head. "It's okay. I'm fine."

"Very well," said Violin uncertainly. She turned away, checked her equipment, and moved toward the door.

"You're leaving?" asked Junie, surprised.

"Yes." Violin nodded to the carnage on the TV. "I am going to see if I can help with this."

"What can you do? They don't even know where this Mother Night person is."

"Well, I can't very well sit around here all night, can I?"

Junie and she studied each other for a long, long time. "Violin," she said softly, "Joe cares very much for you. He really does. We both do."

Violin said nothing.

"I hope we can be friends." When Violin still didn't answer, Junie said, "Stay safe."

Violin simply nodded, not trusting herself to speak. She closed the door quietly behind her as she left.

Chapter Seventy-two

"Who has the capability of making new Berserkers?" asked Rudy.

"Theoretically, anyone," said Hu. "The Jakobys cracked the science. Any lab with the capability to perform gene therapy can replicate their processes if they have the notes."

"And if they don't?"

Hu shrugged. "The Jakobys were so advanced because they used their Pangaea computer system to steal research data from hundreds of other labs around the world. They were, in fact, standing on everyone else's shoulders, and that allowed them to reach higher. Reusing their science is one thing; rediscovering it would take years. Conservative guess, ten to twenty."

"Then we can reasonably conclude that someone has stolen their science, yes?" suggested Rudy. Hu and Church both nodded. "I think we—"

Before he could finish, Nikki appeared on the big screen and gave us the latest information about the crimes happening across the country. Mother Night was not slackening off. We stared in abject horror at what was happening. Murders by skinny kids in anarchist hoodies and Doc Martens, and murders by guys who looked like defensive linemen. The release of a quick-onset Ebola in an Indian restaurant in San Antonio.

Three more backpack bombs. At a flower show in Jacksonville: an estimated seventy dead and three times that many wounded. At a wedding on the beach in Malibu: twenty-eight dead. At a playground in Gary, Indiana, where a bunch of teenagers were playing pick-up basketball: thirty-four dead and wounded.

And more.

Much more. Beatings. Molotov cocktails thrown through windows in upscale neighborhoods in Connecticut and low-rent trailer homes in New Jersey. Random stabbings. More attacks in restaurants by Berserkers.

We watched in horror, but we were not idle.

Church and Aunt Sallie were on the phone, dispatching DMS teams to hotspots, especially those where a suspected bioweapon was being employed. Soon, though, we were stretched so thin that Church began splitting the teams, and then splitting them again. In California there were seven two- and three-person teams rolling out to cover situations where we would normally insert two full teams. SWAT, FBI hostage rescue, ATF, and Homeland's various task forces were also being pushed to the limits. Every biological disaster team in the country was in play. Ordinary police were stretched just as thin, working crowds at each of the crime scenes, and establishing unbreakable perimeters around every site where a biohazard was known or suspected.

It became unreal. It was like running around putting Band-Aids on leaks on a sinking ship when God only knew what was happening below the water line. As we worked to move assets into place, we fought to carve out a few seconds to analyze these new attacks. We worked with limited information, relying on experience, intuition, and guesswork.

Minutes and then hours burned away. It was nearly dawn when we caught enough of a breather to go back to trying to assemble our puzzle.

"Dr. Sanchez," said Church, "yesterday, when we were discussing the stolen Berserker technology, you were going to make a point. What was it?"

"Was I?" Rudy rubbed his eye, which was red and puffy. "Yes, yes . . . God, I'm exhausted." He cleared his throat, looking grainy and old. "It wasn't about the Berserkers per se. It's just that we've been dealing with so many events over the last twenty-four hours that I've begun to wonder how much of that has been orchestrated to have the effect it's been having. By that I mean we are being distracted from a simple progression of logic."

Church twirled his finger in a go-ahead gesture.

"I'm no statistician, but it seems improbably ponderous to me to believe that a single group like Mother Night's could rediscover the Jakoby science for the Berserkers, reinvent pathogens like the *seif-al-din* and quick-onset Ebola, build a microchip like Vox's, and develop a computer comparable to MindReader."

"Well, damn," I said, "when you say it like that—"

"I agree, Dr. Sanchez," said Church, "the timetable for development is as improbable as it is to assume they've merely come up with bioweapons and technologies coincidentally similar to those the DMS has faced."

"Right," I said, "so there *is* a leak?"

"Maybe," said Church and Rudy at the same time.

"Maybe?"

"Sure," said Aunt Sallie, jumping into the conversation. "If Artemisia Bliss stole some of this stuff, and I think we're all thinking that, then she could have handed it off to someone else before the weenie roast in her cell."

"How likely is that?" I asked.

"Not very," confessed Aunt Sallie. "We confiscated her computers, went over every inch of her apartment, even checked her storage unit. Everything we found was turned over to the federal prosecutors, and I can tell you for damn sure that there was nothing there that even touched on the science behind the Berserkers."

"Then explain what's happening."

"I can't."

Rudy asked, "Could Bliss have done that if she was alive?"

"No way," said Auntie. "She was a computer engineer and—"

"Yes," said Hu.

All eyes snapped back in his direction.

"You keep forgetting that Bliss wasn't just a genius, she was a supergenius. That's not a casual phrase. Her intellect was staggering. If she had the information and enough resources, she could either do it or arrange to have it done. That was one of the things we were all afraid of when we discovered that she was copying information and planning on selling it. Her level of genius was profoundly dangerous."

Auntie said, "So what are we talking about? We know Bliss is dead. Could she have obtained Berserker science and sold it elsewhere while she was alive? Sold it and then cleaned up after herself?"

"I don't . . . think so," said Bug tentatively. "MindReader tore her computer apart, and if she'd ever had that information there would have been some record. You can't erase that much data without leaving a trace."

"Couldn't she have bought another computer?"

"We hacked her banking records going back a lot of years," said Bug. "We were looking for that kind of purchase, but there was nothing. We found the stuff she actually stole, and that's why we busted her." He paused and cocked his head thoughtfully. "You know, though . . . if she was still alive, then I could build a pretty good case for her being Mother Night. The level of genius, the subtlety and complexity. She had that by the bagful. And I've played a lot of games with her. She was devious as shit."

"But she's dead," said Circe.

"She's dead," agreed Bug.

"Guys, guys," I said, "let's stick with who might actually be alive. Bug, have Nikki run a thorough background check on Bliss. I know she was adopted from China, so see if you guys can hack Chinese adoption records and—"

"I already did that," said Hu. "She had one sister, but the girl was adopted by a family in Des Moines. School records indicate above-average intelligence, but only just. There's nothing to indicate that she had anything approaching Artie's genius. And there's no indication that Bliss ever had contact with that girl."

"Check again," Church said to Bug. "Find that girl and run a deep background check. Also establish her whereabouts on all dates and times relative to this case."

"On it."

"And send information to all law enforcement agencies about the Berserkers."

Bug hesitated. "Really? That's going to raise a whole lot of questions."

"Do it."

Chapter Seventy-three

The Hangar
Floyd Bennett Field
Brooklyn, New York
Monday, September 1, 5:53 a.m.

I was on my sixth cup of coffee and my hands shook with the aftereffects of violence and way too much caffeine. The last hours of Sunday had burned away and now we were four and a half hours into Monday. We'd spent all night going over every bit of data going all the way back to Arlington and up to the news reports of violence all across the country.

The number of bombings was now eight.

Random acts of violence, fifty-three.

Arsons, eleven.

The release of weaponized pathogens, four. DMS teams were handling each of those, but with plenty of help from local law. Word came down from the White House through subtle channels to drastically but quietly diminish any show of federal involvement in matters that might involve a trigger pull. At the same time, the press secretary and his team were doing heroic spin control. Experts were being trotted out to decry the government's involvement. Those experts included a number of writers, pundits, and scientists in various extreme groups, but people who were willing to participate in a conversation rather than rant and shout. So far it was working. A bit.

The radical right and left, the loudmouth extremists on both sides, were being jackasses. As they usually were. A lot of the moderates were keeping mum for fear of standing on the wrong side when the full story finally came out. If it ever came out.

The president made a few short and very calm statements to the nation, and attended one press conference. Even that, I learned, was staged pretty well, with handpicked members of the White House press corps.

So far, Washington was not burning.

Other places were not so lucky.

At one point I turned to Hu. "Doc, that was definitely the *seif-al-din* down in the subway, no doubt about it, right? One of the early generations."

He nodded. "I know, though my people are running tests."

"Here's the kicker, though," I said, and ran the footage from the subway attack. Not our part in it, but the earliest parts of the video. We watched a sweaty man in a hoodie and yellow raincoat make his announcement about Mother Night and then attack a black teenager. I froze the image. "There! See that guy? He was the patient zero of that attack, right? But he's talking. That means—"

"—he was infected by one of the later strains," said Hu. "I know. I already instructed the forensics team to locate his corpse and take samples."

"My point," I said, "is that someone had access to two *different* strains of the pathogen."

"Obviously."

"How?" I asked.

There was a beat.

"I mean . . . where'd they get them? As far as we can tell, the original lab in Afghanistan blew up. The only person we know of who was infected with Generation Twelve of the pathogen was Amirah, and I put a bullet in her head."

It was true. After El Mujahid tried to release the *seif-al-din* at the Liberty Bell Center in Philly a few years ago, I took Echo Team to Afghanistan and hunted Amirah down. By then she was already infected and driven mad by the experience. I offered her a chance, live as a monster or ride a bullet into paradise. She made the best choice for everyone.

"So who else has both generations?" I asked.

Hu and Church exchanged a look, then Hu said, "There are three places that have both samples. The Locker in Virginia, the Centers for Disease Control in Atlanta, and right here in the Hangar."

The tension in the room was palpable.

"And do we know the status of all three sets of samples?" Rudy asked quietly.

"Nikki conveyed your request for a full security scan of the Locker," said Aunt Sallie. "All the lights were green."

"What about the CDC?" I asked.

"Same thing, and they called in additional security."

"And the stuff we have here?" I asked Hu.

"The samples here are safe," Hu said defensively.

"When you say the lights were green," I said, "exactly what does that mean?"

"It means that all of the dozen or so automatic security programs run system-wide diagnostics and—"

I cut him off. "You mean that we're going on nothing but a computer's word that everything is okay? Jesus fuck, doc."

He immediately whipped out his cell phone to call his senior lab assistant. "Melanie, I need you to check our storage vault. Put eyes on the samples of the *seif-al-din*. All generations. I need a count of how much material is in each vial. Exact numbers, okay? Then run a diagnostic on the log-out computer. I want to know who looked at it, if any vials were touched, when, the works. Go back all the way and get back to me. Then get me somebody at the Locker. I want to talk to the senior researcher on shift or someone in administration." He set his phone down and I gave him a nod.

"What happens if the pathogen is still safely stored in all three places?" asked Rudy.

"Then we're in big fucking trouble," said Aunt Sallie. "'Cause that means someone else has access to it."

"But who else even *knows* about it?" persisted Rudy. "We never fully disclosed the nature of the disease to Congress."

"He's right," said Circe. "And the samples at the CDC are in a special lab with access by only a short list of researchers, all of whom are with either DARPA or the DMS."

"We need to check it all," I said. "Triple the security and dig a fucking moat if we have to."

Hu made another round of calls.

Circe said, "Building on what we were talking about before, about how this may not be as chaotic and anarchical as Mother Night would have us believe, I think her choice of which subway car to hit seems obvious. It's a controlled environment. Going on the assumption that Mother Night knew both the nature of the disease and how we would have to react to it, the stalled subway car gave her a kind of sound stage. The cameras Joe found prove that it was staged so that the drama would unfold in a precise place and manner."

"There's more to it than that," Hu said. "If Mother Night knows about the function and communicability of the *seif-al-din*, then she had to know that if it got out there would be a lot more than anarchy. It would be a feeding frenzy."

"Begins with an A and rhymes with Ohpocalypse," I muttered.

Church nodded. "So the stalled subway car was both a stage and a containment facility. That's very interesting."

"Doesn't that give us a little bit of hope?" asked Rudy. "Clearly Mother Night is not trying to create an apocalyptic event."

"She's trying to take down the president," suggested Hu, but nearly everyone shook their heads.

"I think Dr. Sanchez is correct when he says that damaging the presidency is a side effect," said Church. "Or a means to an end."

"How did she do all that? Is this a cyberwarfare attack? Like Comment Crowd or something like that?"

"It could be," said Circe.

"I asked Bug about that and he put some people on it," said Aunt Sallie. "MindReader can't trace it exclusively back to China."

"Meaning what?" I asked.

"Meaning that his guys have been backtracking the source of these posts and e-mails, and they're linking everywhere. China, yes, but also England, Taiwan, Guam, you name it. One source went to a tiny village in Peru. I asked Bug if he thought Mother Night had a global network or a rerouting system, and his best answer was 'maybe both, probably.' But he couldn't pin anything down."

Rudy leaned forward and placed his elbows on the table. "That troubles me. Why is MindReader having so hard a time pinning this down?"

"I asked Bug that, too," said Auntie. "He's run ten kinds of diagnostics on the system and hasn't yet come up with an answer. One thing he did find, though, is a number of instances when one computer or another has *attempted* to sneak in to MindReader. However, every one of those attempts was rebuffed. No one even dented the outer firewall. Bug is confident that no one has hacked us."

"How would we know?" asked Rudy. "Isn't MindReader designed to hide all traces of intrusion?"

"Not in our own system," said Auntie. "When someone or something attempts to hack MindReader all sorts of bells go off."

"And—nothing?"

"Nothing except failed attempts."

"What option does that leave us?" I asked. "You guys always tell me that MindReader is the only computer system capable of doing some of what we're seeing. How true is that statement as of right now?"

Church nodded, approving the question. "It suggests several possibilities. One is that someone else has built a machine identical to MindReader."

"Which is impossible," said Auntie quickly.

"Why impossible?" I asked.

"Because it wasn't designed following any predictable philosophy or developmental progression," she said. "And it's been futzed with a lot, both to make it work better and to keep its operating system unique."

"The next thought is that someone," said Church, "the Chinese or another group with extraordinary resources, has developed a better computer. Something so much more powerful than MindReader that it's doing to our computer what ours does to everyone else's."

Rudy whistled. "That would be devastating."

"We are experiencing a degree of devastation right now," Church pointed out. "This may be proof that our edge has become blunted."

Auntie gave an emphatic shake of her head. "No, I'm not buying it, Deacon. Part of MindReader's daily function is to scout for anything that even suggests that a lab or design team is headed that way. So much of that kind of research, development, and planning would involve the Internet, even proprietary access setups. We'd have seen it."

"Wait," said Rudy, holding up his hands, "pardon me if this is impertinent or above my pay grade, but perhaps if we understood how MindReader came to be the powerhouse that it is then we might have some chance of figuring this out."

Church nibbled a cookie for a moment, then nodded. "Prior to the formation of the DMS, I was involved in various operations with a team of players from different countries, code-named the List. Our primary goal was to tear down a group of scientists called the Cabal, who had built very advanced systems using illegal technologies first initiated by the Nazis. They had a computer scientist named Antonio Bertolini, who was very likely the most brilliant computer engineer I've ever encountered. A soaring intellect who could have done great good with his work. But he took a different path. The cornerstone of the Cabal's efficiency was Bertolini's computer and its search-and-destroy software package—known as Pangaea. The Cabal used Pangaea to steal bulk research material from laboratories, corporations, and governments worldwide, and much of that research was later used by the Jakobys."

I nodded, familiar with part of the story. "You killed Bertolini and took Pangaea and somehow that became MindReader, right?"

"In a way," said Church. "I was already supporting the development of a similar computer system called Oracle."

Oracle, I thought. *Wow.* That was the computer system Church gave to Lilith and the women of Arklight.

"Oracle was good," Church continued, "but it wasn't Pangaea. However, we were able to combine the best elements of both systems into a new generation, originally designated as Babel. But even that was insufficient for what I believed we needed to create an organization like the Department of Military Sciences. I scouted for the very best software engineers who were also insightful into the current and future needs of cyberwarfare. They wrote the master programs for MindReader."

"Doctor," Rudy said to Hu, "you said that the Jakobys used Pangaea to steal research data?"

"Yes."

"Did they have the *actual* machines built for the Cabal?"

"No," said Aunt Sallie. "Those were destroyed."

"Then they did what? Built their own?"

Bug said, "Sure, the schematics were in Hecate's safe."

Rudy smiled. "Hecate had them? No one else?"

"No . . ." began Bug, but he slowed to a stop, then carefully said, "Not that we know of."

"Let me ask this, then," said Rudy. "If you, Bug, had those blueprints or schematics or whatever they're called for computers and you *knew* about MindReader, could you build a computer that approximates what MindReader does?"

"Hecate and Paris couldn't do that. They were geneticists and—"

"I'm not asking about them. I asked if *you* could do it."

"Me? Well, sure, *I* could do it, but—"

"Ah," said Rudy.

"Wait," said Bug, "what's 'ah' supposed to mean?"

"It means that if you could do it," I said, "then someone on your level could do it."

"They'd have to have some access to MindReader. At least some basic understanding of the software written after Pangaea was created."

Rudy nodded. So did Church. And me.

"But there's no one else I know of who could do it. Even Yoda and Nikki couldn't do it."

"I'm not asking about them," said Rudy. There was another pregnant pause, then Rudy glanced at each person at the table. "We are absolutely certain Artemisia Bliss *is* dead, yes?"

Hu started to laugh, but Church raised a hand.

"I believe you visited the crime scene," said Church. "You saw the body."

"Her body was identified from dental plates and DNA," added Circe. "There's no doubt that it was Artemisia Bliss in that cell."

Hu and Bug gave emphatic nods.

Rudy smiled. "No doubt at all?"

"Where are you going with this, doctor?" demanded Auntie.

That's when I got it, and I slapped my hand down on the table so hard everyone except Church jumped. "Christ on a stick!"

"Joe," said Rudy quickly, "what's wrong?"

"I'm a goddamn idiot is what's wrong." Hu began to smile but I pointed a finger at him. "And you're every bit as stupid as I am. As we all are. Shit, Rudy's absolutely right and this is staring us in the face. I mean . . . we even said it but threw it away."

"Captain," said Church, "skip the dramatics. What are we all missing?"

"Burn to shine," I said. "It's right there."

"What is?"

"This is Artemisia Bliss."

"Um," said Hu, "I'm pretty sure we already covered that, Einstein. She'd make a great suspect if she wasn't ashes in a box."

"No," said Church, leaning forward, "hear him out. I think I know where he's going with this, and I'm afraid I agree."

Everyone looked from him to me. Rudy nodded encouragement.

"Okay," I said, "we all put it on the table. Artemisia was smarter than almost everyone, right? Smart and devious. She was on Auntie's shit list because she tried to hack MindReader. She got fired and arrested because she copied and sold a lot of the information we've been trying to keep the bad guys from using. She was bagged, tagged, and the judge hit her with max penalties. She was going to jail and she'd never get out. She was done."

"And somebody *killed* her," said Hu again, leaning on it so Captain Shortbus could understand the concept. But I shook my head.

"Somebody killed someone."

"No," said Circe, "Joe, you're forgetting that Jerry Spencer collected DNA from her corpse and it was an exact match to hers on file. It was her."

I gave another shake. "Jerry pulled DNA from *a* corpse and it matched DNA on file."

"What?"

"Step back for a second and look at this from a distance. Think about how to do this and let's pretend we're all actually smart for a minute." I said this last part while looking directly at Hu.

Church was already nodding. Rudy and Circe were a step behind him. Hu had to already be there, but he so did not want me to have figured this out.

It was Bug who put it into words.

"The DNA we matched it to was not physical DNA. We matched the samples Jerry collected against data stored in the system."

"Right," I said. "Data stored in the system. We only have the computer's word that it's actually Bliss's."

"No," said Hu, shaking his head, "you're talking about MindReader."

"Right," I told him. "I'm talking about a computer. Computers are basically storage devices. You can put anything in there you want. And Artemisia Bliss is one of the most brilliant computer experts who ever lived, as you're so fond of telling. Fuck, man, you hired her. You want to sit there and tell me that she isn't smart enough to have faked the data in MindReader?"

Hu cleared his throat. "Well . . . she, um, wrote the code for the bio-data retrieval software."

Rudy said, "Oy."

"But the passwords were all changed after her arrest," insisted Aunt Sallie.

"Sure," said Circe, "but I'm sure you didn't go in and change every line of code she ever wrote. Or all of the millions of lines of code she supervised. Joe's right, she could have built her own false evidence right into the code. Hidden it so that it popped up whenever any data was entered for a comparison with hers."

"That would suggest she knew she would be arrested," said Rudy. "And that her own death was planned."

"It could have been planned," I said, "or it could have been one of a dozen contingency plans she built into the system because she *knows* the system. Maybe there are other things that would have come up if something else had happened to her. They could be lurking in the system right now."

Bug began hammering at some keys. There was a *bing-bong* as he received an almost instantaneous reply. "Oh, shitballs. I just sent a second set of DNA to the system for comparison to hers, and it came up as a positive."

"Which DNA?" Hu asked reluctantly.

"Yours," said Bug weakly. "And . . . mine. And Circe's. All three came up as a match to Artemisia's. There was no way we could have known it, but any DNA comparison request that involves Artemisia is going to come up positive."

"*Dios mio*," breathed Rudy very softly.

"Artemisia Bliss is alive," said Hu, just as quietly.

"Worse than that," said Church. "Artemisia Bliss is Mother Night. And that changes everything."

Chapter Seventy-four

Office of the Vice President
The White House
Washington, D.C.
Monday, September 1, 5:58 a.m.

"Do we have an estimate on the number of people on the C train?" asked Vice President William Collins.

Boo Radley opened a blue leather notebook and consulted the top page. "The area is still sealed pending biohazard cleanup, but based on the hour and averages for holiday traffic we're putting the number at around two hundred."

That slapped Collins in the face hard enough to align all of his attention. "Two *hundred*?"

He fumbled for his coffee cup, found it empty, stared into it, set the cup down.

"K-keep me posted," he said, tripping over the words.

"Yes, sir," said Radley. He lingered for a moment. "Will the president address the nation?"

Collins shook his head. "It's too early for that. We don't know enough."

In truth he didn't know what the president would do. His relationship with his two-term running mate had steadily deteriorated to the point where they only ever spoke when it was absolutely politically necessary. Their dislike of each other was an open secret, and was often the substance of jokes by Leno, Fallon, Colbert, and Stewart. No one in the press or the talk show circuit knew the reason for the animosity, and neither

Collins nor the president would respond to questions about it. There wasn't much left to this second term anyway, and soon Collins would be out and would no longer have to endure the disdain—publically or privately—from his boss.

The truth of the schism between the two men ran deeper than the fact that Collins had lost to the president during the primaries and always felt that his vice presidency was a bone thrown to him. And a way for the president to keep his party rival close at hand. The real core of the trouble between them was their view of how best to serve the country. Not run it—serve it. The president was an idealist who kept trying to solve problems. Collins didn't like him any more than he'd liked the two previous presidents. All three of them cared too much about party politics and brinksmanship. Collins saw things from a different perspective, from what he believed to be a big-picture angle that allowed him to see what America really needed. It needed to be strong again. As strong as it was right after World War II ended. A position of power it tasted only once more, when Reagan was in. When the American military was so scary strong that the mere threat of it put the cracks in the Berlin Wall and toppled the Soviet state. That couldn't be accomplished with either the liberals or conservatives trying to cock-block each other. And it couldn't happen if American corporations kept taking a shit on their own soil. Thirty years of poor management—political and corporate—had empowered North Korea and Iran and turned China into the most frightening superpower since . . .

Well, since the United States dropped the bombs on Japan.

What really pissed Collins off was that this was a problem that could be fixed. The balance of power could be shifted where it was supposed to be with so little effort. The primary obstruction wasn't even the war in Congress over who had the bigger dick. It was a lack of courage. A lack of real balls.

It was a lack of the American spirit that built this fucking country.

He shook his head.

His mood was further soured by the body-count estimates. Two hundred dead?

Mother Night had promised him there would be a lot more than that.

And then, as if in response to his angry thoughts, his cell buzzed to indicate a text message. He glanced at it and saw that it was a message from *her*.

MORE TO COME.

THE GAME IS FAR FROM OVER.

It was signed with the letter A.

He sat back in his leather chair and considered the message and its implications. The fact that Mother Night was going to see this through all the way to the end was comforting. Gratifying. The fact that she took the time to tell him was encouraging.

So why had she sent a letter filled with anthrax to him?

He sank into a brooding stillness, teeth grinding, fists clenched on his desktop.

"What the fuck are you doing?" he growled quietly.

Chapter Seventy-five

The Hangar

Floyd Bennett Field

Brooklyn, New York

Monday, September 1, 5:59 a.m.

Once it was said, once it was out there, it made sense. A twisted kind of sense.

Artemisia Bliss was Mother Night.

Too many of our puzzle pieces now fit, but the picture they made was like something out of Salvador Dalí. Or maybe Hieronymus Bosch.

"This is nuts," said Hu, still not buying it. "Artie was corrupt, sure, and maybe she made some questionable choices—"

" 'Questionable'?" echoed Aunt Sallie.

"—but we're talking about Mother Night here. Artie never physically hurt anyone. Mother Night has killed hundreds. That person is either totally deranged or she's outright evil. Where's the evidence of that kind of evolution?"

"There are foundations of it," said Rudy, "but I would need time to work up a profile and—"

Suddenly the big screen on the wall split and Nikki Bloomberg filled the second window. She was a tiny, mousy young woman with enormous eyes and slightly bucked teeth. She was twenty-six but looked like a gawky twelve. "Sorry to interrupt," she said quickly, "but you have to hear this."

"Go ahead," said Church.

"When Rasheen brought us the cameras Joe's guys pulled off the wall, I found that there were two kinds of transmitters inside. Two separate signals. One was the satellite feed that went out to the press, and that one had the fake soundtrack of people begging for mercy. The *other* one, though, was sent via a different satellite to a rerouting system that bounced it all over the globe. The thing is, that second video stream had an additional track, too, but it was a separate video track. A digitally imposed data crawl."

"What did it say?" I think we all asked that at the same time.

"I'll show you," said Nikki, and immediately the screen split into two windows, one with her face and the other with the horrible footage of my team shooting at the walkers. With the false soundtrack off you could hear the moans of the hungry dead, and the effect was far more terrifying and monstrous.

But the data crawl at the bottom is what caught everyone's eye.

It jolted us all and, I have to say, it changed the game right there and then.

It read: *The bidding starts at fifty million.*

Those six words, over and over again.

Rudy said, "*Dios mio.*"

I said, "Holy shit."

"And there it is," said Aunt Sallie. "The anarchy, the destruction, it's all a cover for a fucking sales pitch. This whole goddamn thing is about money."

"It's always about money," grumbled Bug.

However, Rudy shook his head. "Money, maybe . . . but I knew Artemisia. There was one thing she wanted more than money, more than career success, and more than personal fame. No, the thing she wanted most was power."

"Yes," said Church, "and look how powerful she's become."

Chapter Seventy-six

Donny Hauk sat on a square of cardboard that was padded by a folded towel that was carefully wrapped around a thick piece of memory foam. It was a very comfortable seat, and Donny believed that the memory foam remembered him. Or at least it remembered his ass. It welcomed his ass. It comforted his ass. And Donny's ass was grateful.

It had been a long night. Hotter and far more humid than the weatherman had said—and Donny, who did this sort of thing several times a year, hated fucking weathermen. Assholes who were overpaid for being bad at their job. They said that it was going to be mild. Eighty-nine degrees wasn't mild. Eighty-eight percent humidity wasn't mild. It was a frigging sauna.

On the upside, the heat drove off a lot of what Donny called "civilians." Shoppers who didn't know how to wait on line, who hadn't acquired the predatory survival skills necessary to make it through a long night.

Donny had those skills. In spades. They'd been honed over years and were locked firmly into place.

Sure, he'd made rookie mistakes. He'd been a civilian once. First time he ever waited on line for a doorbuster was the release of the unrated director's cut of the second God of War game. Donny spent a bad night in worse weather than this, wearing a hoodie and nearly freezing his nuts off in sixteen degrees with a minus-two wind chill. His fingers and toes were almost dead from cold when they opened the door, and that made him sluggish and slow, and the crowd had surged past him. After eleven hours of waiting, Donny had returned home without the game, so crushed that he sat on the toilet, crapping and crying.

Not his best moment, he knew, but an instructive one.

When he showed up at Walmart for the latest version of Resident Evil, he was wearing a fleece-lined anorak, gloves, earmuffs, and a scarf. He had a thermos of espresso and six power bars. His only mistake then had been to neglect to bring something comfortable on which to sit, and as a result he stood too long and then sat too long on hard ground. The aches born from that slowed him by a step, and despite being third in line he was not even among the first twenty through the door when the lights came on.

Live and learn.

Now he sat on ten inches of foam next to an ice chest filled with food and drinks. He had his iPod, iPad, and iPhone charged, and had extended batteries for each. Donny downloaded fourteen hours of movies from iTunes and made deals with people to watch his flicks via an earjack splitter in return for them holding his spot during bathroom runs to Dunkin Donuts a few blocks away. He also shared power bars and icy cans of Coke with line neighbors who kept an eye on his stuff whenever he dozed.

At 6:00 a.m., when the sleep-deprived sales staff opened the door to the Best Buy in Willow Grove, Donny was on his feet, rested, as fit as his three hundred pounds on a five nine frame would allow, bags packed and eyes bright at the thought of the new game, Burning Worlds, which was rumored to be the toughest video game ever.

Donny was first in line, and by now the other doorbusters—they'd taken that as their name—showed deference to Donny. He had become royalty to then. While not quite a family, the doorbusters had become a community, a "people," and Donny Hauk was their king.

As the store manager appeared and bent to unlock the doors, Donny led the applause. Then Donny turned to the others and in a regal voice declared, "Let the games begin!"

That sparked another round of applause and laughter, but this time it was all for him. With a great beaming smile, Donny picked up his shopping bag, waved to the crowd, turned, and walked through the doors. The crowd bustled like anxious bees, but no one tried to push past him. No sir. Not anymore. Not King Donny.

He waddled along familiar aisles with the horde of doorbusters behind him, heading to the big display for Burning Worlds. They had life-size character cutouts on either side of a kind of cattle chute that opened in a space where a long rack of games had been placed. One hundred copies of the new game were in the center, and all of the other hot products put out by the same company were racked for impulse purchase.

Donny reached out his hand, fingers wiggling, as he selected which copy of Burning Worlds he wanted. There were grunts and a few curses behind him—not directed at him but fired by members of the increasingly agitated crowd. Donny picked one, top row, fifth from the left. The plastic wrapping on the box looked perfect. No smudges or fingerprints, no tears in the cellophane.

When Donny turned and held up his selection, the crowd applauded again.

All hail the king.

Satisfied, happy, and excited, Donny stepped away from the rack, giving only a casual glance behind him as the crowd surged forward and the feeding frenzy began. A few people ran past to be first in line at the checkout, but that was fine with Donny. He didn't need to be first to pay. Instead he drifted over to look at the Blu-ray box sets. He was reading the back cover text on the fourteenth series of *Doctor Who* when he heard one of the staff say, "What the hell?"

Donny looked up in time to see a semi pull to a stop out front, the truck so close to the building that it triggered the automatic door. The truck was big, white, with no markings. Everyone who was near the front of the store stopped what they were doing and looked. Donny frowned because the narrow gap left by the truck was far too tight to allow him to get out. Complaining about that would be awkward, and anxiety immediately began to climb inside his chest.

He turned to the closest salesman to ask a question, but the young man was already in motion, striding toward the front with a firm jaw, an outraged expression on his face, and balled fists. Donny drifted along behind.

A slender Asian woman squeezed though the tiny gap between the open door and the cab. The door effectively blocked any additional doorbusters from getting in, however. The truck and its door formed a bulky seal to the front of the building.

The salesman began yelling questions as soon as he was close, but Donny was bemused to see that the driver completely ignored him. The driver wore a white jumpsuit, brand-new sneakers, and leather driving gloves. A pair of nearly opaque sunglasses clung to the front of her face.

The morning breeze blew under the truck and into the store, carrying with it the stink of gasoline and . . .

And what?

It wasn't skunk and it wasn't the sulfur stink of a troubled engine.

This was more like his fridge smelled when a storm tripped the circuit breakers in his apartment the week he was away at San Diego Comic Con. Everything in the box, from leftover Chinese to the brisket his aunt Helene had brought over, turned into lumps of rot. It took a week, lots of scrubbing, and four boxes of baking soda to get rid of the stink.

That's what the female driver smelled like.

Like rotten food.

The Asian woman seemed to tune in on his thoughts, and while the salesman continued to yell at her, she removed a small spray bottle from a pocket, uncapped it, and sprayed the contents on her clothes.

The god-awful smell of decay suddenly became ten times worse.

"What the hell are you *doing?*" yelled the salesman.

The Asian woman put the bottle back into her pocket, unzipped her jumpsuit, reached inside, and when she removed her hand she held . . .

A gun?

Donny gaped at it. He'd played every kind of first-person shooter game on the market and yet he'd never once seen a real gun.

The salesman froze, his expression caught between outrage and horror. "What . . . ?" he said.

Donny's legs trembled with the desire to run, but he dared not move. The crowd in the store was noticing the gun by degrees. There were gasps and yells. And screams. The Asian woman smiled placidly and watched the effect, apparently enjoying it. She raised her gun and pointed it at the salesman.

"Shhh," she said.

The salesman became a statue, though Donny could see him go dead pale. Then the slim woman in the reeking jumpsuit half-turned and looked at Donny.

No, she looked *above* Donny. Despite himself, Donny turned and looked up, too, and saw one of the store's many security cameras. A small red light glowed beside the black lens.

Without a word of warning, the Asian woman shot the salesman in the chest. It was done with an almost casual disinterest. The bullet punched through the salesman's body and exited with a burst of blood that splashed across Donny's chest and face. The salesman fell backward and crashed to the floor.

Everyone screamed.

The killer raised her pistol and fired the next shot into the ceiling.

"*Shut the fuck up*," she bellowed, spacing out the words for maximum clarity.

Everyone shut the fuck up.

Donny's bladder suddenly let loose and hot urine coursed down his legs and into his shoes. Even with death looking at him, he was wretchedly ashamed and hoped no one would notice.

No one did.

The woman turned in a slow circle with the eye of the pistol following her line of sight. She held a shushing finger to her full lips as she turned. When the store was totally silent, the woman once more looked up at the video camera.

"Now that I'm pretty sure I have your attention, here's the news," she said, smiling, enjoying herself. "The only action is direct action. Sometimes you have to burn to shine."

That's when Donny—and everyone else—understood what was happening. It was more of the Mother Night stuff. The anarchy and chaos that was all over the news. It was here. Right here. For real.

Laughing at the crowd's reaction, the woman walked out to the truck, jerked open the side door, and then came back into the store. People began jumping down from the open door.

But that was wrong. Donny frowned, trying to understand what he was seeing. The truck seemed to be filled with people, but they weren't jumping down or climbing down. They were falling down.

Awkwardly.

Clumsily.

Hitting the ground so hard Donny was sure he heard bones break.

They were dirty, dressed in rags, slack-faced.

And they stank. God almighty, they stank worse than the Asian girl did.

The people kept tumbling out, landing on one another, crawling, struggling to their feet. They all looked stoned.

They all looked sick, Donny thought.

Their faces were pale. Some as white as mushrooms, others as gray as dust,

What was weirdest of all, what disturbed Donny on a level he couldn't understand . . . was why none of them cried out when they fell or when someone fell atop them. Even the ones who clearly broke a hand or arm or leg didn't scream or curse or anything.

However, they did make sounds. Small sounds. Low and so oddly out of keeping with what was happening.

They moaned. Soft, plaintive.

Moans of deep need.

Then the people got to their feet and began shuffling awkwardly into the store. The people inside, the sales staff and the doorbusters, shifted back from them. No one liked the look of them.

There was something intensely wrong here.

When Donny looked into the eyes of the closest of these newcomers he saw . . .

Nothing.

No trace of personality. Not even the deadened gaze of stoners. There was simply—*nothing.*

Like they're dead, thought Donny.

That was the worst thought he'd ever had. It was also the most cogent and accurate observation he'd ever made.

Like they were dead.

Like.

They.

Were.

"Oh, God," whispered Donny.

The Asian woman—the one who called herself Mother Night—smiled as the slack-faced people passed her on either side. They ignored her. Once past her, however, their moans of need sharpened into driving, intense moans of another kind.

Moans not just of need.

But of hunger.

A hunger so deep that it made Donny's bowels ache and throb.

To the camera, the woman said, "Generation Six. Old school, I know, but a classic nonetheless. Now, children, remember what Mother Night said. Bidding kicks off at fifty million euros." Then, as she turned, she said something else, but it was directed to the slack-faced people. To Donny it sounded like, *"Bon appetit."*

Donny was sure of it.

Dead certain.

Donny had seen this before. In games. In movies.

He'd played this before.

As the gray-and-white people rushed him and bore him to the floor, as his own screams drowned out the moans of the dead, as the pain burned down the world in his mind, Donny wondered how he could reset this. Which button did he have to push to get a replay, to get a new life?

How?

How?

That was his very last thought.

Chapter Seventy-seven

Floyd Bennett Field
Brooklyn, New York
Monday, September 1, 6:01 a.m.

Violin sat in the darkness under a tree, feeling lost and useless. The sun was still down, though there were fires over the horizon line across Jamaica Bay and past Flight 587 Memorial Park. Six hundred yards away from where she sat, the humped shape of the Hangar pretended to be a vacant building. Violin knew better. She also knew that Joseph Ledger was inside.

Since leaving Junie Flynn's hotel and coming here, Violin had wrestled with herself as to what to do. And although Lilith had granted permission for her to assist Ledger, Joseph himself had not asked. Nor, technically, had the Deacon. In her brief conversation with him, the man said that he would appreciate her help should the appropriate situation arise, but he neglected to say what that situation might be. This whole country was in turmoil, people were dying, but it wasn't a fight where you could locate the battle lines. It was all random, chaotic. There seemed to be no way to actually help anyone.

So she crouched in the darkness and watched the Hangar and hoped that her cell would ring. As the hours crawled past, she thought about her feelings for Joseph. It was a fact that she loved him, and she was furious with herself for allowing that to happen. It made her madder still that those feelings persisted long after he'd fallen in love with someone else.

Junie Flynn. An ordinary woman? Maybe. A dying woman? Possibly.

The right woman for Joseph?

No.

Violin was certain of it. Junie was soft. Not a warrior at all. A civilian. Joseph was a warrior, a killer. In many ways he was every bit as much a monster as Violin herself.

The most troubling thing of all was the fact that she, a woman of Arklight, daughter of Lilith, soldier in the war against the Red Knights, felt totally defeated by an ordinary woman who would probably waste away and die sometime soon.

Violin tried very hard to hate Junie Flynn.

Chapter Seventy-eight

Westin Hotel
Atlanta, Georgia
Monday, September 1, 6:02 a.m.

Mother Night did not want them to see an ordinary person.

However, deciding what to wear took some time. Although she had no one to confess it to, there were times when she considered wearing a costume. Something outrageous, like a supervillain costume, and she had several in mind. She got as far as the sewing stage for one of them before she realized how totally ridiculous that would be. The real world was never cool enough for anyone to accept a costumed supervillain.

Which sucked.

Some of her people would appreciate it, though, and every now and then she considered doing a Skype chat with them while wearing a costume. The foot soldiers would dig it, and Ludo Monk would probably come in his pants. Especially if her costume included cleavage and a large firearm.

But for the meeting with the bidders, a costume just would not work.

So sad. So boring and commonplace.

She thought about how rich she was about to become. Richer than she was already, and Haruspex had helped her loot tens of millions from groups ranging from Citibank to the Russian mob. After the auction, though, she would be many times richer. As rich as she imagined she deserved to be.

She wondered what would become of all that money.

Speculation about that made her think about everything else she'd leave behind. Apartments, cars, jewels, labs, all the science she'd torn from the Jakobys' computer records. She couldn't take that stuff with her. She'd had no need of it where she was going.

Deep inside her head a small voice tried to whisper to her, but Mother Night didn't listen. Would not listen. That voice was only an echo anyway. A glitch in the system that played a tired recording of someone else's voice.

Artemisia Bliss.

That weak little cow.

That dead bitch.

She forced herself to focus. The outfit she ultimately chose was a simple one, and it was also the first one she'd thought of. A black hooded sweater, black pageboy wig, black glasses. The same one the girls in her street teams used. She darkened her skin with spray tan and painted her mouth with black lipstick. And she took nearly forty minutes using professional stage makeup to change the shape of her face. Padding in her cheeks and behind her upper lip, suggesting an overbite. Plastic-coated wire springs to flare her nostrils, and putty to thicken her nose. Black pencil to add multiple fake piercing holes to her ears and two very heavy earrings to stretch her lobes. Clip-on ring to her nose and one to her lower lip. Then she used latex to give herself a small crescent-shaped scar above her left eyebrow, and a small surgical scar on her throat. More of the spray tan hid the latex and blended it all.

She appraised the final result in the bathroom mirror, and nodded approval.

Mother Night smiled back at her. Haughty, confident, and gorgeous.

The spray tan changed her skin tone from Asian to something more complex, and combined with the reshaping of the nose it suggested mixed ancestry. She'd based a lot of the look on photos of a Congolese fashion model who had been popular in France in the sixties.

Her cell buzzed and she dug it out of her hoodie pocket. It wasn't a call but rather her alarm.

It was time.

Mother Night hurried out of the bathroom and into the dining room, where everything was set up. She opened her laptop, engaged the global rerouter that would bounce the video feed to more than a thousand spots every ninety seconds, and loaded a videoconferencing utility she'd built by hacking and rewriting the Skype software.

One by one, calls began coming in. Most of these were rerouted, too, and Mother Night smiled at that. It was adorable. As they logged in, she engaged Haruspex to begin tracking them down. Rerouting didn't mean a fucking thing to Haruspex. There were eleven bidders. None of them had their webcams turned on, of course; however, Mother Night broadcast her image to all of them.

"Good evening," she said, giving herself a vaguely European accent she'd cribbed from the movies. She'd practiced it for months, listening to playbacks and making adjustments. All part of the "woman of mystery" mystique that made playing Mother Night so much fun. "I trust I have been able to adequately entertain you with today's festivities. Here is how the game will be played. Each of you has access to the conference chat function. No one is required to speak. Type in your questions and comments. Everyone will be able to see the amount you are bidding. If you wish to send me a private message, use the button marked with a W, for whisper. Only I will be able to access the whispers. This session will conclude when I have accepted the winning bid. The winning bidder will then wire me the entire amount to the routing number I will type in now."

She had a different number for each bidder, and quickly cut and pasted those into individual whisper boxes.

"I will warn you now that I am monitoring those accounts. If there is any attempt to trace them I will be very cross. You have each seen what I am capable of doing. Let us all remain friends. We *have* a common enemy."

One of the bidders typed a message into the main chat.

HOW DO WE TRUST YOU?

She laughed, and said, "This is not about trust. At this moment I have my people in each of your countries or inside your groups. Each one of my people has a supply of the pathogen built into a wide-dispersal explosive device. When I have a winning bid, that courier will place their parcel in a protected place and you will be texted the location and the disarming code."

WHAT HAPPENS TO THE OTHER SAMPLES?

"Ah," said Mother Night, "that is another matter. The losing bidders will each wire me a penalty amount of ten million euros. Failure to do so within ten minutes of the end of this conference will result in my people releasing the pathogen in the nearest crowded city. And if any of you de-cide to drop out of the bidding, the pathogen will be released."

She let that sink in.

THIS IS OUTRAGEOUS. THIS IS EXTORTION.

"Of course it is," she said with a laugh. "What's your point?"

There was no answer to that.

"Oh, and one last thing," she said after a moment. "In case you are thinking that this would be a good time to swear one of those tiresome vendettas or fatwas against me, bear this in mind: the *seif-al-din* is not the only item I have for sale. Play fair with me and you will get to bid on other toys. Break faith with me and you will spend the rest of your lives burying everyone you have ever known. Tell me you understand and accept the terms of our game."

One by one they sent her private whispers.

Everyone understood.

"How delightful," she said, settling back. "Now, let the games begin. The starting bid is fifty million euros."

The first bid was for sixty-five million euros.

Chapter Seventy-nine

"We need to reassess everything," I said. "Every reaction we've had, every response we've made. Knowing that this is Bliss changes the game entirely. Bug, if she built something like MindReader based on what she hacked from our system, and maybe schematics for Pangaea, what does that do for us?"

"Puts us up shit creek?"

"No, damn it . . . work the problem. You know MindReader better than her. No matter how smart she is, you know that computer. Are there assumptions she might make that we can use against her? Are there ways MindReader can set a trap? And more important, now that we know she's using those technologies plus Vox's chip, does knowing it give you a way to work around her tech?"

This was the core of any counterattack—knowing your enemy. It's virtually impossible to protect yourself against the unknown. But with knowledge comes understanding and with that comes strategic thinking.

"I'm all over this," Bug said with more edge in his voice than I've ever heard. His screen went blank.

Then I focused on Hu. "No fucking around now, doc. Where did Bliss get those pathogens? You're supposed to be a couple of points smarter than her. Prove it."

If I expected him to get snarky or huffy, he proved me wrong. Hu straightened in his chair. "She could have obtained some samples at the Liberty Bell Center. If she was going crazy back that far, it's possible she pocketed some samples of Generation Six and Generation Twelve."

"Enough to do the damage she's doing?"

"I don't know. Probably, but definitely not enough to sell to bidders. And the same with the quick-onset Ebola released at the bar. Unlike the *seif-al-din*, that strain of Ebola doesn't replicate inside a host. It kills through direct exposure but that's it. It has to be produced in a lab, and it's a very complicated process. I think it's most likely she got some from that lab Colonel Riggs busted in Detroit. Bliss was there running the cleanup team. The reports say that she used water balloons at that bar and in other locations. If that's the case, then she probably added a portion of her supply to each balloon, so she's probably burned through any samples she might have obtained. From what I can put together in my head based on where she was and what she had access to, I think her real weapon is the *seif-al-din*. She's more likely to have enough of that for more hits, and, like I said, she could possibly have harvested more from infected test subjects."

"I never thought I'd ever say that I wish we were facing Ebola instead," I muttered.

No one argued. People infected with Ebola would die, but they wouldn't become carnivorous vectors.

"If Bliss intends to sell these bioweapons to foreign bidders," said Rudy, "and if we can reasonably believe that her supplies are limited to what she might have taken from DMS crime scenes . . . then how can she have enough to sell?"

Hu shook his head. "I don't see how she can. She would need the purest strains to be able to sell them to anyone's bioweapons program."

"Unless she has a source for more pure pathogen," suggested Circe. "Is it possible that all of this chaos and violence is a distraction to keep us from looking for her true agenda? Could this be a screen while she makes a run at getting a supply of the purest versions of each pathogen?"

We looked at one another for a long second, and then Church snatched up the phone. He called Samson Riggs and ordered him to drop everything and take what was left of Shockwave Team and get to the Centers for Disease Control in Atlanta.

Auntie was on her phone ordering Brick to triple the guards on the virus vault buried six levels down here at the Hangar.

That left the site with the biggest array of pathogenic monsters and the largest supply of each.

The Locker.

"Captain——" began Church, but I was already heading for the door at a dead run. Ghost ran beside me, his nails clicking on the marble floor.

Chapter Eighty

By the time Ghost and I reached the prep room, Top had already gotten the word. Everyone was in the process of grabbing gear and stuffing it into duffel bags. We were all wearing borrowed clothes and would be rolling with guns and equipment that wasn't ours.

I tore off the fake police uniform I'd been wearing since leaving the subway and began pulling on a Saratoga Hammer suit. Top was next to me, buckling on a gun belt. "Not trying to dodge all the fun and games, Cap'n, but why are we rolling on this? There are two teams closer."

"Everyone's already deployed," I told him. "There's so much shit going on that most teams are split into two-man squads. As of right now, Echo has more manpower. So it falls to us."

"Even though we're America's most wanted?" asked Montana, who stood next to Top, hooking flash-bangs on her belt.

"That's not how it's playing out," I said. "The public and the press are looking for that team in the subway, but nobody has a face or a name. We're rolling out with DEA stenciled on our body armor. Nobody's looking twice at a DEA team right now."

Doubt flickered in her eyes, but she gave me a tight nod.

We grabbed our equipment and hauled ass to ground level, where Church's private Lear was waiting, engine hot, door open. We piled in, Coop slammed the door, and seconds later we were climbing high and fast, leaving Brooklyn behind. Ghost huddled down by the door, his hair standing on end, eyes filled with a lupine wariness. As we flew, we loaded every spare magazine we had and prayed that we were not already too late.

Church called before we even hit cruising altitude.

"Tell me something good," I asked. Or, maybe, begged.

He told me about the release of the *seif-al-din* in a Best Buy in Willow Grove, Pennsylvania. Mother Night's people had used big tractor trailers to block front and back doors, and then they released a couple of dozen infected into the store during a doorbuster sale of a new video game.

"Are there any survivors?" I asked.

"No," Church said wearily. "But no infected have escaped. The trucks kept everything contained and local SWAT have the area locked down. However, the entire thing was broadcast live via cameras apparently placed inside the store."

My stomach felt like it was filled with raw sewage. "The press is going to keep on this, you know. They're going to want to show everything, maybe hoping for a response like to what we did in the subway."

"No doubt."

"If you wipe out the infected, they'll see that, and if you don't—and people get wind of what's really going on in there . . . Christ, we're screwed either way."

"And all the confusion, public outrage, and panic serves Mother Night."

I wanted to bang my head on a wall. Or maybe toss myself out of the damn jet. Would have simplified the day.

"You know," I said, "thinking back on it, I can see how Bliss got here. Some of the things she asked. The kinds of trouble she got into with Auntie. The opportunities she had. It's not unlike Hugo Vox."

"Yes," said Church, "power corrupts. It's not the first time I've heard that."

He disconnected.

But he was back in less than five minutes. It wasn't about Bliss's possible friends and it sure as hell wasn't good news.

"Captain," he said in a voice from which all emotion and inflection had been crushed, "at 10:01 this morning we lost all contact with the Locker."

Chapter Eighty-one

Reconnaissance General Bureau
Special Office #103
Pyongyang, Democratic People's Republic of Korea
Monday, September 1, 10:09 a.m. EST

Colonel Sim Sa-jeong mopped sweat from his face as he watched the numbers flow from the account he managed for the Democratic People's Republic of Korea and into the numbered account of that witch, Mother Night.

He had won the auction, though barely.

Three-hundred and seventy-eight million euros. Nearly half a billion in U.S. dollars. Nearly one quarter of his yearly operating budget. And all for a weapon that the supreme leader might never have the courage to use. In his private mind, Sim knew that the young leader was more bluster than bite. Would he dare to use a bioweapon of such devastating power as the *seif-al-din*? Apart from the commonsense question as to whether such a weapon could ever be used with even a prayer of controlling it, the knowledge that North Korea had it could be disastrous. The entire world would fear the country, no doubt, and that was what Kim Jong-un truly wanted. But they would also become a unified force against Sim's beloved country. North Korea would become an island in a sea of enemies. No one would dare invade them, but would anyone trade with them? Would fear of the prion-based pathogen force the world to defer to North Korea and treat it like a global supreme power?

Sim had his doubts.

But now the money was paid.

The only grace was that all of the bidders were blind as to the nationality and personal identity of the others. No one yet knew that the Democratic People's Republic of Korea had bought the world's most dangerous weapon. Only Sim, the supreme leader, and Mother Night knew.

For now.

His computer screen changed to indicate that the money transfer was complete.

Sweat ran in lines down Sim's face as he waited for the last part. The coded message with instructions on where and how to take possession of the *seif-al-din*.

An icon appeared. A symbol of the English letter A surrounded by a circle.

Below it were the words, in Korean, CLICK HERE.

Sim did as instructed.

Nothing happened for a few moments, but he waited with all of the patience he could muster.

Then the display changed again. The letter-A symbol expanded until it filled the entire screen. It paused for a moment, then dissolved into a cartoon version of the face of Mother Night. The cartoon image was laughing.

Laughing.

Then everything went crazy.

The computer system isolated and disabled its own keyboard and mouse. He tried pressing CONTROL, ALT, and DELETE simultaneously, but that did nothing.

Nothing that he was aware of at that moment.

In truth, those keys unlocked the Trojan horse that had been planted in his system by Mother Night during the auction. Once unlocked, hundreds of viruses and tapeworms invaded Sim's computer and, via its wi-fi and landline connections, plunged into the intranet used by his department. From there it raced onward, infecting thousands of computers through the Democratic People's Republic of Korea. Copying files, destroying security protocols, interpolating data, shutting down every system and program that could be used to defend against cyberattacks. And in flash-bursts it sent all of that data back out to the Net.

To Britain and Israel.

To Japan.

To South Korea.

To China and Russia.

To America.

To the major press agencies in more than one hundred nations.

And while that was happening, a secondary set of programs reinitiated the banking transfer order, using Sim's passwords for authorization. Three separate sets of transfers began. Each one taking a remaining third of Sim's annual budget. Two billion in American dollars.

It was all so fast.

By the time Sim realized that he could not stop the process and tore the battery out of his computer, the damage was done.

Everyone knew that North Korea had just paid two billion dollars for a doomsday plague.

Chapter Eighty-two

"No, Mr. President," said Mr. Church, "we can't prove any of this yet. However, this is the most credible way for the pieces to fit."

On the big screen the president of the United States looked like the victim of a violent mugging. He was gaunt, his eyes and cheeks were hollowed out by stress, the lines on his face seemed to have been carved there by a rough hand.

"I'll be addressing the nation again in a few minutes," he said. "My advisors are telling me not to, that right now the people don't want to see my face anywhere except with a noose around my neck. In their shoes I couldn't blame them. That video is damning."

"Bug's pulled it apart."

"I know, he sent it to my people and they're trying to decide how best to present that information to the public without it looking weak, phony, and desperate."

"Good luck with that."

The president bristled. "Is that sarcasm, Deacon?"

"No, Mr. President, it's heartfelt. I believe you will need all the luck you can muster, and I sincerely wish you well."

Some of the tension leaked from the president's face, and he nodded. "Sorry. I'm a bit on edge."

"We all are. Right now I have teams on their way to——" His cell buzzed and Church glanced at it. "One moment, Mr. President," he said. "This may be news."

He picked up the phone, listened for a moment.

"Send it to my screen. I'm on with the president." He set his phone down. "Mr. President, I believe you need to see this."

The big screen split and the other half was filled by Anderson Cooper. Two small pictures flanked the reporter. One was a screen capture of the Mother Night video from yesterday. The other was a picture of Supreme Leader Kim Jong-un. The text banner below the pictures read: BIOTERRORISM.

". . . in a bizarre twist on the catastrophic events of the last twenty-four hours, sources now confirm that North Korean president Kim Jong-un has purchased a deadly weaponized pathogen—a so-called doomsday weapon—from the terrorist calling herself Mother Night . . ."

The president of the United States said, "Dear God . . ."

Chapter Eighty-three

The Locker

Sigler-Czajkowski Biological and Chemical Weapons Facility

Highland County, Virginia

Monday, September 1, 10:17 a.m.

He thought it was funny.

He thought everything was funny.

The looks on their faces.

The screams.

The bright blood, red as balloons.

The way they tried to run from him.

The way they tried to play hide-and-seek with him. Well, the way they tried to hide from him.

So funny.

All so fucking funny.

Like the two women who managed the data-processing office. One was as fat as the Goodyear blimp and the other looked like a pencil with boobs. Jack Sprat and his wife. An imperfect comparison, but he didn't care. It was funny to think of them that way. The fat one trying to squeeze into a closet, screaming, crying, snot running down over her lips and chin. As if she could cram her fat ass into a closet that wasn't even deep enough for the skinny one.

And the skinny one. Hiding under a desk. Silly bitch. How can you expect to hide under a desk if you give yourself away by screaming at the top of your lungs?

Silly, silly, silly.

And funny.

The way her hands just came off when he swung the axe. They leaped up and landed on the seat of the leather roller chair. One on top of the other, like pancakes. He couldn't have managed that if he'd tried. He tried to get her head to land up there, too, but his aim was bad and her skull just fell apart.

But that was funny, too.

It was all funny.

The brains were delicious, too. So sweet. Filled with secrets. Better even than the flesh of their breasts, which he thought was the best thing he'd ever eaten. A naughty pleasure that made him chuckle guilty little chuckles with each bite.

Later, he stood in the doorway to the data office. Blood ran in twisty lines down his clothes, and it plop-plopped from the blade of the fire axe. It misted the air when he laughed because there was so much of it on his face.

He was sure some of it was his blood.

But that was okay.

That was funny.

It was all funny.

He turned away from the chunks and lumps, trying to remember their names. He should know their names, having eaten their brains. He was sure they *had* names. He'd known them for three years. But the names slipped away like greasy eels.

He thought about that image and laughed and laughed.

And laughed.

And laughed.

And laughed.

And laughed.

And . . .

Chapter Eighty-four

Pennsylvania Airspace
Sunday, September 1, 10:23 a.m.

I gathered my team and broke the news to them.

"Here's what I know. We've lost all communication with the Locker. That includes landlines, cells, computers, the works. It happened in a way that somehow prevented the automatic systems from notifying anyone. In fact, from the outside during automatic checks by computers it appears as if things are normal. When MindReader pinged the system the automatic status sent back an all-clear message. It was only after Aunt Sallie tried to call them to have on-site security coordinate with us that she hit a dead line. All attempts to reestablish contact have been negative. Because the automatic replies were still functioning there's no way to know exactly when the facility was actually compromised. Last verbal contact of record was nine thirty last night."

"How the fuck are we just finding this out now?" asked Lydia. "I thought Auntie confirmed that the place was secure."

I sighed. "It's set up for computer confirmation rather than person-to-person. It was a design element that keyed a request from the Hangar directly to the Locker's security systems. Ask for a status report and it runs an immediate diagnostic that excludes the possibility of human coercion."

"Except when one of the world's smartest computer experts rigs the system."

"Yup. And I'm pretty sure Mr. Church is going to fry Aunt Sallie for not speaking directly to a human being," I said. It's possible my total lack of sympathy for Auntie was evident in my tone.

Top grunted. "Maybe that was built into the plan. Mother Night's been jerking us in so many damn directions it's likely she knew that this sort of slipup might happen."

That thought had occurred to me, too, though I felt ungracious enough not to admit it. Aunt Sallie had threatened to neuter my dog. Ghost seemed to catch my train of thought and bared a fang.

"Whoa, whoa, wait a minute," said Bunny. "I'm having a hard time buying that the Locker's been taken. I thought that couldn't happen."

"*Titanic* couldn't sink either, Farmboy," muttered Top.

"No, I mean aren't there like ten kinds of redundancies?"

"At least," I said. "There are separate backup landlines for the computers and phones, ditto for wi-fi and cells. The redundancies are both passive and active. The passive ones go active when the primary signal is interrupted; the active ones randomly ping the system and go active when they don't get a reply. And we have some phantom lines that even the people at the Locker don't know about. These can be remotely activated on Mr. Church's say-so."

"Which he gave?" asked Top.

"Which he gave," I agreed. "However, no one's picking up the phone, and now even the computers have stopped responding."

"Is the Locker the prize in this whole game?" asked Noah. "Or is this another way to thin us out to the point where we're effectively useless?"

Of all the newbies he was the one whose personality I hadn't quite grasped. Montana was a tough country woman with the professional skeptical cynicism of the FBI. Dunk was a solid team player with a sense of humor that was probably a façade over some kind of personal hurt. Maybe an idealist wearing the uniform because he actually thought it would make a difference. But Noah was a blank, a mask. In some ways he reminded me of a shooter who'd run with my pack a couple of years ago, a laconic man named John Smith. He'd been the best sniper in the U.S. military, the hammer of God in a firefight; but he kept everything in. He never shared his opinions or feelings, never let anything show. Was Noah cut from the same cloth, another internalizer and self-imposed loner? Or was his bland mask hiding complexities he didn't want to share? Wish I had the time to find out.

"We don't know," I said. "We're operating on guesswork and supposition."

"Is stealing those things from the Locker really a possibility?" asked Montana. "Can that facility be cracked and looted?"

"If you had asked me that question this afternoon I'd have told you no. Not without a computer like MindReader and a security strategist as savvy as Bug. Things have changed, which sucks for all of us." I switched on a tabletop computer and brought up the floor plan of the Locker.

As I loaded the screens, Bunny mused, "I didn't know her real well, but well enough. When the hell did she become evil?"

"Not the first time that question's been asked," I said. "We know she went off the reservation when she started stealing classified materials, but when did she cross the line to the point where she was willing to take lives? I don't know."

I thought back to some of the conversations I'd had with Bliss. About the nature of good and evil, and of where evil came from. About nature, nurture, and choice. She'd brought those topics up. Was she looking for how to put her ethics and compassion on a shelf? Or kill those qualities within her life? I think so, and it made me feel sick to think that I played a part, however small and tangential, to that process. Part of me felt sorry for her. I'd known her pretty well, and I'd liked her a lot. I thought she was part of the family, and even after she'd been arrested, I wished her well. I was sorry when the judge threw the book at her, and sorrier still when I thought she'd been murdered in prison. Those feelings were still inside me, warring with the apparent truth that Bliss had become a murderous monster.

The civilized man inside my mind was appalled and refused to accept that such things were possible. The cop was far more worldly and cynical. He knew about the pathology of all kinds of criminals. After all, everyone is innocent until they commit their first crime. Even Hitler was innocent once. And Charles Manson.

Could we—the experts in the DMS—have spotted this thread of damage in Bliss? Should we have spotted it sooner? Aunt Sallie saw it and stopped trusting Bliss months before she was able to bring charges.

Hu never saw it, though. Nor did Rudy.

I didn't.

And Church? Who the hell knows what he saw, but I know that he couldn't have anticipated this level of treachery or criminality.

This level of evil.

The third voice inside my head—the warrior, the killer—was not trying to figure it out or assign blame. All he wanted to do was hunt that other killer, to find the enemy and destroy her.

He was banging on the bars of his cell, demanding to be let out.

Soon, I knew, I would want to do just that.

Once more Ghost sensed what was in my mind, and the look in his eyes made that subtle and dangerous shift from dog to wolf.

Part Five
First-Person Shooter

When Alexander heard from Anaxarchus of the infinite number of worlds, he wept, and when his friends asked him what was the matter, he replied, "Is it not a matter for tears that, when the number of worlds is infinite, I have not conquered one?"

—PLUTARCH, *Life of Alexander*

Chapter Eighty-five

Centers for Disease Control and Prevention
Special Pathogens Branch
Building 18
Atlanta, Georgia
Sunday, September 1, 11:02 a.m.

Colonel Samson Riggs leaned out the side door of the Black Hawk and studied the target. The building was modern but awkward, with wings of various sizes jammed in together, and with walkways and shrubbery covering the grounds. The streets were blocked off by police vehicles and everything was washed in overlapping red and blue lights. There were already crowds of pedestrians, including a fair number of kids from Emory, but the local law had set their barricades hundreds of yards back. The grounds immediately around the buildings were empty and dark. Inside the building a few night lights glowed.

Nothing moved.

Like the four remaining members of Shockwave Team, Riggs was dressed in an unmarked black battledress uniform. Unlike them, he wore no helmet. Instead, a Chicago Cubs cap was snugged down on his head. He tapped his earbud for a clear channel to the pilot. "Set us down here, Corkscrew."

"Roger."

The colonel felt tired. Usually a mission of this kind would have him jazzed and jumpy, ready to rock and roll as soon as boots were on the ground. But not today. His team was as somber as he was.

What was left of his team.

There had been no time for the shock and grief and wrongness of that to process through Riggs's mind. The only thing that kept it firm was the thought that the people responsible for the deaths of his team and so many

356 | Jonathan Maberry

other deaths around the country might be taking a run at the CDC tonight. If so, then tired or not, he was going to do them ungodly harm.

Riggs was old for the field, pushing forty-five pretty hard, and he could feel every one of those years. He'd been a sailor, a SEAL, a CIA shooter, and for the last seven years he'd run the number-one team in the Department of Military Sciences. Only Captain Ledger's Echo Team was racking up stats like Shockwave, but they were a newer team, assembled four years ago. By the time Echo had turned out for its first mission, Shockwave had already stormed the gates of hell more times than Riggs could count.

As the helo swung into position, Riggs watched his team get ready. Only his sniper, Rico, had been with him since the first mission. So many others had come and gone. It was the way of things when you worked for the Deacon.

The Black Hawk sank slowly toward the macadam.

His second in command, Carrie Marchman, hunkered down behind the minigun, the barrels pointed down at the building. The other members of the team finished their buddy checks of each others' gear and clustered by the door.

"Okay, heroes, listen up. Latest intel says that the building's security system is online, Aunt Sallie has been in direct voice contact with the senior security officer, Lieutenant Neale. He reports all clear. The building has a six-person security force, all armed, all former police officers. Neale will meet us at the rear loading door."

"Neale's a friendly?" asked Marchman.

"We treat him as such, but we are going to ask him to surrender his weapon and stand down while we search the building. No assumptions, feel me?"

"Hooah," they all said.

"Combat call signs from here on," said Riggs. "I want a clean dispersal." He nodded to Rico. "Gangbanger, you take up a shooting position behind that trash can. See it? It offers the widest target range around the door. Hipster and Gomer watch side-to-side. Once we're inside, we'll split into two teams. Wicked Witch and Gomer with me going upstairs; Gangbanger and Hipster go downstairs."

Hipster glanced at the building. "That's a lot of real estate for five people to clear."

"Well, life sucks just a little bit, don't it?" said Gomer.

The wheels of the Black Hawk had barely touched the ground when Samson Riggs was first out, with Shockwave following.

As they approached the rear loading bay, a uniformed man stepped outside. He wore a billed cap, a holstered pistol, and a broad smile. He raised his hand in a friendly greeting as the group of killers converged on him.

Chapter Eighty-six

Maryland Airspace
Sunday, September 1, 11:07 a.m.

We landed on a private airfield thirty miles from the Locker. Bird Dog and his crew from the Warehouse in Baltimore met us with a pair of fully loaded Black Hawks. The helos dusted off as the last of us scrambled aboard.

Church called me with a quick update and I shared the intel with my guys.

"Aunt Sallie was able to contact Dr. Myles Van Sant, the director of the Locker," I told them. "He had the day off and was on a fishing trip, camping in the nearby woods with a friend—Buddy Scarf, the local sheriff. Van Sant was ordered back to the Locker, but his radio and cell phone went dead shortly after entering the building. No way to know if he ran into hostiles or if there was a signal jammer. Bug's working on determining that. There has been no further communication with anyone inside the Locker."

"Dingo balls," grumbled Ivan. He was one of those guys who was never quite happy about anything. Not a complainer in a way that would interfere with team efficiency, but not a cheerleader by any stretch.

"What about Van Sant's fishing buddy?" asked Lydia. "We sending him to see what's what?"

"No," I said. "The sheriff's department is too small to be anything but collateral damage. A Homeland SWAT team is on the ground, and they've secured a perimeter one mile out. Nothing gets in or out, and they've been ordered to stay well clear of the facility. They don't have the same generation of protective gear as we do."

"Wouldn't a hazmat suit work?" asked Dunk.

"No," I said. "There are at least three different bacterial agents stored at the Locker that are designed to specifically feed on the materials used in hazmat suit seals."

"Jesus Christ," said Dunk. "This shit is insane."

Bunny popped his gum and grinned at him.

"The governor of Virginia is rolling out the National Guard," I said, "but we'll be on the ground before them. They'll reinforce the perimeter."

"Nice to know we're not completely alone with our balls hanging out," said Ivan.

"Okay," I said to the group, "questions?"

"What do we know about Van Sant and Scarf?" asked Sam.

I tapped my earbud. "Bug—? Give us the lowdown on Dr. Van Sant."

Immediately photos of two men appeared on screens of our forearm-mounted tactical computers. One man was dressed as a rural cop, the other in a lab coat. "Dr. Van Sant is clean as a whistle as far as MindReader can tell," said Bug. "He's a longtime friend of Mr. Church, and was a thesis advisor for Dr. Hu. His background check is squeaky clean. Couple speeding tickets because he bought a sports car when middle age set in, but otherwise nothing. We're looking at him, but nobody expects him to be a bad guy here."

"What was his relationship with Artemisia Bliss?" asked Montana.

"Van Sant testified against Bliss at her trial. I don't think they're down there doing the dirty boogie together."

Noah nodded at the second picture. "What about Sheriff Scarf? What's his story?"

"Bryan 'Buddy' Scarf did twelve years in the army," said Bug, "the last six as an M.P. at the beginning of the Iraq war. Clean service record and honorable discharge nine years ago. He had people out in this part of Virginia, so he came here and ran unopposed for sheriff, got the job, and he's been doing it as well as a place with less than three thousand people requires in an area where the closest thing they have to capital crime is growing an acre of pot."

"How hard are we looking at him?"

I answered that. "Bug's going deep on *everyone* at the Locker, and anyone even tangentially associated with it."

"Wait," asked Ivan. "If Van Sant was off the clock, who was running the place?"

Bug sent another picture to our screens. A bookish Indian woman with a rather severe ponytail and thick glasses. "The senior researcher on duty was Dr. Noor Jehan. She and Van Sant are the only ones who had the day code to access all of the secure areas. But Dr. Jehan hasn't made any attempt to reach out, or at least no successful attempt."

Lydia popped her chewing gum. "Y'know, Bug, no offense, but I'm finding it hard to believe that you can't find a way into their computer systems."

Bug cursed. A rarity for him, and it wasn't aimed at Lydia. It was simply that he was deeply frustrated.

"I know," said Bug sourly, "but it's like trying to push your finger through a solid brick wall. No doors, no windows, no nothing. We're completely shut out."

"*MindReader*'s shut out," said Lydia, not making a question of it. Putting it out there so we could all chew on it and everything it might mean. "You're breaking my heart, *Bicho*."

Bug sniffed. "We just found out that this was Artie Bliss. I'm shifting mental gears as fast as I can." He paused and maybe there was some edge to his voice. "Don't get me wrong, kids, I *will* beat this *bruja*."

He used the Spanish word for "witch" for Lydia's benefit.

"Bug," I said, "give me the floor plan of the Locker."

A 3D model of the place assembled itself on our screens.

Bug said, "The Locker is built into an old coal mine that played out in the seventies. Government bought it and Mr. Church acquired it when he founded the DMS. The top level has two parts, administration offices in the back and a tractor parts store up front. The store's legit insofar as they actually sell tractor parts, but the staff's ours, of course. Lots of buttons to push if anyone tries to rush the place."

"Any of those buttons get pushed?" asked Ivan.

"Not a one."

"Donkey balls," he said.

Bug highlighted elements of the schematic as he continued. "Once you go past the store, there are a series of security doors. Outer level is keycard, but beyond that you hit doors with retina scans, geometry palm scanners, and variable-signal keycards. You go through those to get to the elevators, and there's a drop of three quarters of a mile. Halfway down, on level two, are the crew quarters. The labs and containment facilities are all on levels three through seven, with the highest-security chambers at the bottom."

"Didn't I see this shit on Resident Evil?" complained Lydia. "I mean, this is the fucking Umbrella Corporation right here."

"You aren't joking," Bug said. "You'd be surprised how many high-tech facilities show up in video games. The design team works them into popular games and then watches to see how long it takes the game geeks to think their way through. The results could make a security expert turn to heroin. Ultra-advanced no-fail designs are beaten by fourteen-year-old kids in a weekend."

"You shitting me?" demanded Dunk.

"No. DARPA's been doing it for a long time. Homeland uses game simulations to work up protocols for terrorist attacks. Everyone does it. And Artemisia Bliss created a killer of a game called VaultBreaker that was designed to test the security of every major facility and high-profile base in the country. It was great, too, because it led to over ninety significant security improvements."

"Bliss did that?" said Montana dryly. "Anyone else getting chills?"

"We made a lot of changes after Artie was arrested," said Bug. "But now that we know it's Bliss and knowing that she might have a system like MindReader, then it's possible she really did read the data on the Vault-Breaker disk Reggie Boyd gave her. A system like that could fool the anti-intrusion programs written onto the disk."

"Fuck me." Montana shook her head. "So this Mother Night bitch could be in there waiting for us."

Bug didn't answer.

Lydia cut in. "Could VaultBreaker be used to crack the security at the Locker?"

When neither Bug nor I answered, Ivan said, "Well, kick me in the balls."

Chapter Eighty-seven

Centers for Disease Control and Prevention
Special Pathogens Branch
Building 18
Atlanta, Georgia
Sunday, September 1, 11:08 a.m.

Colonel Riggs placed the laser site of his pistol on the center of Lieutenant Neale's chest.

"Stand right there, hands out to the side," he warned.

Carrie Marchman—call sign Wicked Witch—angled in from the side and took the security chief's weapon and gave him a fast pat-down. Hipster stood nearby providing cover.

"Everything's fine here," said Neale quickly. He was a nervous man with a sweaty face and bright eyes. Was it fear of what might be happening on his watch or the sudden excitement for a man whose usual day-to-day life was quiet to the point of tedium? In either case, he didn't want the man walking around with a loaded gun. Bad aim and bad intel weren't the only reasons for "friendly fire" deaths; bad nerves and bad aim accounted for a lot of it. "Really," insisted Neale, "my team did two full sweeps since receiving your call."

"This will make three, then," said Riggs.

Neale looked up at Riggs. "Are you FBI or NSA? They didn't say."

Riggs ignored the question. "Where are your people?"

"Everyone's inside. I was told to have them all meet you in the conference room."

"Good. Let's go."

They entered the building. Rico—Gangbanger—moved in and cut left and stood at an angle that offered a clear view of the entire room. It was a large receiving and storage room. Towers of boxed supplies stood in neat rows under the downspill of fluorescent lights. The air was cool and very dry. Gomer raised his BAMS unit and turned in a slow circle.

"Green," he said.

Riggs signaled for Hipster to walk ahead of the line with Neale while he faded back to call in. He tapped his earbud and spoke quietly. "Big Kahuna to TOC, copy?"

Aunt Sallie was managing the Tactical Operations Center with Yoda online for real-time field support. "Go for Auntie. What's your status, Big Kahuna?"

"So far it's all quiet. We're going to interview the security staff. Where are we on thermals?"

"Satellite's in position," said Yoda. "Reading two clusters of signatures. Group of six in the loading bay—"

"That's Shockwave plus one. How's the signal strength?"

"Spotty. Lot of shielding in that structure. Some of your signals are weak."

"What about the other cluster?"

"Reading seven—no, correct that, five—bodies in the first-level conference room. Wait, it's seven again. No. Damn, the signal is really fruity."

"Kick the damn thing," said Riggs.

"It's a satellite—"

"Find a way to give me clear intel. We're expecting five friendlies. I need to know if there are two unknown signals or not."

"The other signals are gone. Might have been ghosts created by interference."

"Big Kahuna," said Aunt Sallie, "proceed with caution. We'll sort out the technical details a.s.a.p."

"Kahuna out."

He checked his BAMS unit and saw the comforting green light.

Neale produced a keycard and opened the door into the main facility, led them down a maze of empty corridors lit only by soft night lights, and finally to the door of a large conference room. The security lieutenant swiped his card and opened the door. Gangbanger and Hipster had their weapons up, covering the room as they entered. Five men stood inside, each wearing uniforms identical to Neale's. They all looked nervous as Shockwave team poured into the room.

No, thought Riggs. *They looked scared.*

The conference room was dominated by a massive oak table and twenty chairs, the walls lined with sideboards and a coffee station. Two big black metal storage cabinets stood against the rear wall, looking incongruous, towering like obelisks.

Four things happened at exactly the same time.

Yoda was suddenly yelling in his ear. "Big Kahuna, confirmed seven signals. Repeat, confirmed *there are seven signals in the conference room.*"

The light on the BAMS unit flicked from neutral green to a bright and burning red.

Every guard in the room tore pistols from holsters and pointed their weapons at Shockwave.

And the doors of the metal cabinets flew open as two figures burst forth, shedding lead-shielded X-ray capes.

They were Berserkers.

Then two more things happened as the moment slid into hell.

Lieutenant Neale, still smiling his nervous smile, flung himself at Wicked Witch and buried his teeth in her cheek.

And the air was rent by the sounds of screams and gunfire.

Chapter Eighty-eight

Virginia Airspace
Sunday, September 1, 11:12 a.m.

"Let's not dig graves yet," said Top. He sat on an ammunition box, running his fingers through Ghost's thick fur. "Even if Mother Night is inside the Locker, that doesn't mean she's strolling through there putting important shit into her purse. There's a thirty-man security team, and none of them are pussies." He touched various points on the floor plans. "And there are airlocks at multiple points. You can't just punch in a code and waltz through. Takes some human interaction."

"So what?" asked Dunk.

"So all of that's going to take time," he said.

"Can we predict how much time?" asked Montana. "I mean, where are the labs with the pathogens?"

Top nodded. "That's my point. The Ark is all the way down at the bottom. On Level Fourteen. Something like eight airlocks between the front door and the prize."

"What's the Ark?" asked Noah.

I tapped some keys to bring up an image of a metal cylinder that looked like a portable decompression chamber. It was heavy, wrapped in bands of tempered steel and studded with massive bolts. The thing squatted on a wheeled cradle.

"The Ark," I said, "is a special containment system in which samples of every bioweapon, pathogen, and genetically engineered disease in the world is stored. It is the single deadliest repository of biological agents anywhere on earth."

Everyone looked as pale as ghosts.

Ivan said, "Dangling gorilla balls."

I expanded the image again to show the airlock that provided access to the Ark. "That's the only door that accesses Level Fourteen. It's four feet thick and armed with thermite charges that can be remote-detonated by the duty officer, the security officer, or Mr. Church. There are similar charges inside the Ark. There are also fail-safes in the event of tampering. The idea was that even if somehow the Ark was ever stolen, those charges could be set off. The door charges would seal the vault where the Ark is stored, but if the thing is removed from the vault the charges inside would incinerate everything. Even the prions in the *seif-al-din* would be turned to carbon dust."

"Shouldn't we just send that signal now?" asked Dunk, then he corrected himself. "I suppose that command function was lost when the place was compromised?"

"Yup," I said. "So we better all pray to God that Mother Night and her team has not breached Level Fourteen. Because believe me when I tell you that if there is a genuine entrance to hell, then that is it."

There was a *bing-bing* and the pilot said, "We're here."

Chapter Eighty-nine

Centers for Disease Control and Prevention
Special Pathogens Branch
Building 18
Atlanta, Georgia
Sunday, September 1, 11:12 a.m.

Samson Riggs heard much more than he could see in those first moments.

He heard Yoda shouting in his ear, warning him of the hidden thermal signatures. He heard Aunt Sallie demanding a sit-rep. He heard gunfire as everyone in the room—the security team, the Berserkers, and his own people—opened up and created a maelstrom of tumbling lead, wood splinters, shattered glass, torn flesh, and flying blood.

He heard Wicked Witch shriek as Lieutenant Neale—if it truly was Neale—tore at her face with his teeth.

He heard the roar of the Berserkers. Massive, ugly sounds that hurt the ears and threatened to crack the world.

And he heard his own voice.

Shouting.

Screaming.

Bullets punched him back against the edge of the door frame, but the Kevlar kept him alive. The impact was fierce, though, and black flowers bloomed all around him. Then something big and dark came at him from his left. A Berserker. Three hundred and fifty pounds of muscle and rage.

It was yesterday morning all over again. Blood and monsters. His people were dying. The world was trying to kill him.

The Berserker's hands filled his vision as it leaped at him.

And that's when Samson Riggs felt that burn, that high, that adrenaline rush. He heard his scream change into a roar, felt his mouth curl into a brutal smile.

At the edge of death he came alive.

He went in and down, twisting right as the Berserker lunged; Riggs chopped sideways with an elbow, knocking the monster's mass over and past him. The creature hit the corner of the door frame, spun awkwardly, and fell outside in the hall. Riggs drew his pistol as he rose. He fired, fired, fired. A security guard with a bloody mouth staggered away from the bullets, his face disintegrating. Another clutched at his throat and vomited blood.

Gomer was beside Riggs, but the young man was not firing. His gun hung limply from one hooked finger as his body juddered and danced with convulsions as the infection from his bites did their terrible work. He gave Riggs one terrified, despairing look and the colonel shot him between the eyes.

He saw a third guard's head snap back as Gangbanger punched a round through his eye socket. But then Gangbanger screamed as the second Berserker plowed into him and bowled him over behind the conference table. Blood splattered the walls.

Riggs fired at the Berserker, but then someone grabbed both of his ankles and yanked with such sudden ferocity that Riggs fell forward. Too hard, and too fast. He got one hand and both forearms out in time to try to break his fall but the force was too overwhelming.

His chin hit his right wrist and his gun went spinning across the floor.

Riggs twisted around as the Berserker from the hallway began climbing up his body. He saw a massive fist driving down toward his face.

And then the world became a fractured dreamscape of red and black and nothing.

Chapter Ninety

We came in low, making maximum use of cover from the forest and the mountain slopes, and we swung around so the sun was behind us. The road leading to the tractor store snaked along, looking like it came from nowhere and went nowhere. The store was a wide spot on it, high up on the mountainside. There were six vehicles in the parking lot. One late-model gray Lexus—Van Sant's car—one SUV, and the rest were pickups. This was Ford country.

Well beyond the building, we could see the SWAT teams at the one-mile perimeter. Lots of guns, lots of backup if this got weird and spilled out into the open.

My earbud buzzed and Church was there. "Deacon to Cowboy."

"Go for Cowboy.

"Be advised, Shockwave Team has encountered significant resistance at the second location."

"What kind of—?"

"We have lost all contact with them," said Church. "It is possible we have lost those assets."

Lost those assets.

I sagged against the door frame as my heart turned to ice. How can three small, clinical words truly carry the weight of their meaning? The assets were people I knew and cared about, including my friend and role model, Samson Riggs.

Lost?

There was only one meaning for that word and it was so huge and ugly that I wanted to close it out on the other side of the door. To deny its reality. The Civilized Man inside my head felt close to tears. The Warrior wanted to taste blood.

Beside me Ghost whined softly.

Church gave me no time for grief, though. "Give me a sit-rep."

In as human a voice as I could manage, I said, "We're at the landing zone."

"Cowboy," said Church, "Shockwave walked into a trap. Expect the same and proceed accordingly."

The words were as clinical as the others, but the meaning was very clear and filled with an anger Church would never allow himself to show. He was telling us that the rule book had just been run through a shredder. The Warrior grinned at that thought.

"We know we're being played," I growled. "Maybe her endgame is the Easter Egg." That was the radio code name for the Ark. "And maybe not. Either way, she has to know we're coming. If she expects to take possession of the package, then she has to clear the road. That means if she's here, then she has to cancel us out. If she's not here herself . . . then we need to determine where the handoff will be. It's got to be a place she can control. Somewhere we can't control."

"Do you have anything in mind."

"Yeah. Tell Bug that this is on him. Mother Night is his to find. He needs to crawl inside her head and figure out where she will be to take possession of the Easter Egg."

"Yes," said Church. "And Captain . . . good hunting."

I looked at my team. We were all on the same channel, so they heard the news, too. There was hurt on their faces. And fear. And one hell of a lot of murderous rage.

"Listen to me," I said, keeping my voice level. "I know that we all want a piece of Mother Night. We want to tear her world apart. But we can't go in hot and stupid. That will get us killed and guarantee her a win. We keep our shit tight. We watch each other's backs, we pick our targets, conserve our ammunition, and if we have to pull triggers then we kill the enemy. But we do it cold. You hear me?"

"Hooah," they said. They all said it. That might have been the moment when Noah, Dunk, and Montana stopped being newbies and became Echo Team for real. I thought that's what I saw in their eyes. I hoped that's what I saw.

"Then lock and load," I told them.

I tapped my earbud. "Cowboy to Birddog."

"Go for Birddog," he replied. He was the crew chief on the second bird.

"Status on the stinkbots?"

"They're scratching at the door, boss."

"Then let 'em out."

The pilot of my chopper went high and wide, turning to give me a better view of the other helo. The side door on the second Black Hawk rolled back and I saw two figures crouching there, the folds of their hazmat suits whipping in the rotor wash. They each held a small machines that looked like a metal wasp. Elegant in an ugly way. Birddog—the biggest man on the tech team—leaned out and flung one of the drones into the wind. It swirled out of control for a moment, then as it reached the outer edge of the rotor wash its own engines stabilized it and it flew away smooth and straight. Another followed, and another.

The official designation for them was some gobbledy-gook like man-portable hand-launched self-propelled aerial bio-aerosol mass spectrometer. Flying BAMS units, for short. We called them stinkbots. Birddog gave them individual names. Huey, Dewey, and Louie.

Understand, Echo Team had to go in there, we had to see what was happening in the Locker even if the sensors on the stinkbots lit up like Christmas trees. However, there was a splinter of comfort in know exactly how high and how smelly was the pile of shit we were about to step in.

When the last of the stinkbots was deployed, Birddog rolled the door shut and the helo lifted high into the air. Top and Bunny huddled with me over the screen display on the tactical computer strapped to my forearm. Three small windows opened up to display the data feeds from the drones. Each box included a sliding color scale, safe green on one side and alarming red on the other. We were all clustered together so tightly that I could feel the waves of tension rolling off of the others, and it was a match for my own.

"What happens if we get a hit now?" asked Dunk. "Outside the containment?"

"Then you'd better be right with Jesus, son," muttered Top.

Dunk tried to laugh it off, tried to smile through it. No one else matched his grin, and it drained away pretty quickly.

I pointed at the ceiling of the Black Hawk. "Mr. Church is keyed in to the telemetry from the stinkbots. If the *seif-al-din* or any of the other class-A pathogens is out, then there's only one fallback plan. Total sterilization of everything within six square miles. Somewhere up there are fighter bombers carrying fuel-air bombs. And if that doesn't get the job done then to save the country they won't hesitate to turn this part of Virginia into a big, glowing hole in the world."

"That's some total wrinkled yak balls," observed Ivan.

Bunny gave them a frank stare. "If you were in the driver's seat on this, how would you play it?"

Ivan shook his head. "I'm not saying I'd do it any other way, Hoss. What I'm saying is that this is some total wrinkled yak balls right here."

Bunny considered. "Yeah. Can't argue with that."

Top snapped his fingers. "The stinkbots have processed the first air samples."

We looked. The feed was coming in from Huey. We stared at the sliding arrow and willed it to stay in the green. Dewey and Louie sent their data. The arrows on all three 'bots trembled.

Trembled.

But they stayed green. For now.

"I don't know whether to feel relieved," said Lydia, "or not."

"Not," said Bunny. "'Cause it means we still have to go in there."

"Yak balls," Ivan said again.

We all nodded.

"Okay," I told the pilot, "put us down."

Chapter Ninety-one

Residence of the Vice President of the United States
One Observatory Circle
Washington, D.C.
Sunday, September 1, 11:17 a.m.

Collins walked through the rooms of an empty house.

His wife was in Boston with the kids. It was a publicized event for her, a speech at a fund-raiser for one of her causes. Education or some such shit, he really didn't know and didn't care. All that mattered was that she was there and he was here. It was the forty-third day out of the last forty-nine that she'd been somewhere else. As he poured a scotch he had to admit to himself that she knew.

Somehow, despite all his precautions, she knew.

Not specifically about Bliss. Nor did she know, he was sure, about the two pages, the reporter from *USA Today*, or that French broad—what the fuck was her name? Amy Something?—from the European Trade Commission. There was no way for her to know specifics about any of them. No, it was simply that she knew. Knew he was screwing around. Knew their marriage was a joke, a thing that existed in name only. Knew that it was over for them. Just as he knew she would not officially leave him while there was even the slightest chance that he could become president. The power was too juicy. After all, Hillary didn't leave Bill even though everyone in the world knew he was dicking around. No, she wouldn't divorce him. She was married to the power.

But goddamn if the place didn't seem empty without her and the kids.

The Secret Service thugs downstairs and outside didn't qualify as company.

He went into his study, turned on the TV to watch the latest on the C-train thing, freshened his drink, and flung himself onto the couch. The press, in a remarkable and unprecedented show of solidarity, was frying the president for the slaughter. U.S. Special Forces in a mass execution of citizens. That was going to change the entire shape of the government.

His cell rang, and when he looked at the display it said MOM. He always appreciated that. If, for any reason, his phone records were subpoenaed they would show that the call did, in fact, originate from his mother; however, it was all part of the magic Bliss did with her little mutant computer

He debated whether to answer it or not. Every bit of contact with Bliss—or with Mother Night, as she insisted on being called—was a deadly risk.

"Fuck it," he mumbled, and punched the button.

"Hello, sonny boy," she said.

"Don't call me that," he growled. The voice simulation software she used as part of her scrambler technology did way too good a job of making her voice sound exactly like his mother's. It was freaky and it made him feel like he wanted to go wash his hands with strong soap.

She said, "Are you keeping up with current events?"

"Funny. Remote tribes in the Amazon know what's going on. You certainly went whole hog on this, honey. Talk about market saturation."

"Power of social media," she said. "They'll probably impeach your running mate. I may have just made you president."

"Yeah, yeah, yeah."

"Why are you so sour?" she asked.

He sipped his scotch and crunched some ice. "Really loved the anthrax thing. That was a bit of a surprise. They said there was enough anthrax in there to kill half of Washington."

"Not really. Maybe half of Congress, which wouldn't be as tragic."

"Tragic? Really? Do you even know what that concept is all about?"

"Of course I do," she said. "I'm immoral, not amoral."

"I wish you wouldn't sound so happy about it."

"Aren't you? Not about the anthrax, I mean. About the whole thing?"

"Happy? Of course I'm not happy. Christ, don't you know me yet?"

"Yeah, I know. You've given me the speech. It's not about destroying America, it's about rebuilding America. A patriot's revisionist view. Necessary evils, like performing an emergency amputation to prevent gangrene from spreading. Yes, Bill, I know the story."

"It's not a 'story,' damn it," he said, anger burning in his chest. "This is the only way to save—"

"—America from itself. Yes, I know," she insisted. "I really do know. Calm down."

"Don't fucking tell me to calm down, you crazy bitch. And don't you dare trivialize this. We're doing God's work here."

The silence on the other end of the line was profound and heavy, and it went on so long Collins thought she'd hung up.

"Are you there?" he demanded.

"Yes."

"Then fucking say something."

"What do you want me to say? We've always known that we come at this from two different places. What are you trying to do here? Try and convert me? It's never been about politics for me, so let's not pretend that I give a wet fart about it. Yours or anyone's."

"I can't believe that," he said with a gentleness that surprised even him. He lay back on the couch and stared up at the ceiling. "No matter what else you are, Bliss, you're an American. Maybe not by birth, but America gave you everything you have, everything you—"

"Don't even try," she interrupted. "You're going to give me that same tired old speech about how someone of my intellect would never have been allowed to shine if I'd grown up in China. How, as a woman, I'd never be given rank or status. Well, here's the newsflash, honey, I didn't get a lot of that here, either. I worked my ass off for America. I helped save the country from one threat after another, and if it wasn't for me, half of the DMS operations would have failed in whole or part. That means I saved millions of lives, Bill. Millions."

"I know and—"

"Let me finish," she snapped. "You always cut me off, you always think I'm just ranting. I let you go on and on about your New American Revolution, and you say I don't understand you. Well, now it's time for you to try to understand me. I put the best years of my life into the DMS. I even tried to work around their antiquated procedures in order to make them more efficient. And what did I get for it? I was never allowed to file patents and I was never allowed to publish. With my gifts I should have been world famous. I should have been on the cover of every magazine. When was the last time there was a superstar scientist of my caliber who wasn't an old white guy? I'm young, I'm pretty, and I deserve more than I was given. For every life I saved, for keeping the world from going to hell, for keeping the world from fucking ending, I deserved so much more than a pat on the back and a paycheck that amounted to pocket change. And let's not forget that I was fired and arrested because I was helping you. If you hadn't insisted on trying to take down the DMS I would never have been caught with my hand in the cookie jar. I literally gave my life for you. Artemisia Bliss died for you and your American dream. Mother Night won't make that kind of mistake, Bill. Not for you and not for anyone. America has let me down too many times. Now it's time for me to get what I deserve. And everything I deserve."

It was such a surreal thing for Collins to hear this passionate rant spoken in his mother's voice. He closed his eyes and rested the icy whiskey glass on his forehead.

Into the crushing silence, he said, "I hear you."

"Do you?" she asked harshly.

"Yes," he said, "I really do. And, no matter what else you think, please believe that I honestly want that for you. I want you to have all the things you deserve."

His words seemed to throw her, because the next thing she said was

"Look, Bill . . . about the anthrax. I knew it would never get anywhere near you. I thought it would help you, help reinforce you as a victim of this. Maybe point a finger at the presidency. Him as bad guy, you as one of the many Americans enduring the terrorist attacks, et cetera. You know?"

"It was clumsy."

"Was it? It worked, didn't it? People are glad you're alive. They see you as one of the targets of the wave of violence. That put you solidly into the good-guy category."

"Sure, sure," he said, sitting up so he could finish his drink. "Nicest present anyone ever gave me."

She laughed. A little too quickly, showing nerves and uncertainty. He made himself laugh, too.

"Seriously, Bliss, I appreciate the gesture. Really. As weird as it sounds right now, it's nice to know you have my health and well-being so much in mind."

"Always, big guy."

He sighed, long and slow. "You know . . . I'll miss you, you crazy bitch."

"We'll see each other again."

"Sure," he snorted. "In like two years if I don't run for the big chair. Longer if I get in. Probably never."

"We'll see each other."

"Even if we do, you won't even look the same."

She chuckled. Low and throaty, the way she used to. "Depends on how closely you look."

"Damn. Wish it was now. Where are you holed up?"

"C'mon, you know we can't play that game."

"Right, sorry. Guess I meant to say, 'What are you wearing?' "

She laughed again. A real laugh. "Trite and sleazy, but cute. I'm wearing a big smile, how's that?"

"Good enough. Keep smiling."

"Bill . . . ?"

"Yeah?"

"I hope you get what you deserve, too."

The line went dead, and Collins slumped back against the cushions and did not move for ten minutes. Then he sighed once more and punched in a number on his cell. The call was answered almost at once, as he expected it would be.

"Yes," said a male voice. Neutral, soft.

"Did you trace the call?"

"Yes."

"Where?"

The man gave him an address.

"How soon can you take care of this?"

"Local assets are already in motion."

"Call me when it's done."

Collins switched off the phone and got up to build one more drink. On the TV, reporters were interviewing people who wanted the president to be impeached and arrested for the subway massacre. A scrolling banner promised that the president would address the nation at one o'clock in the afternoon. Collins could imagine the roomful of speechwriters and spin doctors trying to make sense of the situation enough to be able to draft a speech that didn't sound like the patronizing horseshit it would have to be.

He walked over to the window and looked out at the morning sky. A Secret Service agent noticed him and turned to give him a nod. Collins saluted with his whiskey glass and continued to stare out at the endless blue sky.

"Goodbye, you crazy bitch," he murmured.

The words were mean, but his tone was filled with love and regret.

Chapter Ninety-two

Westin Hotel
Atlanta, Georgia
Sunday, September 1, 11:22 a.m.

She sat on the edge of the bed and stared at her cell phone.

The call to Bill Collins had been strange. She'd expected him to appreciate the anthrax ploy. It was just the sort of thing that he needed to separate him from the president. A victim, standing with the other victims in an America under assault. While at the same time the president, whether deemed innocent or guilty in the court of public opinion, would forever be seen as the man who reacted wrongly, with too much power and a total disregard for human life. She was sure that no amount of spin control could repair that kind of damage.

Thinking about that made her feel immensely powerful. It drove back the monsters of doubt that kept trying to nip at her. It drove nails into the slinking remnants of her conscience that kept trying to crawl after her long past the point where it should be dead.

Ledger had been wrong about that. So had Riggs. Conscience couldn't easily be carved out and strangled into silence. It was a persistent little bastard.

Only power—more power—kept it at bay.

Her thoughts, however, kept drifting back to Collins.

Was there something in his voice?

She was sure there was. But what was it?

Bliss trusted him a great deal. After all, he had engineered her false death and escape from prison. That had been all him, and it must have been a difficult and necessarily dangerous operation.

Which meant that he had to care enough about her—love her enough—to take such a risk.

So what was that in his voice?

She opened a can of Diet Coke and sipped it. CNN was on the TV and AP on her laptop. The country was going nicely out of its goddamn mind. It was close to chaos out there. More bombs went off. The last doses of the quick-onset Ebola were released in a cab filled with Japanese businessmen—let the State Department make something out of that. They'd have to assume it was Chinese agents acting on American soil. The last wave of random street attacks was pushing police and other first responders to the outside edge of operational efficiency. Just a couple more pushes and it would be chaos in point of fact.

Her cell rang, and she answered it on the first ring.

"Hello, Ludo," she said, smiling.

"Hello, Mother."

"Are you in position?"

"Yes."

"Is this going to be a problem?"

"Nope."

"Good. I'll text you with a go code. You remember which is which?"

"Yes, Mother. One is go, two is execute, and three is drop and run."

"Very good. You deserve a biscuit."

"Thanks."

"And, Ludo—"

"Yes."

"I don't want a bullet for this one."

"Oh."

"Something was left in the safe in your room. Use that."

"Okey-dokey."

"Ludo, for Christ's sake stop saying okey-dokey. We're master criminals. We're supervillains. Can't you for come up with something that doesn't sound like we're a couple of hicks?"

"Yes, Your Exalted Evilness. How's that? Or should I call you Dark Lady?"

Mother Night sighed. "Take your meds and stay by the phone."

She disconnected the call.

Between the bittersweet call to Bill Collins and the surreal call to Ludo, Mother Night felt odd and lonely. Tears burned in the corners of her eyes.

A voice whispered into her ear. The ghost of a voice.

Walk away.

"No," she told the voice. It was her old unevolved self. The voice of Artemisia Bliss. The weak self. The old self. Though now that voice sounded strangely firm and powerful.

You can do it. You have enough money. The bank transfers cleared. You're richer than you ever dreamed. You have the power. Take it and go.

It was true in a way. The bank transfers had cleared and she'd transferred the funds again and again, filtering them through dozens of accounts she'd set up over the last few months. The buyer, North Korea, was being buried under a landslide of political backlash and would probably never recover. And even if the Koreans hadn't been such suckers it wasn't like she would have had to deliver anything. Everything was bullshit.

She could run.

Right now. Just up and go and never look back.

It was so tempting.

And yet . . .

"No."

If you stay here they'll catch you, warned Bliss.

And there it was. Like a flash; like a switch being thrown. As shocking as a bucket of cold water in the face.

They will catch you.

They.

Aunt Sallie. Mr. Church. Bug. Dr. Hu.

They.

They had caught her before. Caught her and shamed her in her own eyes. They had made it seem like she wasn't strong enough or quick enough or smart enough to stay one step ahead. They'd caught her. They'd laid a trap for her. They'd outwitted her.

That fact screamed inside her head every night and every day. It had been like a knife in her mind from the moment of her arrest.

They had outsmarted her and stolen her power.

If she walked away now, how could she ever prove to them that she was stronger, quicker, and smarter? And if they closed in on her and she had no weapons left, then how could she fight back? Her stock of the pathogens was almost gone. All she had left were what she thought of as party favors. To absolutely insure her safety she needed much bigger supplies, and a greater variety of them. If she had those, no one would dare harm her. They could never be sure she didn't have something poised to go off in a gavotte of mutually assured destruction. After all, hadn't she already proved that she was crazy, that she would do absolutely anything?

Yes, she damn well had. Ask anyone.

Walk away . . .

"Shut the fuck up!"

Mother Night screamed it so loud it filled the whole suite.

"No—no—NO!"

She snatched up the TV remote and hurled it with savage force at the screen, which exploded in a shower of glass and sparks.

Mother Night glared at it, hunched from the throw, chest heaving as if she'd run up a steep hill, teeth bared.

"No."

That time her voice was so soft, so small, so cold. Like a bullet waiting to be fired.

Chapter Ninety-three

The Locker

Sigler-Czajkowski Biological and Chemical Weapons Facility

Highland County, Virginia

Sunday, September 1, 11:27 a.m.

From the air the Locker looked exactly as nondescript as it was supposed to look. A small tractor parts store with a wraparound parking lot. Pair of green metal Dumpsters on the west side. Scattering of vehicles in the lot, mostly pickup trucks. Ghost whuffed softly at the apparently empty terrain.

"I thought a lot of people worked there," said Montana. "Where are their cars?"

"Secondary parking lot close to town," I said. "Staff comes in on a bus and they stay down in the Locker for three-week shifts. Bus drops them off when the store is officially closed."

Top nodded to the pickup trucks. "We can scan their plates once we're down, but from here they don't look like the kind of vehicles an infiltration team would use."

"Maybe the bad guys came in a bird, too," suggested Dunk, but I shook my head. "The staff at the tractor store would have seen that and hit the alarms. No, they either came in nondescript vehicles or they came over the hills."

We pulled on the hoods of the Hammer suits and fitted the visors into place. They had clear lenses with night-vision goggles mounted above, ready to swing down should the lights go out. I ordered the pilot to set us down by the heavy Dumpsters. They would provide cover while we offloaded.

"Then dust off and stay on station," I told him, "eyes open and weapons hot."

He set down as light as a feather. The rotor wash picked up dirt and old trash and swirled it around in a cyclone of detritus, but it all whipped away and fell out of sight. With the stealth mode engaged, the nearly silent landing of the helicopters had a ghostly and unreal quality that provided no comfort.

Top jerked the door open, and Sam leaped out first, fading left, kneeling with his rifle to his shoulder to offer cover as the rest of the team hit the ground and ran for the cover of the Dumpster. They looked like gray shadows in their Hammer suits.

Ghost fidgeted and whined, eager to get out and bite something, but we were going to do an infil into a potentially biohazardous site, and they don't make hazmat suits for dogs. They should, but they don't. I told him to stay topside with Sam. Ghost gave me a look of such hurt and personal affront that it let me know in no uncertain terms that he would poop in my shoes at the first convenient opportunity.

"Don't give me that face," I said. "If the bad guys get out I promise that you can track them down and go all Hound of the Baskervilles on them. But you're not going inside."

We jumped down from the bird and ran fast for cover. Top took Lydia and Noah with him and headed around back. Bunny, Dunk, and Montana ran straight to the front of the building and flattened out in a blind spot of the security cameras. Or, what would have been a blind spot if the cameras were functioning. They sat there, unmoving, their little red lights gone dark.

Sam Imura broke right and ran to a tumble of three cracked boulders and laid his rifle in a cleft where two of them had smashed together. When he gave me the nod Ivan and I made our run. Sam's weapon of choice is a 408 Cheyenne Tactical sniper rifle that fires .338 Lapua Magnum supersonic rounds. Getting hit by one of those rounds is like being swatted off the planet by God. And if Sam fires at you, you will get hit. It's easy math. Sam's worst day on the range makes my best day look pathetic, and with him there I felt confident in running the distance from the helo to the iron Dumpster.

Behind us the Black Hawk lifted up and away, rising to a height of two hundred yards and making a slow circle of the building.

Ivan and I found a secure location and he took up a firing position while I did a visual sweep of the terrain. Nothing moved but dragonflies, grackles, and a squirrel who panicked and ran like a gray streak when Ghost materialized behind him.

Bunny's squad moved to the parking lot and quickly went from vehicle to vehicle, using helmet cams to send images of each license plate. Nikki's team ran them through MindReader.

"Cowboy," said Nikki, "every plate checks out as either an employee of the tractor store or a farmer from within a twenty-mile radius."

The terrain continued to be empty and uninformative. I headed to the far side of the front wall and knelt in a cleft between two withered decorative shrubs, then crabbed slowly sideways toward the front door. It stood slightly ajar, blocked from closing by something I couldn't yet identify. I tapped my earbud. "Report."

"Sergeant Rock to Cowboy," said Top. "Nothing going on back here. Rear door is closed and locked. No recent footprints in the dirt leading to or from. No windows back here."

"Copy that. Leave a door prize and converge on me."

Top clicked off. "Door prize" was another name for a blaster-plaster, which was a sheet of flexible material saturated with high explosives. When it was inactive it could take a rifle bullet and not detonate. But there were small wires running through it that, when the material was stretched and placed over the seam of a closed door, leaked compounds that combined to form a chemical detonator. You peeled off plastic film to expose a strong adhesive that bonded it to almost any solid surface. Left undisturbed, it could sit there for hours. Left too long and the detonator chemicals oxidized and became inert. However, if anyone opened a door or window sealed with a blaster-plaster, then it went boom. It packed a lot of oomph per inch.

A few seconds later, Top's squad came running around the far end of the building, moving fast, with a lot of small, quick steps so that their aim wasn't jarred. They squatted down behind me, Lydia facing back the way they'd come, Top shoulder-to-shoulder with me.

"Something's blocking the door from closing," I told him, "but I can't get an angle on it. Watch my back."

I leaned out and took as close a look at the door as I dared. A mailbox blocked my view of the obstruction and the front of the building was in shadow. Too dark to see well but not dark enough for night-vision glasses. I slung my rifle and drew my Beretta, which is easier to fire when moving in a low crouch and which has a powerful flashlight mounted below the barrel. Four slow crabbing steps got me to the right spot and I trained the flashlight beam on the obstruction.

"Shit," I whispered.

"What are you seeing, Cap'n?" asked Top.

I said, "It looks like a hand."

Another step, then I changed the angle of the flash in order to see inside. It was a hand, no doubt about it.

But it wasn't attached to anything.

Chapter Ninety-four

The Locker
Sigler-Czajkowski Biological and Chemical Weapons Facility
Highland County, Virginia
Sunday, September 1, 11:31 a.m.

The hand lay in a pool of dark blood. It had been cut off a few inches above the wrist. Not a clean cut, either. There was a heavy silver school ring on the pinky. I used the zoom function on my helmet cam to pick out the details.

"Nikki? Can you see the ring?"

She had clean-up software that—as Ivan once put it—could count freckles on a gnat's balls. "Highland High School," said Nikki. "Class of '92. A local, probably a farmer."

I felt a dart of sadness bury its needle in my chest. Some poor bastard, maybe working his dad's farm instead of going off to college, comes in here to buy parts and walks into a nightmare. Walks off the cliff at the end of his life. Sometimes the hardest deaths to take aren't those of fallen heroes but of innocent bystanders who, had they stopped at Starbucks for a cup of coffee, might have missed this whole thing and gone on with their lives.

"What's the play, Cap'n?" asked Top.

I didn't answer immediately. We now knew for certain that this was no technical glitch, no industrial accident. Sure, we knew that coming here, but there had been a tiny fragment of hope. Ah well. Our luck had been running piss-poor for a while now. Why change? Mind you, I was still hoping that there were only one or two maniacs hiding inside, waiting to give up peacefully and get right with Jesus. And turquoise warthogs might fly out of my ass.

I took two devices from my pockets. The first was the size of a deck of playing cards. I thumbed a button and adjusted a dial, then held it toward the door, moving it back and forth slowly, first from side to side and then up and down. The small green light didn't change, didn't moderate toward orange or red.

No electronic devices.

That was the first relief. This doohickey didn't scan for jammers, it scanned for devices keyed to electronically detonate bombs. So far so good, but still not the time to do the happy dance. The second device looked like a collapsible cane for the vision-impaired, and when I unfolded it the lightweight hollow sections fit into place exactly like a cane. Except this one was nearly ten feet long and ended with a small red rubber ball that looked like a clown nose. It wasn't. It was actually about twenty thousand dollars' worth of sensors suspended in a ball of foam. The alloy of the cane was nonconductive, the handle wrapped in rubber.

If we'd had more time, if there wasn't a clock the size of Big Ben ticking as loud as gunfire in my ear, I could have logistics send me a bomb disposal robot. That wasn't going to happen, so I waved everyone else back and then crunched myself into as small a size as possible, angling so that my body armor offered the greatest degree of protection in case I was dead wrong about that whole bomb thing. Then I extended one arm, holding the rod like a conductor with a baton. The red tip hovered an inch away from the door and then lightly brushed it. If it picked up anything—such as a trembler switch being activated by my opening the door—it would send a sharp warning to the electronics detector I still held in my other hand.

I took a breath, offered a generic prayer to whichever god was on call, and pushed.

Then froze.

The door didn't move.

Was there a wire somewhere I didn't see? Would further pressure snap it?

I licked my lips and pushed just a little harder.

The door swung inward.

I waited.

Nothing went boom.

I pushed again.

It wasn't that there was resistance from a wire; the door was simply heavy. I waited some more. I could almost feel each of my team waiting, eyes sharp, breath held, fingers laid along the curves of trigger guards, hearts pounding.

There was no explosion.

After a thousand years I withdrew the rod and collapsed it, then stowed it and the detector into my pockets. I ordered Ghost to go find Sam and stay with him. Then I tapped my earbud to open the team channel. "Everyone get ready, I'm about to get loud."

I pulled a flash-bang.

"Flash out!" I yelled and lobbed it side-arm in through the open door.

The flash-bang did what the catalog says it'll do. It flashed and banged. I squeezed my eyes shut, buried my head, and clamped my hands over my ears. As soon as the blast was over I was in motion, Bunny and Top swarmed up behind me, and the others followed. We broke right and left, guns up, yelling at everyone and anyone to drop weapons, raise hands, not get shot.

However, everyone in that store was beyond caring or complying.

There were nine people in there. Eight men and a woman. The woman wore an apron that had the name of the tractor company on the bib. She sat on the floor behind the counter. Four black holes were stitched across her chest.

Everyone else was just as dead.

Shell casings littered the floor. They looked like little metal islands in an ocean of red. But not all of the killing had been done with guns. Someone had used a heavy, bladed weapon in here. Long wounds were gouged across bodies. Heads and limbs were hacked off. Top nodded to a wall display of fire and woodcutting axes. There were clips for six axes but only five were on the wall.

"Check the air," I said, but the others were already looking at the screen displays of the portable BAMS units clipped to their belts.

"In the green, boss," said Bunny from the far side of the room.

"Green here, too," said Ivan, who stood by the door.

"Green and good," confirmed Top.

I glanced down at mine. Green.

I wondered how long it would take my nuts to crawl down out of my chest cavity even if it stayed green. Maybe by Christmas. Definitely not today.

We checked the whole store and found only the echo of pain and the persistence of death. The people here had died hard. Maybe the counter woman had it the easiest, she was the only one who looked to have been shot to death. We were all silent as we took this in. We weren't shocked into stillness. It wasn't that. We were assessing the situation, gauging our unknown enemy. We'd expected there to be bodies here. The level of savagery was surprising. The efficiency with which this installation had been invaded spoke to a brilliant and calculating mind; the butchery spoke of passions that were out of control.

"No sign of Dr. Van Sant," observed Montana. "Does that mean he made it into the facility?"

"Don't know," I admitted. "Be real useful if we found him alive and able to talk, though. He knows the day code, and without those we have to blow open a lot of doors. I'd prefer not to have to do that."

"Because of the damage?"

"No, because if any of the fail-safe systems are still functioning then the shock might trigger them. In which case we don't get out."

Montana studied me for a moment, then nodded. "Then I guess we better find him."

Top walked over to one corpse whose body had been hacked almost beyond recognition as human. I watched Top's eyes as he took in what little information was left.

"Boy," he said. "Fifteen, sixteen."

He didn't say anything else, didn't fill the air with any macho threats, but we all knew and understood. Top was the only active DMS team member who had kids. Well . . . one kid, his daughter, who'd lost both her legs when an IED exploded under her Bradley. His son was buried in Arlington. They'd found enough of him for funeral purposes. Those tragedies had been the impetus that made Top apply for the DMS. The memory of a son torn apart by enemy fire and a beautiful, brave daughter living her life in a wheelchair made Top into a different kind of soldier than the rest of us. His fury was cold, calculating, and enduring. He never lost control or fell prey to battle madness, but if he had his sights on the bad guys who did this, then they were going to come to watershed moments in their lives that they would not enjoy.

I moved past Top and he followed in my wake as we rounded the counter and went through the open doorway to the back room. The curtain partition was on the floor, tangled around the dead woman. Bloody footprints tracked past her.

"What do you figure?" I asked him, nodding to the prints.

"Too many to count," he said. "The overlap. But they're all wearing the same shoes."

The tread was unmistakable. Not military boots, or even the pseudomilitary stuff the wannabes and militiamen favored. These were all Timberlands.

Dunk looked over our shoulders. "Tims? All new, too. No signs of wear. Weird."

"They're dressing for this job," said Top. "Probably changed in a van. We catch them, they'll have civvies to change back into and the clothes they wore in here will go into a bonfire."

Lydia pressed her foot down next to one of the intruder prints, then lifted it away to compare the marks. Our shoes had a distinctive pebbled tread, the kind you see on tactical footwear made by companies like Saratoga.

We all saw what she meant us to see.

"They're not wearing Hammer suits," said Ivan.

"Or anything like Hammer suits," said Montana. "Pretty sure Timberland doesn't make biohazard versions of their shoes."

Dunk said, "They could have hazmat suits on with the booties tucked into their shoes." He paused, frowned, shook his head. "No, that's stupid. Sorry."

"Well," said Bunny, blowing out a breath as he looked around, "this is either very good or very, very bad."

The good would be if the bad guys just wanted to steal the pathogens without immediately releasing them. The bad would be if they were on a suicide mission and didn't give a fuck about protective equipment.

Top, who was always in the same gear as me, touched my arm and said, "If these jokers came down here to die for the cause, then why try for anonymity with the new shoes? I think they're here to take the Ark, not open it."

It was a glimmer of hope. But a little hope can be like a splinter in the mind. It can lure you into believing in a positive outcome, and that can take the edge off your skills.

"We're not making any assumptions," I said to the team.

We were in a small dummy office that held two desks, a water cooler, and a file cabinet. Enough for appearances. A door marked "Employees Only" hung by one hinge. The lock assembly had been torn out by a savage kick. The footprint on the door wasn't huge—maybe size ten—but whoever had delivered that kick knew their business. Single kick, too.

We went through into the next room and then wasted five minutes checking and clearing the administration offices that comprised the rest of Level One of the Locker. As we passed from room to room the stink of cordite clogged the air, and the gun smoke was almost thick enough to block out the sheared-copper smell of blood.

Almost.

There was simply too damn much blood.

Bug's intel said that there were fourteen support staff members working in the Locker's topside offices.

We found all fourteen. With the nine in the store this added up to the twenty-three cooling thermal signatures.

Twenty-three people whose lives had ended. Unexpectedly, terribly.

In bits and pieces.

Body parts were strewn around on the floor. Some of the secretaries and staff members were sprawled across their desks, their bodies torn open in a final indignity worse than rape. The walls were spattered by arterial sprays. Blood dripped from the overhead fluorescents.

"Christ's balls," murmured Ivan.

Bunny said, "What the fuck?"

You'd think that people like us wouldn't or couldn't be shocked by yet another example of man's potential for appalling brutality. You would be wrong.

"Berserkers?" mused Bunny.

"Got to be," said Top.

Bunny waggled his combat shotgun. "Glad I brought my boom-stick."

"*Jefe*," said Lydia, "how many ways are there out of this place?"

"Two," I said. "This way and a service corridor."

"Okay, 'cause I'm only seeing footprints going into this elevator. I haven't seen anything coming out."

I nodded and tapped my earbud. "Cowboy to Ronin."

"Go for Ronin," said Sam.

"Any movement from the service exit on the east side of the building?"

"Negative."

"Very well, but get close and tell me exactly what you see," I said.

There was a rustling sound and then Sam said, "Okay, I've got eyes on it. Confirming that it's undisturbed. Exterior screws are intact."

"Lift the cover plate."

The service corridor was a tunnel big enough to wheel parts down. From the outside it looked like a big electrical junction box, the man-sized ones that county power companies put up. But those doors opened to reveal a cubicle in which were the same kind of high-tech hand and retina scanners we had down here. And there were several levels of security behind that, including a length of reinforced corridor that could be filled with fire at a moment's notice.

"Everything is intact," he reported. "No one's come out this way. Even the weeds are undisturbed. Your bad guys are still inside."

In light of all the vicious slaughter, that news should have scared us. But I felt a weird little smile carving its way onto my face. I avoided meeting the eyes of the others, or even looking at their faces. They'd be wearing the same killers' smiles. It was an ugly thing to see on the faces of good people.

I looked at the main security doors that provided access to the elevators. The built-in scanners—hand, retina, and keycard—were junk. Wires dangled from what was left of them.

"Okay," I said, tapping my earbud again, "Ronin, put a blaster-plaster on the grille and find cover. You're our eyes topside. If you see anything hinky—I don't care if it's a bobcat walking with a limp—put it down."

"You got it, boss," he said. "Me and Ghost will watch your backs."

I heard a soft *whuff* in the background.

"Green Giant," I said, "let's get those doors open."

Bunny applied a magazine-sized blaster-plaster to the heavy doors. "Ready."

We moved away and hid behind desks.

"Fire in the hole!" yelled Bunny as he triggered the detonators. Bigger the bomb, bigger the boom. The steel double doors blew apart, open like the petals of a flower to reveal an elevator shaft. No car.

"Gear up," I said, but everyone was already rigging rappelling equipment. I did a quick look down the shaft and saw nothing but concrete, greasy cables and a few small utility lights. The hole was so deep we couldn't even see the top of the car.

Top dug into his pack, removed a lime green tennis ball, and let it drop. Then he flipped open the small tactical computer strapped to his forearm and tapped keys. The tennis ball was filled with several small sensors packed in Styrofoam beads. We watched the meter count off the distance of the drop.

"All the way down," Top said again.

A series of numbers flashed across the screen, giving us ambient temperature, negative elevation, motion detection, audio, and thermals. But the meters had nothing to read. No sound, no movement, and no heat signatures for anything human or animal.

"Hellboy," I said to Ivan, "you're on point. Drop to within fifty feet and if you hear anything drop a flash-bang. Once you're down, give us a shout."

Bunny anchored him with a powerful hand on Ivan's belt that allowed him to lean out and clip on to the main elevator cable. He gave Bunny another nod, adjusted his gear, then stepped out into the shaft and was gone.

Top and I leaned out to watch him rappel down with practiced ease. At fifty feet he stopped, reported all clear, and went down the rest of the way. Lydia went down next. Then Top, Bunny, and me. The newbies followed.

We crouched atop the car and bent to the access panel to listen.

We heard nothing at all.

"Dead down there," said Ivan.

Bunny gave him a withering look. "Really bad choice of words, dude."

Ivan colored. "I meant . . . no gunfire. Nobody yelling."

I removed the access panel and we pointed lights and guns into the car. Nothing.

No, not exactly nothing.

There was a dripping red handprint on the wall by the control panel.

"Listen up," I said quietly, "we go down, open the doors, and then make our way into the facility. We have to assess the situation and react based on what we encounter. There are a lot of civilians down there."

"We hope," said Dunk.

"Yes, we hope."

"Mission priorities?" asked Top.

"It's all about the Ark," I said. "We have to protect it at all costs. The civilians down there are secondary to that, though if the Ark is safe, then we do whatever we can to protect and evacuate the staff."

"Rules of engagement?"

"Nobody pulls a trigger unless you have no choice. Return fire and protect yourself, but don't approach this as a target-rich environment. We want to protect the staff and we want to take prisoners. Check your BAMS units, but make sure someone's watching your ass whenever you do. If you so much as encounter a common cold germ you sing out."

They said, "Hooah."

I tapped Ivan's shoulder and nodded to a junction box on the wall. The door hung open and wires trailed out like guts. "See if you can fix that, see if you can get this elevator in operation."

He nodded and unclipped a toolkit from his belt.

To the others I said, "Let's do it. We all go in, we all come out."

"Hooah."

One by one we dropped into the car. Lydia and Ivan took up stations to either side of the double doors as I took a shooter's stance off center of the opening, my Beretta up in both hands.

I gave Lydia a nod and she pressed the button to open the doors.

They parted and rolled back and Dr. Van Sant stood there.

He was smiling.

Laughing.

His clothes were disheveled, his thin hair messy, and there was a streak of blood on one cheek. But he was laughing.

He held a bloody fire axe in trembling hands. He stared at us in shock for a moment, then a single laugh burst from his chest.

"Dr. Van Sant," I began, "I am Captain Ledger, DMS, and we're here to—"

That was as far as I got before he screamed at the top of his lungs and tried to bury the axe in my skull.

Chapter Ninety-five

The Locker
Sigler-Czajkowski Biological and Chemical Weapons Facility
Highland County, Virginia
Sunday, September 1, 11:42 a.m.

"Captain—watch out!"

Lydia shoved me hard and I staggered sideways as the axe blade whistled down with incredible force and speed. It gouged a huge chunk out of the poured linoleum floor and rebounded, staggering Van Sant.

He was laughing all the time. Bloody bubbles popped at the corners of his mouth.

Lydia and I hit the deck and rolled over; I pushed her away and kept rolling until I was on fingers and toes. Bunny rushed the doctor and then had to suck back his stomach to keep from getting sliced open. The others crowded back and put guns on Van Sant.

"No!" I bellowed. "Do not fire. He has the bypass codes. I repeat do not fire."

Van Sant kept swinging at Bunny, driving the big young man backward. Bunny was fast for all his size, and he ducked and dodged until he got the timing right, then he stepped inside the arc of the next swing, grabbed the shaft of the fire axe with both hands, and with a savage grunt tore it from the scientist's grip. There was absolutely no pause between that action and Van Sant's response; he instantly lunged forward and clamped his jaws around Bunny's muscular wrist.

Bunny screamed in pain and backed away, trying to wrench his arm free. There was a note of hysteria in the big man's voice.

Lydia shrieked in terror and threw herself at Van Sant, hammering the doctor's face with a vicious flurry of punches. Van Sant's face disintegrated under the assault. I saw blood and teeth fly as the doctor reeled backward.

He lost his hold on Bunny, but as he fell back there was a long streamer of protective material clamped between his teeth.

The doctor, far from subdued, suddenly whirled, grabbed Lydia by the hood, and slammed her face-forward into the wall. A crazy, high-pitched cackle of laughter bubbled continuously from him.

Noah shifted around to take a kill shot and I slapped his barrel down.

"We need him, goddamn it," I barked.

"He's going to kill—" began Noah but then Van Sant shoved Lydia at him and laughed as they crashed into me and we all went down.

That's when Top made his move, sliding in sideways between Van Sant and us to deliver a brutal side-thrust kick to the doctor's knee. The bones broke with gunshot clarity, but as Van Sant fell he took Lydia with him. He snapped at her like a rabid dog and then slammed her head down against the ground. Once, twice.

I pushed myself off the wall, grabbed Van Sant by the collar, and hauled him backward. He snarled and whirled toward me and suddenly I had teeth lunging for my throat.

"Fuck this," growled Top, and he swung the stock of his M14 around and smashed it into Van Sant's face. More bones broke, the doctor's left eye socket lost all shape, his body trembled at the edge of terminal shock.

And yet . . .

He did not go down.

He did not slow down.

He leaped at Top, clawing at the visor of his hazmat suit, biting the air because he couldn't yet bite the flesh.

Van Sant and Top hit the wall side-by-side and collapsed to the floor. Top was unable to bring his barrel to bear, so he used the gun as a bar to keep the deranged scientist from trying to bite.

There was a *krak!*

Van Sant was plucked away from Top and knocked into the wall. His head no longer looked like a head. He collapsed down, his rage and his madness and that awful laughter stopped.

Stopped.

We all lay there for a broken moment.

Dunk stood ten feet away, a smoking rifle in his hands.

He said, "I . . . I had to . . ."

And the access codes were lost to us. And all I could say was "I know."

The moment seemed to freeze around us into a tableau of impotence, horror, and violence. Top and I were covered with blood. Lydia was dazed, hanging at the edge of consciousness. Montana and Noah crouched over her. And Bunny stood apart, the sleeve of his Hammer suit hanging in tatters, a hand clamped over the spot where Van Sant had bitten him.

We all stared at him.

"Bunny . . . ?" Top asked softly.

He looked down at the hand he was using as a patch. "Oh, God . . ."

Chapter Ninety-six

Centers for Disease Control and Prevention
Special Pathogens Branch
Building 18
Atlanta, Georgia
Sunday, September 1, 11:48 a.m.

Jacen Rolla knew that this was going to be his story. He was the first reporter on scene and he'd been sending in regular sound bites to his editor at *Regional Satellite News*. His cameraman told him that four of those sound bites were already getting serious airplay on the networks. For a second-stringer like Rolla that was God whispering to him that his time had come.

He'd done two other stories at Building 18—one during an anthrax scare last March and again for a zombie apocalypse bit for Halloween. He knew the best place to stand so that the complex would loom behind him. He had his jacket and tie off, sleeves rolled up, and hair ever so slightly mussed, as if he'd been in the trenches all night. It was the kind of image that sold Anderson Cooper during Katrina. A no-nonsense reporter who cared more about the story than good grooming or personal safety.

All of which was pure bullshit, but it played so damn well on TV and the Net.

The cameraman gave him the nod and Rolla pitched his voice to convey authority, concern, and a hint of the ominous.

"We can now confirm that a SWAT team from Homeland has entered Building Eighteen, and there are reports of gunshots coming from inside the facility."

That was unconfirmed by any source, but Rolla knew shots when he heard them, even if they were muffled by walls and doors. There were also flashes from inside the building, and if they weren't muzzle flashes then he'd eat his microphone.

Because there was nowhere else to go with the immediate story, Rollo began a recap of the Mother Night campaign of terrorism—his verbiage—in which he connected dozens of events. Much of it was conjecture and wild guesswork, but Rollo was absolutely dead-on when he made his assumptions. Of all the news coverage during those events, in retrospect, Jacen Rollo's was the most accurate, both in chronology and supposition.

It was the kind of gut-instinct journalism that all reporters wish they had. The kind that Rollo was unaware that he possessed. Suits at the various networks were watching his coverage and taking note. So was a huge portion of the American TV-watching population.

It was therefore later estimated that more than sixty million people saw him blown to bloody rags when Building 18 exploded.

Chapter Ninety-seven

The Locker
Sigler-Czajkowski Biological and Chemical Weapons Facility
Highland County, Virginia
Sunday, September 1, 11:50 a.m.

Top scrambled to his feet and pushed past me. "Talk to me, Farmboy. Are you bit?"

Bunny stared at his arm.

"*Are you bit?*" Top demanded, and as he said it he brought his rifle up.

Pointing it at Bunny.

Ivan gaped at Top. "What the fuck are you—?"

"Stay out of it," I warned. To Bunny I said, "Top asked you a question."

Bunny gulped in a huge lungful of air and as he exhaled I could hear him shudder at the edge of tears. Panic was a howling thing that screamed in his eyes.

"It . . . it d-didn't break the skin," Bunny said, tripping over it. "The arm pads . . ."

We all wore Kevlar limb pads over the Hammer suits. They'd deflect a bullet but they were for shit against knives. I doubted it, because I've seen Ghost rip through similar padding on hostiles more than once.

"Farmboy . . . you know we got to see that bite," said Top gently, though he didn't lower the gun.

"I'm telling you, man, it didn't break the skin."

"You know you got to show us."

"Boss," said Ivan, "check your BAMS."

I did.

I wished I hadn't.

The orange glow had deepened. It was almost red.

Bunny's eyes flared with panic. "What's in the air? Christ, what's in the air?"

Ivan held his unit out and turned in a slow circle, letting the little intake motor suck up particles. When he checked the reading again I heard him make a small, sick sound.

"Shit," he said. And that was all he needed to say.

"But the air . . . the contaminants . . ."

Top and I just looked at him.

"Show me the motherfucking arm," said Top through gritted teeth.

There were tears in Bunny's eyes. Even through the plastic visor I could see them. It took about a thousand years, but he finally raised his hand to expose the bite.

The sleeve was torn.

The Kevlar was torn.

The skin was bruised.

But there was no blood.

Not a drop.

We all looked at it.

"Oh Jesus, please . . ." breathed Bunny.

Then Top was in motion, shoving his rifle into Dunk's hands, pushing Bunny back against the wall, tearing open his pack, pulling out the small roll of black electrician's tape we each carried, winding it around Bunny's arm, turn upon turn upon turn, sealing the ragged hole in the protective clothing. And all the time talking in rapid fire under his breath. ". . . can't fucking take you anywhere you stupid cracker farmboy, don't know how to wipe your own ass, ought to knock you *on* your ass and see if I can kick some sense into you . . ."

Bunny was still praying to Jesus.

On the floor Lydia groaned.

I clapped Ivan hard on the shoulder, knocking him in her direction. "Help her."

He snapped out of his shock and dropped to his knees to help her.

I touched Top on the arm. "That's good," I said. "That's good."

But Top seemed reluctant to step back. He gave the tape two more turns then angrily tore it off and slapped the end firmly down. He stepped back awkwardly, almost a stagger-step, and stared hollow-eyed at Bunny.

"Top—?" I asked.

He gave me a wild look for a moment, then he seized control of himself and slammed his control back into place.

I squatted over Van Sant's corpse. His clothes were torn and it was clear he'd been brutalized. The question was . . . in what way. Top and Bunny stood on either side of me looking down at the body.

Noah asked the question. "What was wrong with him? Was he a walker?"

"I think so," I answered.

"But he was using an axe . . . I thought they were mindless."

I sighed. "It depends on which generation of the *seif-al-din* they had. This looks like Ten, maybe. If it was Twelve he'd have his full intelligence."

"Jesus," he said, appalled. "Why would someone create something like that?"

"It was a doomsday plan. A small group of radical extremists wanted to dose their own people with Generation Twelve and everyone else with Generation Six."

"That's insane."

Ivan punched him on the arm. "Dude, what part of 'doomsday plan' sounds sane to you? If you're going that far out and trying to kill everyone, is it really that much crazier to leave some thinking zombies behind? It's all fucked up."

Noah almost smiled. "Zombie balls."

It took a two-count but despite everything everyone cracked up.

The laughter was brittle and short-lived, and as I pulled back the collar of Van Sant's shirt it died completely. There two ragged half circles torn into his flesh. The marks of human teeth.

He'd been bitten.

Then I touched the BAMS unit to his throat. It had a small panel for reading surface temperatures. The meter said ninety degrees.

"Dead," I said.

"I had no choice," began Dunk, but I cut him off.

"No. His body temperature is already down five degrees. He's been dead for a while."

Montana helped Lydia to her feet and she leaned heavily on her as they came to join us.

"Talk to me, Warbride," I said.

There was a glaze in her eyes but it was fading. She looked around to orient herself and then those eyes flared when she saw the damage to Bunny's suit. She pushed past Montana and grabbed Bunny, checking every inch of the tape to look for the smallest flaw.

"*Canejo!*"

Dunk looked at Noah. "Big guy's popular around here."

Bunny gently pushed Lydia back. "I'm okay," he said, though he still sounded breathless and scared. "It's cool."

It wasn't cool, and we all knew it. He may not have been bitten, but the BAMS unit told the tale about the ambient toxicity. The air was a soup composed of at least four different pathogens. We had no way to know if the tear in Bunny's suit was going to prove as fatal as a bullet to the heart.

The others gathered around me.

"What's that mean?" asked Dunk, looking as scared as he should be. As we all were.

"It means that you don't want to unzip to scratch your balls," said Ivan.

"No," he said, "does that mean they've already opened the Ark?"

That was a tough damn question.

"We can't know," I said. "This place is a research facility, so the BAMS could be reading stuff released from labs on any of the lower levels. We're going to have to get to the Ark to make sure that it's intact."

It was news I didn't want to say and they didn't want to hear.

I was going to say more, but the lights suddenly went out, plunging us into absolute blackness.

"Night vision," growled Top, and we all snapped the devices down over our goggles. The darkness went from a stygian nothingness to that weird and disturbing green.

"I got movement!" cried Montana.

I whirled and saw that she was right. Someone stepped into view from one of the small offices that lined the far wall. A woman. Tall, slim, dressed in a white lab coat that was spattered with black dots. Black in this light, red if we still had normal lighting.

"Freeze!" I yelled. "American Special Forces. I need you to put your hands over your head and—"

The woman bent forward at the waist and bared her teeth at us. The shriek she uttered was in no way human. It sounded more like a mountain lion.

Then she rushed at us.

Not a slow, shambling gait.

She ran full tilt at us, hands reaching, fingers hooked to grab, teeth bared to bite.

"Damn," murmured Montana.

She raised her rifle and shot the woman in the chest.

The rounds punched through her and knocked her back and down.

But she immediately began climbing to her feet.

Ivan reached out in an almost intimate way, touching Montana's arm to raise the barrel.

"The head," he said. "You know this."

Montana took the shot and the left half of the infected woman's head disintegrated into pulp. Her next step was meaningless and she pitched forward, landed hard, and slid to within a few feet of where Montana stood.

"Faster," she said softly. "They're faster."

No one answered.

There was no chance.

Doors opened all along the wall and people began pouring out. Some running. Some staggering. All of them marked by the wounds that had killed them.

Just as we had in the subway, we raised our weapons and moved into a shooting line. It was hell for me, and I'd had years to fit the reality of this into my head. For my team it must have been a hotter hell because this was an insane rewind of yesterday.

But then the game changed on us.

One of the running figures suddenly dropped to one knee, raised a pistol, and began firing at us.

"Gun!" yelled Ivan.

We broke left and right, firing as we dived for cover.

Except for Dunk.

His head suddenly snapped backward and black wetness flew up from the ruin of his face. He fell hard and did not move.

"Goddamn it!" howled Noah and he hosed the shooter, knocking him down and back.

Before the body hit the ground two other guns opened up from beyond the crowd of running infected.

I had an angle on one shooter and took him with a double tap to the chest and head. He pitched sideways, careening into two walkers and dragging them down. Their heads whipped around at the sight or smell of fresh blood, and the monsters fell on him, tearing at his clothing to expose the meat.

Not sure if that meant that there was some chemical on their clothes that masked their smell, but whatever kept the shooters safe during the charge was for shit when there was blood in the air.

Works for me. Something to bear in mind.

Bunny, Lydia, and Noah were crouched down in the open elevator doorway, firing continuously. Montana and Ivan had ducked behind a desk. I knelt next to the desk, taking whatever shelter its corner offered.

The first wave of the dead reached us and their screams tore through the darkness, challenging the thunder of our guns for domination. Montana and Ivan both copied my double-tap method, using first shot to stall the mass of the oncoming infected and thereby allowing an easier headshot. The others were sawing back and forth with automatic fire, trying to kill or cripple enough of the dead to create a barrier.

"Frag out!" I yelled as I pulled the pin on a grenade and hurled it into the center of the oncoming mass. The infected caught in the center of the blast radius were torn to pieces. Others lost limbs and went down.

One of the opposing guns went silent, too.

It was the moment we needed to take charge of the situation.

Bunny, Lydia, and Top moved forward, using the brief advantage to take better shots while the rest of us covered them. Noah concentrated his fire on the third shooter and he had to drop three infected before he took the money shot. The third gun went silent.

That opened another door for us. We all rose from cover and moved into the diminished crowd of walkers. I still had my Beretta and the others switched to handguns, allowing the dead to close to point-blank in order to guarantee a head shot.

We fired and fired.

They fell.

One by one, they went down.

Then there were none.

"Reload!" bellowed Top.

Dunk lay sprawled between Top and I. A short, squatty ATF agent from Boston. A man I'd been in two horrific battles with, but about whom I couldn't really recall a thing. Not one personal detail. A bit of a sense of humor, some genuine astonishment at the things he was experiencing. A good soldier. A brother, fallen in battle.

There was no time to react, to acknowledge, or to grieve.

With the night-vision goggles in place I couldn't see anyone's eyes, couldn't tell how they were dealing with this. One by one they turned away to focus on the room.

Top and Noah knelt on either side of one of the shooters. The man wore a lightweight hazmat suit over street clothes. The white protective material was tucked down into the Tims.

"That's some weird shit," said Top.

"Would that even work against this stuff?" asked Noah, gesturing to indicate the pathogen-filled air.

"Not for long," I said.

"Wonder if they knew that," mused Noah.

It was a good question, and it opened up a very interesting line of speculation.

I called up the floor plan of the Locker, picking the fastest route to the Ark.

There was no "safest" route.

"Let's go," I said. "Clock's ticking."

Chapter Ninety-eight

We had several levels to go down to reach the Ark. Twice we had to use blaster-plasters to blow open sealed airlocks. As we ran I tried to reach Nikki or Church or anyone on the command channel, but there was nothing and we hadn't found the jammers.

I thought about Samson Riggs and his team. Was this the kind of thing they'd walked into?

Riggs was older and more experienced than me. He was a superior team leader in all regards. If Mother Night had taken him out, then what chance did I stand?

Doubt of that kind is an ugly, ugly thing.

The warrior in my head snarled at me.

We ran down level after level. Four times we encountered infected, all of them employees of the Locker. We tore them down with guns and grenades.

We made it all the way to the airlock on Level Fourteen.

We were a long way down, and as we crept into the room it became apparent that we had just stepped into one of the inner rings of hell itself.

The chamber on our side of the airlock was big and dark, with hundreds of metal packing crates stacked in rows. Some of the crates had been pulled down and pushed together to form a barrier directly in front of the Ark airlock. Thousands of shell casings littered the floor all around the barrier and everything—cases, floor, and airlock façade—was splashed with blood. This was clearly where the Locker's security forces had made their last stand. Thirty men and women, all highly trained, all combat veterans, had tried to hold this position.

And that is where all of them died.

Now they stood there, around and behind the barrier, their faces slack and white, their eyes dark, their bodies torn by bullets and blades. Here and there among them were a few of Mother Night's people, as damaged and dead as the rest.

The dead turned toward us as we entered the room.

They bared bloody and broken teeth at us.

Behind them, the airlock to the Ark stood ajar.

We were too late.

Chapter Ninety-nine

The Locker

Sigler-Czajkowski Biological and Chemical Weapons Facility

Highland County, Virginia

Sunday, September 1, 12:38 p.m.

The infected guards milling in front of the Ark were all looking at us now. Maybe it was the heavy stink of gunpowder hanging in the air, but even though they were aware of us in the room they seemed confused, not yet reacting to us as prey.

I wanted to take that moment and use it.

"Echo Team," I said sharply. "*Take them down.*"

We opened fire. Bunny had switched from an M-4 to the big shotgun with the drum magazine. Fully loaded, it was a brute of a weapon, but it was a toy in his hands. The gun bucked and bucked as he fired round after round at them, aiming head-high and blasting snarling faces into meaningless red junk. The others let out a howl of savage hunger and rushed us, all hesitation shattered.

It was a slaughterhouse.

Another fucking slaughterhouse.

How many times would this happen? How many times would Mother Night force us to massacre people who had already suffered, people who had died in fear and pain from the pathogen, or from the bites of their friends who'd been infected first? How many rungs down were we required to climb into the pit? Nietzsche wrote, "Battle not with monsters, lest ye become a monster." Was that the endgame here? Was Bliss somehow punishing me, the killer with whom she philosophized about the creation of monsters, by making me kill so much that I lost my humanity?

I could feel it slipping.

I was screaming. No. Yelling with a weird and savage joy.

It was a dangerous, dangerous place to be.

The dead came at us and we—did what? Made them deader? Desecrated their corpses? What would you call this?

"Kill them!"

It was my own voice shouting.

The voice of the Warrior, the Killer who lives inside of me. The one who gets stronger with every trigger pull.

I obeyed his orders.

I killed.

And so did the people who followed and trusted me.

As the infected rushed us, we met their charge and as a group began angling to one side, forcing them to attack us on our flank as we edged toward the open door of the Ark.

That's when Mother Night sprung her trap.

Bright lights flared on all around us, blinding us, stabbing through the optics of the night vision, tearing cries of pain and confusion from us as we scrambled to raise the devices away from our tortured eyes.

On either side of us, two stacks of metal cases leaned out and fell with mighty crashes as six huge figures sprang out from hiding.

Berserkers.

Chapter One Hundred

The Hangar
Floyd Bennett Field
Brooklyn, New York
Sunday, September 1, 12:30 p.m.

Bug sat in front of the big MindReader monitor, fingers hanging poised above the keys. The screen was broken into dozens of smaller windows, each filled either with images of the disasters or data about Mother Night and Artemisia Bliss. His eyes jumped from window to window so fast that anyone observing him would think he was having a seizure. His mind was whirling with information, trying to do what MindReader does. Look for patterns. Make connections.

MindReader was a computer, though. Possibly the most powerful one on earth. But a computer nonetheless. It could not make true intuitive leaps. It could not speculate or imagine. It was not capable of abstract thinking. A box of circuits and storage slots could not, by definition, think outside of itself. Not even this one.

Bug, however, could.

And if he didn't exactly know Mother Night he damn well *knew* Artemisia Bliss. They'd worked together for four years. Every day. Designing and scheming together. Solving problems like this together.

"What's your damage?" he asked the Bliss who dwelt in his mind. The remembered version of her.

Then he grunted.

That, he realized, was the wrong question.

This wasn't about her damage.

This was about her hunger.

That was the truth because it had always been the truth about her. She was always hungry.

For knowledge?

No. That was data, a means to an end.

For recognition?

Maybe. That was close, and he knew it.

People coveted what they saw. They lusted for specific things. They envied specific people. They hated people who had what they wanted.

So . . . who did Artemisia Bliss hate?

And why?

What did those people have that she wanted?

The answers to those questions were the answers to *this* question.

He knew that.

Bliss hated Aunt Sallie.

Why? Auntie was older. No. She was black. No, race had nothing to do with it. She was a combat veteran. Something there. A tickle. She was . . .

If he had to pick a single word that defined her. Just one. What would it be?

Dangerous?

Close. Very close. But . . . wasn't that a side effect?

Yes. She was dangerous because she was powerful.

That was so close.

What about Church. Pick a word.

Powerful.

In every way, powerful.

Dangerous, too.

Power and danger.

Bliss hated *him*, too. Bug. He'd testified against her, too.

Why would she hate him? She would have to know that he was compelled to testify, and her hatred wasn't born in the courtroom. It had to be there for her to do this kind of damage. It had to have been there for years, cooking, changing her.

So why would she hate him. He wasn't powerful. He wasn't dangerous.

Any power he had came from MindReader.

Bug stopped and cocked his head, reappraising that thought.

Was it true?

Was it an accurate assessment?

No. Maybe it wasn't. If MindReader was only a computer then it was no more powerful than whoever put it to work. That was no different than a gun. It could not pull its own trigger.

Bug was the power *behind* MindReader. Something he had always known but never realized or considered.

And that's why Bliss had hated him, too.

Because Bug was allowed total access to MindReader. Only two other people on earth had that privilege. Church and Auntie. How that must have galled Bliss. She always thought she was smarter than Bug, that she knew more about computers than he did, that she could do more than he ever could had she been allowed that freedom of access. She'd begged to show that to Church, to Auntie. To Bug.

It all came down to power.

He thought back to all the times the two of them played video games together. She won more than he did. And made a point of telling everyone about it.

That she'd won.

That, at least on those terms, she was more powerful than he was.

And something else flickered in Bug's mind. Something that Rudy had said in his testimony at her trial. Bug closed his eyes as he pulled those words out of their storage slot in his mind.

"Her pathology clearly indicates that winning is of critical importance to Miss Bliss. That manifested in a number of ways, from using a variety of psychological manipulations to win arguments, even over minor points, to posting video game scores on the corkboard in the lunchroom. She needed to win and to be seen to win. To be acknowledged as the winner. It was one of the ways in which she felt empowered."

That was part of it, but Bug was sure there was something else. Another point Rudy had made later during cross-examination. What was it?

"Come on," he told himself, tapping his feet nervously on the floor. "Come on."

Then it was there, like a file pulled from a nearly corrupted folder in a buried subfolder. There was only a fragment of it. Something Rudy had disclosed under protest because he felt it violated doctor-patient confidentiality. Only a federal court order was able to make Rudy say it.

"I counseled Miss Bliss about her drive to obtain power—as she defined power—and about her need to be recognized as the winner. She is not without a significant history of psychological problems. There are two documented suicide attempts from when she was a teenager. In both cases the attending psychiatrist concluded that these were cries for help or for recognition, or for acknowledgment of the power a child has when endangering their own life. She controls, for a short duration, the attention and actions of all adults around her. In light of my own sessions with Miss Bliss, I do not entirely agree with the conclusions of those early therapy sessions. It is my considered and professional opinion that she continues to be unstable and that she barters with herself for her own continued existence. Existence is predicated on winning. I cautioned her that one day she might either fail in so spectacular a way as to rob living of its richness, or that she would win too big a prize, because if you have climbed Everest, whither then?"

Chapter One Hundred and One

Westin Hotel
Atlanta, Georgia
Sunday, September 1, 12:31 p.m.

Mother Night paced back and forth in her room.

Everything was going exactly right.

Like clockwork.

Perfect.

Ever since Collins had managed to free her from prison, she had worked toward this moment. Using Huge Vox's screening software and his massive database of information culled from tens of thousands of businesses, she had compiled a master list of disenfranchised and emotionally damaged people. She'd used Haruspex to troll the confidential records of hospitals, police departments, and foster care agencies to find even more of them, winnowing her list down to a few hundred. The ones who had been abused and discarded, or marginalized because they were statistically inconvenient to a system that did not allow for creative care of its fringe elements. She'd cultivated them with gifts, empowerment speeches specifically designed to play on their needs, be they anarchism, extreme socialism, radical patriotism, religious mania, or something else. There were so very many lost ones out there, and many of them—despite claiming to want or need no one—clung to Mother Night because she validated their existence. And her gifts were always well received. Food, money, video games, drugs, weapons. All paid for with money siphoned from accounts in banking and trust corporations whose security was no match for a system like Haruspex, whose parents were Pangaea and MindReader.

For two years Mother Night crafted her own persona and drew her minions to her, letting them suckle at the milk she provided. For two years she built the master plan of Burn to Shine. The greatest terrorist attack in history. That's how it would be remembered. Through her faceless, broken minions she would be the most feared and powerful person on the planet. Even if that was only for the span of a weekend.

She. Mother Night. Artemisia Bliss.

More powerful than the president of the United States.

More powerful than Mr. Church.

As she paced she had to keep telling herself that this was exactly what she wanted. That she had already won.

But just as it had done earlier, that awful inner voice, her unevolved self, kept needling her, nagging her.

Run, it would say.

And she would scream at it.

She stopped pacing and went to the window. From the sixty-ninth floor, the city of Atlanta was beautiful. Sunlight and blue skies reflected from all the glass, and she could see for miles. It was a shame that she could not see the smoke curling up from the Centers for Disease Control. Wrong view for that, and it was a mistake she regretted making when picking this room.

She thought about calling Ludo Monk, and it took her a long moment to realize why that had occurred to her.

It wasn't because she needed to give him instructions.

No.

It was because she had no one to talk to.

There was no way Collins was going to take any further calls from her. And . . . who else was there? Yesterday she'd had some fun sending blind texts to Samson Riggs and Joe Ledger, but the novelty wore off. That wasn't real conversation.

There was no real conversation.

There was not even the possibility of real conversation.

Any conversation.

She felt a tear dangling from her jaw before she even realized that she was crying.

Then a thousand thoughts fluttered through her mind like a flock of starlings. Strange thoughts. Bad thoughts. Thoughts of dying, of suicide—though those thoughts were always with her. Other things, too. Like maybe she should call someone in the press. Give someone the interview of a life-time. Make the most important call ever. Tell the whole story. Wow them.

Would that work?

Would that ease the pain?

Maybe.

For as long as the call lasted.

And then what?

Then what?

She placed her palms against the big glass window. It was sealed, no way to open it. She wished there were a balcony.

Or maybe not.

It was too tempting to simply swan-dive out of the pain and into the nothing.

Instead she turned and put her back to the wall and slowly slid onto the floor.

And wept because she was lonely.

She wept because she had won.

She wept because there were infinite worlds.

She wept because she believed she could conquer them all.

She wept.

Chapter One Hundred and Two

The Locker

Sigler-Czajkowski Biological and Chemical Weapons Facility

Highland County, Virginia

Sunday, September 1, 12:33 p.m.

The Berserkers rushed us. They were all as tall as Bunny—six six or larger—with monstrously overdeveloped muscles. They wore black body armor, head to toe, that left only a triangle of their face visible through a clear plastic shield.

The belt slipped on the gears of time. The speed and insanity of the fight shifted as the Warrior became the Killer and he shouldered all other parts of me aside.

I had my Beretta in my hands and I spun and moved into the line of attack of the closest Berserker. I'd fought these monsters before. I knew that if they had one chance, one fragment of advantage, then they would win. They were immensely powerful, designed by cutting-edge science to be ferocious and savage, driven to the point of madness by chemical adjustments and drugs.

But the point of madness was now somewhere behind me.

As the Berserker grabbed me I rammed my gun against the plastic covering over his mouth and pulled the trigger. The round went straight through the clear cover but the dense bulletproof material of the Berserker's head cowling prevented it from exiting, so instead it bounced around inside the thing's head, turning monster into meat.

But as it fell, its fangs locked inside the trigger guard and tore the weapon from my hand. I let it go and whipped out my rapid-release folding knife as I turned.

Bunny was down, rolling on the ground with another of the monsters. Noah was down, too, but he was trying to fight his way out from under a pile of infected. Top and Lydia were running and trading shots with the Berserkers. Montana and Ivan were behind the stack of fallen cases. All I could hear were curses, screams, and howls of bestial fury.

A Berserker smashed one of the zombies aside and ran at me, raising a Ruger Blackhawk and firing. I shoved another of the infected into the path of the bullets, ducked low, and came in hard and fast. I head-butted his shooting arm up so that its next round exploded one of the overhead lights; and as I did so I used both hands to drive my blade through the plastic guard and into one flaring nostril. The blade bit deep, blood exploded over my hands as I gave the blade a vicious counterclockwise turn and then ripped it out.

He screamed so high and shrill that I thought my eardrums would burst. I dodged left, jumped, and kicked him in the side of the knee, landing as much of my weight as I could on the joint. It shattered audibly, and the Berserker was falling sideways into the hands of a half dozen of the zombies, who bore him down.

A dead-white hand grabbed at my goggles, trying to pull them off, but I kicked out and the infected fell away. If I lost those then the mucus membranes around my eyes would be an open door to the pathogens in the room. If that happened I was dead no matter who won the fight.

There was no time to think about that as a third Berserker came wading toward me, swinging for my head with the stock of his rifle. But he staggered as a fusillade of rounds hit him in the side. The foot-pounds spun him but didn't drop him. His armor was too solid and he had enough mass to bull through any bruising from the impact. He whirled toward the shooter and I saw Montana kneeling atop one of the crates, her rifle tucked into her shoulder. There was a jagged crack across the front of her goggles. The Berserker was caught in a moment of indecision—take me or go for her.

Montana made him pay for that with six rounds through his face.

Three Berserkers down.

I leaped over the falling body to try to help Bunny, but I saw the big kid from Orange County drive a Ka-bar up under the soft palate of the Berserker. As he did it, they both roared like monsters. The mercenary flopped over dead, temporarily pinning Bunny to the ground. White hands reached down, tearing at the corpse, trying to find purchase on Bunny's Hammer suit.

Then Top was there, unarmed, rushing in, scooping up Bunny's shotgun, firing, firing as he bought Bunny the chance to worm his way out.

A piercing scream made me turn and there was Ivan, fighting hand to hand with a Berserker. The big creature was bleeding from the mouth, big gouts of blood splashing on his chest and Ivan's. I couldn't tell what injury Ivan had inflicted, but then I saw something that drove an icy blade into my heart.

There was a long, ragged gash down Ivan's chest and the layers of his Hammer suit were parted like the obscene lips of a terrible wound. I could see Ivan's bare chest and there was no visible mark on him, but all of his protection against the monsters in the air was gone.

Gone.

Ivan must have known it, too, because he went absolutely insane with combat rage. He drew a bayonet and a short fighting knife and he attacked the Berserker, chopping pieces of padding and flesh away, ripping the life from the killer.

"Cowboy! Watch!"

It was Noah's voice, and I darted left and spun as two zombies came hurtling at me, propelled by a mighty shove from the remaining Berserker. Noah had his gun up, but I was inside his field of fire. I waved him off as I closed on the zombies from the outside, slashing down at the knee tendon of the closest one and shoving him into the other. They went down. The Berserker threw himself at me. Nearly four hundred pounds of brute strength and crushing weight. I dropped flat and then kicked up, spoiling his lunge, sending him spinning into a bone-jarring fall.

I back-rolled to my feet, but Noah was there, aiming past me now, sighting along the barrel. He emptied half a magazine into the Berserker. The first bullets pounded the thing into forced immobility, and with that freeze-frame, Noah used the last four rounds to blow out its lights.

The gunfire was thinning as Echo Team chopped the last of the infected down.

I reached for a fallen rifle, but as I straightened, the last of the walkers fell over, a black dot painted on its pale forehead.

Thunder echoed through the cavernous room, bouncing back and forth, diminishing with each collision, and finally fading into a terrible silence.

We stood there, each of us frozen in whatever posture of combat we'd been in when the silence caught us.

We did not look at the fallen walkers.

We did not look at the dead Berserkers.

There was only one thing any of us could see.

Ivan stood by the pile of overturned cases, his dripping knives in his bloody hands. Where his uniform was torn we could see his skin. It was no longer untouched. Now huge blisters as big as walnuts were expanding, straining the thin layers of skin, and finally bursting to seed the air with tiny droplets of blood. Black lines of infection raced crookedly up his stomach and chest and vanished beneath the undamaged part of his mask. Blood ran in lines down from that hood.

With a cry of horror he tore his mask off and flung his goggles away. The blisters had turned his face into something out of nightmare. His eyes were bright red and he wept tears of blood.

"Help me!" he said, but his throat was so thick with wet wrongness that it came out as a strangled gurgle. He pawed the air in our direction, imploring us to do something even though we all knew there was nothing that could be done.

Nothing.

Not even if he was in a medical bay with the world's top doctors around him. These were bioweapons of the worst and most terrible kind. No cure, no treatment.

No hope.

Ivan sank slowly to his knees.

Top handed the shotgun to Bunny and took the pistol from Noah. He looked at me.

It cost me a lot to give a single nod.

It cost Top every bit as much to see it.

He raised the pistol and sighted on Ivan.

Ivan reached out to him. Begging him for the bullet.

Montana yelled, "No!"

But the madness of the moment demanded a different answer.

Chapter One Hundred and Three

We stood over Ivan's body for as long as we could. I knew that there was little chance he would receive a proper burial. Even if the technicians and biohazard teams would somehow sterilize this place and bring it back online—an event I did not believe possible—any organic material would have to be incinerated and the ashes treated with chemicals and then sealed in ceramic-lined steel drums. We'd bury a box under a stone with Ivan's name on it.

Top knelt and placed the pistol on Ivan's chest. None of us would ever want to fire the gun that had killed our friend.

And besides, a warrior needs his weapon as he rides into Valhalla.

Finally, I turned away and walked to the door of the Ark vault, pushed it open, stared inside.

There was a heavy set of industrial-grade acetylene tanks and a welding mask. The whole front of the Ark had been cut open, the locks melted away, the steel panels for each compartment pried up. My BAMS unit was picking up traces of everything. Every single goddamn virus and spore and bacterium and prion that was stored at the vault was now swimming in the air.

But as I studied the storage slots I could see that even though they had been opened, they were still full. The Berserkers had not stolen the pathogens. They'd merely released them. They'd totally contaminated the Locker. Top and Bunny came in and saw what I saw.

"I don't get it," said Bunny. "They opened these up before we got here."

"I know."

"That makes no sense."

Top backed up a step and looked out through the door at the mass of bodies outside. I could see his eyes through his goggles and they were narrowed. Intelligent and calculating.

"Talk to me, Sergeant Major," I said.

"I don't think this was a theft, Cap'n," he said slowly.

"No," I agreed.

"What are you talking about, old man?" asked Bunny. "They sent a whole team in here."

"You saw the team they sent in. A bunch of thug shooters and those fucking Berserkers. Tell me, Farmboy, which of them look like highly trained technicians capable of safely transporting the worlds deadliest pathogens out of here?"

Bunny said nothing. He kept looking at Top.

"Tell me where the vehicles are for this team," added Top. Then he shook his head. "Hell, no, boy. This was a trap set for us. Or for a team like us."

"Almost worked, too," said Bunny as he nodded out the vault door to where Ivan lay.

"That's where you're wrong, Farmboy," Top said. "It worked exactly right. Just like whatever Shockwave walked into in Atlanta. There were only two DMS teams left and Mother Night took them both clean off the board."

"But we won this," insisted Bunny. "We ain't dead."

I said, "What Top is trying to tell you is that we've been manipulated into wasting time we don't have to waste. What do you call it in video games when you go off the main level of play?"

"A side quest?"

"Yeah," growled Top, "and another term for that is *wild goose chase*."

I kicked the side of the Ark so hard that hollow metal echoes shouted back at me. "We're down here fighting the wrong goddamn fight."

"Then where's the real fight?"

I tapped my earbud but there was no signal. "I don't know but we need to get out of here to find out, and I think our clock is just about out of time."

We turned and we ran.

Chapter One Hundred and Four

Westin Hotel
Atlanta, Georgia
Sunday, September 1, 12:41 p.m.

Mother Night looked at her watch and saw that it was time to get ready. She showered and dressed in the Lucy Kuo costume she'd hand-sewn.

For ten long minutes she did nothing but stand in front of the full-length mirror and look at herself.

Then, with a sudden rush of white-hot anger, she tore the costume off, ripping it, pulling it away from her skin as if it were diseased. The top was taped to her breasts, and as she ripped it off the tape left angry red welts across her naked skin. She threw the rags on the floor, then got a knife out of her bag and knelt over the costume, stabbing it over and over and over . . .

Time seemed to go away for a while.

A long while.

She blinked.

Blinked again.

She was no longer in the bedroom.

Mother Night was huddled in the back of the shower stall. Naked. Bleeding from cuts on her forearms and thighs, her face swollen and sore, eyes burning from tears.

"Wh-what—?"

Her voice was thick. The way a sleeper's is after a long night.

The vomiting began then.

Without warning, without the slightest twitch, everything in her stomach surged upward, burning her throat, bursting from between her lips, spraying the shower walls with garish red.

Red.

For a terrible second she thought she was throwing up blood, but it was too much and too thin.

Wine?

When had she drunk wine?

When could she have had this much?

There seemed to be no food mixed in with the wine, but the liquid was lumpy with . . .

She stared.

Another rush spilled out.

And another.

Then her body convulsed with dry heaves as if it were trying to rid itself of her stomach lining. She strained so hard that white sparks detonated at the edges of her vision. Blood roared in her ears.

She kept staring at the lumps in the red mess.

There were pills mixed in with the wine.

Lots of pills.

"What?" she asked again, as if the vomit itself could provide an answer. It took a long time.

The dry heaves ground slowly to a halt, leaving her breathless. She gasped for air, tried not to pass out.

Trembling fingers fumbled for the spigot and she turned it with a cry of effort.

The water was ice cold.

It punched the air out of her lungs and tore a scream from her.

Inside, deep inside, a voice laughed at her.

An old voice. The hated voice. The unevolved voice.

You killed me.

"What . . . ?" she asked aloud, giving it different meaning now. Directing it somewhere. Inward. Backward in time.

You killed me, said her older self. *You stole my life. You threw everything away, you pathetic bitch.*

"Fuck you, you weak little cow," sneered Mother Night. "You were nothing. You had no power. Look what I've done!"

You stole my life and made yourself into a monster. A hag.

Mother Night gripped the shower's safety bar and pulled herself to her feet. It took a lot and her legs did not want to hold her. She tried to lift her leg over the edge of the tub, bungled it, and then she was falling, clawing at the air, finding only the shower curtain, clutching it, tearing it loose, dragging it down to the floor. She landed hard, striking the point of her left elbow on the closed toilet seat.

You're pathetic. A psycho bitch who doesn't deserve to live.

"Fuck you fuck you fuck you fuck you . . ."

It was all she could say as she fought her body onto hands and knees, gripped the edge of the sink, and pulled herself to her feet again. When she looked into the mirror it was not her own face she saw. It was not Mother Night.

Artemisia Bliss stared back at her. Sensibly dressed for work. Hair pulled back into a ponytail. Glasses on the end of her nose. Eyes filled with hate.

You're nothing but a loser.

"You're a goddamn liar. You were too weak to speak up for yourself. Pretty, clever little Artemisia Bliss. Crying into her pillow. Mad at the world. Boo-fucking-hoo. I won the game. I beat everybody. *I* made us into *this*."

She beat her fist against her chest. The pain was shockingly hard and it felt so good. So delicious.

So powerful.

"I fucking won!"

In the mirror, Artemisia Bliss shook her head.

This isn't a game.

"Everything's a game, asshole. You were always too stupid to know that. It's all a game and I won. I beat them all. Church, Aunt Sallie, Bug. The field teams. Everyone. I fucking won."

The face in the mirror looked at her with such sadness.

So what?

"What?" Mother Night asked again.

Who cares if you won or not? Why do you think it matters?

Mother Night's mouth opened but she couldn't find the right words to explain to this phantom what it all meant. To make it crystal clear what every detail meant, why it all mattered, and the value of her victory. "I . . . I . . ."

And then someone knocked on the door.

As if a light switch had been thrown, the image in the mirror vanished to be instantly replaced by Mother Night's face. She looked into those eyes—*her* eyes—and told herself that this was her true face. This was the only truth.

Mother Night.

Another knock.

A man's knock.

But not, she was sure, a police knock. If the police knew she was here they'd have knocked the door down and she'd be in handcuffs or sprawled in a pool of blood.

Her body was streaked with wine vomit. A few pills clung to her skin.

Mother Night took the white terrycloth robe from the peg on the door, pulled it on, belted it, walked into the hall and out to the living room of the big suite. Her laptop was on the bed and she paused to hit a few keys. The screen display immediately showed the hallway outside her room via a video stream from the cameras she'd mounted there.

Two men stood in front of the door. They were dressed casually, in Hawaiian shirts, jeans, dark sneakers. They could have been conventioneers at the hotel, or they could have been conferees there to attend DragonCon, the big science fiction and fantasy convention that spilled across five hotels. Not everybody at the conference wore costumes from movies, comics, or games.

They could have been ordinary men.

But they weren't, and she knew it.

Mother Night recognized one of them. The last time she'd seen him, he'd been dressed in a dark suit, white shirt, and dark tie, with sunglasses and a wire behind his ear. In her memory, the man stood beside a limousine, watching up and down the street as a man got out of the car.

The man this fellow was guarding was Bill Collins.

This man at her door was one of the Secret Service agents whose loyalty to the vice president extended far beyond his role to the country. This man was owned by Collins, heart and soul. His companion would be as well.

And yet they were here.

Knocking on her door.

As if to punctuate that thought, one of the men rapped his knuckles on the door.

The realization of who they were was so intensely painful that Bliss nearly collapsed. Her legs, already wobbling from the wine, the pills she'd taken in her fugue state, and the aftereffects of vomiting, tried to buckle, but she caught herself.

"No," she snapped. "Don't you fucking dare."

She kept her voice low. She didn't want the killers at the door to hear her.

The pain didn't abate even though her legs grew more steady.

"Bill . . ." she whispered.

On the level of pure human emotion—a level she felt floated at an immense distance—there was heartbreak. Bill. How could he do this?

On all other levels, however, there was a cynical amusement. How could he *not* do this? It was neither surprising nor unforgivable. In his place, she would do the same.

Probably *should* do the same, time allowing.

Still, it did hurt.

Oddly, she knew that he loved her, and she him. So strange. Maybe that's how gods love. It was all very Shakespearean.

She waited, watching as they listened and finally nodded to each other. One man shifted to watch the hall as the other removed a keycard. Both men drew pistols from under their Hawaiian shirts and held them down by their legs, out of sight even though the hall was currently empty.

Mother Night spent one moment listening inside her head for the voice of Artemisia Bliss, but there was only silence.

She smiled and waited for the men to enter.

Because the hallway was deserted, no one heard the two men scream.

Chapter One Hundred and Five

The Locker
Sigler-Czajkowski Biological and Chemical Weapons Facility
Highland County, Virginia
Sunday, September 1, 1:02 p.m.

It took twenty-two minutes to climb flights of stairs and scale the elevator shaft. We encountered six wandering walkers and put them down. With each encounter it was simply a matter of one of us making a head shot. There was no drama attached to it, which is surreal. We were so numb, so terrified, so humiliated that the infected we killed had become little more than irritants.

In a flash of thorny precognition I knew full well that this was going to come back to bite each us on the ass. Once we were past the heat of the fight—and providing Mother Night didn't destroy the fucking world—we were going to visit those killings in our dreams, in our quiet times. The infected were victims. Colleagues in the DMS. Scientists, technicians, office staff, maintenance, cafeteria staff. People. Humans whose lives had been stolen from them and whose bodies had been hijacked by a parasitic bioweapon that made them into monsters. Yeah, sure, we had to kill them.

And no, there was no way we could stop and mourn or even regard their humanity in our haste to get out of there and back into radio contact, but you can't write bad checks like that without them bouncing. We would all have to pay those penalties someday, somehow.

But for now, we climbed, we ran, we killed, we fought, and we prayed.

The hardest part was the decontamination process. One full hour of being blasted by steam and chemicals and foams and God knew what else. Eventually we staggered out of the offices into the Tractor Store, wearing sweat-soaked underwear. We even had to leave our guns behind.

We reeled into the sunlight of a Monday afternoon.

Ghost came racing and barking toward us, then slowed and stopped as he smelled the chemicals on me. He growled at me and even bared his fangs.

Fair enough.

Sam broke cover and ran to us, his rifle ready, face twisted into doubt. He looked past us, waiting for Dunk and Ivan to come out of the building. Looked in vain, and I saw pain flicker across his features. He and Ivan were close. I took his earbud and tapped it to get a command channel. First thing I did was call for the Black Hawk and order the pilot to have the Lear fueled and ready. Then I called Church and told him what had happened.

"I'm adding Bug to this conversation, Cowboy," said Church. "He has something you need to hear."

Bug came on the line. "Are you okay?"

"Doesn't matter," I snapped. "What do you have?"

"Okay," he said, "you told me to get inside Artie's head, right? Well, I went back over everything I knew about her. What she wanted, what she did. I thought about the stuff said about her at the trial. Stuff about her psychiatric history."

"Cut to it, Bug. Tell me you have something."

"Yes," he said, "I think I know what she's going to do. I think I know how she's going to win this."

It was hard to hear.

It hurt.

Not because it was surprising. But because there was so little time to do anything about it. Even as we crowded into the Black Hawk, I was certain that Bug was right.

About Mother Night's plan.

And about the fact that she was going to win.

Chapter One Hundred and Six

Westin Hotel

Atlanta, Georgia

Sunday, September 1, 1:50 p.m.

Mother Night took a long, hot shower, washing away the dried wine she'd vomited all over herself. Washing away the blood from the two Secret Service men.

Every time she thought about the looks on their faces as they died it made her laugh. Their arrogance was insulting. They'd come in, holding their guns down at their sides, smiling, expecting her to do what? Faint? Fall down and cry? Beg?

Fuck that.

With their first step across the threshold they snapped the silver wire she'd placed at ankle level and that triggered a pair of compressed-gas dart guns. The chemical dropped them in their tracks. Dying, but not dead. A little fun with chemistry.

She pulled them into the room, closed the door, wrapped duct tape around their ankles and wrists and across their mouths, and let them watch as she carved pieces off, bit by bit, from each. They tried so hard to scream, but paralysis kept their pain and terror trapped inside. Afterward she'd covered them with a blanket. It was fun while it lasted, but overall it was pretty disgusting.

It was the first time she had ever killed anyone with her own hands.

She'd done it as a challenge to her inner voice, daring Artemisia Bliss to say something. To try to *do* something.

But that voice seemed to be gone.

Pussy.

Before taking her shower, she called her teams at the CDC and the Locker. One call was answered, and she heard what she wanted to hear. The other call was not. Ah well. That could mean anything.

Off to the shower.

She turned off the water, dried herself, spent some time to get her makeup right, and then stood for almost twenty minutes in front of her open closet, trying to decide what to wear.

The original plan had been to go over to the Hyatt in costume, dressed as Lucy Kuo from the video game Infamous 2. There was all sorts of subtext and meaning in that. All about betrayal and revenge.

The costume was in ragged pieces scattered all over the room.

She could remember destroying it, but not quite exactly why. The fugue had started then, and events at the edges of it were fuzzy.

The other costumes had less meaning, though some were very sexy and would look great on TV.

Which was the problem, as she now considered it.

If she wore a costume to the final act, that meant she was playing a character. Would the character eclipse her?

Probably.

Not entirely, of course, because—hey, she'd spilled blood, coast to coast. The name Mother Night was never going to be eclipsed.

The face, however, might.

And wouldn't that suck?

It would certainly suck some of the meaning out.

So, in the end, she dressed as Mother Night. The wig, the sunglasses, the skin tones and piercings. It was, after all, what her fans would want. What they'd appreciate. She had no doubt at all that she would have fans. Her anarchist fruitcake children were all devoted to her, even though— let's face it—she didn't give a stale fart about them. They should all have had "means to an end" tattooed on their foreheads. Useful, fun, occasionally charming, but dumb as hamsters. And yet, fans, every last one of them.

There would be others.

That was the nature of power. People idolized it, mythologized it. People showed up at events like DragonCon dressed as Hannibal Lecter, as Freddy and Jason and Pinhead. As Darth Vader and Dracula. As Nixon and Bin Laden. As killers both real and unreal. There were always those among the vast sea of disempowered who wanted to borrow power by wearing a fake identity. That was the central pillar of fandom, and Bliss knew that in earlier years she was as guilty of it as anyone.

So the best way to use that, as well as honor it, would be to give them the role model in point of fact.

And so, as Mother Night, from gleaming black Betty Page hairdo to spike heels, she was the über-terrorist, Mother Night.

It would not surprise her one bit if there weren't already three or four girls in the seething crowd of conferees dressed as her. Certainly no one would look at her in this environment and believe her to be the *real* Mother Night.

Not yet.

Soon, though.

God, yes. Soon.

Her clothes were fun. A short plaid skirt that showed a lot of leg. White stockings that ended two inches below the hem and were clipped to a cream lace garter belt. A half-shirt that showed her hard-muscled bare midriff, and a vest with lots of pockets. Gunbelts slung low over her hips. The guns were bright yellow water pistols. Lace fingerless gloves with a frilly ruff at the wrists. A blood-red circle-A on her shirt. No bra. Lots of jangly bracelets with gold and silver zombie-head charms. The last touch was a backpack crammed with goodies.

Her lipstick was the most whorish red she could find, and she bent and kissed her own mouth in the mirror.

Her mouth. Not the pouty mouth of Artemisia Bliss.

Before she left the suite, she picked up her cell, typed a single digit in a text message, and sent it off. She smiled, thinking about how much fun Ludo Monk was going to have.

As she reached for the door handle the voice was there again.

Please! it screamed.

"Go away, you stupid bitch."

She tried to reach for the door handle but her hand wouldn't move.

No. I won't let you.

The darkness started closing in around Mother Night. Like before, only she saw it coming this time.

I won't let you.

Mother Night screamed.

Chapter One Hundred and Seven

"It's called DragonCon," said Bug. "It's one of the largest science fiction and gaming conventions in the world. Something like sixty or seventy thousand people."

"And you think Mother Night is planning a strike there?'

"Yes," he said quickly, "and for a couple of reasons."

"Hit me."

I was dressed in black BDUs that didn't fit well. Everyone had found clothes except for Bunny, who only had pants. Our jet hurtled through the skies at unsafe speeds, flanked by F-15s, with a path cleared by executive order. The National Guard and every cop with a gun was massing in four separate staging areas, waiting for the word.

"They spread it over five hotels in Atlanta," Bug continued. "The Hyatt Regency, the Marriott Marquis, the Hilton and Towers, the Sheraton, and Peachtree Place. Brings in about forty million in tourist dollars. And it raises tens of thousands for charities and—"

"I don't need the sales pitch," I barked.

"No, you need to hear this. One of the things they do every year is a massive blood drive. Auntie thinks that might be ground zero for Mother Night."

"You sound skeptical. Why?"

"Well . . . as devastating as polluting the blood would be, it wouldn't stand out as the biggest event of the last two days. I think she has something else planned."

"They have a mass gathering of zombies to do the dance from Michael Jackson's "Thriller." They had more than fifteen hundred people there last year. A bunch of celebrities from zombie movies and TV will be there, including the cast from *The Walking Dead* and George Romero, the guy who did *Night of the Living Dead*."

"Are you fucking kidding me?"

Beside me, Top shook his head like a sorrowful hound dog.

"No," insisted Bug. "It's part of the event every year."

"That's where you think Mother Night will hit?"

"I do. At least . . . I think so."

"Why?"

"Because it's the only way she can absolutely win."

He told me why.

He talked about Bliss's need to win. About her suicidal tendencies, fueled by boredom and a fear of not being acknowledged as the best. About her growing dissatisfaction because she could not publish anything about the ultrasecret work she was doing, even though that work—inarguably—had helped guys like me save the world. About a child who was so freakishly smart that she could not help but grow into an oddity. Sure, some people—a rare few—manage their genius. But many do not. That old saw about there being a fine line between genius and madness wasn't bullshit. Bug cited the documentation and case studies.

As he told me this I knew that Church was listening, and I wondered how this was hitting him. The entire success of the DMS was built on having the very best. The smartest, the most insightful, the fastest thinkers, the innovators. Was he wondering if his own desire to have an irrefutable A team of the best and brightest was somehow flawed? That it was appropriate to the job we had to do but maybe inefficient when it came to saving the people who did that job. I knew for sure that I had lost psychological ground since going to work for him. Every time I went to war with the kinds of people we had to fight, and every time I faced the horrors that those people inflicted on the world, I went a little crazier. Even Rudy was showing some cracks around the edges, and he was a rock. Christ, he was *my* rock. He kept me sane, but every day he had to face secondhand horrors as field guys like me unloaded on him in therapy sessions.

Was Church examining his own conscience, wondering if this was somehow his fault?

Was Hu? After all, he'd hired her.

Was Aunt Sallie, who'd taken Bliss on despite personal misgivings?

Was I complicit? I'd let her use me as a sounding board for her explorations of the evolution of evil within a person's soul.

"Deacon," I said, "we have to shut it down. The convention . . . we have to shut it down."

Church's voice was heavy and slow. "Cowboy, there are sixty thousand people there. Most of them are tourists staying at those hotels or surrounding hotels. I've been on the phone with the governor of Georgia and the mayor of Atlanta, as well as advisors from Homeland and the National Guard. They believe that any attempt to shut the conference down will likely result in a panic that would send all of those people into the streets. If Mother Night releases a pathogen during that panic, then we will lose all possible control. There would be absolutely no way to contain the outbreak."

"We have to do something."

"We are. National guard and police are moving into position now. Truckloads of barricade materials are being brought in and we are going to try to create a quarantine zone around those five hotels. We have people coordinating the logistics. However, I spoke with the president five minutes ago and he has authorized a fleet of helicopters for air support and we're scrambling bombers from Robins Air Force Base."

"To do what?"

"To sterilize the area." It sounded like those four words were pulled out of Church's mouth with pliers.

Sterilize.

"How?" I asked, though I already knew. It was simply that my mind rebelled at conjuring the word.

"Fuel-air bombs. In the event that we are certain the *seif-al-din* has been released at the conference, we will burn everything within a six-square-block radius. And if it comes to that, Captain . . . God help us all."

"Then we have to damn well make sure it *doesn't* happen," I snarled. "We need spotters in the crowd. We know what Bliss looks like, in or out of her Mother Night getup."

"Cowboy," said Bug, "you don't understand. You don't go to events like this. These are fan conventions. At least one out of every three people is in costume."

My heart, which had been teetering on the edge of a long drop, toppled over into darkness.

The jet flew on.

But toward what?

Chapter One Hundred and Eight

Grand Hyatt Hotel
109 East Forty-second Street
New York City
Sunday, September 1, 3:46 p.m.

Junie Flynn sat on the bed, legs crossed, shoulders against the headboard, eyes closed. Meditation was the only thing that kept her from climbing the walls. And even then, inside the calm space she had created while the minutes and hours passed, tension nipped at her with rat teeth.

No calls.

No word.

Nothing.

Not from Joe or anyone at the DMS. The only call she'd received had been a short, awkward one from Violin asking if they could talk sometime, maybe. Junie agreed, of course, but before she could ask what Violin wanted to talk about, the strange and moody woman had hung up.

Apart from that, Junie's cell remained as silent as if it were broken.

She knew that this was how it had to be. Secrecy was paramount for the DMS. If anyone ever suspected that she knew something about one of Joe's missions, then she would become a liability. She could be used as a lever against Joe. It broke her heart to know that she was the one chink in his armor.

Love was such a wicked thing at times. How like a blade. Used one way, it could carve and sculpt and prune, it could remove a tumor or harvest a flower. Used another way, it stole life and scarred beauty and destroyed hope.

Love was like that.

In Junie's view it was the most powerful force in the universe, the core of creative energy, the shaper of all things, giver of life and author of possibilities. However, it could be turned to wicked purpose.

Mr. Church knew that, she was certain. The two men stationed outside her door were not there to protect her. Not really. They were there to protect Joe.

To protect the mission.

She understood that, appreciated it, and hated it, too.

The minutes grew like weeds to become hours, and Junie fought her panic. Moment by moment, the calm space around her withered and contracted.

When someone knocked on the door she jumped and cried out in a voice like a startled bird.

Chapter One Hundred and Nine

Peachtree Center Avenue
Atlanta, Georgia
Sunday, September 1, 3:47 p.m.

"Now that's really in poor damn taste," growled Police Officer Michael Feingold.

His partner, Officer Carol Daniels, was standing a few feet away, arms wide to keep the crowd from crossing while traffic crawled past. He followed Feingold's line of vision and didn't have to ask what he was referring to.

Mother Night was crossing the street.

It was a young woman dressed exactly as the one from the video. Betty Page wig, sunglasses, painted lips, and an outrageous costume that pushed the envelope of modesty. Here at DragonCon they saw a lot of people push that same envelope, and occasionally tear it open. Earlier that day they'd busted two men dressed only in blue body paint and carrying plastic spears. They claimed to be ancient Celtic warriors. Even tried to argue that a layer of paint constituted clothing. It didn't. Daniels and Feingold made them sit in their cruiser for a couple of hours and then gave them a citation and fine.

The girl in the Mother Night costume was wearing a high-cut midriff top that exposed the bottoms of her breasts.

"She shows even half a nipple and I'm busting her for public indecency," said Feingold.

Daniels grunted. "That costume's what's indecent."

The crowd parted to let the woman pass, and there were equal amounts of boos and cheers.

The woman held a sequin-encrusted leash that connected to studded leather collars on two men who stumbled along behind, hands bound behind their backs, pillowcases over their heads. The men were covered in realistic-looking wounds. Both of them wore blood-soaked white dress shirts, the flaps hanging. On the back of one, the words GOVERNMENT LACKEY were written in red lipstick. The other had GOVERNMENT STOOGE. Two other men followed behind, dressed in hoodies and gorilla masks.

The light changed and Daniels dropped her arms to let the crowd cross the street, rivers of people going from the Hyatt to the Marriott or the other way. It amazed both officers that these people still wanted to dress up in costumes, go to panels, cruise the dealers' rooms, stand in line for celebrities, when half the damn country was in flames. At the morning role call, the sergeant said that the mayor was considering shutting down the convention but no one had a workable plan for what to do with sixty thousand tourists. The fear was that to stop the con would be to create doubt about a possible terrorist attack and that would result in immediate panic.

And, of course, chaos.

A plan was being worked out, according to the sergeant, and most likely this evening, as the activities of the day wound down, they would coordinate with event staff, hotel security, and some National Guard to shut it down and more or less tell everyone to stay in their rooms.

The plan, Feingold and Daniels agreed, was horseshit. No way it would work. There would either be a panic or a riot.

Having a fruitcake dressed as Mother Night was not likely to help matters. It was socially irresponsible as well as potentially dangerous. Riots have erupted over less.

As the woman crossed the street she passed within a few feet of Feingold and Daniels.

"I have to," murmured Feingold, and then stepped into her path. The woman stopped.

"Is there a problem?" asked Mother Night. The two men in gorilla masks stopped also, flanked her as if they were bodyguards. The men with the pillowcase hoods milled as if drunk.

"Miss, I feel I need to urge you to reconsider your costume," said Feingold, trying to sound calm and authoritative. "Some people might take offense."

The woman tugged her sunglasses halfway down and looked at him with big, innocent brown eyes. "Oh, my. It's just for fun."

"People are dying," said Feingold, his tone shifting into harshness. "Not everyone would think what you're wearing is fun. Some people might get pretty angry about it."

"Oh, it's okay," said the woman. "They're going to kill me later on anyway. All part of the fun."

"What?"

"It's part of the show. Good guys and bad guys. Big dramatic finish and, oh, poor me, I die. Don't you know that's how it goes?"

"That's not funny."

The woman pushed her glasses back into place. "Oh, no, you're wrong there. It's hilarious."

With that she moved around Feingold, nodded to Daniels, tugged on the sequined leash, and sauntered off, giving the crowd something to look at with absurdly exaggerated hip swagger. Lots of catcalls, whistles, obscene comments, shouts, and laughter. Her slaves staggered along behind her, their awkward balance occasionally steadied by the big men in masks.

Daniels came and stood next to her partner, who had his fists balled at his sides and whose face was now the color of a boiled lobster.

"She's asking for trouble," grumbled Feingold.

"Well, shame on her if she finds it and needs our help," sniffed Daniels. "I might just not see her. Bitch."

The crowds surged back and forth and the officers had to shift their focus back to the management of all those people. Feingold, unable to completely let it go, kept throwing looks at the hotel that Mother Night and her entourage had just entered.

Then something else caught his eye and he looked up as a phalanx of helicopters moved slowly from east to west above him, no more than a hundred yards above the hotels. They were military birds. Feingold had done a tour each in Iraq and Germany, and he knew helicopters. Those were AH-64D Apache Longbows and UH-60 Black Hawks. He counted at least a dozen of each, and four AZ-1Z Vipers. They vanished behind the buildings.

"The hell was that all about?" asked Daniels.

"Don't know. Something with the attacks."

Suddenly there was a burst of static from their radios and the dispatcher said, "All units, call in for instructions."

Chapter One Hundred and Ten

Junie crossed to the door. The lock was in place. She leaned close.

"Yes?"

"Agent Reid, ma'am."

"Is everything okay?"

"Shift change."

"Oh, okay."

She peered through the peephole and saw an agent dressed in a dark jacket, white shirt, and dark tie. He had a long, lugubrious face and the kind of bland, expectant expression people had when waiting for someone to answer the door. He turned and said something to someone else Junie couldn't see. Probably Reid.

Junie flipped the lock back and opened the door.

"Do you guys need to use the bathroom before you . . ."

There were three people in the hallway. Agents Reid and Ashe.

And someone else.

Reid and Ashe lay on the floor. Blood pooled under their heads.

The other man stood there, and his bland expression changed into a slow smile. He raised a pistol and pointed it at Junie.

"People like you make this too easy."

Chapter One Hundred and Eleven

She walked through madness leading her slaves on a leash.

Her costume was perfect, and she knew it, showing enough skin to attract the eye, and because she was dressed as the infamous Mother Night from yesterday's video, every eye that fell on her lingered.

In any other place, she and her hooded slaves would create a screaming panic or have witnesses calling the police. But this was DragonCon, and there were hordes of bloodthirsty vampires, storm troopers from the 501st Vader's Fist, Cenobites from the hell dimension, and far worse. By comparison, the gruesome and humiliating nature of her costume was understated.

Everywhere Mother Night looked she saw a deliberate insanity, a willful detachment from the ordinary. The atrium of the Marriott Marquis was vast, soaring four hundred and seventy feet above the lobby, and seeming to ripple and flow. Mother Night always thought it looked like the inside of the spacecraft from *Alien*. The one designed by H. R. Giger. Like this was the throat of some titanic dragon rather than the lobby of a hotel. The entire lobby, wall to wall, was crammed with people. But also not people. There were Orcs and Hobbits, Vulcans and Klingons, Vikings and spacemen, dead presidents and celebrity monsters. This late in the day, the panels were shutting down and the parties were kicking into high gear. Every tier of the atrium was abuzz with people going from room to room, in costume and in street clothes, sober and drunk, stoned and abstinent. Laughing. Everyone laughing.

She saw a line of teenagers in hoodies and backpacks with anarchy symbols spray-painted on their backs. Impromptu costumes. People shook beers and doused them, and they retaliated by throwing handfuls of confetti as if bombing the crowd. Hotel security and police scowled, and several times they stopped the kids to check their backpacks. They found beer and some pot. A few kids were dragged off. The rest were absorbed into the party.

Mother Night estimated that the lobby was packed with four thousand people. The fire codes were a joke. Thousands more shouted from the balconies.

The costumes changed as the day faded and night came on. There were fewer kids and a lot more booze. Costumes got smaller, more risqué, occasionally obscene, always delightful.

Strolling among them was such fun. Especially once the crowd began to *get* her costume. People with toy guns pretended to shoot her. The kids dressed in hoodies immediately fell into step behind her, appointing themselves as her entourage. She knew that her beauty and skimpy costume were as much a draw as her "character." By playing Mother Night on this weekend, in this town—with the destruction of the CDC the buzz everywhere—she was a walking cause célèbre. Cameras flashed, flashed, flashed.

It was so delicious. Even the people—and there were many—who thought that her costume was in bad taste and far too soon, reacted to her. Their disapproval and contempt was evident on their faces, in their shouts, in the fact that they followed her in order to berate her. Once the crowd was aware of her, everyone reacted to her in one way or another.

Everyone.

She constructed a haughty half-smile interspersed with flashes of a broad "yes-we're-all-in-on-it" grin.

It was so thrilling.

To be out in public as Mother Night.

What surprised her was how long it took for any of the police officers to approach her. Most of them gave her a glance and turned away. It made her wonder if some of them had lost colleagues in the current wave of chaos. *Poor babies, if they did,* she thought.

Lots of people wanted to take photos with her, and she stood smiling with them, striking an imperious pose.

People wanted her autograph, and she signed convention programs, newspaper headlines, T-shirts, and even skin.

People began offering to buy her drinks, and she let them. They toasted her, and she toasted chaos, and everybody raised their glasses and shouted the word.

Chaos.

Then she turned to one of the teenagers in the hoodies.

"You, minion, come here . . . Mother wants you."

He obeyed as if he truly were her minion, and that made the crowd laugh. He came and dropped to one knee before her, head bowed like a samurai waiting on the pleasure of his daimyo.

"Hold this," she said, handing the leash of her slaves to him.

She signaled another of the hoodie crowd, and he imitated what his friend had done, the way sheep will so quickly and reliably follow each other even into a bog. Mother Night shrugged out of her backpack and handed it to the second of her new minions. He extended his arms and held the pack while she rooted through it. Mother Night removed a double handful of chocolates, each wrapped in colorful plastic. She tossed them to the crowds and they went crazy grabbing at them, snatching them out of the air, playing a vicious tug-of-war when two people grabbed one at the same time. Mother Night laughed and laughed. She scooped out more and threw them, wildly and sometimes with precision toward a specific person whose costume she admired. Hands reached for the treats. Some hands reached past the candy to try to touch her, so she obliged and danced her fingertips along theirs, gracing each of them with the gift of contact.

Contact with *her*.

Then she removed one last thing from her bag. A pair of scissors with big, happy, pink plastic handles. She snipped them in the air a few times.

"Okay, monkeys," she yelled, "who wants to help me free my slaves?"

The crowd roared.

Chapter One Hundred and Twelve

Peachtree Center Avenue
Atlanta, Georgia
Sunday, September 1, 3:55 p.m.

When Officer Feingold received the call from dispatch he thought it was a change of assignment. He and Daniels had been outside for hours and it had been a long, hot day in the unrelenting August heat. The dispatcher told him to leave Daniels in charge of traffic control and that he was to report to his supervisor, a sergeant who was around the corner. He was told to do this quickly but without causing undue alarm.

He understood the wisdom of that. No one reacts well to the sight of a policeman running down the street.

"You going to be okay?" he asked Daniels.

"Yeah, let me know what's up."

Feingold patted her on the shoulder and headed up the street, moving at a brisk walk that was not quite a run. As he neared the corner he saw other officers converging on the same spot. He followed them around the corner and nearly jerked to a stop. There were four trucks parked in a row, engines on and idling, while lines of National Guardsmen were off-loading dozens of sawhorse barriers. Down at the far corner Feingold could see other trucks being similarly off-loaded. The crowds that passed glanced curiously at the soldiers and cops, but when one of the passersby—a young black woman dressed as Lieutenant Uhuru—asked what was going on, a huge white man who looked like an oversized California surfer said, "Getting ready for the parade."

"Parade?" laughed the young woman. "That was this morning."

"Different parade," said the surfer, and he gave her a big, white-toothed smile. One of the soldiers, a slender Latina, punched the big man in the arm and said something in rapid-fire Spanish. The young black woman shrugged and walked on.

Feingold found his sergeant-supervisor, who was preparing to address several dozen cops. "What's with the barricades, Sarge? Did I hear something about a parade?"

A man in poorly fitting black BDUs answered his question, and it was immediately clear that he, not the sergeant, was in charge. The man looked around to make sure that there were no civilians within earshot before he spoke.

"Listen to me," he said. "We have reason to believe that the woman who calls herself Mother Night may be somewhere here at DragonCon. As soon as we're set, we are going to shut down all streets leading into or out of Peachtree Center. You will work in pairs and when the signal goes out, every team will move into position at the same time with the barricades to block the streets. The trucks will then take up position behind the lines of barricades, and the National Guard will establish defensive positions between the vehicles, the barricades, and the walls of the corner buildings. That's a whole lot of people moving all at once. We need to snap the lid shut on this area and we need to do it without mistake."

"Excuse me," said an officer, "but is there a bomb threat here?"

The soldier, who had neither name tag nor rank insignia, said, "We have to assume that as a possibility, but our major concern right now is a biological threat. You saw the videos of the Brooklyn subway. That was a biological attack."

He then told the officers about something called the *seif-al-din*; and about what it did.

"This is not a drill," he concluded, "and it's not a joke."

"What about the people inside?" asked the same officer. "How do we get them out?"

"Once we seal the area we'll have filter points at each corner. The crowd will be directed to those points and we'll evaluate them and process them through as quickly as we can." He held up a small device. "You all know what a BAMS unit is, well, this one is portable. We have thirty of them here and another hundred on their way."

"People are going to freak," said another officer.

"Yeah, they will, so it's your job to manage that. Announcements will be made inside each hotel asking people to return to their rooms or, if they are not booked at the hotel where they are when this goes down, they will be asked to sit down and await further instructions. The exact wording is being worked out and it will sound better than what I just said. But over-all, crowd control is critical, not just to save lives but also to give us a chance to find—"

"I saw her," said Feingold, and instantly every pair of eyes turned to him.

"What?" demanded the soldier.

"I—I mean I think I saw her," stammered Feingold. "Mother Night. I think I just saw her go into the Marriott not ten minutes ago. Oh God!"

Chapter One Hundred and Thirteen

Grand Hyatt Hotel
109 East Forty-second Street
New York City
Sunday, September 1, 3:55 p.m.

The stranger kept walking forward, his gun barrel against Junie's stom-ach, forcing her backward to the bed. There was a sound suppressor screwed onto the barrel, which gave him an extended reach.

"Please," said Junie. "Please, don't."

For a moment the man appeared confused and then alarmed. Then he smiled. "What, you think this is a rape? Christ, lady, do I *look* like a rap-ist? God. Don't be so rude."

"I—I—"

He jabbed her with the gun. "Where's your cell phone?"

Without meaning to, Junie's eyes flicked toward the bed. He spotted the cell, nodded to himself.

"You have anything else? iPad? Laptop?"

She said nothing, unsure as to the kind of answer he wanted, or which answer would keep her safe. He solved the problem for her by raising the pistol so that the barrel touched her cheek below her left eye.

"Lie to me and I blow a hole through your head," he said quietly. "Tell me the truth, the day goes a whole different way."

"Laptop . . . over there." She made a small, vague gesture toward the desk. "What are you going to do to me?"

He didn't answer. Instead he moved around her and scooped her cell off the bed, then backed up until he stood by the desk.

"Just these two? Nothing else? No?"

She shook her head.

"Good. Now go sit on the bed."

She hesitated for a moment, then obeyed.

"I have to do something and while I'm doing it I want you to stay right there. If you move I'll kneecap you. Understand? Good."

He pocketed the cell and tucked the pistol into the waistband of his trousers, then he stepped halfway into the hall, looked up and down, and dragged the two bodies in, one at a time. Then he took a newspaper from the desk, opened it, and laid it on the hall floor over the spilled blood. There was surprisingly little, but Junie knew that corpses didn't bleed. The two men had single bullet holes in their heads. No exit wounds. She understood what that meant, too. Assassins used small-caliber weapons like .22s because the bullet lacked power to exit the skull and instead bounced around to do fatal damage. Less mess, too. The gun this man carried was a silenced .22.

The man closed the door, hooked the wheeled chair from the desk, pulled it to the middle of the floor, and sat. He removed his pistol, unscrewed the sound suppressor, pocketed that, and laid the gun on his thigh. He removed her cell phone from his pocket and weighed it in his hand for a moment, and then tossed it onto the bed. It landed near Junie but she dared not touch it.

"Here's the thing," he said. "If this had gone a different way you'd have never met me. Plan A was for me to put a bullet into your head from across the street. Not here, but at FreeTech. Bang. Single shot, your brains are one of those splash paintings by that guy. What was his name? Jackson Pollock. That was Plan A." He took a deep breath and raised his eyebrows for a moment before exhaling. He removed an object from his pocket and held it up between thumb and forefinger. "Plan B is I come here and use this on you."

The item was a syringe filled with green liquid.

"Personally, I don't dig this whole thing. I already have enough monsters in my head, you dig? No? Doesn't matter. The thing is that Mother Night thinks there's a chance your action hero boyfriend may actually survive all of the stuff she has planned for him. Guy's a wild card, so I can see her point. So she wants him to have a really interesting homecoming, if you follow me. Yeah," he said, smiling, "I can see you do."

Junie stared at the syringe. Her mouth was totally dry and her heart felt like it was going to burst from her chest.

"But," continued the little man, "I'm not a bad guy. Not really. Not completely, anyway. I personally think you should get a choice. You're a nice lady, and this isn't about you anyway."

"Please don't . . ."

"So, the choice is this. You get to pick the way this ends. This way," he said, holding up the syringe, "or this way." He held up the pistol.

"God, please."

"God ain't part of this conversation, miss. It's just you, me, and a choice. Mother Night didn't authorize me to give you this choice. This is me being a nice guy." He smiled. "So what's it going to be?"

"You don't understand," said Junie. "It's not about me. I . . . I'm pregnant."

Chapter One Hundred and Fourteen

Marriott Marquis Hotel
265 Peachtree Center Avenue
Atlanta, Georgia
Sunday, September 1, 3:56 p.m.

The crowd jumped and roiled around Mother Night, and she laughed to see them writhe. She held the pink plastic scissors over her head, waggling them back and forth. The action made the underside of one breast peek deliciously from beneath her cutoff shirt. Men and women hooted and whistled.

"I need a volunteer!" she called, and they pressed forward, all of them totally caught in the moment even though none of them had any idea of the payoff to this game. It didn't matter. The world seemed to be going crazy and this was their reality. The rolling, endless party that was DragonCon and this beautiful, sexy, wild woman.

"Me! Meeee!" cried a girl dressed as an anime character with fuzzy pink cat ears. She was closest and her voice soared through the din. "Me!"

Mother Night smiled at her. A big, wide, wonderful smile. She hooked a finger under the girl's chin, lifted her face, and kissed her on the tip of the nose. "You win."

Then she handed the scissors to the girl.

The crowd thundered its appreciation, though there were cries of disappointment threaded through the noise.

Mother Night made a twirling gesture to the boys in hoodies and they spun the slaves around in a full circle. Once, twice, again.

"Snip, snip!" yelled Mother Night, and she stepped aside to give the girl in the fantasy costume access to the slaves. Their hands were tied with strips of red cloth.

As she approached, the girl pretended to be grossed out by the wounds all over the slaves, but it was all comedy and every time she made a face the audience laughed harder.

"Snip, snip, snip," said Mother Night.

The girl flourished the scissors—and received cheers—then she turned and gently inserted the blades between the bound hands of one of the slaves. The cloth was wet, the slave was struggling, and it took a bit of doing to cut through the material. But suddenly the bonds fell away and the man's hands were free. He swayed as if very drunk.

"Now take off his hood and give Prince Charming a big kiss!"

Lots of hoots and rude comments followed that.

The girl with the fuzzy cat ears blushed, a hand to her mouth, as she tentatively reached up, took hold of the pillowcase that had been used as a hood, and with a great dramatic flourish whipped it off.

And screamed.

The face below was slashed and hacked and covered with blood. His skin was pale, his eyes dull and empty.

The crowd gasped and stepped back.

Then they cheered even louder, shouting their praise of the great, life-like, professionally accomplished zombie makeup.

There were shouts of "*The Walking Dead*!" and "George Romero is God!"

The applause was massive, it shook the walls and rose high into the atrium. People on balconies threw confetti and colored scarves and anything else they had. Mother Night moved out into the center of the floor, waving at them, encouraging them, ignoring the guards who told her to dial it down. There was no dialing this down. It was like Mardi Gras times ten, and the whole place shook with laughter, yells, and applause.

The girl with the fuzzy cat ears grinned and blushed, and it was all so wonderful, so much fun.

Until the man she had just freed grabbed her by the shoulders, yanked her forward, and tore out her throat with his teeth.

Most of the crowd did not see it, could not hear it, did not know it for almost five full seconds. Then, like ripples from a stone dropped into water, the yells of the crowd turned to screams. Mother Night flicked out a switchblade and slashed the bonds of the second slave, whipped off his hood, and shoved him toward the boys in the hoodies. The dead thing, which had once been one of Bill Collins's assassins, snarled and flung itself at the boys. Biting. Tearing.

The girl with the fuzzy cat ears sank to her knees, blood pouring from her throat. In her veins, in her flesh, the infection was already taking hold. The *seif-al-din* had been engineered to work at blinding speed. Nature could never have created it, only science twisted to awful purpose could have done this.

Before her mind and body were truly dead, the infected girl with the fuzzy cat ears snaked her hands out, grabbed the arm of a woman who was trying to help her, and sank her teeth into the soft flesh of her inner arm.

Mother Night cried out in nearly orgasmic joy.

This was power.

This was her victory.

The end of everything started right here, with her as the zero point, the center of the new big bang, the author of this red madness.

Inside her head the old, unevolved voice cried out, but that voice went unheard and unheeded.

Around Mother Night the slaughter began.

Chapter One Hundred Fifteen

White House Press Room
Washington, D.C.
Sunday, September 1, 3:57 p.m.

Vice President William Collins stood a few feet behind the president and to his right. The posture he affected was intended to convey a separation between the commander in chief and himself—head bowed, hands clasped in front of his body, positioned to the extreme edge of what would be the televised image. The attorney general, Mark Eppenfeld, stood next to him. On the other side of the podium were the director of Homeland Security, the secretary of state, and the surgeon general.

The press was relentless. Asking the hard questions, tearing apart everything the president said, chewing at the edges of his credibility. Collins tried not to fidget, aware that the press—and the American people—would be scrutinizing him for complicity, for guilt, or for distance. He wanted to convey distance while at the same time looking like he wasn't a rat deserting a sinking ship. It was delicate, and he gave every movement, even subtle changes of facial expression, serious thought.

At that moment, the NBC correspondent was asking which provisions of law allowed the president to order troops to open fire on the "sick and wounded" in the Brooklyn subway.

Ouch, thought Collins, *that one's going to leave a mark.*

The president paused before answering, letting his famous penetrating stare do some of his work while he organized his answer. He had scripted answers for a lot of questions, but so far the man had gone off-script a dozen times. Trying for the personal touch, relying on genuineness and spontaneity to reconnect with a truly hostile audience. Every reporter in the place, even those who were friends of the administration, smelled blood in the water and they wanted to tear him apart. Careers were being made today, or would be if their program of attack journalism played out in their favor. This question was a killer and it was the fulcrum on which everything turned. Collins didn't know how the president would handle it.

"I would like to be able to tell you that the video which was broadcast today was a total fabrication, that no such tragedy occurred and that I played no part in the decision to use lethal force. However, I promised the American people that I would tell them the truth, and that I will do. That I am prepared to do."

He paused and his dark eyes moved slowly across the sea of faces.

Good luck selling it, asshole, thought Collins.

The president stood very straight, his head high, eyes clear. "Since the tragedy of 9/11 our nation has been engaged in a so-called War on Terror. That war is ongoing. It has never gone away. It makes the headlines less often even when bombs explode in our cities. We, as a society, have lived with terrorism for nearly a generation. It has become a regular part of our lives, and even though it is a part of our shared American lexicon, too often we forget to consider its nature or its scope."

The press grew very quiet, and Collins could see some doubt on their faces. This wasn't going the way they expected and they, like he, didn't know where the president was going with this.

"Many people seem to believe that we have won the war on terror, that groups like the Taliban and al-Qaeda are on the run. They continue to be threats," said the president, "but there are greater threats out there, dangerous enemies whose identities are not household names. These enemies wage a constant war against the American people and our ideal of freedom and democracy. The weapons they bring to bear are often far more sophisticated than are commonly associated with terrorist groups or cells. Exotic bioweapons, genetic weapons, designer pathogens, weaponized diseases designed for the purposes of ethnic genocide, and other threats of equal complexity. To some, these weapons may appear to be the stuff of science fiction, but I can assure you they are not.

"The only way to oppose such weapons and to insure the safety of the American people, our country and our allies, was to form a group under special charter. That group is composed of some of the most brilliant scientific minds of our time and the most elite and courageous special operations forces gathered from the SEALs, Marine Force Recon, Army Special Forces, FBI Hostage Rescue, the ATF, SWAT, and other groups. These men and women are the best of the best and it is their job to fight this war on terror with every weapon we can put into their hands."

Holy shit, thought Collins, *he's outing the damn DMS. He's actually going to use the DMS to save his own ass.*

The president spoke for several minutes to a stunned audience. He did not name names, but he gave a general description of the Department of Military Sciences. And he described some of the bioweapons the DMS had tackled.

"Mr. President," said a reporter, "don't you think the American people have a right to know more about this organization?"

The president fixed him with a considering stare. "In a perfect world there would be no secrets and no need for secrets. In that perfect world our enemies could not use knowledge about the inner workings of our covert special forces against us. In a perfect world all battles would be fought on a level playing field and according to a set of rules. This is the twenty-first century and there are no rules of fair play and good sportsmanship. Precious documents like the Geneva Convention and the Bill of Human Rights mean less than nothing to our enemies. The tragedy that occurred yesterday was not the result of a military coup, it was not an example of excessive force by a corrupt administration, nor was it military or police brutality. What happened yesterday was a tragedy. The terrorist who calls herself Mother Night released one of the world's deadliest pathogens into that subway car. That pathogen infected and killed every single person. All of those deaths, every one of them, can be laid at the feet of this enemy of our country. What was shown on the video was a distorted version of a terrible, painful, but necessary response."

He called the surgeon general up to describe the function of the *seif-al-din* pathogen. He was frank, calm, precise, and terrifying.

Then the president returned to the podium. "It's sometimes difficult for us to grasp the realities of this disease because its very nature is one of deception. The parasites that drive the pathogen manipulate the central nervous system of the victims, making their bodies move and act in an aggressive manner. But in that state, at that stage of the disease, the person who once inhabited that body is dead. That person has been murdered by the cowards who released this disease. Because this disease is one hundred percent communicable and the mortality rate is also one hundred percent, the only possible response—the only safe, sane, and moral response—is to destroy the central nervous system. That is what the people of our joint specials forces team did. It was a tragedy for everyone involved. For the victims of the disease, our innocent brothers and sisters murdered by these terrorists; and for the brave members of our Special Forces."

He paused.

"Now, imagine for a moment what they felt. Imagine how they felt. Having to open fire on what *appeared* to be their fellow citizens. Imagine the pain and the horror they felt." He shook his head. "Those soldiers are victims, too. They have had injuries inflicted on them in this war. Emotional hurt that they will have to carry with them for the rest of their lives."

Another pause. Even Collins held his breath.

"I am going to play a five-second clip from that incident. As you will see and, more important, what you will *hear* is a false audio track overlaid onto the actual audio. You will see that Mother Night intended to use this video to make everyone who watched it complicit in her attempt to drive us apart. We were able to separate that false soundtrack, and you'll hear it and then the original."

He nodded to a technician and a movie screen slid noiselessly down from the ceiling. The lights dimmed and the video began.

However, it was not the video from the subway.

It was something radically different, and only later would the White House cybercrimes team be able to determine that it was planted in the system using a type of computer intrusion alarmingly similar to Mind-Reader.

The video was clearly taken from a camera mounted on a bedpost, and it was equally clear that one of the two people in the video was unaware that a camera was rolling. That was evident because no sane person would say the things he said.

". . . and you're sure you can get that video out to everyone?" asked the man.

"Of course," said the woman.

"It's got to go every-fucking-where. I mean it. I want the American people storming the White House with pitchforks and torches. I want them to hang that sanctimonious motherfucker by his balls. And then, by God, I am going to take this country back to its roots. Even if I have to roll tanks down Broadway, I'll do whatever I have to do to bring America back on track. Born in fire, reborn in fire."

"Oh," said the woman, "you know what I think. Sometimes you have to burn to shine."

There was more, but by then the video had done all the damage it could do.

The man in the video was William Collins.

The woman was Mother Night.

They were naked, in each other's arms.

When the lights came on, everyone looked to where Collins had been standing, but he was gone.

The Secret Service eventually found him. It was the sound of the single gunshot that drew them to the spot where Collins lay, the barrel of a pistol in his mouth. His suit was blue, his shirt was white, and his blood was bright red.

Chapter One Hundred and Sixteen

Marriott Marquis Hotel
265 Peachtree Center Avenue
Atlanta, Georgia
Sunday, September 1, 4:00 p.m.

When I heard the screams I knew we were too late.

I was already running toward the Marriott, pistol in my hand, a swarm of shooters behind me. People came running out of the hotel. Some of them were in costume, some weren't. No one looked hurt but that didn't mean anything. Not really. Even a small bite would do it. Or blood in their eyes or mouth. We'd have to trust to the techs at the barricades to make judgment calls. God help anyone who had so much as a cold sore, because no one was getting a break today. We were in hell, and nothing good happens in hell.

Top and Bunny flanked me as I raced toward the Marriott entrance, and the rest of Echo was seeded through the crowd. People screamed when they saw us and they scattered like birds. Some of them ran back up the steps to the hotel. Others ran to the Hyatt and more ducked down behind cars. A few stood there, stupid and immobile with shock, as people with guns ran past them.

Overhead, I could hear the choppers coming. We had every military bird we could muster. Sixty-three helos. Apaches, Black Hawks, Vipers. All of them heavy with missiles and rockets, machine guns leering out of side doors. Behind and in front of me the National Guard was slamming the barricades shut. The crowd surged toward them and I prayed the barricades would hold.

The crowds flooding out of the hotel were like a tidal surge and we had to fight our way up each step, bashing people aside. Some of them were so intensely terrified that they didn't even react to the guns in our hands. They just wanted out.

Yeah, and we were trying to get in. How smart were we?

Bunny got in front of me and literally smashed people out of our way. We finally got inside the hotel and that's when we realized just how bad things were.

People lay bloody on the ground, trampled by the panicked crowds. Some of them were clearly dead. Others lay crippled and screaming.

Down the hall and around the corner the screams were even louder, though, and we fought our way through the human tide. We were battered and struck and careened into and tripped by people who were so much less afraid of us and our guns than they were of whatever was happening inside the atrium.

I realized suddenly that Top and Bunny were no longer with me. Somehow, the crowd had separated us. Ahead, though, I could see a woman standing on a marble wall, waving her arms and shouting at the crowd. Mother Night—but too far away for me to take a shot. All around her was a scene that my mind refused to connect with the real world. After everything I've seen, this was too much, too far, too strange. People dressed in Starfleet costumes, people dressed as Dorothy Gale and her companions, people dressed as characters from video games I couldn't even name, were *eating each other*.

It was already far too late.

There were scores of infected.

Hundreds.

And more people died every moment, dragged down and bitten, their flesh torn away, blood everywhere. Screams and pain everywhere.

Horror everywhere.

I tapped my earbud. "Echo Team, look for Mother Night. If you see her, take the shot."

If there were any replies, it was too loud for me to hear them.

I jumped up onto the lip of an abandoned information desk, trying to understand the pattern of this. Trying to see Mother Night.

And there she was, dressed like one of those fantasy characters in Japanese comics. Little-girl clothes recut as a statement of sexuality. I'd always thought that kind of thing crossed the line into some publicly acceptable species of pedophilia, a Lolita lust for the comic book crowd. Never my thing. I like my women grown up. Never had a desire to troll for sex on the school yard. But Mother Night was playing it up. She stood on a high marble wall, well above the grasping hands of the dead, dancing, waving her arms, laughing at the carnage she'd wrought.

It was at that moment that I realized Bug and Rudy had been right about her and I'd been as wrong as Aunt Sallie, Church, and Hu. Until that moment I'd been looking for clues to her endgame. The chaos in the streets had to be a distraction for something else. The bombs, the release of the pathogens, the videos, all of them had to be carefully planned components of some grand scheme. I'd become even more certain of it when we realized that Mother Night was Artemisia Bliss. She was the master strategist; someone as brilliant and calculating as her had to be working toward a goal every bit as big, as evil, as devastating as what the Jakobys and Hugo Vox had planned.

Had to be.

Nothing else made sense. Even Hitler had a damn plan.

But now I knew what Rudy had understood all along. He'd told us about it at her trial. Maybe Bliss herself had told Aunt Sallie and the others during her initial job interview. I read a transcript of that session, heard her talk about suicide attempts, about the need to stand out. To shine.

And hadn't Mother Night told us over and over again?

Sometimes you have to burn to shine.

The whole world was watching now. The subway video was probably playing on every TV and computer monitor in the world. The bombs had been like finger snaps, making people turn to listen. The controlled releases of the plagues had set expectations of her power. The destruction of the CDC and the total pathogenic pollution of the Locker were not the result of bungled attempts to secure the bioweapons. She already had what she needed. She used the CDC to kill Samson Riggs and tried to killed me and Echo at the Locker. Perhaps if the Warehouse in Baltimore hadn't been destroyed last year, resulting in all DMS field offices tripling their security, she might have tried to take out the Hangar.

Maybe she knew that she couldn't take on Mr. Church and Aunt Sallie in head-to-head battle. Or, more likely, she left them alone so they could be her witnesses. The most important witnesses. Sure, there have to be witnesses for something to have importance. Church and the others had to see her win and know that they lost. That was the end of the equation.

That was her endgame right there.

So what was this? What was it Bug and Rudy thought was going to play out here?

Sometimes you have to burn to shine.

If you're the one who's burning, what's left afterward?

Only the memory of that brilliant light.

Mother Night stood above the crowd, literally atop the wall, and figuratively as the conductor of the mad symphony playing out below.

I raised my pistol and fired at her. Handguns are great at close range but they suck ass beyond fifty yards and she was all the way across a sea of the living, the dying, and the hungry dead. I fired anyway.

For a moment I thought the gods of war had granted me their grace, because she jerked sideways. Then I realized that the bullet had hit the wall nearby and she flinched from the point of impact. She crouched, looking wildly around, and I think she spotted some of my people fighting their way through the crowd. A moment later she was gone, leaping down behind the wall, out of sight.

So I did the same thing, jumping from the information counter and diving into the crowd. I was still mostly in an area of screaming people caught in a human gridlock as they fought to flee and in their panic became the enemies of survival for everyone. Bodies lay trampled everywhere. Small knots of people huddled together in corners. I saw several people standing stock-still, their eyes glazed, colorful candy wrappers in their hands. No idea what that was all about, but I had a bad feeling I'd find out.

Here and there were pockets of resistance. A bartender held his ground behind the counter and used heavy bottles of top-shelf alcohol as clubs, smashing them over the heads of a mass of infected who were trying to crawl past him to get at several cowering patrons. A fat man in chain mail was swinging a sword, except that the sword was still in its sheath, held in place by a peace bond. Even so, he swung the weapon like a cudgel and he laid about him with a will. There were several dead or crippled walkers piled around him. Thirty feet past him, three police officers stood back-to-back in a shooting triangle, firing at anyone who came near them.

But these pockets could not last.

Did not last.

I saw one of the cops begin to reload an empty pistol, and in the few seconds it took for him to drop his magazine and swap in a new one, a teenager in a dark hoodie threw himself at the cop in a tackle that knocked all three of the officers down. Four more infected piled atop them.

Somewhere off to my left came the big boom of Bunny's combat shotgun. Again and again. Then more gunfire to my right and behind me. Echo Team and the rest of the shooters. But the crowd was so thick I couldn't see any of them.

I began fighting my way toward Mother Night. I needed to stop her. She was the driving force for everything that was happening and I needed to switch her off.

I tried to push my way toward her, but a new surge swept me sideways.

I thought I heard someone speaking through my earbud. I pressed the bud deeper into my ear and caught some of it. ". . . streets secure . . . crowd surge . . . need more trucks to block . . ." Then a note of rising panic. *"They're out! They're out! I have walkers on . . . oh God!"*

And then a different voice.

". . . going weapons hot . . ."

I recognized that voice. The pilot of my own Black Hawk.

Even through the roar of the crowd I could hear a new and terrible sound. The thunder of heavy-caliber automatic guns all around the buildings.

God help us.

The infected had escaped the building and the helicopters were opening up on the crowd.

Cursing, I tried to shoulder into the melee. A shrill scream made me spin, and a walker had a woman dressed as an elf and he was trying to bite her. She had her forearm jammed under his chin, but he was much bigger. I bashed him in the temple with my pistol butt, and as he staggered off I jammed my barrel against the bridge of his nose and blew off the back of his head. Blood sprayed the face of a second walker, momentarily blinding him. I shattered his knee with a side-thrust kick and as he fell I axe-kicked the side of his neck. He landed in a sprawl, his head tilted awkwardly on a shattered spine.

When I turned to help the girl up, she was gone.

I heard Mother Night shouting to the crowd, making crazy jokes with pop-culture references that were lost on me. I elbowed a bleeding man aside and turned to look. She was above me, leaning over the rail from the fifth floor. No idea how the hell she got up there. She must have had some of her anarchist crew with her to help clear out an elevator car. I raised my gun to fire again, but a powerful arm came whipping out of the crowd and slapped my pistol from my hands. The shock jerked my finger and there was a single bang, but I had no idea where the bullet went. As I lost the gun I spun toward the asshole who'd hit me. He was a real bull of a guy in a hooded sweatshirt and a rubber gorilla mask. He went to grab the front of my shirt, but I slapped his reaching hand away and drove a two-knuckle punch into his short ribs.

I might as well have been punching a brick wall for all the good it did.

He laughed.

The son of a bitch actually laughed.

So I tried to change his mood with a palm-heel shot across the chops that knocked the gorilla mask from his face.

The blow did not drop the man, as I had every right to expect.

It didn't even stop him from laughing.

The face that leered down at me was brutish, almost a match for the mask I'd just knocked away. A heavy brown, flat nose, overgrown incisors.

It was a Berserker.

But it was far worse than that.

The skin was a pallid gray-green and he stank like rotting meat. Drool ran from the corners of his mouth, and in that bubbling spit I could see tiny maggots writhing and twisting. Its eyes, though, were filled with a terrible awareness and a dreadful hunger.

The Berserker was a Generation Twelve walker.

Oh shit.

Chapter One Hundred and Seventeen

Grand Hyatt Hotel

109 East Forty-second Street

New York City

Sunday, September 1, 4:01 p.m.

Ludo Monk stared at her for several seconds, his eyes seeming to go in and out of focus.

"Pregnant?" he asked.

"Yes."

"Mother didn't say anything about you being pregnant."

"No one knows."

"Joey-boy doesn't know?"

"No one knows. Please . . . don't hurt my baby."

"No," said Monk. "You're lying to me. You don't even have a baby bump. This is a cheap trick and I've heard crap like this before."

"It's the truth! Please, you don't have to hurt me."

"Yeah," said Ludo Monk, "I'm pretty sure I do. That's how it works. Baby or no baby. That's what Mother Night needs me to do. It's just your good luck that I'm giving *you* a choice. A quick bullet or the needle. But I got to tell you, I don't think you should even consider the second option, because then you're this ugly monster lady and when Joey-boy comes home you'll get all bitey on him, and that's a downhill slide. There's no happy ending to that romance, you see where I'm going with this?"

"You can just leave," begged Junie.

"We covered that already. Don't make me make this decision myself. I'm already pissed that I wasn't allowed to do this my way. I hate personal interaction, and you're sitting there with those big eyes and those sun freckles looking all innocent and wholesome, and I'm going to feel like a total piece of shit either way. At least the bullet is quick and clean."

"Listen to me," said Junie, trying to keep her voice level, "if you know who I am, then you know who Joe is."

"Sure."

"Do you know *about* him? Do you?"

"Yeah. He's crazier than I am, and I'm really out there."

"Do you know what he's capable of?"

"Yup."

"Do you know what he's done to other people? People like criminals and terrorists."

"Yeah, he's killed more people than God. That's why Mother Night wanted him taken out of the picture. But now I hear that he slipped her punch. So if she can't kill him, then she wants to do something worse."

Junie's heart suddenly lifted. Joe was alive. Whatever that woman had tried to do, he'd escaped or survived it.

"If you hurt me," she said, "Joe is going to find you and he will—"

A knock on the door interrupted her words. She and the man both froze, eyes darting to the door.

And in that moment Junie moved.

She screamed at the top of her lungs, slapped the syringe out of the man's hand, and drove her shoulder into his chest, driving him backward into the desk. The movement was much faster and harder than either of them expected, and as they hit the edge of the desk the force spun them around and toward the floor. He tried to club her with the gun and break his fall and grab her all at the same time, and he failed in all three things. The gun struck the carpet, bounced, and hit the door with a thud. Then he and Junie crashed to the floor. His hand darted out and snagged her hair, and he jerked back to try to break her neck.

The hair came away and he fell back as Junie flung herself sideways.

Without her hair she was bald except for a dusting of peach fuzz on her scalp.

A fist pounded on the door and Junie screamed for help as the man lunged for the fallen gun. She tried to kick it away, missed, and he snatched it just as the door burst inward in a spray of wood splinters and twisted metal.

Chapter One Hundred and Eighteen

The Berserker swung a fist at me with blinding speed but I got an elbow up in time to save my skull from being crushed. The force was incredible, though, and it plucked me clean off the ground and hurled me into a group of people trying to flee the carnage. We all landed badly and I felt something break under me. Someone's leg, I think.

I scrambled to my feet, shoving fleeing conferees out of my way. There was a man dressed as Thor from the movies and I grabbed his hammer, hoping to smash the zombie Berserker into roach paste. I was already in full motion, taking the hammer, swinging it, aiming, hitting, and all the time realizing that the hammer was made out of rubber and plastic. It exploded into empty debris. I would have done more damage blowing him a kiss.

He snarled at me, showing his big gorilla teeth.

Shit.

Generation Twelve of the *seif-al-din* allows the infected to retain their full mental capacities even while the rest of the body begins a sloweddown process of decay. If there were a worst-case scenario for a zombie plague, genetically altered supersoldiers would be way at the top of my list.

He swung a punch that would have turned my head into pulp.

I got under it and hooked a punch into his groin.

It staggered him, just a little. He stumbled back a step and roared at me.

Roared.

Yeah.

You'd think a guy like me wouldn't be fazed by something like that. You'd be wrong. Like I said, mutant zombie supersoldier.

Find a comfortable corner of your mind for that to curl up in.

But . . .

Damn if it didn't feel like my knuckles punched actual balls instead of combat padding.

Inside my head the Killer let loose with his own roar. Fuck it. If this monster wanted to fight dirty, then I was willing to get all sorts of dirty.

Maybe he thought he didn't need armor with the *seif-al-din* cooking in his bloodstream.

I snatched my rapid-release folding knife from my pocket. It was the third one I'd had this weekend. The first was in a barrel along with my Hammer suit, either still down in the subway or in storage wherever they put toxic waste. The second was with my second Hammer suit in the decontamination unit at the Locker. This one was borrowed from Bird Dog, the DMS logistics utility infielder. He had good taste in knives, too. A Wilson Tactical Rapid Response knife with a three-and-three-eighths stainless blade. Not a lot of reach but it was so light that it moved at the same speed as my hand. My hands are very fucking fast.

I moved in and left, ducking low and slashing at the side of his knee, feeling the tendon part. I don't care if you're a muscle freak, a zombie, or a mutant, you need your leg tendons. He went to one knee but chopped at my head with his elbow. Bastard was fast, but I took the impact on my shoulder and used the force to propel me forward and out of range. I banged into a walker who was biting Captain Kirk. I grabbed him by the collar and jerked him backward and down. The back of his head hit the edge of a bar table. I sidestepped the mess. Captain Kirk wandered off, bleeding and screaming and weeping.

The Berserker rushed me on wobbling legs, arms wide to scoop me into a crushing embrace. I met his rush with a flat-footed stamp-kick to the front of his hips. The effect is like running into a fireplug—everything below the waist stops, everything above the waist cants sharply forward. As his head bowed forward I jammed a palm against his shoulder and for a split second he was frozen in that bent-forward position. A split second was all the time I needed to bury my blade into the top of his skull. I knew the right spot. The fontanelle. That area of the skull that's soft on babies and never quite firms up. I drove the knife in all the way to the hilt and then wrenched it a quarter turn.

The Berserker died. Right then. There was no death spasm, no struggle to stave off the reaper. He simply stopped living. Everything that made him a monster, a person, and a threat was gone. I stepped back and let the fall of his body help me pull my knife free.

"On your six!" I heard someone shout, and I turned to see Montana behind me. She was bleeding from a broken nose, and one eye was puffed nearly shut. She had her rifle up and fired three shots past me, dropping two walkers.

"Give me your sidearm," I snapped, and she pulled her Glock and handed it to me along with two magazines. There was considerable gunfire to our right, and we turned to see Bunny plowing the road with round after round from his drum-fed shotgun. Noah was with him, but there was no sign of Top.

Outside, the sound of machine-gun fire was intensifying.

The look in the eyes of my team was probably the same as what had to be in mine. Despair and fury in equal measure.

"Mother Night's up on the balcony. Where's Sam?"

Bunny jerked his head to the far side of the lobby. "Lost him and Top somewhere over there. They saw her running for the elevators with one of those Berserker assholes."

"The Berserkers are infected with Gen. Twelve."

"Well . . . fuck me blind."

A voice began speaking in my ear and I covered my ears to listen while my team circled up, their backs to me, firing into the crowd to try to stop the unstoppable tide.

"Deacon to Cowboy . . ."

"Go for Cowboy."

"The infection is in the streets. We are working to contain the spread. Have you acquired the target?"

"Not yet."

"Give me an assessment. Can the civilians inside that hotel be saved?"

It was such a hard, cruel, necessary question.

"If they're in their rooms, maybe. I think we're losing the lobby."

"Be advised that the president and the governor have authorized sterilization of that building if there is no hope of preserving significant numbers of uninfected."

"Not yet, damn it."

"Give me another option."

"We need boots on the ground. Not out there—in *here*. Send in the damn cavalry."

Church paused. "I'll see what I can do."

"And Mother Night may have video cameras in here."

"She does," said Church, "the feed is leaking to the Internet."

"Shit. You got to find some way to—"

"Bug is close to cracking her system and is confident he will be able to jam all the cameras. I will alert you when that happens."

"Make it fast. We're going after Mother Night and I don't want her gloating to the world."

"Captain, listen to me," said Church, "we're not interested in an arrest. Not this time."

"Preaching to the choir."

"Then good hunting, Captain. And God bless."

He was gone and I looked at the lobby. Maybe I was asking for help for something that was already helpless. But damn it, this was still a fight. There were still more people uninfected than transformed.

And I needed to get to Mother Night. Goddamn it, I needed to look into her eyes and determine for myself if there was any shoe left to drop. Was this slaughter what she wanted or did she still have one last game to play?

"We need to get to the elevators," I yelled. "Clear me a path. Right now."

Bunny swapped in a new drum and everyone fished for fresh magazines. The elevators were thirty yards away. They might as well have been on the dark side of the moon.

Even so, we had to try.

We raised our weapons at the seething crowd and began firing.

I would like to say that the only people we killed were infected. I would dearly love that to be true.

But that would only be a lie.

Chapter One Hundred and Nineteen

Grand Hyatt Hotel
109 East Forty-second Street
New York City
Sunday, September 1, 4:04 p.m.

As the door burst open, Ludo Monk snatched up the pistol, turned, fired without aiming. The figure coming through the doorway moved with blinding speed. There was a second shot. A third.

A scream.

No, screams.

A woman's scream. High, shrill, filled with pain and terror.

And his own voice. Nearly as high, screeching so loud that the sound of it burned away the clouds in his mind, leaving him clearheaded for a moment. No intruding voices, no peculiar patterns of thought. In that moment he could see and hear and understand everything with a clarity that was so rare and . . .

And lovely.

It was beautiful. Never once in his entire life had there been such fidelity of vision and perception. Never before had something stilled the voices in his head. Not even the pills did it this completely.

Monk tried to understand what was happening.

He turned his head and it moved very loosely on his neck. Too loosely. He knew that his neck was not broken, yet the muscles were strangely slack.

"What——?" he asked.

A figure moved from left to right in front of him. Tall, slender, female, and familiar. He didn't know her name, did he?

Something . . .

Something musical.

He was sure of it.

"M——Mother——?" he asked, hoping it was her. Needing it to be her.

There was no answer. Not to his question. But the woman with the musical name was speaking. Shouting.

Monk turned his head again, trying to see who was talking. Why was it so hard to remember who was in the room with him? He knew that he should know this. It was just a few moments ago.

A few moments.

Everything had changed in those moments.

His mind became clearer and yet he could not fill it with names or meaning.

The woman was kneeling now and he saw her bend down over something . . .

No.

Over someone.

Another woman.

A woman who seemed to be lying on a red blanket.

Or floating in a red pool.

Monk could not tell which, but as he watched the blanket or pool it grew larger and larger.

"Mother?" he asked again.

The women ignored him. Neither was his mother.

He heard the tall woman yelling something.

"Junie! Junie, stay with me. Stay with me . . ."

That was funny to Monk because it was clear that the other woman, the bald woman, wasn't trying to go anywhere. So strange.

The lights in his mind began to go out as if someone were walking through a room and flipping switches. The darkness was soft and cool and it covered him completely.

Chapter One Hundred and Twenty

Marriott Marquis Hotel
265 Peachtree Center Avenue
Atlanta, Georgia
Sunday, September 1, 4:11 p.m.

It took two or three thousand years for us to fight our way across the lobby. Halfway there, Lydia joined us. She had a Sig Sauer in one hand and a Glock in the other and her face was flecked with powder burns.

We kept going, kept fighting.

This was so much worse than the slaughter outside the Ark chamber down in the Locker and worse even than the subway slaughter. Some of these people stared at us in horror, the hurt of betrayal in their terrified eyes. Some of them begged us for help even as their eyes began to glaze from infection. There were people of all kinds there. Adults of every age. Children.

Tears burned like acid in my eyes as I fired.

Then we reached the elevator. The door was jammed open by a knot of corpses and three walkers who crouched over them, feeding messily.

"Yo! Dickheads!" yelled Montana. Their heads jerked up and she blew them back against the wall and out of this version of hell. Bunny grabbed the dead and flung them into the lobby, tripping two other walkers who were rushing us from behind. Before I could bring my gun up, the two walkers pitched sideways, red spray blowing from the sides of their heads. I never even heard the shot and I wasted one moment looking around for the shooter. Had to be Sam, but I couldn't see him.

We crowded into the elevator.

The lights on every floor were lit and at each stop we had to shove back the living and the dead. It was as heartbreaking as it was terrifying.

"I don't know how much more of this I can . . ." began Montana, her voice low and fragile, but then she stiffened. "No," she snapped, directing it at me or herself, or both. "No."

We reloaded.

"I'm sorry," I said to her. "If there had been some other way to ease you into this. Or to let you know this is what we did . . ."

"No," she said again, and there was a bright—almost fevered—ferocity in her eyes. "This has to be done. If not us, who?"

Behind her, Noah laid a hand on her shoulder and said, "Hooah."

"Hooah," echoed Bunny, Lydia, and I.

The doors opened and we stepped out onto a balcony that was completely crowded with the infected. There were at least five Berserkers among them, towering like titans above the throng of ordinary walkers. Beyond the Berserkers, standing against the balcony wall, was Mother Night.

The crowd of the dead let out a deafening moan of raw, unending hunger, and rushed at us from both sides.

Once more we formed a shooting line, Bunny and Noah facing forward, Lydia and Montana facing behind us, and me looking for a way to get to Mother Night. I had the irrational feeling that this was actually hell. The real hell. And it would be nothing but this. Red slaughter and the roar of guns, blood and pain and death.

Some of the infected seemed to be whole, without bites or marks to indicate how they'd died. And I recalled the woman I'd seen downstairs, looking like she was on the edge of becoming a walker. I remembered the candy wrapper in her hand. There were other wrappers, and plenty of unopened candies down there on the floor. It didn't require a leap of genius intellect to come up with a theory on that. The *seif-al-din* pathogen could easily be added to food, or injected into a tasty piece of chocolate. It fit with the "love me while I destroy you" vibe that Artemisia Bliss had constructed within her Mother Night persona.

I saw an opening and left the shooting line, using the borrowed pistol and knife to carve a path to Mother Night.

A Berserker saw me trying to do an end run around the pack of dead and he began wading toward me, pushing walkers out of his way. He gave me one of those mind-numbing roars. He had a pistol tucked into his waistband but he came at me with those big, bone-cracking hands.

"Dumb ass," I said, and shot him through the eye.

Behind him, a second—perhaps smarter—Berserker raised a handgun and fired three shots at me, forcing me to dive behind a metal trash can while I returned fire. I hit him in the chest, which did nothing to the undead son of a bitch, and when he opened his mouth to laugh at me, he vomited blood, tissue, and a high-powered rifle slug.

Sam.

I still couldn't see him but right them I wanted to kiss him. If I had a sister I'd let him marry her.

Two other Berserkers closed in on me, both firing handguns. A bullet punched me in the chest and knocked me back. The Kevlar stopped it, but from the sudden, grinding pain I knew that something was broken. When I raised my gun, the pain jumped to the top of the scale and I realized that the raw impact of the Berserker's bullet had cracked my sternum.

But a split second later I saw the Berserker wheel away as a dark form rose up from the press of bodies. There was a flash of silver, over and over again, and the Berserker seemed to fall apart. Then I saw Top moving away from him, two sturdy fighting knives in his fists. He had no gun and the front of his Kevlar vest was torn open and hung down, exposing brown skin crisscrossed with old scars and purpled with new bruises.

The battle raged on.

Mother Night saw me coming and she turned and ran, but it looked less like she was fleeing in panic and more like a catch-me-if-you-can flirtation.

So I ran after her.

I fired my gun dry and swapped and fished for my last magazine. Fired and fired.

Then I was at the edge of the crowd. I stabbed a walker in the eye and flung his body behind me to slow down pursuit. The balcony curved around and I pelted after Mother Night, though each step was screaming agony. My chest felt like it was on fire.

Then I rounded the next corner and there she was.

She'd climbed up onto the rail and had her arms spread wide to steady herself. Four of her small video cameras were mounted on the walls, their lenses aimed at her, little red lights burning.

Bliss turned to me and blew a kiss. "Hello, Joe."

In my earbud I heard another voice. Bug. He said, "It's done."

I slowed to a stop, gun pointed, waiting for her last trick. "Hello, Artie."

"Don't call me that."

"What would you prefer? Psycho Bitch? 'Cause that seems to work."

She actually smiled. "Been called worse."

"Yeah, me, too. Side effect of being a functional psychotic."

"You should know," she agreed.

"Yup."

She nodded to the gun. "Aren't you going to shoot me?"

"Good chance of it."

There was a playful twinkle in her eyes. "But——?"

"Need to ask a question first." I said. "Why?"

Mother Night seemed genuinely puzzled by the question. "Why? You mean you really haven't figured it out yet?"

"I've got some theories." The pain flared in my chest and I winced.

"You bit?"

"Broken sternum. Stood too close to a bullet."

"Not bit?"

"Nope."

"Mm. Ah, well. Can't have everything."

"Seems you got everything you were after," I said, making it casual. "Or is there still a cherry you're looking to put on top of it."

The question seemed to push some unusual buttons in her psyche, because a whole series of emotions wandered across her face. Doubt, happiness, triumph, anger, and even something that appeared to be innocent wonder. Finally, her brow wrinkled and she said, "I thought you would understand, Joe."

"Really? Why me?"

"Because you're the only one crazier than me."

"I might be nuts, kid, and I might have a whole committee shouting inside my head, but I never wanted to burn the world down."

Her frown deepened. "Neither do I."

I gestured to the madness down in the atrium. "You tried to release a doomsday weapon. Surely at some point you looked up *doomsday* in the dictionary."

She cocked her head to listen to the sound of gunfire from the swarm of helicopters. "They'll stop the infection. Even if they have to burn Atlanta to the ground, they'll stop it. There was never any doubt about that."

"What if we hadn't figured out that this was your big finale?"

She shrugged. The action caused her to wobble on the rail, but she regained her balance. "Whoa. But, no . . . I left you enough clues. Step by step there was enough for the DMS to figure it out in the right order and at the right time. Everything happened exactly right."

"Really? You're standing on a rail and, honey, there is no way out. And in case you're wondering, I didn't bring a pair of handcuffs."

"Of course not. Terminate with extreme prejudice. That's the phrase you guys like to use. Very manly, very macho."

"Yeah, it makes our dicks hard. You going somewhere with this? Is there some big dramatic speech you want to make? Any last shoe to drop to prove to us how smart you are and how dumb we are?"

"First, I know you're smart. What would be the fun of winning against a group of morons. You, Church, Aunt Sallie, Willie Hu, Bug . . . you're all the best. No one can stop you. You've proved it over and over again. The best of the best of the best."

"Except for you."

"Except for me."

"So . . . we're, what? We're Moriarty to your Holmes?"

"Close enough."

I nodded to the rail on which she stood. I lowered my gun, let it hang at my side. "And that's the Reichenbach Falls? Am I supposed to climb up and plunge over with you in the big finish?"

"Oh, would you?"

"Fuck you."

She sighed. "Hey, a girl can ask."

We actually smiled at each other. For just a moment.

Then she said, "Holmes killed Moriarty at the Reichenbach Falls. His archenemy fell and Holmes survived. Except that's not how this plays out. I've already killed you."

"What?"

"Not physically. No . . . after everything that's happened, I'm beginning to think that you can't be killed. You're like James Bond. You always walk away, even if you're busted and broken. You survive and live to fight another day."

I said nothing, waiting, cringing for what she was going to say next, now that we were really up to it.

"The only way I could kill you was to hurt you, Joe," she said. "I read your files. I know what happened when you were a teenager, what turned you into the maniac, the killer you've become. I believe that if something like that happened again, it would push you all the way over the edge. All the way. You'd be like me. Maybe worse."

"What are you talking about?"

"I hope you loved her, Joe," she said. "I hope you loved her with all your heart."

I felt a sudden, blinding pain in my chest that had nothing to do with a cracked sternum. I realized, I understood now. My body swayed as the enormity of it opened a big mouth in the floor that threatened to swallow me whole.

"Junie . . . ?" I whispered.

Mother Night's red mouth widened into a huge, insane grin of absolute triumph.

"I win," she said. "Everyone in the world is looking at me right now. Everyone. You didn't defeat me, Joe. Not you or your goon squad. Not Willie Hu or Aunt Sallie. Not Bug and not even Mr. Church. I made you all play my game exactly the way I wanted it. You wouldn't even be standing here if I hadn't allowed it to happen. I'm Mother Night," she said triumphantly, "and I win this game. There's nothing else left for me. No worlds left to conquer, because I beat this one. I did what no one else could ever do. And everyone watching me right now will know that Mother Night *won*."

I smiled at her. Despite the pain in body and soul, despite the terror that wanted to crush me down to my knees, I smiled.

"No, Artie," I said, "you don't get to win."

Doubt flickered in her eyes. "What?"

"Look at your cameras," I said.

She did.

All the little red lights were dark. "Bug hacked your system. He figured it out and cracked it like a walnut. The video was cut before you opened your mouth, so no one heard your big speech."

She pulled her sunglasses off and let them fall over the rail. Her eyes were huge.

"Here's how this ends," I said. "You spent so much time building up the Mother Night character that it's become a symbol. You used a couple of doubles already. At the Cyber Café and elsewhere. People think Mother Night is a group, not a person. And we're going to make sure that's all anyone ever knows. A terrorist organization created a fake identity and various nondescript, faceless agents assumed the role of Mother Night. There will never be a *real* Mother Night. No one will ever know that a woman named Artemisia Bliss ever existed. MindReader is already systematically erasing all records of you. You think you won? Fuck you. We're going to edit you out of the world. You're going to be forgotten. You're going to be the nothing you deserve to be. None of the victims or the survivors will ever know you even lived."

Her eyes grew wider and wider and filled with tears. "You . . . you can't . . . . . ."

"It's already done," I said. "You lose."

I raised my gun and put two rounds through the center of her cold, black heart.

She fell backward and damned if there wasn't a smile on her face as she plunged over the railing and fell.

All around me there were shouts and moans and the sound of gunfire. I heard none of it, saw none of it. All I could see or hear was the lingering image of her smile and the sound of my own screams.

Epilogue

Chaos.

After all the theories, after all the psychological profiling and strategic models, it came down to chaos. In the end, just chaos.

That's what Mother Night brought to America. That was her endgame.

God.

The DMS has spent so long fighting religious fundamentalists and terrorist splinter cells, kill squads from enemy states and domestic militiamen. Each time there is some kind of agenda, some clash of ideologies.

For Mother Night, all she wanted was to be recognized as the winner, and then lie down on her pyre and let it all burn.

Megalomania is the word Rudy used to describe her, but it's too thin and shallow to say what needs to be said. Though in truth I don't really think there is a word for what Mother Night was.

No, I'm wrong about that.

There is a word.

Monster.

The threats about erasing her from history had been spur-of-the-moment, but Bug and Church made it happen. Even her prison record and trial were expunged by MindReader. You can look for some trace of Artemisia Bliss, but you won't find a damn thing. Nothing. And Aunt Sallie built a thoroughly convincing story about a legion of nameless, faceless people using the Mother Night name and costume as part of a terror campaign. The real person was so deeply buried in the new "official story" as to become individually irrelevant. Did that mean we actually won? I'll let social philosophers figure that out.

Historians may well call the last two days the worst in U.S. history.

There have been days with bigger body counts. Fifty-one thousand died in three days at Gettysburg in 1863. Thirty-four thousand died in the Battle of Chickamauga, twenty-two thousand at Antietam. But they were casualties during battles in a war. We were not at war on Labor Day weekend. We were supposed to be at rest. At play.

Six thousand, eight hundred and four people died in Lexington and in Brooklyn, in Willow Grove and in Washington, and in a cluster of four hotels in Atlanta.

It could have been so much worse.

If the police and military in Atlanta hadn't done their jobs, it would have been the end for us. It would have been the first night of the apocalypse and no one would be alive to tell the story.

But we prevailed.

Prevailed.

That word showed up in a lot of speeches over the next few days. It sounds like a heroic victory, and sure, there were plenty of heroes, but I'm not sure there was a victory. Not in the truest sense.

None of the pathogens escaped the quarantine and free-fire zones.

The bioweapons never fell into the hands of our country's enemies. Mother Night never really intended to hand over those pathogens. It was all a lie, a theft, an illusion to make her feel powerful. To prove that she *was* powerful.

As a result of that auction, though, the enemies of the United States have become significantly weakened. North Korea most of all. Virtually every nation on earth has ceased trading with them and most have imposed incredibly harsh sanctions. Even China has distanced itself from North Korea. There's speculation as to whether the government will last.

The other countries in that auction claim that they were involved either under duress because of Mother Night's threats or to remove those items from the black market and thereby insure the safety of the world. Total bullshit, of course, and off the public radar the State Department was beating them up pretty heavily because of it. So, in a weird, twisted way Mother Night actually helped the United States. In political terms. In all other ways she did unbearable harm.

So . . . did we win or lose? Was that a victory?

You tell me.

3

Before Bliss's body had finished its long fall to the floor of the atrium, I was in motion, running for the closest exit, screaming into my microphone for Bug or Church or anyone to send people to my hotel.

To Junie.

God.

Junie.

A maniac had killed her guards, broken into her hotel room, and offered her the choice of *seif-al-din* or a bullet. She'd pleaded with him.

Not for her life.

For a life I didn't even know was there.

A baby.

Our baby.

Oh, God . . .

Violin had busted down the door. I'm not even sure if I have it straight in my head why she went to the hotel at all.

There was a fight. Shots.

The killer, Ludo Monk, died.

Junie was shot.

She did not die.

Did not.

Did not.

But the bullet did terrible damage. Awful damage.

Irreparable. Cruel damage.

I sat in Junie's hospital room, drinking bad coffee, watching her sleep, watching the news on TV. All regular programming was canceled. Everything was news coverage except on the movie and cartoon stations. The reporters all managed to do stand-ups in front of debris, or rows of bodies under sheets, or with flaming buildings behind them. Their producers cooked up catchphrases and labels and did everything they could to buzz them out into the social media floodwaters.

Fox News called it the Battle of Atlanta. They went out of their way to make sure they painted the current administration as villains willing to go to war with their own people.

MSNBC went with the Fall of Atlanta. They demonized the warmongers who were willing to rain fire down on U.S. citizens. In substance, it was no different from what Fox was saying.

All the other networks followed suit, and since the war itself was over, the press as a whole whipped public opinion into a frenzy of outrage that was unbelievably powerful but aimed in the wrong direction. They demanded that the president be impeached, despite the fact that his actions had likely saved the entire country and probably the whole human race. They wanted to crucify the Joint Chiefs and everyone in uniform. They wanted heads to roll.

But they were all pointing their arrows at the wrong target.

When the story of Vice President Bill Collins's suicide broke—a story intentionally delayed because of the national emergency and while his wife was being notified—there was a moment during which all the screaming, yelling, and finger-pointing ground to a halt. The press and the congressional witch-finders were like a pack of bloodhounds that suddenly had to decide which trail to follow.

As for the president . . . he addressed the nation again that night with a speech that was perhaps the most eloquent I've ever heard. The press, of course, cynical as ever, tore the speech apart and nitpicked the soul out of it.

I was genuinely surprised, though, that over the next few days several of the more intelligent politicians from both sides of the aisle stepped up to support the president. Perhaps they realized that to continue tearing him down would weaken the nation as a whole and likely crash the stock market. And perhaps they had some quiet coercion from people behind the scenes. Mr. Church comes to mind.

But I'd like to think that it was evidence that, as fractured and flawed as our system is, there are still some good people working to keep the ship of state sailing and to steer her out of dangerous waters. Maybe that makes me naïve and idealistic. If so, that's fine with me. I need something to believe in, something to fight for.

Deep into the heart of the third day after the battle in Atlanta, Junie finally addressed the thing that neither of us had dared talk about.

The baby.

"Joe—?"

I turned to see that Junie was awake. I kissed her tenderly on the forehead and on her lips.

"Joe," she whispered, "I'm sorry. I'm so sorry."

"No," I told her. "No."

Then I knelt beside her bed, laid my head on her chest, and we both wept for a long time. My broken sternum hurt so bad; my broken heart hurt so damn much worse.

Later. So much later, she said, "Maybe . . . we can adopt."

She said those four words in a small and fragile voice. My breath caught in my throat and for a moment I dared not reply for fear of saying the wrong thing. At times like these even well-intentioned words can destroy.

So I said, "Is that what you want to do?"

Junie was a long time answering. "You've never once said anything about wanting kids."

I said nothing. Waiting.

"I mean . . . we're not even married. I'm being so presumptuous. This would never have even come up if . . ."

She didn't say it. How do you say "if an assassin's bullet hadn't killed our baby and robbed us of ever having our own kids"? How do those words fit into your mouth?

I got up from my chair and sat on the edge of the bed and looked into her eyes. I brushed away a tear, looked at the wetness on my thumb, pressed it into the flesh over my heart.

"I love you," I said.

It was the first time I'd spoken those words to her. It was not the first time I'd thought them.

"Oh, God, Joe," she said, "I love you."

It was all I said. For that moment, though, it was enough. There would be time for the rest, for anything else. For now, this was the firm ground beneath our feet.

It was the only safe place to stand.

4

On an unseasonably cold afternoon in late September, I went to an Orioles game with Rudy Sanchez. I'd barely seen him since Atlanta. As a specialist in postviolence trauma, he was in high demand. When I called to ask if he wanted to help me watch the Orioles spank the Red Sox, he surprised me by leaping at it.

I had season tickets right behind home plate. A gift from Mr. Church, who has a friend in the industry. Rudy and I got there early. Ghost was allowed in because he was dressed like a service dog and pretended to help Rudy with his one eye and bad leg. In truth, Ghost likes baseball as much as any sane American. Being a canine doesn't change that fact. We bought hot dogs and big cups of beer and for a while it was just the three of us in the box. Ghost dismantled his hot dog the way he does, eating each side of the bun first, then licking off the mustard and relish in turn, and finally eating the hot dog. He wasn't even finished before he began eyeing mine.

Rudy looked older than his years, and worn to a brittle thinness.

"How are you doing, brother?" I asked him.

He took a bite of the hot dog, chewed it thoughtfully, sipped some beer. Finally, he said, "It's not just the statistics, you know."

I said, "What?"

"This thing, Joe . . . it's not just about how many crimes were committed, how many bombs went off, or how many died. It's not about that."

I nodded.

"This has done something fundamental to the American people," he continued. "In some ways it's completed a process that began with the fall of the Towers. It's like the gradually stripping away of innocence as the result of a pattern of abuse. We've lost so much of our optimism, so much of the belief that we can survive anything."

He sighed and drank more beer. People were drifting into the stadium now, walking in ones and twos, dads with kids, groups of friends. There was a lot of laughter.

"I hear what you're saying, Rude, I do, but I think you're saying that because you're worn out. You've been at this twenty-four/seven. But you're standing so close to it, all you can see is the pain. I think you've gotten yourself a nice dose of PTSD."

He started to object, then raised his head as if listening to something, and gave me a small shrug. "Maybe. I'll consider that. However, I do think that it's partly true. We have lost some innocence." He nibbled his hot dog. "I remember reading articles in psychology journals about similar losses of innocence after Kennedy was killed. And Martin Luther King. And after John Lennon."

"Violence always leaves a mark," I reminded him. "A pretty smart guy told me that once upon a time."

"And now we are all badly marked." He shook his head. "I don't know, Joe, but I'm afraid that I'm beginning to lose faith that the good guys will actually win in the end."

I set my beer cup down—well away from Ghost's inquisitive snout— and placed my hand on Rudy's shoulder.

"Sometimes they do," I said.

He kept shaking his head.

I leaned close and very quietly said, "Junie got the results of her last panels."

He winced, preparing for the worst.

"She's totally cancer-free."

I don't know what reaction I expected. Laughter, shouts, a bromance hug. Instead Rudy put his hot dog and beer down, placed his face in his hands, and his shoulders shook with silent tears.

"Hey, man, I said . . . don't, it's cool . . ."

And then I realized that he wasn't crying.

He was laughing.

It was the kind of laughter that comes from way down deep on the cellular level. On the soul level. A laughter that has to brew a long time before it bubbles to the surface. Sure, there were some tears mixed in with it, but there was also a lot of relief. A lot of hope renewed.

Corny?

Sure, fuck it.

But under the September sun in a Baltimore ballpark, with my dog drinking Rudy's beer and the stands filling up with people, Rudy Sanchez and I laughed and laughed and laughed. Soon, without understanding anything about who we were or why we were laughing, the people around us started laughing, too.

Oh, yeah . . . and the Orioles kicked serious ass.